LUNAR LOVE

a novel

LAUREN KUNG JESSEN

FOREVER

New York Boston

Copyright © 2023 by Lauren Kung Jessen
Reading group guide copyright © 2023 by Lauren Kung Jessen and Hachette Book Group, Inc.

Cover design and illustration by Sandra Chiu
Cover copyright © 2023 by Hachette Book Group, Inc.

Forever
Hachette Book Group
1290 Avenue of the Americas, New York, NY 10104

Forever is an imprint of Grand Central Publishing. The Forever name and logo are trademarks of Hachette Book Group, Inc.

The publisher is not responsible for websites (or their content) that are not owned by the publisher.

Interior design images © 2023 by Lauren Kung Jessen

ISBN 978-1-63910-583-0

Printed in the United States of America

For those who are also mixed and have felt like
they aren't enough or don't belong.
You are and you do.

CHAPTER 1

In my almost eight years of matchmaking, there's one thing I know to be true: love is like the moon.

Case in point: love moves in phases. New love is a barely there whisper in the night sky, a slow burn into brightness. The relationship matures in the first quarter, advancing into full illumination—two compatible people becoming whole. The immediate passion wanes but doesn't disappear. Instead, the initial flash evolves into a steady glow. Like the moon, love is dependable. You don't have to see the moon or love to know they're there.

Both the moon and love are romantic and enchanting, can be moody and mysterious, possess dark sides, and have gravitational pulls on us that we just can't control, no matter how hard we try. The moon was formed when a large object collided into Earth, a happenstance so cataclysmically devastating that produced something so beautiful. When two people collide, there's the possibility that love will be created. There's also the potential for us and everything we've ever known to be thrown out of orbit.

As a matchmaker at Lunar Love, my family's Chinese zodiac matchmaking business, it's my duty to keep clients and their relationships rotating on their axes and revolving in orbit. I make thoughtful and personalized matches based on people's compatible animal sign traits. My years of hard work have paid off because I'll officially be in charge of Lunar Love in just a few hours. By the end of today, its legacy will be my responsibility.

I've dedicated myself to my craft, so one day, I can be half as good as Pó Po, who has grown Lunar Love through the decades. Expectations to make matches is one thing, but when you're the granddaughter of Lunar Love's famously successful matriarch, whose match rate for Chinese zodiac matchmaking is near-perfect, expectations reach truly celestial heights.

I park in my usual spot in the public parking garage a couple of blocks from Lunar Love and weave through early-bird tourists on the hunt for breakfast in Los Angeles's Chinatown. In the eight-minute walk from my car to Lucky Monkey Bakery, I watch vendors roll their boxes of vegetables and fruits on hand trucks and bump against early morning shoppers eager to beat the crowds. Burnt orange lanterns are strung between colorful pagoda-style shops, dotting the light blue, cloud-speckled sky. Vivid murals recount Chinese legends, the colorful mosaics popping against the dulled brick.

An incoming call from my mom glows on my phone screen. Before I can say hello, a voice at the other end frantically speaks. "Where are you? Never mind. I need you to make a quick stop!"

"I'm grabbing a late breakfast at Lucky Monkey," I say, quickening my pace.

"Oh, perfect! I need you to pick up extra buns." The stress in Mom's voice practically makes my cellphone vibrate.

"Don't you think the cake I made will be enough? Plus all the pastries Dad made?" I ask, sidestepping a man carrying a tub of fish. "Lucky Monkey's been open for a couple of hours already so I don't know how much will be left."

"Pó Po wants cocktail buns for her birthday breakfast. Just choose an assortment of items, but don't forget cocktail buns. Apparently, she's having a coconut craving."

I nod to myself. "Got it."

"And a few Bo Lo Baos for me. One second." At a lower volume away from the phone, I hear Mom bark out more orders, to my father most likely. "Have you decided on the balloons for Nina's Cookie Day?" Mom asks, a question directed at me this time.

"Of course. I'm finalizing the details on that today," I say, making a mental note. "Okay, I'm here. See you soon."

As I approach Lucky Monkey Bakery, my stomach grumbles in excitement. The bakery hasn't changed much in over five decades, with its unassuming façade featuring a single identifying sign written in Chinese characters. Behind its doors is a wonderland of sweet and savory baked goods with a variety of fillings and cakes and tarts that look too pretty to eat.

A wave of unexpected heat greets me when I step into the shop, the ringing of bells above the door the soundtrack to my entrance. Near the entryway, the yellow walls are lined with framed photos and articles from magazines featuring the bakery. A Polaroid photo of me, my sister, and my old best friend from twenty years ago catches my eye. Our noses and cheeks are covered in flour, our smiles almost bigger than our faces. I inhale the scent of butter, egg, and sugar and continue on with my mission.

The owners, Mae and Dale Zhang, a husband and wife who started their bakery around the time Pó Po first set up shop here, pack as much as they can into the small space. They became fast friends with Pó Po, and I've known them my entire life, so while they're not technically blood related, they're as close to family as they can get. To me, they're just Mae Yí-Pó and Dale Yí-Gong and are practically my third set of grandparents.

Mae Yí-Pó and Dale Yí-Gong have established a reputation for making colorful cakes and offering the widest variety of Asian baked goods. Once they sell out of something, it's gone for the day, so regulars know to show up early to get first pick.

"Olivia!" a voice shouts over the bustle of hungry visitors. "Nǐ hǎo! It's nice to see you!"

I wave to Mae Yí-Pó as she carefully slides a freshly frosted cake into the display case.

"Nǐ hǎo!" I call out as I make my way to her. "How are you doing today?"

"I can't get the damn oven to turn off. So other than being drenched in sweat, great!" Mae Yí-Pó says, sweeping her bangs over to the left.

Last summer, she chopped all her silver hair off into a pixie cut, which has accentuated her cheekbones and complemented her petite but strong frame. Mae Yí-Pó twists another fruit-topped cake on a pedestal so that her piped whipped cream designs are prominently displayed.

"I hear Monday's a big day for you," she says.

I nod. "I'm really excited."

"It feels like yesterday that you and Nina were tiny little

things coming in here and eating all of our steamed buns." Her eyes flick over to the wall of photos. "How's your friend Colette doing?"

I hesitate before answering. "I'm not sure," I admit, tensing up. "I've been busy."

"Well, of course you are! You're in charge of the family business now," Mae Yí-Pó says. In the air in front of her, she draws an arch with her hands. "Olivia Huang Christenson, Chief Executive of Love. That's got a nice ring to it."

"That's not bad. I may need to have new business cards printed up," I say, playing along.

"It's about time you were in charge. Though I remember June starting Lunar Love like it was yesterday. Do I look as old as I feel?" Mae Yí-Pó wipes her hands on the towel hanging from her apron. She's the one who taught me how to bake when I was younger. When Pó Po and Auntie Lydia, my mom's sister who took over Lunar Love after Pó Po retired, were busy with clients, I'd sneak over here to help mix icing and watch dough rise.

"Not even a little," I say. "Are you still coming to Pó Po's birthday party today?"

"I wouldn't miss it. Dale won't be there, unfortunately, since he'll be covering for me."

"Sounds like he's finally feeling better?"

"Much better. The doctor says it was just stress. I'm sure you know the pressure to sell has been increasing all over town, and with new restaurants coming in, it's hard to compete with shiny things." Mae Yí-Pó swipes crumbs off the counter into her hands as she talks. "Very dangerous to his heart. Have you been approached by the vultures yet?"

"Who?" I ask, confused.

"Real estate agents," she clarifies.

"Oh. Not that I know of," I say, thinking back on recent non-client visitors.

"They act all sneaky and try to befriend you, but at the first sign of weakness, they swoop in and try to buy your land out from under you." Mae Yí-Pó claps her hands together, startling me. "It happened to our friends at the bookstore next to you."

"We need to hold strong so we don't lose the essence of what makes Chinatown special," I say.

Mae Yí-Pó pushes her glasses up the bridge of her nose. "Exactly! Good girl. Anyways, go, go! We know you're going to do great things with Lunar Love. We're so proud."

"Thanks, Mae Yí-Pó." I smile at her, grateful for the support. "See you at the party!"

I select a pair of tongs and a small cream-colored tray lined with parchment. I take count of what remains after the early morning rush through the illuminated plastic cases presenting the day's fresh creations. My eyes fall over the seemingly endless options: sweet and savory buns, steamed and baked buns, egg tarts, mochi doughnuts, sesame balls, and Swiss rolls.

I squeeze past a woman loading up her tray with red bean buns and bend over to grab two ham and cheese buns with my tongs. They look identical, their browned tops glossy from baked egg wash. I open the case door directly above the ham and cheese buns to pick out Bo Lo Baos for Mom. She loves these sweet buns because they resemble pineapple skin with their scored yellow tops, even though there's actually no pineapple in them. They're Lucky Monkey's bestselling item, so Mae Yí-Pó always makes sure to bake triple the amount compared to other treats.

Having already memorized the pastry placements, I take two steps to my right and secure the last baked pork bun. Then without hesitation, I open the plastic case door next to the now-empty tray of meat-filled mounds and reach in for the last cocktail bun for Pó Po. Before my tongs reach the puffy pastry, another pair of tongs swoops in before my eyes to grab the sesame-seed-sprinkled treat.

"Oops! Excuse me!" I look over at the offender who just swiped Pó Po's breakfast. I expect to see the woman with the full tray of red bean buns, but instead a tall man stands beside me. I nod toward the cocktail bun on his tray. "I didn't see you there, but I was actually here first. Would you mind?"

The man looks at me with a surprised expression. "Would I mind...moving? Sure!" He takes a couple of steps back from the wall of cases.

"Uh, no. The cocktail bun. It's mine."

The man looks down at his pile of food. "I had my tongs on it first. Therefore, I have first pick. It's a law."

"My tongs were on that bun before you ripped it out of my cold metal grip," I casually explain. I eye up the cocktail bun, the sides still looking soft from recently being pulled apart. Across the surface of the bun, which is baked to golden perfection, are two white lines of sweet cream.

"That's quite the dramatic retelling of what just happened. I'd love to hear your version of what happens when I keep the bun." The man smiles, his cheeks pushing crinkled lines up around his delighted eyes.

I gesture with my tongs to signify my personal space. "I was clearly here before you."

The man raises both eyebrows. "If you move too slowly, you

miss out. What's that saying? If you're browsing for fun, you don't get the bun."

"I think it actually goes: When you cut me off, things are going to get rough," I retort, slightly amused.

"Mmm, nope," he says, "haven't heard of that one."

"You see, it's my pó po's birthday, and if I don't get her that cocktail bun, well, I'll be a disappointment to her. You wouldn't want that for me, right?" I ask sweetly. I look into the light shading of his deep-set eyes, and for a moment, I'm at a loss for what color they are.

"How do you know that I'm not taking this bun to *my* pó po?" the man asks. His use of the Chinese term for maternal grandmother surprises me.

"You have a pó po who also happens to be obsessed with cocktail buns?" I ask suspiciously.

"Actually, my pó po prefers egg tarts. She's got a thing for puff pastry and butter," he replies, glancing over at the cases next to us. "But that's beside the point."

Before I can make my rebuttal, a young boy pushes past me to snatch the last Swiss roll out of the case. "Great, there goes the last one!" I shout, looking at the vacant platter and throwing my hand up to overemphasize my distress. Maybe this approach will work.

"I can tell you need this bun more than I do. If you really want it," he says, "we can make a trade."

"A trade?" My pulse begins to race. His eye color is on the tip of my tongue.

"Yes. A good old-fashioned barter," he says, looking entertained. He studies me with his color-I-can't-quite-place eyes, unnerving me. There's a soulful depth to them that draws me in, making me forget why I'm staring at him in the first place.

The man clears his throat, and I refocus. "Sure. You can have my Bo Lo Bao, and I'll take your cocktail bun," I offer. I make a move for my prize, but the man gently clutches my wrist with his tongs, guiding my arm back to my tray.

"Whoa, hold on! No deal. There's still a pile of those. I could grab five of them right now if I wanted to. Therefore, your trade is worthless," he says.

On the tray, he has two slices of Swiss rolls (one rainbow and one vanilla), a Chinese hot dog bun, two curry beef puffs, and *my* cocktail bun.

"You clearly have an agenda," I say, "so what is it you want? Ham and cheese? They look extra delicious this morning."

The man vocalizes his thinking with a *hmmm*. "The cocktail bun for your pork bun," he finally offers.

I hesitate and look down at what was going to be my breakfast, fully knowing it's the last pork bun. "Your cocktail bun *and* Swiss roll for my pork bun," I say firmly, throwing in a curveball. "That's my final offer."

He glances over at the empty Swiss roll case and pauses before finally agreeing. "I normally have a ninety-two percent success rate with negotiations. This is hands down the worst deal I've ever made, but I'm impressed by your bargaining skills, so you've got yourself a deal."

"And I want the vanilla one," I add, studying him. He has a kind face, his quick-to-smile demeanor disarming me. On his upper right cheek is a small coffee-colored beauty mark.

"What's the difference? I'm pretty sure the rainbow Swiss roll tastes like vanilla, too," he says, poking the dessert with the silver utensil. "How do you know this one's better?"

"It's not that it's *better*. I just have a particular preference for the golden one," I say flatly, holding my tray out toward him.

"Whatever you want." A dimpled smile spreads across his face. I barely manage to pull my gaze away from the deepening, shadowed spots. I bet those dimples have broken hearts before.

He places the cocktail bun on my tray and hesitantly grabs his Swiss roll with his tongs, looking pained to be parting with it. "Goodbye, new friend. It was nice almost enjoying you." The man places the slice of Swiss roll onto my tray and, in the same smooth movement, grabs the pork bun.

"Enjoy that," I murmur. I can't help but smile.

"Nice doing business with you," he says, snapping his tongs playfully like lobster claws.

A snorted laugh sneaks out. The man gives a slight wave before heading to the register. I grab a few more baked goods before paying, lingering a while so the man can leave and so my heart can stop fluttering.

When I push the door open, I realize I didn't wait long enough. The man from the bakery loiters on the sidewalk, staring at his cellphone. The damn bells above the door jingle, betraying me by giving up my location.

Bakery Guy looks up at me. "You back for another barter?" he asks with a pleased look.

I lift the heavy bag of food. "I do have more leverage now."

We both turn in the same direction.

"I'm not following you, but I have to go the same way," I say with an awkward laugh.

The man's hair is a lighter shade of brown than it looked in the bakery's yellow fluorescent lights. I sneak a look at his eyes once more. Hazel. His eyes are hazel. In the sunshine, I see that there's a fleck of gold around the pupils. He stretches to adjust his posture, his shoulders broadening and expanding his evergreen-colored polo, which looks soft from years of wear. He comes off as someone who wants to remain low-key but still appear put together.

"No problem," he says, sliding his sunglasses on.

I walk at his pace but stay about six feet to the right.

"What brings you out here this early?" Bakery Guy asks, filling the silence.

"Picking up breakfast. I meant it when I said I was bringing food for my pó po's birthday. You almost denied a ninety-year-old woman her favorite bun."

The man's eyes widen. "Yikes. She's lucky to have a clever granddaughter to win it back."

I grin to myself. "What about you?"

"I just had to pick up something from my office downtown. I like to grab breakfast here sometimes. We're looking for offices in the area since coworking spaces are expensive."

"On a Saturday? Your boss must love you," I say.

Bakery Guy looks over at me. "Work never really shuts off for us."

I nod slowly. "Chinatown's really changing. I can't imagine your coworking space is more expensive than here."

"At least here there's room for negotiation," he says with a smirk.

"I hope your future negotiations go better than today," I say, thinking about Mae Yí-Pó's warning of vultures.

My stomach grumbles louder for breakfast, and I dig around my tote bag for the vanilla Swiss roll and a fork. I pierce the roll, breaking off a bite with an even ratio of cake and filling. From the weight of the buns, my tote slips down my shoulder, sending my arm off balance. The vanilla roll wobbles precariously as my arm instinctively reacts to stabilize my bag.

Bakery Guy is quicker. He closes the distance between us and reaches out to grab my canvas bag. His hand brushes against my forearm, sending unanticipated tingles up the length of my neck. He slides the tote up smoothly, cautiously moving my hair back so it doesn't tug under the handles.

My cheeks warm. I'm at a loss for words. Something resembling "thanks" stumbles out of my mouth.

"Can't risk losing that roll, too," he says with a smile. "Mind me asking your name?"

I glance over my shoulder and look him up and down. "My friends call me Liv," I say. "What do your friends call you?"

"You have nice friends. Mine call me *asshole*," he says with a joking tone. Bakery Guy reaches into his plastic bag and pulls out his own vibrant Swiss roll slice. Slinging the handles of the bag onto his forearm, he uses his palm as a makeshift plate. "I'm going to open this. Can I count on you not to try to swipe this one, too? I'm really hungry."

There's nothing in this moment I want more than to also take *that* roll from him, just to prove a point. Obviously, I won't. Plus, his boyish excitement for his Swiss roll is too endearing. I nod, and he starts unrolling the swirly slice into a flattened cake layer.

"What are you doing?" I ask, perplexed.

"What do you mean?" he asks.

I nod toward his hands. "That!"

"I'm eating my breakfast?" he says. The confusion on his face is priceless.

"This cake requires delicate rolling to achieve the perfect spiral," I explain.

"Really?" Bakery Guy uses his fork and gently scrapes off the filling from the center of the now-flattened spiral.

"I did not just see you scoop the filling out," I groan. The colors of the rainbow cake glow in the morning light, the sides bending up and looking sad to not be living their full spiral potential.

The man scrapes, eats, scrapes, eats. "Did you see that?" he asks playfully.

"The cake and filling are meant to be enjoyed together, so you have an equal ratio of creamy filling to chiffon cake. And their flavors are complementary to one another."

"I like eating the sweetest part of the dessert first," he explains, taking another bite of the sweet cream. "I know it's a bit different, but I like different."

My lips lift into a smile. "Just for fun, or ...?"

"I like knowing that the first bites of my meal will be good. And this way, I know I'll have room for it. Don't judge me!" he says dramatically.

"When you do something like that, you're begging to be judged," I say with a laugh. "I'm just trying to understand what motivates a pastry thief to do such a thing." I wiggle another well-balanced bite off my roll.

Bakery Guy lets out a full, genuine laugh. It's a warm sound that unexpectedly and instantly puts me at ease. He shrugs and then takes another bite of filling. "I've never met anyone so passionate about baked goods," he says before diving into the cake itself.

"I enjoy and respect the process of baking. And it de-stresses me. Well, normally. Swiss rolls are tricky. I'm still trying to figure out how to roll the cake without it cracking."

"Once you get the hang of it, you can keep your hands off my rolls," he says humorously, his cheeks turning rosy. "What else do you like to bake?"

We walk side by side, the crowd around us growing. A bicyclist barrels down the sidewalk in front of us, weaving through people jumping out of his way. Without thinking, I reach up and place my hand on Bakery Guy's shoulder, guiding him out of the man's unpredictable path. He feels warm and sturdy, his shoulders sculpted but not so much that I'd think he spends every off-hour at the gym. I should not know this. I immediately pull my hand back, crossing my arms tightly.

"You might've just saved my life," he quips.

"All in a morning's work," I respond with a smile. I squeeze my hand that touched him into a fist. I remember his question and try to pick the conversation back up smoothly, as though I hadn't just caressed his shoulder. "As for what I like to bake, um, anything with chocolate like cookies or brownies. Cinnamon rolls. Sourdough bread."

The man nods. "Very nice. Did you know that sourdough is the oldest form of leavened bread? Food historians believe that the use of leavening was discovered by the Egyptians. Until there was commercial yeast, all leavened bread used naturally occurring yeasts."

"I...why do you know that?" I look up at him, amused.

"I love learning about history. Mostly so I can whip out interesting facts and sound smart at parties." He grins.

"I'm sure these random facts come in handy when you're

trying to impress the ladies," I say, looking away and rolling my eyes at myself. The ladies? Did I just say that out loud?

"Rarely," he says. "Only when there's someone worth trying to impress." He gives me a lingering look, and now *I* blush.

We curve around tourists taking photos and lines of workers waiting for their breakfast orders. Six minutes later, I realize I've completely bypassed my car.

I slow my steps. "I'm that way," I say.

"The real world calls. Maybe I'll see you around?" he asks tentatively.

I pull my sunglasses off to get one last good look at him. "Maybe...if you're even able to afford office space here," I say.

Bakery Guy takes a step closer to me and pushes his sunglasses above his head. "Then let's hope prices aren't *too* high," he says with a smile.

My pulse quickens at the nearness of him. I look down at his chest to confirm that I'm just imagining the electric field vibrating between our bodies.

"It was nice meeting you, asshole," I say with a smirk, sneaking one last glance at his hazel eyes.

Bakery Guy raises his eyebrows, his startled look transforming into a throaty laugh. "Meeting you was a very nice surprise."

I reorient myself and walk back to my car, reflecting on our interaction. As I think back on Bakery Guy's traits, I come to a horrifying realization: For the first time in my entire career of being a matchmaker, I didn't think to consider this man's zodiac animal sign for a single second.

CHAPTER 2

I stand in my parents' kitchen with a box of matches in hand, replaying this morning's exchange with Bakery Guy. I snap out of my daze and give the giant horse-shaped cake I baked for Pó Po's ninetieth birthday one more look over. It's salted caramel chocolate—my specialty and Pó Po's favorite. At three feet wide and two feet long, the platter takes up the entire kitchen island. Shaping the cake to look like a horse was no easy feat, but given that Pó Po is Year of the Horse, like me, I thought it would be a special and memorable dessert to honor her. The horse lies flat with three layers of chocolate cake, two layers of chocolate and caramel frosting, and an outer layer of chocolate frosting sprinkled with just the right amount of sea salt.

I wiggle the ninetieth candle into the cake and pull a match from its small box. I strike it once. Twice. No spark.

"I'm usually a lot better with matches," I joke to Auntie Lydia, who's preoccupied with taming stray hairs back into her shoulder-length bob in the reflection of a frying pan. At sixty-six, she still has flawless, glowing skin. Her youthfulness and elegance remind me of the actress Joan Chen.

"You just have to swipe it right. Isn't that what the rage is all about nowadays?" Auntie quips. There's a hint of bitterness in her voice. Like me, she believes in the power of a personally made match, not one made through a cellphone.

A spark ignites at the tip of the match, and I quickly move from candle to candle. A few matches later, I light the last candle while trying to remember where Dad told me he keeps the fire extinguisher.

Auntie and I carefully carry the flaming horse through the dining room's sliding doors to the backyard where the party is in full swing. With over fifty people in attendance, it's practically a Huang family reunion. Pó Po's sisters, children, nieces, nephews, grandchildren, and close clients came from all over the world—China, England, France, South Africa, New York, Texas, and Washington—to join us in Pasadena, California, for her special day.

Mom and Dad transformed their two-thousand-square-foot bungalow for the birthday party, using the backyard as the festivity's stomping grounds. And because Pó Po's birthday usually falls within range of the Moon Festival, she prefers to celebrate both at the same time. Under vibrant red-and-gold globe paper lanterns, crescent moon balloons, and string lights, family and friends hold cool drinks and cluster in groups. When they see us with the cake, everyone in unison starts singing the first low chord of the Happy Birthday song. We sound like an off-key chorus.

Guests part to create a pathway for us as we navigate around wooden folding tables decorated with bud vases. The chorus grows louder as the kids and the ones who were too shy to join in at first contribute their voices, belting out the words with enough gusto to make Andrea Bocelli proud.

When we finally reach Pó Po, my heart swells with emotion. Delighted, Pó Po grins from ear to ear and places a hand over her cheek. When she smiles, her entire face lights up, the creases around her twinkling eyes deepening.

Auntie and I set the cake on the table in front of Pó Po, her face illuminated by the fire. As expected, a few singers go rogue and change the song's ending, but Pó Po claps along anyways. I give Pó Po a side hug, and we link pinkies and press our thumbs together. It's a gesture we've been doing ever since I could form a fist, as a promise that our love for each other will never change. I don't know who I'd be without her in my life.

Pó Po closes her eyes for a few moments, wax slowly dripping down onto the top layer of the cake, giving the horse's coat a healthy sheen. She blows out the candles, resting between each extinguishing to catch her breath. Everyone bursts into cheers and claps when she puts out the final flame. I make some noise for the woman whose past decisions have provided me with my future.

After Pó Po makes her wish, Auntie and I carry the horse cake to the winner's circle, conveniently located at the dessert table. Mom strategically placed the dessert table by her blooming roses so Sān Pó Po, one of Pó Po's sisters, could admire her handiwork. The sweet scent of the flowers wafts up in the light breeze. Beside the cake are trays of mooncakes, egg tarts, sliced apples and oranges, fruit tarts, red bean sesame balls, and Bo Lo Baos from this morning's bakery run. I smirk at the memory of Bakery Guy instigating a trade. I may have lost my pork bun, but at least it was on my terms.

Dad turns Pó Po's moon-themed playlist back on and Frank

Sinatra's "Fly Me to the Moon" blasts from the outdoor speakers. Pó Po slowly waltzes her way over to me. She's the proud leader of the local senior-citizen dance team and finds every opportunity she can to show off her moves. She holds up two sideways peace signs in front of her eyes and pulls them apart. I extend my arm diagonally up to the sky with a disco finger and then bring it down across my body.

"Are you ready?" Pó Po whispers. She adjusts the cornflower blue vest she's wearing over her white polo, her signature daytime look. Her short hair is freshly waved from hair rollers, a style she's preferred for decades. "I'm going to make the announcement after the cake is served."

"I think most people already know, Pó Po. Was it supposed to be a big secret?"

"Aiyah! I guess I should've expected the news to spread. This is the Huang family, after all. No respect, even at ninety-one years old." Pó Po laughs and reaches out to rub a rose's soft blush petal. "Ah well, I'll still give a little speech. It'll be nice."

"Pó Po, you're ninety! Not ninety-one," I say, holding her gently by both shoulders.

Pó Po gives me a subtle wink. "When I was born in China, children were considered to be one year old at birth. That would make me ninety-one, but yes, let's go with ninety. Oh, Liv? The cake. It's hilarious. Thank you. Can I put in an early request for a unicorn next year?"

"They're becoming harder to find, but if that's what you want, I can make it happen," I say with a mock-serious tone.

She pushes a loose strand of my dark brown hair behind my ear and takes a moment to study my face. "Why do you look so radiant? You're practically glowing!"

I bring a hand to my cheek. "Am I? Well, I'm excited about today!"

"For the announcement?" she asks probingly.

"What else?" I say casually, fiddling with a plastic fork. I'm *definitely* not glowing because of Bakery Guy. That would be ridiculous. I don't even know his sign.

"Okay. Well, good." Pó Po nods slowly. "Ah, before I forget, there's someone I think you'll want to meet. Should I set up a date?"

It's one of Pó Po and Auntie's favorite pastimes to introduce me to people they think I might want to meet. Really, they're young men *they* want me to meet.

"Do you really think now is the best time for me to be dating?" I ask. "There's going to be too much to do with Lunar Love."

Pó Po narrows her eyes at me. "We'll revisit this later. Auntie also has someone you might like. Choices are never a bad thing! One way or another, we need to get you matched," she says before fluffing her hair and twirling off to find more family members to charm.

I pluck the melted candles out of the horse and smooth over the icing. When I cut into the cake, it becomes apparent that this looks very wrong. In its entirety, the cake looked great. Dismembered, not so much. I divide the tail into six pieces, placing each one onto small round paper plates. I line the plates up next to each other and attempt to re-create the shape of the horse so that it doesn't look like a bunch of body parts scattered on the table.

A bracelet-covered arm jingles past me to grab half a hoof. Without needing to look, I smell Alisha's gardenia perfume and know it's her. Alisha Lin, my co-matchmaker at Lunar Love, always looks put together in stylish clothing. She sweeps her long, dark brown hair over to the side, the curls cascading over her shoulders. Ever since Alisha was hired at Lunar Love three years ago, she's quickly become one of my closest friends and confidants.

Randall Zhu, Lunar Love's finance, admin, legal, and human resources teams all wrapped into one, follows closely behind. Randall joined as an intern around the time Pó Po retired and worked his way up, so he knows practically everything there is to know about Lunar Love.

Alisha and Randall deeply inhale the chocolate-on-chocolate cake scent. "Your Pó Po is major goals. She doesn't look a day over seventy. What's her secret?" Alisha asks.

"Full-moon milk baths, red wine, and dark chocolate," I reveal.

"I'm lactose intolerant, but I've got the other two covered," Alisha jokes.

"It's working. You don't look a day over thirty-three," Randall says, teasing Alisha.

"These days it takes skill to actually look your age," she says with a mock-defensive tone. Alisha takes a bite of cake and groans. "This is perfect. Not too sweet."

"Yeah," I mumble, half my mind still stuck on the man from this morning. Why is this happening?

Randall takes a step back and shoots me a concerned look. "Are you okay? You feeling nervous about your first day as Head Matchmaker on Monday? It'll be fun since we have that conference to attend."

"I'm not nervous! You know that's my favorite event of the year," I say. I try to find the words to explain what happened this morning, but they jumble in my head. *I met a man* is all that comes out.

Alisha gasps. "Ooh, who is he?"

"No, it's not like that. It was at the bakery. He took Pó Po's cocktail bun, I made a trade for it, and he works downtown. That's really all there is to know."

Alisha's eyes glimmer as she closely watches my face. "What sign is he?"

I fiddle with the cake server. "I didn't ask for his birthday or analyze him that closely," I admit.

"*You* didn't analyze him?" Alisha asks. Her widened eyes are as round as full moons. "I don't believe you."

"I didn't expect to be engaging in negotiations this morning," I say. "It caught me off guard."

"Okay, well, what were his traits? Could he be a candidate for one of our clients? Let's debrief," Alisha says, taking another bite of cake. "You said you made some kind of trade? Maybe he's a lawyer."

I cross my arms. "Let's see. He's overconfident and engages in social behaviors that are a little too forward for my taste. He told me he likes to go to Lucky Monkey for breakfast, but he works all the way downtown, which indicates that he puts his needs before his company's. Yes, he was eventually charming and was surprisingly good-looking. He had stunning eyes. Hazel! Well-dressed. But he probably knows that, and in a relationship, he'd likely want to be told those things. I wouldn't tell him what he needed to hear; we'd fight about it."

Without stopping for a breath, I add, "I can see it now: A couple of months into the relationship he'd be frustrated that I prefer doing things the way I want to do them. I'd be annoyed that he can't sit quietly with himself and that not everything can be a negotiation. That kind of dependency, paired with my need for alone time, would never work."

Alisha and Randall look stunned for a moment. Then they finally break the silence by clapping against their plates. "You continue to impress us. But who said anything about a relationship?" Alisha says, wiggling her eyebrows.

"Oh, I didn't mean relationship. They're just always on my mind for our clients," I hurriedly reply, fumbling over my words. "You know how I feel about being matched."

She sighs. "Right, of course. You're the matchmaker who can't be matched."

I shrug. I know how people will act—and how things will turn out—because I know their traits on a deep level. I've accepted my fate. For everyone else though, there's hope.

"By the way, we were debriefing about *him*. You brought yourself into this," Randall adds with a gooey smile.

"I was just trying to put it into context. Enough about him," I add defensively.

Alisha wags her finger in thought. "You're right. Enough about him, more about you. Monday is coming up, and we need to get you out there more. Podcasts, listicles, interviews with young professionals–type stuff. You're the new face of Lunar Love. Let's show the world that. Maybe the media, and a younger clientele, will find it interesting that the new owner of LA's original zodiac matchmaking company is a gorgeous young woman."

"That's exactly what we should do. Try to reach a younger market," I agree.

"I have a contact at WhizDash. They've become really popular. I'll let her know that we want to get something up on the website," Alisha says. She crams the rest of her cake slice into her mouth, licking the crumbs off her lips along with some of her berry-colored lipstick. "If you want to write something, I can send it to her."

"I'll start thinking of article ideas," I tell her, ideas immediately flooding my mind.

"Perfect. I—ooh! Randall, there's Aunt Vivienne!" Alisha says, becoming distracted by my aunt across the yard. "She has that list of art documentaries for us to watch. Liv, we'll catch you in a bit!" The two of them shuffle through the grass, leaving me alone with my thoughts.

My sister, Nina, catches my attention from the outdoor dining table, and I rush over to her. Her arms are filled with bowls and plates stacked on a large platter where, just an hour ago, eight Peking ducks sat among steamed buns, cucumbers, green onions, and hoisin sauce. My mouth waters at the memory of all the flavors melting together. I can tell she's stressed by the thin layer of sweat forming on her upper lip.

"Do you need help?" I ask, extending my arms to assist.

"So. Many. Dishes," Nina huffs, keeping the pile to herself. "Mom wants them cleaned before the big announcement." She lifts her elbows as high as she can as I fan her with my hands to cool her down. "It's October! I'll never get used to the fact that it's still eighty degrees in autumn."

"It's only going to keep getting hotter every year," I mumble bleakly.

Nina sticks her tongue out and adds, "I can't wait for my Cookie Day when I won't have to do any of this. Enjoy the view. You're looking at your future."

"I'm going to be a sweaty bride-to-be with hoisin sauce on my shirt?" I ask. We both start cracking up.

"I need to get back there before I make a scene. Save me a

piece of cake. And if you see my future husband, tell him to refill the jasmine tea." She slowly walks toward the kitchen, carefully balancing the remains of this afternoon's meal.

I grab a slice of cake for Nina and retrace her steps to the kitchen. I swing the kitchen door open to find my dad leaning over the sink with his head turned toward a small television under the cabinets featuring reruns of *Seinfeld*. The stack of dishes Nina brought in looks untouched. My footsteps startle Dad, and he jolts, his hands quickly resuming position with the scrubber. He lifts a plate out of the bubbly water and starts moving the brush counterclockwise in efficient strokes.

"Are there any leftovers?" I ask, hopeful for a honey-glazed prawn.

"Oh, hi, sweetie. I thought you were your mother." His eyes shift back to the screen, and he absentmindedly drops the plate into the sink. "I think there's a bit of broccoli left. And birthday noodles. Or maybe I already ate those."

"Why do I hear so much chatter when I should hear more scrubbing?" Mom asks as she sets empty cups and wine bottles onto the kitchen island. Her eyes shift over to the pile of dirty dishes. Dad picks the plate out of the water as quickly as he dropped it, his eyes now glued to the dish. Though only five foot three compared to Dad's six-foot-three frame, Mom's the one who commands the room.

Dad hangs his head, a strand of sandy brown hair flopping over his face, and speaks in the voice of an omniscient narrator. "At that moment, Marty looked at those dishes, not as a pile of porcelain and stainless steel, but as a direct representation of the failure that is his life." He lifts a dirty soup bowl from the dish mound.

Mom and I look at each other and shake our heads. Dad finds joy in making people laugh by occasionally speaking as though he's writing a script. For him, it comes with the territory of being a screenwriter.

"The dessert portion of the afternoon seems to be a hit," Mom says to me. "Has Sān Pó Po come by for a slice yet?"

"I saw her sneaking around the dessert table with pruning shears."

"Ha ha. Very funny," Mom says, checking the time on her watch. "Pó Po's getting ready for her speech. How are you feeling? If you change your mind, I can get you out of whatever contract you signed." Mom smiles to show me she's kidding. As a public defender, Mom never meets halfway in any negotiation and delivers tough love like a pro.

"In that case, can you renegotiate my salary?" I ask. "I want double what I make now with a guaranteed annual bonus." We share another laugh.

"Is this cake for me?" Dad asks, nodding toward Nina's slice.

"You already finished the last of the long-life noodles. I think you've had enough," Mom says with as much tenderness as she can muster in a family reunion setting. She wraps her arms around Dad's waist and hugs him from behind. To me, they have a marriage I've only dreamed of one day having. They're respectful of each other, communicative, and most importantly, compatible.

A high-pitched noise rings from the outside, and I follow my parents out to the backyard. It's time.

"Everyone, please gather around. Closer!" Pó Po shouts to the group. She stands in front of the backyard's circular fire pit as everyone slowly forms a U-shape around her. Pó Po taps her glass with the edge of her knife once more. The group falls silent. "Thank you all for making your way here to join me on my birthday. I only wish Gōng Gong could be here with us." Pó Po's eyes become glossy. "This entire day has been about me. I'm tired of me at this point, and I know you are, too." Polite laughter ripples through the air.

"Nǐ zhǔnbèi hǎole ma?" Pó Po asks Auntie.

Auntie lingers for a moment. Then she gives a quick nod and joins Pó Po. "Ready."

"Other than me lasting this long, I have more good news," Pó Po continues. "When I first started Lunar Love, I could never have imagined it would become what it has. After twenty-five years, I passed the business down to my daughter Lydia." Pó Po wraps her arm around Auntie's waist. "Lydia took over the business in the mid-nineties and ran it for another twenty-five years. And now, it's time for Lydia to pass our business on to the next generation. Olivia, my granddaughter, will be Lunar Love's new guardian Cupid."

Pó Po and Auntie signal for me to join them. My heart beats faster as a few heads in the crowd turn to look in my direction. The moment isn't lost on me. Pó Po coordinated the timing of the announcement so that the entire family could be here to witness not only her birthday but Lunar Love's emergence into a new era. I stand up straighter knowing people are watching.

"It has been my life's great honor to carry my mother's legacy all these years," Auntie says emotionally, dabbing the corner of her eyes with a paper napkin. "Her vision has lasted over five decades. That is a true testament to her ideas, her work ethic, and who she is as a person. We both feel comforted knowing that Lunar Love will be in great hands."

Pó Po positions me between her and Auntie. "Truthfully, there have been more than a fair share of challenges lately," she says. "It seems young people these days have greater trust in their phones to find them true love than experienced matchmakers, but after all these years, I know in my heart that it's just a growing pain. A phase." Pó Po grabs my hand. "It goes without saying that Liv will do an excellent job bringing Lunar Love into the future."

I give her hand a squeeze. *Challenges* is putting it lightly. In recent months, more clients have left Lunar Love complaining about the high cost of services and lengthy matching process. They say they want to explore other options. More modern options. I have my work cut out for me.

I watch Mom pour small amounts of whiskey into glasses that Dad passes around.

"And now, in following tradition, this necklace is yours." Auntie flips the gold crescent moon pendant between her thumb and pointer finger one last time before reaching behind her neck to unfasten the dangling gold chain. I'm beaming with excitement, and in this moment, I allow myself to feel it. The anxiety can wait.

Auntie extends her arms to place the necklace around my neck. I twist the little moon back and forth between my own fingers. The necklace itself is lighter than I imagined, but the weight of what it represents feels like a cinder block.

Before this necklace was Auntie's, it was Pó Po's. She bought it for herself with the money she made from her matchmaking practice in China, a one-woman show at the time. She wore the necklace when she moved from China to Taiwan, and ultimately over to America. Pó Po felt proud being able to not only support herself and her family but celebrate her small but good fortune with a special piece of jewelry. When she successfully transitioned her business to America, she attributed the accomplishment to hard work, late nights, single men and women who were willing to take a chance on an immigrant who promised true love, and good luck in the shape of a little crescent moon.

I turn to the crowd to say a few words. "I'm over the moon to be a part of Lunar Love's legacy in this way. All I want to do is make Pó Po and Auntie, and all of you, proud. I am ready and excited for this next chapter in my life and for Lunar Love. If you know anyone who's looking for love, you know who to talk to."

All three of us hold our glasses up to our friends and family. They hold theirs high in return, and we toast to the future and good health. I take a sip of the amber-colored liquid, notes of oak and caramel dancing on my tongue.

Tears sting my eyes as I lean in to embrace Pó Po and Auntie in a group hug. "Thank you both," I whisper. "For this opportunity, for believing in me, for everything."

An overwhelmed laugh of disbelief escapes my mouth. I absorb every last detail of this moment, taking a second to appreciate how far this journey has taken me. Starting Monday, I'll no longer be following in the footsteps of a well-worn path. A new adventure begins, and with all the challenges ahead, I'll be forging my own path. I can hardly wait.

CHAPTER 3

As a matchmaker, I stay on top of my game by reading (and rereading) every English book on the Chinese zodiac and by attending as many relevant events as I can to stay in the know.

Today's event is the one I look forward to most, and it's just my luck that it falls on my very first day as Head Matchmaker of Lunar Love. Every fall, the annual Matched with Love Summit takes place in Los Angeles. The day-long conference captures the magic of new beginnings, optimism, and unspoken *what if*s. If you're a matchmaker, it's the queen of all conferences. Thousands of matchmakers, behavioral scientists, CEOs, marketers, and investors from around the country attend to learn about the state of the industry, how to increase profits, and the science behind attraction. Basically, we gather to talk all things love and matchmaking.

This year, Matched with Love is being hosted on the outskirts of Chinatown, which Lunar Love has called home for the last fifty years. The speaker of this afternoon's session, Dr. Annie Goodman, paces back and forth on layered carpets at the front of the event space. Rows of chairs facing her are lined up neatly in the outdoor veranda of an industrial warehouse that's been painted all white. Flower garlands drip from the overhead beams, casting floral shadows on the concrete floor in the natural light. It's all very romantic.

"Raise your hand if you believe that opposites attract," Dr. Goodman instructs in a loud voice. "And be honest!" With silver hair, tortoiseshell round glasses, and her fingers steepled in front of her, Dr. Goodman looks like a glamorous therapist only seen in movies. She commands the room with her quiet confidence as she speaks methodically about the psychology of love.

Opposites attract? Not a chance.

I turn in my seat near the front, looking around at the number of arms that shoot up into the air. In a room of two hundred professionals, a little over half of them have their hands raised. I shake my head in disappointment.

"You in the back, can you share with us why you believe opposites attract?" Dr. Goodman gestures toward a man in a burgundy long-sleeve shirt sitting in the rear of the space.

I angle my head to try to see who's speaking when the man stands to answer. "Differences in personalities can make for interesting relationships," he says. "One might call it opposite, another might call it complementary. It's not that I *only* think opposites attract. I just don't like limiting who can be attracted to who." The man addresses the room as he speaks, rotating to seemingly make eye contact with everyone in the room.

Dr. Goodman nods her head in slow, long dips, looking as though she's forming her response. "And do you think complementary personality traits help the relationship long-term?"

The light makes it difficult to see his features from where

I sit, but he appears to stand with confidence. "A recent study showed that over eighty-two percent of people found those who were their opposite attractive. I think that's because differences create chemistry. The way I see it, there's not a lot of excitement or room for growth if people are with others who are just like them," he says, running a hand through his dark hair.

"Thank you. And what about you?" Dr. Goodman cradles her chin in her hand and looks in my direction. "I saw you shaking your head. You don't think opposites can attract?"

I feel everyone's eyes turn on me, and I hold my notebook against my chest and remain seated, facing the people in the first few rows. "I've personally experienced and witnessed what happens when two opposites come together," I say, quietly at first.

Dr. Goodman makes a noise. "Go on."

"It's fun for a short period of time because the other person is exciting and shiny and new, but it's lust versus love. If people are too opposite in values and interests, that's how conflicting, contentious partnerships are formed. Don't get me wrong, I'm not saying that people have to agree on every single thing, because that's rare. But just because people have similar traits doesn't mean they're in boring relationships."

"Mmhmm," Dr. Goodman hums.

"My job is to find those similarities *and* flaws in clients and pair them with well-suited matches," I continue. "This way, people can bypass all the wondering and initial skepticism. I'm there with clients through the new moon, I mean, the beginning of their relationships so I can better understand the dynamics of their interactions."

"Sorry, but whoever's speaking right now, you really don't

think two opposites can balance each other out?" the voice of the man who spoke before me calls out.

I turn to face him, but the man's already seated, his face lost among the crowd. "Only if—and that's a big if—both people are willing to keep that balance in check and are open to transformation. It won't just happen. Change is hard and requires work. Certain flaws can be dealbreakers," I respond.

"Your point being what? That opposite traits are flaws?" the man yells again.

"Complementary traits and opposite traits are not one and the same," I say loudly so the man in the back can hear me. "If you're looking for excitement in your life with someone who is wildly different from you because you can't be with someone so similar to yourself, well, then, best of luck to you."

Take that, Opposites Attract Guy.

"And if you're scared to be with someone who's too different, I respectfully wish you all the best," the man says, his tone assertive but not unfriendly. My jaw drops as I face back toward the front.

"Thank you both for the dialogue. I appreciate the passion. You give us a lot to think about," Dr. Goodman says as she repositions herself behind a podium. "Now, to go back to something else that was mentioned: love versus lust. Let's explore that." She resumes her presentation while I take notes.

After the session, I meet up with Alisha. While waiting for her, I watch as attendees shake hands, embrace in hugs, and tap their phones. I slide my fingers down my heart-patterned lanyard and admire the dangling glossy badge printed with my name and fancy new title.

I've played Cupid for over three hundred clients. It's a beautiful thing when two people come together from various corners of the world and are matched based on their truly complementary personality traits, just as the moon and Earth complement one another. With as many people as there are out there, finding your person can be overwhelming, to say the least.

I love creating love and seeing relationships go from a spark to a raging bonfire. Sure, sometimes the fire goes out in relationships, but sometimes, even after a few missteps, the embers still glow hot, and the fire remains in a steady state of potential, needing just a single gust of air to reignite. It's all part of the process of finding and falling in love.

Alisha startles me when she sweeps her arm around my shoulder.

"Happy first day! That should really say CLO!" she says in a singsongy tone. "Chief Love Officer. How do you feel?"

I laugh and nod my head toward a bouquet of overfilled giant heart balloons, the glistening red foil practically bursting at the seams. "Like that. I'm so excited I could burst."

Alisha laughs. "How was your session? I learned about so many different attachment styles in relationships, I feel like I just got out of therapy."

"I was put on the spot but I'm always eager to talk shop," I say. "Ready for lunch? Randall says he'll meet us there."

"Can you get a couple of quick shots of me? This outfit's a bit over-the-top," she says, referencing her puffy red sleeves, "but it matches the color palette of my feed."

With Alisha's phone, I snap a few photos, crouching low to capture every angle. When she's not busy matchmaking, Alisha runs her Instagram account where she features first-date outfits styled and modeled by her. With over thirty thousand followers, Alisha's in tune with what's happening in the social media world. Her expertise will be invaluable for our upcoming marketing efforts.

We stroll through the outdoor veranda to the stage kitchen where countless cookbook photoshoots have undoubtedly taken place. Situated next to the long community tables is a photobooth with the words *Love at First Aura* scrawled across the side.

The woman at the booth gives us a warm smile as we pass by. "Welcome. Would you be interested in trying *Love at First Aura*? First we read your aura, then we find you a match based on your aura color."

Alisha looks fascinated by their concept. "I love how spiritual this is. Get in!" she says, nudging me.

"What! No!" I use both my arms to push off the booth. "Great concept, though!"

"Come on!" Alisha begs. "I'll bet you're a deep blue and violet. Don't you want to know who you'll match with?"

I laugh. "Good one. Aura compatibility isn't quite my thing. Besides, it's not about me. Love is in the air, Alisha. Can you feel it?" I raise my hands and spin around.

She raises her eyebrows in amusement. "For everyone but you, I suppose."

I let her comment roll off my back. Many moons ago, I did love being in love. I used to fall in love easily. Too easily. Now I know better. I'm wiser. More careful.

Randall is already behind the counter picking out his lunch, which is standard conference to-go fare, a turkey and cheddar sandwich with a bag of chips and an apple. I cherish every single bite because, even though the bread's stale and the apple's bruised, I'm surrounded by people who are trying to bring more love into the world. Today might as well be a holiday in my calendar.

"These sandwiches are cut into hearts!" Randall says, looking amused. His expression morphs into confusion. "What do they do with the crusts, though? Seems wasteful."

We eat and wander, stumbling upon the designated booth section for online dating and digital apps, or in other words, Dating Purgatory. With new apps popping up all the time, I feel at ease knowing that Lunar Love focuses on in-person match-making where clients aren't caught straddling the fine line of ghosting or playing the waiting game. Because we're hands-on with our clients, no one is ever left wondering about the status of their love lives. Humans deserve more than being relegated to names like *users* and being worthy only if they contribute to data and bottom lines.

Alisha, Randall, and I wind through people waiting for free swag from online dating apps both big and small. I hear founders and CEOs pitching their products to the media, interested customers, and potential job candidates. In the midst of the chaos, I hear the words *Chinese zodiac* spoken by a person at one of the booths. I stop in my tracks as Alisha bumps into me from behind. A chip flies out of my hand and under the heel of a man's sneaker.

"Oof! Are you okay?" she asks. "What's up?"

"Did you hear that? Someone just said *Chinese zodiac*."

"Maybe you were thinking out loud again, and you heard yourself say it," Randall says as he looks around the crowded room. "It wouldn't be the first time."

"There it was again!" I say, leading them closer to the row of booths. As I push my way through the crowd, I can see just enough of the company's sign over people's heads.

My eyes scan over the words *ZodiaCupid: Compatibility is in the personality.*

Alisha gasps when she reads the sign. "Does that sound like what I think it sounds like?"

"It can't be," I say, trying to get a better look at the man speaking from the booth. He wears the confidence of a CEO and a burgundy long-sleeve shirt. It's the Opposites Attract Guy.

I step closer to listen and get a better look at his face. A feeling of familiarity washes over me when I realize I've met this man before.

"No...way," I say slowly. The air collapses out of me as though I'm a shiny heart balloon that's just been popped.

"We're excited about our new app that matches users based on their Chinese zodiac animal signs," Opposites Attract Guy announces.

My heart plummets from my chest to the bottom of my stomach. Opposites Attract Guy is none other than Bakery Guy.

"Pinch me," I squeak. "Ow! I didn't mean both of you!"

"Any time," Alisha and Randall say, both of them transfixed on the man.

"I can't believe this." I grab Alisha and Randall by their forearms. "That's him. That's Bakery Guy."

"Which one?" Alisha asks eagerly, scanning the room.

"Him! The one in the booth. The guy talking!" I stare at the man in disbelief. "He was so...nice. So charming."

"He still seems nice and charming, no?" Randall asks.

"Not anymore! Do you think he was spying on me?" I say, my mind racing.

Alisha snorts. "Liv, you taking over Lunar Love hasn't been announced yet to the public. How could he have known? Besides, if he asked for your number at the bakery, then I'd worry. But he didn't, so it doesn't sound like he knows who you are."

Her words hit harder than they should. "Uh-huh." I can't take my eyes off Bakery Guy. "It's not like I would've given him my number anyways," I justify. Why *didn't* he ask for my number? Any onlooker would've thought there was a connection there. But with his magnetic personality, he probably connects with everyone like that.

Bakery Guy speaks animatedly, waving his hands around when he shares vague data points and ideas. He's careful not to give away too many details, sticking with loose explanations of what the app is and how it works.

"To us, compatibility has a broader definition. We're doing things a bit differently, as you'll see," he announces to the crowd.

I clench my jaw. "Different? Different how?"

"Maybe they've made up twelve different animals completely," Randall offers. "I always thought Dolphins and Pandas were unfairly left out."

"Are they seriously calling themselves ZodiaCupid?" I huff. "He basically stole the idea of our business and digitalized it. He can't do this to Pó Po's legacy! And those poor people in Digital Purgatory!"

I cross my arms and watch as Team ZodiaCupid high-five each other and toss branded T-shirts and zip hoodies into the enthused crowd. Bakery Guy's features don't look so appealing anymore. Instead, he just looks smug and deceitful.

"Their marketing budget must be insane," Alisha says, nearly knocking a woman over in a desperate attempt to catch a hoodie in midair. "Ooh, these feel like eco-fleece!"

"Wow, that's soft," I say, running my hand along the arm of the hoodie.

"They're just wannabes," Randall says.

"Right. Lunar Love is the original. You want quality love, you go to quality matchmakers. Why let an algorithm have so much control when you can have a real, experienced person that you can trust?" I say confidently before realizing I'm still stroking the eco-fleece.

Alisha nods. "That's the damn truth."

Bakery Guy continues his presentation, matching the energy of the crowd now decked out in ZodiaCupid swag. "We're in the beta testing phase," he says proudly. "For everyone who's at our booth right now, we're giving you immediate beta access. Just use the code CHINESEZODIAC. Being mixed race, I hope to share my Chinese culture with you all and work toward bridging communities with ZodiaCupid. It's my hope that you'll join us on this journey."

So Bakery Guy is mixed race like me.

Alisha, Randall, and I immediately huddle in the corner and download ZodiaCupid onto our phones using the beta code. I keep one ear on the founder, who's fielding questions from the group.

"Thanks, everyone, for your attention," he says, offering the crowd a giant, suck-up grin. "Again, I'm Bennett O'Brien, and we're ZodiaCupid!"

Sounds and chatter around me fall away. Bennett O'Brien. Finally, Bakery Guy has a name. Bennett. My lips touch for a brief moment to form the *B* of his name. I silently repeat the words to myself. I hate the way his name feels on my tongue.

"Let's see what all the hype is about," I say, focusing on the task at hand. I type in the code. My screen glows with ZodiaCupid's logo, a single connected line of a cursive *Z*, its last loop turning into an arrow and piercing through a heart. I add my first name and last initial and a fake birthday within my Horse year so my animal sign can populate into the system. I don't have to worry about finding a decent photo of myself since the app apparently doesn't let people upload any.

"I hate to say it, but this actually looks good," Randall says as he taps through the app. "It's unbelievable how quickly these matches happen. What takes us days takes them seconds."

I groan. "That's exactly the problem. Instant isn't better."

Around us, more women have gathered to catch a glimpse of the handsome man peddling false hope.

"I read that he's LA's most eligible bachelor. Apparently he uses his own app," one woman says.

"In that case, maybe we should try matching with him," another woman responds with a giggle. "He just made some list of, like, top ten up-and-coming Asian American entrepreneurs. Pretty impressive."

I roll my eyes and then continue filling in my empty profile. As soon as I hit Save, matches start trickling in. That *was* fast. I skim through the animals I'm paired with, expecting compatible Dogs and Tigers to my Year of the Horse. Instead, a variety of animal signs and noises appear. They don't even know my birth hour, yet they're providing me with this wide range of animals.

"I think a Snake just hissed at me," Alisha says, stunned.

This is all wrong. I return to the match page and continue scrolling to see what other signs I've been paired with. While my compatible animal signs appear, there are also Monkeys, Pigs, Snakes, and Oxen.

"I never thought I'd know what sound Dragons make, yet

here we are," I mumble. A few more seconds later, a Rooster crows at me.

"Maybe they're bots. Or it's the company's back system flattering users and making them feel like the app works. Or," Randall says conspiratorially, "it's a ploy to steal users' data."

"It's impersonal and inaccurate. People won't fully understand who they're being matched with and why, let alone what their signs mean. Without a matchmaker, people lose the human element of falling in love," I say, trying to steady my shallow breathing.

Alisha nods. "People are more complex than what these animal traits imply," she says, her lips forming a tight line. "And there's so much variety within each animal sign."

"Welcome to the twenty-first century," I say with a sigh. "I guess all animal signs will be matched in one way or another instead of following tradition." This thought pains me. "We can't let them take advantage of people like this! Maybe they'll never make it through beta because of terrible reviews. It'll be so bad that people will realize that there's a lot more to zodiac matchmaking than simply pairing animals together."

I watch as the crowd continues growing around the ZodiaCupid booth. Bennett shakes hands with a few audience members, his face beaming with pride. From my corner, I can hardly see his dimples, but I remember them so vividly that he might as well be standing right in front of me.

"Their app will crash and die a fabulous death before ever making it to launch," Alisha snickers.

I narrow my eyes at Bennett from across the room. "I guess we'll just have to wait and see."

CHAPTER 4

Turns out, I'm not so good at waiting. After a long day of conference sessions and networking, I'm still obsessing over ZodiaCupid. At least now I have my cat, Pinot, take-out pizza, and an actual bottle of Pinot. I lean against my velvet pink couch in my apartment as Pinot purrs in my lap. I finish off my first glass of wine, a celebratory drink for my first day and for remaining calm and collected about the whole ZodiaCupid disaster.

My mind recalls the two women's words at the conference about matching with Bennett. Like that'd be fun. All he'd probably do is talk about his business nonstop, the latest features, and how ZodiaCupid is going to change the world. That's not . . . wait.

That could be useful. But I'd have to match with him first, and what are the chances of that? I would need to know what animal sign he is, though that probably doesn't matter since ZodiaCupid matches anyone and everyone. Of course, I wouldn't tell him who I am. Or is that not ethical? But if I pay for the date? Then it's more of a work lunch. Or a business dinner. Or a work meeting, or whatever.

If I *could* match with him, I'd test out the app, go on a date, and crush his ego so much that he doesn't want to do the app anymore. Or I could be so horrible that he'd feel wary about sending any other users out on dates with complete strangers. I pour myself a second glass of wine and swirl it around in the glass.

On my phone, I tap into a press release from today to read more about ZodiaCupid.

NEW DATING APP MATCHES ZODIAC ANIMAL SIGNS TOGETHER

By Miranda Moore / October 5, 2020 / 11:30 am PT

Move over, Cupid, there's a new matchmaker coming to town. His name is Bennett O'Brien, and he's created an app to help others, and himself, find love. Inspired by Bennett's Chinese roots, ZodiaCupid is a dating app that pairs people based on their Chinese zodiac animal signs. It's coming to an app store near you on the Lunar New Year, which happens to fall just two days before Valentine's Day next year.

Based out of Los Angeles, ZodiaCupid is currently in beta testing. O'Brien, LA's most eligible bachelor and Year of the Rat, is a tech-savvy entrepreneur who has helped guide other start-ups to success in his roles as founder, consultant, and investor.

Of course the founder of our new competition is a Rat, my exact opposite sign. I guess it makes sense. Rats do tend to have an inborn entrepreneurial sense. Clearly, he's a self-made man and a natural-born leader. In normal circumstances, Horses and Rats would never be matched, but this is ZodiaCupid. Anything goes.

I could set up a date and then stand him up. No one likes to be ghosted. But that doesn't help me. I can go on a date, order the most expensive meal, pre-order my dessert, head to the bathroom, and then never come back. Diabolical, but not strategic. Maybe I could write an exposé about how ZodiaCupid is a total scam. They'll call me Olivia Farrow. Alisha does know someone at WhizDash. I need to match with this man, go on a date, milk him for all the information he's got, and then write a scathing tell-all.

That's it!

With my beta Horse profile activated, there's only one way in. I just need to make some minor changes. I read the press release again slowly, fixating on each and every word to find ones I can use in my profile to match with Bennett. I throw in a few personal ones so that the algorithm doesn't flag me as a bot or something.

To some it's unpopular, but I'm a sucker for . . . nights in with a good book. Baseball game soft pretzels. Pinot Noir and pizza nights.

The best place I ever traveled was . . . Rome. They say Paris is the City of Love, but true love is actually pasta.

I'll try anything once . . . like ZodiaCupid and celebrating Valentine's Day.

He's probably the type of person who would share the who, what, when, where, and why of his own app *in* his dating profile. That's easy promotion. I wouldn't put it past him.

I'll pick up the tab . . . if you can actually tell me, in order, the Chinese zodiac animal signs.

Midway down the screen, a pop-up box interrupts my flow.

Prepare those paintbrushes, Horses! You share an animal sign with Rembrandt. You're artistic by nature.

"Oh, look. Generic fun facts about the animal signs," I say sarcastically. "This is where we can play to our advantage. We take the time to get to know our clients, Pinot. We don't brush-stroke their animal signs over them." Still, I'm momentarily distracted by what Horse traits Rembrandt must've possessed.

I take a sip of wine. A sinking feeling whirls in my stomach. What if people using the app match with my fake profile? Then they'll feel led on and think that the nonexistent person on the other end is purposely ignoring them. I'm not trying to break anyone's heart. Pó Po and Auntie would be so disappointed if they knew what I was up to.

Pó Po's advice when we were in initial discussions for me to take over Lunar Love echoes through my head. *If you take on more than you can chew, you'll choke,* she instructed. I push her words out of my mind. In order to survive, we have to eat everything. I suppose it's a small sacrifice for exposing the truth.

I feel like I'm trying to fly to the moon on a sailboat. I take a deep breath. I can't bring love to the world if Lunar Love doesn't exist. I tap Save on my profile and watch as more animal noises trickle in, waiting to see if a certain Rat will squeak at me.

I flip through the channels on TV to find a new distraction, landing on a docuseries about the deep sea. It feeds into my curiosity *and* fears. But being *in* the ocean is different than observing it from the comforts of my studio apartment. The distraction attempts don't work for long. I let the episode play in the background as I continue studying the press release. Another form of feeding my curiosity and fears.

"One thing that differentiates us is that we aren't showing images of users in the profiles. Eighty-five percent of people we surveyed preferred not to show photos, so we eliminated the need for it. We're about personality traits, not how people look. Our concept is based loosely on the Chinese zodiac animal sign traits, but we do things our own way," O'Brien shares. "After all, traditions were meant to be broken."

Traditions were meant to be broken? Who does this guy think he is?

"It's the Great Race to Lunar New Year. That's only four months away," I calculate. "It's fine. There's still time for them to fail before then."

Pinot stares blankly at me.

"I know the Great Race is a sore subject for you cats. Oh forget it. I thought you'd at least care because a Rat is involved!"

February is our biggest month of the year with Lunar New Year and Valentine's Day. If ZodiaCupid successfully launches then, we may not see the boost in client numbers we're used to. We'll need to rethink our strategy and make the most of the next few months. Lunar Love counts on that annual increase.

I grab my laptop and double-check Lunar Love's spreadsheets. Luckily, we have enough savings to keep us afloat for about two or three more months, but we don't have time to waste.

ZodiaCupid is running a closed beta where a few thousand lucky users can test the product early and experience most of the features ZodiaCupid will offer, with lots more additions to come. Meanwhile, ZodiaCupid is taking beta tester feedback into consideration and working on improving their product.

"We're excited about the overwhelmingly positive feedback we've received so far. We don't take the work we do lightly or for granted. It's been a wild ride, and we're just getting started," O'Brien adds.

It wasn't until the past two weeks that they announced their presence to the world with a creative social media campaign. They've already received over 25,000 email signups from people hoping to be accepted into beta during this campaign. If you haven't yet found love, sign up on their website to be a beta tester and give this clever and unique dating app a try—this could be your Year of the Match Made in Zodiac Heaven!

I unintentionally clench my jaw as I read phrases like "The start-up world's newest darling" and "Fresh concept for those looking for tradition in a modern world." If people cared about tradition and the Chinese zodiac, they would've found us. Lunar Love has been here for half a century, but because we're not some flashy new app, we get overlooked. Apps are soulless and impersonal. Love is between two people, not two avatars. Lunar Love is a business that's built from the heart.

Another headline, "Chinese Zodiac Expert Helps Masses Find Compatible Matches," stops me in my tracks.

"You think you're an expert, Bennett? You're not an expert! The only thing you're an expert in is stealing other people's business concepts and buns." My shouts annoy Pinot, and he jumps off my lap, settling into the far corner of the couch.

I wander into the bathroom and rip open a sheet mask. I

carefully drape the mask over my forehead, nose, and cheeks. How are they measuring success? The number of oinks and barks people receive? Messages? How are they even tracking that without knowing who's going on dates? My skepticism remains. There's no way this app works.

I scroll through more matches that appear in my dashboard on the app, keeping a close eye out for one in particular. "Let's see your so-called expertise in action. You're not fooling anyone, Bennett O'Brien!"

I peruse the profile of the Rooster that crowed at me earlier and evaluate the contents of the profile of Parker T., the owner of a hip new Italian restaurant in downtown Los Angeles. According to what he's written, he's obsessed with anything that has to do with Italy (especially the food) and is a proud Angeleno.

Truthfully, if our animal sign personality traits didn't clash so much, Parker T. might actually be interesting. After all, I'm a fan of carbonara and the Italian Riviera. Clearly their system is pulling words from profiles and matching people that way. I used the word *pasta* in my profile. But that's profile matching, not necessarily personality matching. I could've written in my profile that I despise pasta, and according to the app's logic, based on those words alone, we still might've matched.

"That's what I thought!" I fling my wineglass up in the air, and the liquid sloshes around dangerously. "Not a match, not an expert." This wine hit harder and faster than I anticipated. I walk over to the kitchen and eat another piece of Hawaiian pizza.

Over the speakers, the narrator's voice grows ominous, drawing my attention back to the television. A hideous creature pops out of the center of a fish's mouth, its worm-like body looking like it's made itself at home. As disturbing as it is, I can't look away. Instead, I turn the volume up.

"The tongue-eating louse, or *Cymothoa exigua*, is a parasite that enters through the fish's gills. The parasite severs the fish's tongue and attaches itself, becoming the fish's tongue itself," the narrator informs viewers. An ice blue fish with squiggly lines on its head swims through the water. Suddenly, a small creature pokes out of its mouth.

"Ew! Pinot, look at that!" I slide the slipping sheet mask up my forehead and cheeks.

Pinot looks over at me from the couch and lets out a husky meow. Curious what I'm doing, he saunters into the kitchen and jumps onto the counter.

"This process doesn't harm or kill the fish, though it may be slightly unpleasant for a while," the narrator continues. "The parasite finds a way to survive in its new host by replacing the fish's tongue and feeding off blood and mucus in the fish's mouth."

I open the camera on my phone and flip it to face me. With the sheet mask on and my tongue sticking out, I look and feel like I've officially lost it.

"Pinot, show me your tongue." I reach for Pinot, who's decided that the cutting board is an ideal sitting spot, but he leaps away before I can grab him.

This process is disturbingly poetic. These parasites find a fish to live in, and the fish learns to adapt to its new tongue. Meanwhile, the parasite survives because of its new host. Will Lunar Love become the fish's tongue that shrivels up and dies because of companies like ZodiaCupid? Realization dawns. Or am *I* the parasite?

"Bennett, I'm gonna find you, and then I'm gonna secretly attach myself to you and survive off your various fluids," I say. "Wait, that doesn't sound right." I laugh out loud at my ridiculous thoughts.

The docuseries is cut off by commercials. I see a cursive *Z* fly across the screen and hear the pitch I've read a dozen times about ZodiaCupid.

"No! They're running commercials now? Boo!" I yell at the screen. I'm tempted to throw my pizza at the TV, but ZodiaCupid isn't worth giving up even one slice.

Well, I have to do what I can in order to survive. And that starts with infiltrating the system to get to the founder. As my mom would say, *Always know what the other side is thinking. You don't want to be caught off guard by new information that could knock you off your feet.*

It's sink or swim.

If I can match with Bennett, I can become one with the fish and suck its blood. Okay, that's a bit much. I'll find out everything I can about ZodiaCupid so Lunar Love isn't caught off guard again. Bennett is simply the fish gills.

Hours later, just before midnight, I stir to the sound of Pinot using the couch as his scratching post. I groggily check my phone for emails, texts, and ZodiaCupid updates.

There are fifteen new matches. I flip through each one, hoping for a miracle. There are a few Rats in the list. I carefully read through each profile, finally landing on one that looks promising. Could this actually be Bennett? I sit up with newfound alertness.

I like to spend my days . . . bringing love into people's lives.

Wait, what? That's *my* job.

My favorite books to read are . . . business books and nonfiction.

An entrepreneur?

The thing I care most about is . . . making ZodiaCupid, a Chinese zodiac matchmaking app, number one in the industry (launches on Valentine's Day).

Bingo.

The name at the top reads B.O.B. Bob? Or . . . Bennett O'Brien? Apparently I'm a drunk algorithm wizard. I was able to figure out how to beat their system with a bottle of wine in me.

If this really is Bennett, there's only one way to find out. Without a clear plan or time to overthink what I want to say, I send: Hi B.O.B., Something in the lunarsphere matched us up. Let's meet.

I obsessively refresh my phone every few minutes in hopes that B.O.B. has responded. Finally, a message materializes below the one I sent.

Hello, Olivia. Nice hearing from you. A date sounds great.

I shudder at the thought of going on a date, but this isn't for me. It's for Lunar Love. I'm on a mission. Agent Olivia Huang Christenson, reporting for duty. It's all suddenly much more real.

I tap out my response: Tomorrow too soon?

CHAPTER 5

I'm the first to arrive at the cooking school for my "date" with B.O.B. I claim a seat at the community table tucked against the wall of the classroom, situating myself in the middle so there are plenty of open chairs on both sides of me for my target—I mean, date.

After some back and forth, my idea of attending a baking class won out. Over the years, I've learned that clients feel more comfortable in first-date settings when they're elbow deep in cake batter. There's flexibility to be flirty, but if the chemistry's not there, clients can focus more on their crème brûlées than each other. Plus, if the date is a bust, they still get dessert, the sweetest of consolation prizes.

Luckily, there aren't any clients booked for dates here tonight, so I won't be exposed. When there's the opportunity to have the home field advantage, always take it. In my case, I won't have to pay much attention to the baking part and can get straight to the grilling.

The classroom looks like a commercial kitchen with stainless steel appliances and workbenches, but the space has clearly been designed for private events and photoshoots. White subway tiles cover two walls in the room and a large chalkboard hangs on the other.

I examine the board so that I know what to expect for the next two and a half hours. In cursive pink chalk, I read: Mochi (Japanese rice balls with red bean filling), Bái Táng Gāo (Chinese white sugar sponge cake), Dàntǎ (egg tarts), Bánh Chuối Nướng (Vietnamese banana cake), and Yuèbǐng (mooncakes). I've made two of the five desserts before, which gives me a small boost of confidence.

B.O.B. said he'd wear a salmon-colored shirt. Within minutes, two men and one woman arrive, all three of them taking seats at opposite ends of the table. No sign of him yet.

A few more students quietly walk in and fill the seats. Nerves start to get the best of me. Maybe this wasn't such a bright idea. I'm acting like a lowlife parasitic organism that takes and takes without giving anything in return. *That's* what I'm trying to be?

Focus, Olivia! You're here to find out information about your competition.

I'm rubbing my moon pendant for good luck when a man in a coral cashmere sweater who looks to be in his mid-thirties takes a seat next to me. He turns, and I find myself staring into the eyes of my enemy. Turns out B.O.B. was Bennett, after all. The stars and the moon have aligned. I can almost hear the sound of singing baby cupids. My plan to match with Bennett worked.

"You?!" we both say at the same time. I overplay my surprise, though his looks genuine.

"What are *you* doing here?" he asks.

"Are you B dot O dot B dot?" I ask.

He laughs. "I am. Bennett O'Brien. Are you O-L-I-V-I-A?"

I smirk. "Liv is short for Olivia."

"First the bakery, now this. Either you're following me or fate keeps bringing us together," Bennett says.

He only remembers me from the bakery, which means he didn't see me in the audience at the conference. I breathe out in relief.

"Why in the world would you call yourself B.O.B.?" I ask.

"Probably the same reason you go by Liv, *Olivia*," he says, emphasizing my name. "So I guess we're here for the same date then."

"By the look of the flowers you're holding, it looks like you're going to a funeral, not a date," I say, nodding to the white chrysanthemums in his hands.

"I'm still mourning the loss of my cocktail bun," he says solemnly. "Since you're my date, these are for you. Sorry for your loss?" He holds the flowers out toward me slowly. "Is there a better flower I could've gone with?"

"I personally prefer peonies, but it's, what do they say? It's the thought that counts. Thanks." I tentatively reach for the bouquet and tuck the flowers into my bag. "Why are you not wearing salmon? That's coral if I've ever seen it."

Bennett looks at his shirt. "This is most definitely salmon," he says. After a moment, he adds, "I know this is weird, but I think we should stay. Let's start with a clean slate. I'm Bennett. You're Olivia slash Liv slash Bakery Girl."

So he nicknamed me, too.

"You can call me Olivia. We can stay, but I'll start with the questions. What do you do for work?" I ask, not wanting to waste any time. I need to squeeze everything I can out of this man.

Bennett looks slightly startled. "Uh, I'm actually the founder of ZodiaCupid. That's why I think we should stay," he admits. "My algorithm is good."

"Wow, your algorithm has taken the place of fate, huh?" I say. He's probably also someone who looks in the mirror and tells himself he's handsome. "I had no idea you were the founder of the app we matched on." Little does he know, I've read every single press release ever published about him and his company. And he doesn't need to find out. Playing ignorant might get me more information.

"I guess you couldn't look me up because of my name. Or lack thereof." Bennett rests his foot on the base of the stool. "My algorithm works, and I trust it. There's a reason we keep meeting. And you're interesting in a weird sort of way."

I put a hand over my heart and give him a mock-serious look. "That's the nicest thing anyone's ever said to me."

Bennett laughs. "That came out wrong. It could've just been me, but I felt like we hit it off at Lucky Monkey. I realized after I should've asked for your number. And now you're here."

Before Bennett can say anything else, the instructor claps her hands to capture the class's attention. She welcomes everyone and explains that we'll break into teams and make one of the recipes on the board. Bennett and I are assigned mooncakes. When we push off our stools to find a spot near the stove, I'm reminded of how tall he is standing next to my five-foot-four height. He's in dark blue jeans that slightly hug his thighs, the cuffs folded above his light brown leather boots. Put together, yet casual. At least the man's consistent.

We claim the space next to the team assigned with egg tarts. Bennett and I awkwardly make eye contact as we move around each other. I remind myself that I'm doing this for love and for the greater good of single people everywhere.

Bennett reads through the recipe, whispering the list of ingredients out loud as he compares it to what's provided in the ingredient bucket on the table. I stare at him in suspicion and pleasure that *he's* the one here in front of me.

He pulls up an image on his phone and tilts the screen so I can see. "I think we should follow this recipe instead. I can attest that they're the best mooncakes. Similar ingredients, slightly different process."

I bristle at his confidence. "Why do you have that on your phone? You couldn't have known we were making mooncakes tonight."

"I looked up the class beforehand and pulled recipes for all of the potential desserts. I've made mooncakes before and happen to have my own recipe. I have a one hundred percent success rate with this."

I put my hand on my hip in defiance. "Well, I've made mooncakes, too, and I think we should follow the class recipe." His line from the press release about how traditions were meant to be broken echoes through my mind. "It looks like some of the steps have already been started because of time constraints."

"You don't want to try it my way?" Bennett asks with a look of surprise. "I *know* my recipe works. This other recipe doesn't even have the salted duck egg yolks in it."

I don't want to try anything his way, dating app or otherwise. "It's out of our control. We paid money to be here, to make the mooncakes the cooking school's way," I say, pushing back. "If they're not as good as yours, then you can gloat all you want."

Bennett's jaw clenches, but after a moment, he slides his phone into his pocket. "Sure. We'll do it your way," he says, a hint of annoyance detectable in his voice. At least he's finally agreed. "How about we get started and see where it goes?"

"Let's try to get through the steps without it being too weird," I say, secretly pleased. I should not feel this satisfied at unnerving him. "This recipe says we should start with the syrup, but that's already been done. So we should do the dough."

"I think we should start with the filling," Bennett counters. "It looks like the teacher already started boiling the presoaked lotus seeds so we can finish that up."

Oh for Cupid's sake! We're not even five minutes in, and we're already going head-to-head. I wrap an apron around my waist. "Like I said, we should follow the steps. They're written in this order for a reason."

"Recipe instructions are meant to be reinterpreted," he says, hooking his apron around his neck.

I sense a theme. "How about this? You do that while I get the dough going."

"You don't want to follow the recipe together?" he asks. "Isn't that the point of a date? Doing things together?"

I reach for a towel, cringing slightly at his use of the word *date*. "Right, but it's not as efficient. We can get a couple steps done at once if we divide and cook."

"Here." Bennett brings the food processor over from a shelf and plugs it in. He checks the simmering lotus seeds and drains the liquid, adding them to the food processor. As they whirl together, a smooth, thick mixture forms. Bennett looks as though he's memorizing every texture and scent. He scoops the mixture into a pan and sets the heat to medium low. "See? Now that's done! We can follow the rest of the steps together."

"Great," I murmur.

"Did you know that, years ago, people were worried there'd be a 'mooncake bubble' in China?" Bennett says as he mixes the puree with a spatula, filling the tense silence between us. "Luxury mooncakes took over the market and were selling for upwards of ten times as much as a traditional mooncake."

I grab a silver bowl from one of the nearest stands. "Why do people feel the need to change a good thing? There's nothing wrong with tradition."

"It's not about wrong or right. Sometimes people like trying new things," Bennett offers.

I try not to let irritation show on my face. There are more important topics at hand, like extracting important intel.

"Is the Chinese zodiac your life's passion or are you just in it for a quick buck?" I blurt out.

Bennett scrunches his nose. "Is that a joke?"

"Let me rephrase: Where did you take, I mean, get your idea from? And don't give me the canned response that I'm sure you're giving reporters." This response I already know from the press release. *I started ZodiaCupid to help give people a shot at love based on who they really are. On our app, there's no need to pretend or perform. All you have to do is be you.*

"What I say isn't canned," he says with his eyebrows scrunched. "I wanted to make something special and specific in the dating app market. I like our concept. It's fun."

"Fun," I echo. I think back to the days when the Chinese zodiac was so new to me that it did feel fun. Mysterious. Rooted in practicality. The magic's still there, but it's mostly become business. I add syrup, lye water, and oil to the flour and fold the ingredients together with a spatula. "Have you always been into the zodiac or is it a recently acquired interest?"

Surprisingly, Bennett looks unfazed by my line of questioning. He focuses in on my eyes and deadpans, "I've just been learning about it through Wikipedia. Really good stuff on there."

Against my better judgment, a laugh slips out. I can't be laughing at my enemy's jokes. It's a sign of weakness.

He laughs and shakes his head, a strand of hair falling across his forehead. "If you're wondering if I grew up learning about the zodiac, no. I learned it on my own. My mom was into the zodiac, but—no, I didn't," he says, cutting himself off. He doesn't elaborate. "I've studied the Chinese zodiac deeply, even though my app takes a looser approach."

He's bluffing.

"Go ahead, you can ask me anything," he says as if reading my mind.

When I shake my head and stay silent, he asks, "Did *you* grow up learning about the zodiac?"

"Not really," I lie. I'm glad Pó Po and Auntie aren't here to witness my betrayal. I push harder into the dough to release some of my anxiety. Once the texture is smooth, I wrap the dough in plastic and place it in the fridge to cool.

"If you're reimagining how the Chinese zodiac works and charging people for it, don't you think you're misleading people?" I add, rejoining Bennett at the stove.

"You think what I'm doing is cultural appropriation?" he asks, quickly glancing up at me.

I think for a moment. "Well, I don't know. Not necessarily."

"I have both Chinese and Irish heritage and have been interested in and studied the zodiac for a long time. It's my culture, my family's culture," Bennett says, a hint of defensiveness poking through. "I don't have to justify myself to anyone who thinks I'm not Chinese enough because *they're* uncomfortable with me being mixed race."

"No, I totally understand that," I confess.

The thing is, I really do completely get it. I fully relate. With Chinese, Scottish, and Norwegian heritage, it wouldn't be fair for me to think that. If I did, wouldn't that mean I was doing the same? I'm working on modernizing Lunar Love, sure, but I'm trying to do it in a way that honors what Pó Po started.

"Our names don't always represent *all* of who we are," Bennett says, speaking toward the range. "I have an Irish last name, and I understand that might be confusing with what I do. But it doesn't negate the fact that I'm Chinese, too. I know that my existence, what I look like, and my name sometimes mystify people."

"Names can be complicated," I say, nodding along. "Assumptions are too easily made."

Bennett stops mixing the filling for a second to face me, his eyes holding intense contact with mine. "I've always thought the Chinese zodiac was a fascinating approach to understanding humans. And a big part of the zodiac is about who pairs well with who. With the rise of dating apps, I saw a business opportunity that I had a personal interest in," he adds, rotating back toward the task at hand and giving the pan a small shake. "I'm trying to be a smart businessman. I have a decent amount of experience in the tech industry. A big part of running a start-up is learning on the job and knowing when to pivot."

Way to state the obvious.

"I just don't buy that ZodiaCupid's concept hasn't been done before," I press.

Bennett looks over at me. "What I'm doing isn't new. There

are dating apps with filters that include astrological signs, and even the Chinese zodiac, as one element of the matching. For us, though, that's our main element."

"Really? Just some dating apps, huh?"

A glimmer spreads across Bennett's hazel eyes, and I'm momentarily sidetracked. "There's also this place called Lunar Love," Bennett says. "Have you heard of it?"

My core is shaken hearing him say those words. I didn't expect him to actually know about us. I open my mouth but nothing comes out. I shake my head no. I can't verbalize another lie.

"Huh," he grunts. "From my impression of you so far, it seems like Lunar Love would be something you'd be into instead of ZodiaCupid, but if *you* haven't even heard of it, then I guess I don't need to be worried."

There he goes saying those two words again. His mention of Lunar Love and his total disregard for us is maddening.

"Uh-huh," I mumble, running my fingers along the design of the mooncake mold.

"Do you typically grill all your dates?" Bennett asks, turning to face me. His shoulders are more relaxed, his tone more casual than before. I look at him straight on, and from this angle, I see that his smile is slightly crooked, the left side of his bottom lip tilting higher over his teeth. It's infuriatingly adorable.

"Just the ones I'm particularly skeptical, er, intrigued about," I say, catching myself. "So it seems like you just let all the animals loose, free to mingle and date who they want. No foundation of compatibility to help guide people."

Bennett laughs and pauses before he speaks again. "Zodia-Cupid takes the animal sign traits into consideration, but it mostly matches users by what they write in their profiles. It opens users up to more potential matches," he explains. "I know it's different than the traditional and limited way of matching compatible signs exclusively. Some people won't like that but I hope they'll still give us a try."

I breathe out heavily. Keyword: *try*. But when people are ready for something serious, they'll settle down with us.

Bennett gives me a funny smile. "Sorry to break it to you," he adds, "but Horses and Rats aren't typically compatible. But we're getting along!"

I grumble noncommittally. "So your app isn't actually making compatible matches." I narrow my eyes at him. "Sounds to me like false advertising."

"Depends on your definition of compatible." Bennett lifts a filling-coated spatula out in front of me as he speaks with his hands. "If you have a problem with our animal signs matching, then why did you ask me out on a date?" he asks curiously.

I reach out to lower the spatula just as lotus puree splats onto the ground. My hand unintentionally touches his, and I quickly pull back as though he were a hot stove. He glances down to where our skin touched and then back up at me.

"As a user of your app, I guess I trusted that you know best," I respond, almost choking on the words.

Bennett smirks and places his palm on the table, bending closer toward me. "You have pretty eyes," he says. "There's a fire behind them."

I look up at his face, my eyes roaming over his smooth, light skin. I place my hand on the table, mirroring his stance. "If you think you're successfully distracting me with compliments, think again."

The corners of Bennett's mouth tilt up as he refocuses on the lotus seed filling. "If you're not happy with this date, you get your money back, no questions asked," he jokes. A bigger grin appears, and I feel my guard start to slowly dissipate. That's not supposed to happen.

The door to the classroom opens, and two latecomers walk in.

"Sorry we're late. We got caught in rush hour traffic," the woman says to the instructor, her voice sounding eerily familiar. "Can we still participate?"

I sneak a look at the two people joining the class, recognizing one of them. My body tenses up. Colette? When did she get back in town? My old best friend and her date are guided by the instructor across the room to a clean workbench.

"What is that? What are you doing with your head?" Bennett asks, twisting his body to get a better look at me.

"Shhh!" I tilt my head lower, trying not to attract any attention to myself. "Don't make any more noises or sudden movements," I whisper.

"Uh, okay." Bennett holds his breath and freezes for a few seconds before bursting into laughter. "Seriously, what are you doing?"

Think, Olivia!

"My ex-boyfriend just walked in," I blurt out. It's the only thing that would make sense. Nothing can save me now. "It ended badly. I do not want to see him right now."

Because then I'll be exposed without getting the information I came here for. And I'd have to confront my past. I am not prepared for either of those things.

Bennett subtly looks up at the couple. "That's awkward. And it looks like he's here with his new girlfriend."

Unexpectedly, a voice calls out across the room. "Olivia?"

I don't need to see who said my name to know whose voice it is. I hunch down under Bennett's bowl and slither toward the back sinks pretending to look for something on the racks.

I peek through the back shelves into the room, trying to figure out my next move. Suddenly, there's a loud clatter of trays. I see Bennett on the ground, surrounded by lotus seed filling and towels. There are gasps all around as the students surround Bennett to help him up.

Perfect. Now Colette will definitely see me.

Or not.

I almost don't notice Bennett looking up at me and nodding toward the exit. I clumsily remove my apron and tiptoe to the door.

Outside, I debate leaving but decide to stay. A few minutes later, Bennett walks out of the building with light orange filling crusted on the parts of his sweater that the apron didn't cover.

"I wasn't sure if you'd still be here. You forgot your bag," he says, offering me my tote and flowers.

"Thank you. For this and that," I reply. "Are you okay?"

"I'll be sore for a couple of days but I'm fine. I moonlight as a stunt double for Keanu Reeves so my body's used to it," he deadpans. "Are *you* okay?"

"Please. Everyone knows Keanu does a lot of his own stunts," I say, trying to stifle a laugh. That entire encounter upstairs was just…bizarre. "I think I'm okay, too."

I was so close to being outed. Bennett helped me cover up my own lies.

Bennett stretches out his back. "You better not be laughing at me!" he says with a grin.

I take a deep breath. "I don't mean to laugh. I really am

appreciative of your distraction, and I know how excited you were to make mooncakes. Let me buy you ice cream as a thank-you."

"I'd be a fool to turn down ice cream," Bennett says. "But I'd be an even bigger fool to let you pay. You covered the class. Ice cream is on me."

"I can't argue with that, but you did throw yourself on the ground for me."

"It's my honor falling for you," he says sweetly.

I feel a blush creep across my cheeks.

Pull yourself together!

We head to the nearest ice cream shop, where I order a scoop of chocolate and one of vanilla while Bennett enjoys two scoops of peanut butter ice cream. We eat and walk side by side to the nearest park as the sky settles into a pink and purple tie-dye dusk.

"This feels strangely familiar," Bennett says.

I give him a look. "Yeah. I can't get over how weird this is."

"Meeting me again or playing hooky?"

"Both! I've never ditched anything in my life!" I say, still stunned by the sudden escape. Adrenaline pumps through my veins. This was not how I saw the evening going.

"Even though one of your traits as a Horse is spontaneity?"

"Well, spontaneity is actually one of the traits I don't really resonate with." I lick my ice cream.

"Interesting," he says, wrinkling his eyebrows. He takes a bite out of his cone. "I'm curious to know more about you. What do you do for work, Olivia?" Bennett asks. He says my name familiarly, as though it's always been part of his vocabulary.

"I'm...in recruiting," I say, which doesn't *feel* like a lie. I recruit single people all the time for Lunar Love. "I'm taking over the family business." There. One truth. Now I can rest easy tonight.

"Is that so?" he asks.

I look at him with my nose crinkled. "It is so."

"What's that like?"

"Honestly, I love it," I say. "There have been some challenges lately, but it's nothing I can't handle."

"Hard to find good talent?" he asks, taking a step closer to me to move out of the way of a skateboarder and her dog.

"Something like that," I admit.

"That's impressive. Congrats. Depending on how quickly we grow, I may need to enlist your services. We'll see how things go with the business."

I want to ask how fast they're growing and what plans they have for ZodiaCupid, but I can't bring myself to interrogate him any further. I don't know why I thought Bennett was going to divulge his company's secrets to someone he just met. Well, met again.

When our elbows distractingly brush against each other for the fifth time, I know it's time to call it a night. "I should get home. I have a busy day tomorrow. Thanks for the ice cream."

"Absolutely." Bennett checks his watch for the time. "I didn't realize how late it was. This was fun, Olivia."

"It was something, B.O.B."

Bennett laughs. "Yeah, sorry about that. My engineer convinced me to make a profile. He said it would be good for me to know what's happening on the ground level. My team has been encouraging me to go on dates to try the app out. Work has been pretty busy, so this is my first."

A sliver of me is thrilled that he wasn't trying to go on dates with someone who wasn't me. I finish my cone and throw this thought away along with my napkin.

"I can imagine. So you're here to do research for work," I clarify, leaving out the "too." The irony is slightly amusing.

Bennett stuffs a hand into his pocket. "You could say that, but I'm really glad I came. I wasn't sure if I'd ever see you again. Maybe I can get your number this time? Then we'll need a little less fate to see each other."

"You mean a little less algorithm?" I tease, taking his phone from him.

His cheeks turn rosy pink. I reluctantly type my number into his phone so we can take our conversation off ZodiaCupid. The only conversation I ever plan on having with him is about what plans he has up his coral-colored sleeves.

Bennett awkwardly holds his arms out and pauses, signaling that he'd like to give me a hug. I hesitantly reach up and hug back. My arms rest against his firm shoulders, and in this close proximity, I learn that he smells like musk. And mooncake filling.

It takes a second before we realize we've lingered. We pull apart, and I adjust the strap of my bag, the chrysanthemums swinging to the side.

"It was nice officially meeting you," Bennett says.

We smile at each other. I'm in denial that I actually enjoyed myself.

"It was nice meeting you, too, asshole."

CHAPTER 6

My instincts guide me as I follow the path I've walked for years. With Lunar Love in sight, I step off to the side to admire the building. Four days into my first week and I still have butterflies tumbling and turning in my stomach. Lunar Love's red exterior, pink window trim, and pink door have remained the same since the very beginning. Pó Po was insistent on the shop's colors symbolizing luck and happiness.

When I was younger, both the inside and outside of the building felt old-fashioned, as if all the shops in Chinatown were supposed to look a certain way. Now I appreciate the parts of the neighborhood that still exude tradition among a growing influx of trendier eateries and art galleries. To the right of our building, what used to be a bookstore is now a to-be-determined renovated office or retail space. The construction hasn't started yet for the day, so I'll have some quiet time to myself.

It was only a year ago that the inside of Lunar Love looked completely different than it does now. Since Day One, the walls and ceilings were painted a deep crimson. The furniture was dark and heavy, and there was an overabundance of stuff: boxes filled with client documents from decades prior, books and torn posters, and bags of donations. It took me eight months to convince Auntie to let me redesign the place.

My design goals were simple: clean and aspirational, yet still traditional. When clients visit, I want them to feel like anything is possible. That a new chapter is just beginning. This meant repainting the walls off-white and hanging local artists' work that reflected the tangled, abstract, beautiful emotions of love. Clunky chairs were replaced by the minimal sets of mid-century modern ones I scored at flea markets. Finding love is stressful enough. The place you go to find it should be calming and reassuring.

Even the name Lunar Love is simple and straightforward yet full of significance. The lunar horoscope was created because of the moon's movements and phases, which people interpreted and assigned meaning to. Each of the twelve animal signs and its accompanying personalities rules a lunar year. The lunar calendar, based on the moon's phases in a month, is the guide for determining the most auspicious dates for momentous events.

When Pó Po chose the name, she wanted her business to reflect the power of the moon, both physically and figuratively. More than just making the name modest, Pó Po also simplified the business concept in an attempt to keep it alive. She realized that Westerners were more interested in zodiac matchmaking when it wasn't too complicated. She figured out how to streamline the magic of it all in order to avoid losing intimidated clients.

Just as she did, I need to figure out which changes to make that feel right for Lunar Love. The speeches and toasts and gold necklaces are special, but that's not what any of this is about.

I'm carrying Pó Po, Auntie, and Lunar Love's legacy into the future. What I do from now on is the true test of what I'm made of and what the business can withstand in these changing, challenging times.

I walk toward the rear of the space where one of the three rooms in our building is designated as an office. Across from the waiting area is the Session Room, where we meet with clients.

I flip through the pile of mail, assessing the damage. Some marketing, some wrong address, but mostly bills. I drop them onto the teetering pile of mail Auntie left on my desk, which I discover contains even more bills. Before I have the chance to tackle my emails, I hear the front door close, followed by the sound of a woman calling out into the waiting area.

"Hi there. Can I help you?" I ask, rushing out of the office to greet the unexpected guest.

"Yes, I'm looking for Lydia. Is she here?" the lady asks. She looks professional chic in her baby blue pantsuit. Inside her oversized leather bag, I spot two eyes shining back at me and then hear a small yip. The woman lifts the bag to her face and coos into the small opening. "Don't mind Poppy. She's friendly."

"Lydia's not here. Did you have an appointment?" I ask, thinking I might have overlooked one of Auntie's clients. "We're transitioning all of her clients over to me and my colleague. Sorry if we—"

"Oh, no," she says, furrowing her eyebrows. "Quite the opposite." The woman hands me a business card accompanied by a dazzling smile. "I'm Carol."

I review the shiny silver words on the card: "Carol Rogers, Realtor, Silver Linings Real Estate."

"So you're not a client?" I confirm.

"Darling, is Lydia here? I have some important business matters to discuss with her. I tried emailing but didn't get a response." She lifts loose fuzz from her sleeve and lets it float through the air until it finally lands on the carpet.

I bend the business card back and forth between my fingers. "Lydia's actually no longer with Lunar Love. If there are business matters to discuss, you can do so with me. I'm the new owner."

Carol's eyes flicker in disappointment. "Oh. I didn't know you were...are you Korean? I thought this was a Chinese company."

"I'm half-Chinese," I say hesitantly. It's the answer that will satisfy her. An easy categorization. When she dips her head in a nod as though she's had an epiphany, I feel like I've failed at something.

"In that case, I wanted to discuss this property. As you may know, this area is very popular," she says with a wink. She hands me a slip of paper before grabbing my business card from the reception desk. "Here's what I think this land is worth."

I scan the surprisingly high number on the paper but maintain a look of neutrality. This is what Mae Yí-Pó had warned me about.

"Let's set up a time to chat. I'll email you! Stay silver!" Carol sings as she heaves her purse up her arm and waves goodbye. The head of a brown Pomeranian pops out. "Say bye, Poppy!"

Back at my desk, Operation Destroy ZodiaCupid is off to a slow and confusing start. I stare at the blinking cursor on my screen trying to come up with bullet points for my "10 Reasons Why ZodiaCupid Is Flawed" article for WhizDash. Obviously, I need to make it clear that ZodiaCupid is a total scam. What did

Bennett tell me? Oh, right. His app is the opportunity he saw as available and seized it without care or concern for anyone else.

This should be easy, yet I can't seem to find the words. Why couldn't Bennett have been completely awful? A horrible villain who wants to match incompatible people together just to watch them suffer while he laughs maniacally under a green snowfall of dollar bills and scrapes icing off the top of every dessert he can find. Children wouldn't have frosting on cakes because he got to it first. Chefs, cookbooks, and cooking schools would be destroyed because *he* has all the best recipes in the world, and no one dare try to say otherwise.

Instead, the man threw himself on the ground for me. He made me laugh. Multiple times. Then he had the nerve to ask for my number. How can I try to hurt a seemingly decent man with an unforgettable smile and a soft spot for the Chinese zodiac? I roll my head back and groan. What's gotten into me? It's a workday, and I'm daydreaming about Bennett. Of all people! In an alternate world, maybe I could entertain thinking about him without consequence. But that's not the world we live in.

The still waters of my pond have been disturbed by Bennett. I can't let the ripples throw me off balance. I have to get back to a state of calm. And what this man does to me is the opposite of that. He's cannonballed into the pond and splashed around, slapping his hands against the surface of the water. It's just plain rude.

Bennett is a Rat, and I'm very much a Horse. Whatever that "date" and our meeting at the bakery was doesn't matter. It can't matter. I can't go down that path again. Even if I wanted to, I know better. Spending more time together wouldn't be good for either of us. In fact, I'd be doing a good deed by putting this to an end with my article. Bennett might be hurt by it, but any brief aggravation he'll feel is nothing compared to the heartbreak he'd feel when it all comes crashing and burning down, as incompatible relationships inevitably tend to do.

I peek at the photo of a fish with a parasite tongue on the background of my phone and remember the mission. *Be the parasite.* I'll just start with a little Vent Drafting where I'll type out all of my feelings and allow myself to be angry and mad. After that, I'll write the nicer version that I'll actually send out. If I don't let myself vent, my frustration could evolve into something more destructive from the inside out.

I summon the words from within, wrangling each word out into the open. My fingers move cautiously over the laptop keys as my emotions find their voice. Before I know it, I'm pounding furiously against each key, pouring my wrath into the sentences.

There. Vent Draft done. Seeing the list in its entirety, there's no way I could've actually sent this out. Especially not with my real name on it. It's way too cruel. But now I feel better. Does Vent Drafting count as self-care? Because it totally should.

I exhale a long breath, clearing the air of any pessimism. Now I can focus on hyping up Lunar Love. I tap out a happier article focusing on the positive of what we do instead of getting sucked into the negative vortex of ZodiaCupid.

I lose track of time, only realizing that the workday has started when Alisha and Randall walk into the office together bubbling with excitement.

"Guess what?" Alisha asks breathlessly.

"What?" I ask, drawn into her enthusiastic tone of voice. I quickly save the completed version of the Lunar Love article into a folder in our shared company Google Drive. I move my Vent Draft to the trash, deleting it so that it never sees the light of day.

"I booked you on the *Dating in La La Land* podcast!" Alisha shares. "They're doing a live panel interview with an audience. It's on Saturday. I hope that works for you."

I clap my hands together. "That's amazing! I love that podcast. Consider all plans canceled. Plans being a TV marathon. Wait, who else is on the panel?" I ask, nervous that a certain competitor might be in attendance. If Bennett's there, I'll be exposed. But then again, I'm outed when the episode airs. If I want more information on ZodiaCupid, I'm going to have to do my digging before Saturday.

"It's an all-women panel on dating in Los Angeles. There will be a relationships editor, a consumer research manager, some reality TV producer, and you. Sounds cool, right?" Randall joins in, plopping his bag into his chair.

I breathe out in relief. "Very. Nice work. An audience, too. I'm already nervous."

"You're going to be great! We'll get you prepped before the big day. I'll email the details over," Alisha says, writing on a pad of paper.

I jot down the event into my planner. "Thank you! Also, I wrote an article for WhizDash. I dropped it into the shared Lunar Love folder. Search for *listicle*, and you should find it."

Alisha shoots me a thumbs-up. "Good! I'll send that to my contact. She said she was Team Lunar Love and excited to promote us."

With the listicle out of the way, I turn my attention to my upcoming client meeting. This is where I should be putting my energy, not on some wannabe imitator app. With what feels like a tsunami wave of cancellations, I need to be at the top of my game.

At 11:00 a.m. on the dot, Harper Chen breezes through the door. Harper, founder of a boutique public relations firm specializing in the culinary world, discovered Lunar Love on her way to meet a chef to discuss details for opening day of his new restaurant just a few blocks away. When she stopped by last week, I thought she wanted directions to the restaurant, but really she was looking for more direction in her love life.

People come to us feeling optimistic, heartbroken, anxious, and motivated. Some are knowledgeable in the Chinese zodiac while others have no clue what to expect. We see it all. In times of anticipation or hopelessness, many of us look to the stars for answers and comfort. In our case, we look to the moon.

"Olivia! How are you?" Harper says. She looks sophisticated wearing a lilac linen dress that ties around the waist and a few pieces of delicate jewelry. She reaches out to give me a hug.

In the Session Room, we take seats opposite one another at a table made from reclaimed wood (another flea market score).

"It's been eventful. Sorry about the construction noise next door. Sounds like they're on lunch break so it shouldn't be too distracting in here. How have you been since we spoke last week?" I ask.

"Wildly busy but in the best way. It feels like there are national food holidays happening every single day, so I've been pitching clients constantly for different opportunities. And there's another big client I'm trying to land." Harper sweeps her dark hair into a loose bun. "But I'm excited to do this. I feel the need to be honest with you, though. I'm also using dating apps."

"Oh!" I plaster a smile on my face and keep my tone neutral. "Any in particular?"

"Just a couple of the big ones that have been around forever, and ZodiaCupid. That one's still in beta, though."

"I've heard of it," I say.

Harper places a jeweled hand on the table. "I hope that's okay. I figured, why not? Try multiple avenues of dating. Your way sounded charming and nostalgic, so here I am. Just giving you a heads-up. It felt kind of wrong to not tell you."

"I appreciate that," I say. "I have complete faith that Lunar Love won't let you down, so don't get too invested in ZodiaCupid."

Harper laughs. "Well, good! I'm excited for more context about the zodiac. That's something ZodiaCupid doesn't do. My family celebrated Lunar New Year on and off over the years, and my dad would teach my mom, brother, and me about the upcoming year's animal sign, but that's pretty much the extent of it."

"That's a great start! Let's dive into it," I say. "You were born on October 10, 1988, which makes you Year of the Dragon. This is a highly desired and respected animal sign. In fact, some women opt to have C-sections so their children are born in the Dragon year."

"That's dedication," Harper says, looking impressed.

"Exactly. I'll walk through the traits of the Dragon with you, and let's see how you identify with them. The Chinese lunar horoscope depicts Dragons as direct, enthusiastic, loyal, strong tempered, and no-nonsense. Practical. You want respect from others and will do anything to earn it."

Harper listens carefully to each trait, nodding along and

sometimes shaking her head in disagreement. Not all traits are immediately obvious and take some time to find in people, both from their perspectives and mine.

"Did you ever find out what time you were born?" I ask, propping open my notebook against my crossed leg.

"My mom said it was sometime between twelve thirty and one p.m. Definitely during lunch hour because she remembers being hungry. Maybe that's why I love food so much," Harper ponders.

"That's a narrow enough window for me to work with." I calculate her ascendant, the animal sign that rules her specific birth hours. "People sometimes demonstrate more dominant traits from their birth hour animal signs. You were born in the hours of the Horse. This means you're not only compatible with Monkeys and Rats as a Dragon but also to animal signs that Horses are compatible with, like Tigers and Dogs. It's something we look at, but it's not always part of the equation when matching."

"Like a loophole!" Harper says as though she's figured out something.

"Kind of?" I say.

"That's amazing!"

And that, my friend, you don't get from an app.

We spend the rest of the session discussing what's important to Harper in a future partner. Later, I'll type my handwritten notes into Lunar Love's archaic but dense database. The system may be old, but it contains valuable information and contacts from the last fifty years. To convert the system to a new one without losing that precious knowledge would take time and money that we don't have right now. If this database had a system or software that could complement our in-person match-making, we'd be unstoppable. In the meantime, it's all manual, all the time.

I review Harper's traits, habits, hobbies, and preferences all listed out on the page. "This is what I'm hearing: It's important that the person you're with has a stable job where shifts don't last fourteen hours. And it sounds like you want someone to share your passion for food, whether it's cooking together or eating at a new restaurant. And someone who's honest, speaks his mind, and isn't afraid to go after what he wants."

Harper nods, her gold hoop earrings jiggling back and forth. "I like the sound of all of that!"

"Based on your birth year, your sign's fixed element is Earth. As an Earth Dragon, this makes you stable and fair. And mixed with what I know about you so far, you seem to work hard on self-development, but sometimes you feel the need to control your environment and other people. Does this sound like you at all?"

Harper laughs and nods with a shrug. "Incredible."

"I tell you this just so you're more aware of yourself. As we get to know each other better, I'll have a better sense of what traits you personify," I explain. "This knowledge tends to come in handy when relationships are developing because Earth, Fire, Wood, Metal, and Water are elements that all react to one another. Once you go on a date, we can get into specifics so that it makes more sense in context."

"How long until you find me my first match?" Harper asks.

"Because of the specificity of traits and preferences, there's no way to put a timeline on it. We're not as fast as ZodiaCupid, but I'll get to work today and will keep you updated along the way."

"Exciting! So, I'm curious," Harper says, leaning in closer to me. "Do you have a special someone? You must know right away when a person would be good for you or what to look for in a partner."

My eyebrows shoot up in surprise. "Me? No! There's no one. No, I...no. It's not as clear-cut for me," I say. "It's more difficult to find someone compatible in the right ways than you'd think, especially when it's for yourself."

Harper watches on amused as I dance around her answer. "Sounds like the matchmaker needs a matchmaker," she says.

I laugh. "I've got plenty of those in my life. Besides, I prefer to focus on my clients, like you. My time and energy are focused on finding you someone compatible."

Harper waves her hand in front of her. "I was only wondering! It's incredible how dedicated you are. This is going to be so fun. I can't wait to see who you'll find."

CHAPTER 7

On Friday morning, I exhale a deep sigh of relief. I survived the very first week, which is saying a lot, all things considered. I start working my way through emails when a new one materializes at the top.

Hello Olivia,

I have to cancel our session today. Work is keeping me busy these days, and I have to focus on that for now. I'd also like to suspend further sessions until my schedule clears up. Apologies for the last-minute notice.

Regards,
Greg

Damn Greg using "Regards" like we're colleagues in a corporate setting. I've known the man for a year! I even helped him decide between festive ties for his company's holiday party!

This is the third cancellation this week. I want to revel in a successful onboarding session with Harper, but we need more sign-ups. The tug-of-war on my emotions won't end.

On the edge of my desk, Lunar Love's planner is filled with crossed-out sessions. Auntie preferred not to rely on technology for appointments so we would all mark our meetings on the designated planner. Alisha and I now track our client sessions digitally, but we're still in the habit of maintaining the paper calendar. Updating our client management system is yet another thing to add to my to-do list.

I cross out Greg's session, adding one more tally to the series of recent cancellations. I refuse to let this moonquake shake me. My mind drifts off to what I'm going to stress-bake tonight. Something fudgy.

Needing a change of scenery and a more productive distraction, I decide that the only thing that can make me feel better right now is a Singles Scouting. When I first started working at Lunar Love, I learned about the lengths Pó Po would go to find clients love. She could talk her way into and out of anything and everything. She once secured two invites to the members-only magician clubhouse, The Magic Castle, for her clients who were obsessed with magic by obtaining and calling the entire list of magicians who were set to perform that month. She offered dating services in exchange. All but one magician thought it was an illusion, and Pó Po got her clients in. It was happy ever after for all parties involved, including the magician.

Stories like that have inspired me to be more hands-on, not only with creating unique dates but also in finding the matches themselves. Ideally, we're pairing Lunar Love clients together, but if we don't have someone already in our database who might be a good match for a particular client, I go out and actively find them myself. There have been a lot of laughably awkward encounters at yoga classes, movie theaters, and parks, but I do it for love. For every ten who say no, there's one who says yes. I just need a yes from the right person.

As I walk down the sidewalk in downtown LA, I habitually check my phone for new emails and tap into a link from a Google Alerts email to see what's happening with ZodiaCupid. Looks like there's action in the press. New articles surface about the company hoping to raise funding from investors.

"We're looking to raise a small seed round," says founder Bennett O'Brien. "We'll be pitching at Pitch IRL in November." O'Brien says that the funding will be used to double its design and engineering teams and to expand their marketing efforts. With a rollout strategy already in place, he plans to dominate a few markets and hone their messaging. "We're offering a service in the market that wasn't being met," O'Brien says. "Our users are looking for relationships that work best for their personalities. It's based on a system that's been around for over two thousand years. We're rethinking online dating and adding a new level of interest. Lots to come, so I hope you'll stick around!"

If they raise money, they're going to be able to grow fast. Put us out of business fast. I fume quietly. The blatant disregard for Lunar Love is infuriating. Bennett may come off as a decent person who's incapable of stealing ideas and faking ignorance, yet in every interview, he comes off as overconfident and tactical. I need more information about this pitch.

I remember that he works in a coworking space downtown. I start a new text message to Bennett.

> I just wrapped up a meeting in downtown. Have time to say hi?

It's worth a shot.

While waiting for him to respond, I do another lap around the block. When Bennett sends me his coworking space address, I fast-walk over three blocks.

"Hey," Bennett says when he meets me downstairs, "this is a nice surprise."

"I was just in the area," I say casually. "This is your coworking space, huh? I've never been inside a start-up's office before."

"Is that your way of asking to see it?" he asks.

"Do I want to see it? Sure, my schedule's wide open," I say, pretending to look at my phone's calendar but instead scrolling through images of Pinot.

Bennett hesitates outside the building. "We're pretty busy. I don't know if this is a good idea."

I look past his shoulder, exaggerating my movement. "What are you, a supervillain? You hiding something up there?"

He looks dramatically from side to side to make sure no one's listening. "I've got a couple of blueprints and top-secret codes that are for my eyes only."

"I promise I won't tell anyone what I witness or hear."

He sighs. "Okay, come on," he says, finally agreeing.

Three levels later, we're winding our way through narrow hallways in the coworking space. Bennett gives me a brief tour as he shows me through the office. I peek into the spaces of other businesses, where two-person teams sit back-to-back speaking into headsets. I wonder if the businesses willing to pay more get the bright, sun-filled rooms closer to the building's tall windows, printers, and kitchen area.

The ZodiaCupid headquarters looks more like a dim, over-sized conference room where five desks are crammed against walls. It's located in the back of the building that surely has never seen sunlight, about a mile from the common area.

In the room are four others who are eating lunch at their desks.

"This is Elmer. He's in charge of development, growth, and payroll," Bennett says, pointing to a man wearing bright red glasses. "And that's Carrie, Christof, and Jingwen. They make up our design and engineering teams." Everyone looks up from their monitors and simultaneously waves.

"That's Carrie's pup and our office mascot, Elvis," Bennett continues, gesturing toward a sleeping bulldog who doesn't seem to mind my presence.

"Clearly he runs a tight ship around here," I joke.

"I blame him for the unpaid overtime. This is where I sit." He gestures toward his astonishingly clean desk. So much for swiping any important documents.

"It's not what I imagined," I say, looking around trying to find something, anything, that will give me an indication for what they're launching next. The only hint of Bennett in this space is the coral sweater from the baking class draped over his chair in a plastic dry cleaning bag. Not a speck of mooncake filling is left, all traces of Bennett's nice gesture for me wiped away.

"I liked the look of the filling, but I started getting some weird stares so I had to have it cleaned," Bennett says, catching me looking.

"Too bad. You pulled it off so well," I joke.

"Can I know the real reason why I had to pay twenty dollars for dry cleaning?" he asks in a slightly amused, curious tone.

I straighten my shoulders, carefully thinking through my word choice. Colette was a former client, but I can't tell him that. "She was someone I used to know a long time ago," I share. There. Truthful and vague.

A flash of surprise crosses Bennett's face. "She? So it wasn't your ex-boyfriend, like you said?"

Great. My past lies have come back to haunt me. "No. It wasn't. She was my best friend growing up. But we're not friends anymore," I admit.

Bennett nods in understanding. "Well, anytime you need an out, I'm your guy."

I huff out a quiet laugh. "I'll keep that in mind. This place is...sterile," I quickly add, using the change of topics as an opportunity to take another good look at the place. It's a plain, undecorated room strictly intended for business. No personality on the walls or desks, except one matte black electric kettle in the corner of the beverage nook.

"Yeah, it's a bit gloomy, but hopefully we'll be out of here soon. We're participating in Pitch IRL to attract interested investors."

Perfect. This is my opening. "Aren't those highly competitive? How are you feeling about your chances?" I ask. "I thought you'd already have the ins." Maybe he's not as seasoned of an entrepreneur as the media claims him to be.

"It's not how I'd normally go about it, but a local college is hosting the event so business students can watch and learn how to pitch. They asked if we wanted to be involved, and it was hard to turn down. I would've loved to attend something like that when I was in school. I even got some of my investor buddies and former business partners to be involved for the Q and A at the end."

Why does Bennett have to be such a good guy? It's making my life very difficult.

"What happens if no one invests?" I continue.

"Then we keep trying. I've poured my savings into this business, so we'll be able to keep going for a few months. Ultimately, failure isn't an option."

"It's better optics for us to launch on or before Lunar New Year," Elmer adds. "After all, it's, you know, the holiday that ushers in the next year's zodiac animal."

"It's a great time to launch," I acknowledge reluctantly. "So, what's everyone working on?" I step closer to the engineers' desks, hoping to see something that might provide some clues. There's just a bunch of code against dark screens.

"We're gearing up to ship a big feature for the beta. If users like it, we'll improve upon it for the app's official launch," Bennett shares.

"Ooh, what is it?" I ask, making sure to sound overeager.

"I can't share the details just yet, but I'm hoping you'll like it. Though we did recently implement an algorithm that connects users based on the good feedback other users give after dates." Bennett sounds excited. "If a user is looking for a particular trait, let's say good manners as an example, and another user writes that their date had good manners in the feedback, we can use that information to better connect them if the first match doesn't work out."

I nod, soaking up every last word. Inside, I shrink. How can we possibly keep up with an algorithm? We *are* the algorithm. *I* am the algorithm.

Suddenly, Elmer sits up in his seat and shouts, "Yes!" His red glasses sitting on top of his head fall in front of his forehead.

"What've we got?" Bennett asks, walking over to Elmer's desk. I edge closer so I can see his screen. On his monitors are colorful graphs moving in a mostly upward direction, high numbers, and well-portioned pie charts.

"We just hit match three thousand!" Elmer says, grinning.

"That number will be a lot higher when we launch nation-wide. How can we get that number even higher before the next press release?" Bennett asks as he hurriedly reviews the data analytics charts on Elmer's screen.

If we sacrificed quality and could work as fast as an algorithm, we'd have that many matches, too. It's quality over quantity, I repeat to myself.

Bennett pumps his fist in the air. "And sixty users deleted their accounts with feedback saying they matched and no longer need the service."

Oof. I bet he won't be happy about that. I can't imagine quitting clients fits into his future investors' business plan. "That fast?" I mumble. I don't try to contain my surprised look.

Bennett somehow hears me. "You look shocked by that number, but quitting clients is a good thing usually. It means they've successfully matched. We'll be able to use this data for the pitch. We want these metrics for our marketing to attract more users."

I can practically see the money signs in his eyes.

"When you lose people—users, sorry—how much do you

anticipate that affecting your bottom line?" I ask, cringing at my own use of corporate-speak. "Do you try to win them back?"

Bennett looks at me curiously. He leans back and crosses his arms.

"We have hundreds of people signing up to be in the beta every day. It's hard to keep track of them individually. And when we launch, we anticipate there being way more users. Eighty-seven percent of surveyed beta users have expressed interest in upgrading to the paid service to get more of our benefits once we have it ready," he explains. "We're doing well, but of course there's always room for improvement."

"I see," I say, smiling wanly. Quality over quantity. Quality over quantity. "Sounds like everything's working out."

"It's...working. Either way, we try to celebrate milestones both big and small. Yesterday we celebrated putting a new verification system into effect to validate animal signs. We had some data indicating that users weren't being truthful about who they were on the site. Now we confirm birthdays to prevent any funny business. You know what I mean?"

"Can't trust anyone," I say, looking him straight in the eye. They have to verify because they never meet people face-to-face and get to know them. "Do you think asking for proof of identity will scare people away?"

"If it does, good," he says. "Ultimately, we want our users to choose us because they want to find love in an honest and safe way, even if this limits sign-ups or leads to drop-offs. It might sound obvious, but these are the lessons we're learning as we go."

"Super," I say. "That's just super."

"We want users to be into the Chinese zodiac, but not *too* into it," Elmer chimes in from across the room. "If users try to get all introspective about which of the four zodiac elements they are, then they'll probably be disappointed."

"Five," I murmur.

"What?" Elmer asks. He pushes his glasses back on top of his head.

"Never mind," I say. It's not worth the energy.

Instead, Bennett speaks up. "There are actually five elements. Metal, Water, Wood, Fire, and Earth."

"Exactly," I say. I can't tell if I feel good that he knows more than I thought about the zodiac, or worse.

"Uh, yeah. Right," Elmer says, his face matching the color of his glasses.

Delight sparkles in Bennett's eyes. "You're learning! Looks like the zodiac bug is contagious! The point is, we want users to trust us. We're trying to make connections, after all," he says, looking at me expectantly.

"Oh, man. You've gotta see this," Elmer says, his tone more serious than before. He starts reading off his screen. "ZodiaCupid is a gimmicky take on a centuries-old horoscope system..."

Bennett and I take a few steps back over to Elmer's desk and crouch to read along with him. I feel my face burning as I scan down the list. It's my WhizDash article. But it's the version I deleted. How is that possible? That draft was never meant to be seen by other human eyes. When Alisha sent the email, it was obviously my Vent Draft—not the Lunar Love article—attached.

Alisha's contact at WhizDash didn't waste any time getting this article up. Riding the wave of ZodiaCupid press, probably.

Tunnel vision takes over as I read my words written in a moment of passion.

TEN WAYS ZODIACUPID WILL DESTROY YOUR LOVE LIFE

1. ZodiaCupid is a gimmicky take on a centuries-old horoscope system that is believed to be the oldest in the world. The only thing the app gets right about the Chinese zodiac are the twelve animal signs. Other than that, it's a generic brushstroke analysis of its users.

2. What stops users from manipulating the system and pretending to be different signs? Careful users. That Rabbit you're flirting with might actually be a Rat.

3. If you think winking is bad, try being hissed at. Are you a Snake or a human? People don't like to be cat-called at, so why would they want to be barked at?

4. Don't count on users to know too much about the Chinese zodiac. If you're a true believer, this is not the right platform for you.

5. Users are matched based on the words in their profile more than the actual traits of their animal signs. What's new?

6. Get ready to ask, "Excuse me? Are you so-and-so?" because users have to uncomfortably guess who their dates are. Give or take a few profile prompts that are supposed to capture people's personalities, the awkwardness of meeting in person is heightened by the fact that due to the no-photos-allowed policy, we have no idea who we're actually looking for.

7. Personalities aren't one-size-fits-all. They're a combination of the temperament we have from the beginning and the character that we build for ourselves through our choices and behaviors. ZodiaCupid doesn't even begin to scratch the surface.

8. Full Moons, New Moons...this is just a replacement for the anxiety- and judgment-inducing swiping. Won't people just be biased toward their preferred animals?

9. To Bennett O'Brien, real people become users, line items in an Excel spreadsheet, and money in his pocket.

10. ZodiaCupid is a digital identity crisis. It doesn't know who it is or what it wants to be.

"A digital identity crisis," Bennett says, the brightness in his face dulled. "Ouch."

"Brutal," Elmer says. The rest of the team shake their heads. "This person didn't even have the nerve to use her first name. CakeGirl. What are we, in fifth grade?"

Long gone are the days of AIM screen names, yet here we are.

"You know you're doing it right when people have strong reactions," Bennett says in a forced upbeat tone. There's a smile on his face but it's obvious he's not happy. "Eighty-two percent of our surveyed users have been happy with the service overall, and that's what matters. Not this personal attack on us."

"This CakeGirl is just trying to get attention," Elmer says with a genuine look of empathy. "This is just the first of many who will try to tear us down. Don't take it personally, man."

"It's personal to me," Bennett says quietly, his mood deflated.

The article worked. It worked better than I thought it would. I was successful.

Shit.

I shouldn't feel upset. I should be thrilled that my little plan is working. But the look on Bennett's face makes me feel otherwise. He has his hands stuffed into his pockets and is slouching gloomily, and I wish I could take it back. Control+Z. Unsend. Delete. Something *I* did hurt this man, and for some baffling reason, that hurts me. I suppress a sick feeling in my stomach working its way up my chest and look away.

"That's just one person," I finally say, trying to lighten the mood and change the subject. "You said people are happy with the service. That's good."

"Bad press comes with the good. I should be used to this. It was only a matter of time," Bennett says, pulling his attention from Elmer's screen. "And yes. Happy users are always a good thing. Are you happy with the service? When you use ZodiaCupid, or apps in general, what do you like to see?"

Right. Back to business.

I think for a moment. "I want to see lots of pop-up ads. Ask me for reviews as often as you can. The more cookies the better. Give me lots of push notifications. Multistep login? Yes, please!" I say, listing the worst things I can think of off the top of my head.

A genuine smile appears on Bennett's face, accompanied by a small laugh. I'm relieved by the sound. I feel too powerful being able to make him both sad and happy. He raises one of his eyebrows. "Cookies, got it. I'll make sure we add all that in," he says in the warm tone he had before reading my soul-crushing listicle.

"Well, thanks for the tour. I should get going," I say, waving to everyone. "Nice to meet you all."

"Don't want any trouble with the boss," Bennett says.

"She's not too bad," I start to say, forgetting for a moment that the boss is in fact me and not Auntie. "Actually, she's tough and has high standards and expectations. So I really should get back to it."

Bennett walks me out to the front of the building. Midday traffic speeds past us as we stand facing each other on the sidewalk, lingering.

"Before you go, I know our first date was a bit...unexpected. Normally, I'd just let it go and forget about it, but ever since first meeting you at Lucky Monkey, I haven't been able to make myself forget. About you." Three shades of pink bloom across Bennett's upper cheeks. "I had a great time with you, but I was hoping we could have a redo?"

I bite my lip hesitantly. "I don't know about that..."

"I don't like making bad first impressions. I felt completely off guard and unprepared. I know I can do better." Bennett runs his hand through his hair, the strands landing in all the right places despite the breeze from the passing cars. "Of course, it's your call. I could take you to the place where I get my best ideas. Or is that weird?"

For the life of me, I can't think of anywhere this could possibly be. Maybe it's in his car, where he drives around looking for other fifty-year-old small business ideas to steal. "I'll admit I'm intrigued, but..."

"It's up to you," Bennett says. He shyly grins, and my heart rises in my chest like a soufflé.

I debate this. I'm trying to learn more about his company, not

date him. But today's impromptu office visit was actually fruit-
ful. Now I know there's a big feature coming. That's something
the press releases didn't share. After this article debacle though,
it feels wrong to keep seeing him. Unless I can use that time
to tell him who I am. A guilt weed has started growing roots
within me, and I need to rip them out. I just hope the damage
isn't irreparable.

"Okay. Sure. Let's do it," I say apprehensively.

My agreement wins me a dimpled smile from Bennett,
and my choice feels like the right one. "Really? Okay! How
about I pick you up tonight, let's say at Lucky Monkey? Seven
thirty p.m.?"

"Tonight?" I ask. "I didn't realize it would be tonight."

"We could do tomorrow night if that works better?" Bennett
suggests.

I'll be exhausted after tomorrow's podcast interview. If we do
it tonight, I can use what I learn to craft better talking points
and explain to him who I am before my identity is revealed on
the podcast.

"Tonight's fine," I say.

Bennett exhales and smiles. "That's really great! See you later."

I wave goodbye, my breath catching in my chest. Saving
Lunar Love is going to be like trying to grow peonies in the
winter. And I'm no gardener.

CHAPTER 8

That night, Bennett picks me up from Lucky Monkey as promised. He drives us out past Pasadena in his old Ford Mustang convertible that looks like it should still be in the shop with its half-painted and patchy body.

"Is this car road-safe?" I ask, gripping the front of my seat. My waved hair lifts in the wind as we fly down the highway.

"Of course it's road-safe," Bennett says. "Just remember when you eject through the windshield, you want to go headfirst. You don't want to slow things down because then there's a chance you might survive. And you don't want to survive something like that."

I tighten my seat belt over my lap.

"That's just to keep up appearances," he jokes.

I run my hand over the cream-colored leather seat. "The article from earlier," I say tentatively, "I'm sorry about that. That was a lot."

Bennett casts his eyes in my direction and shakes his head. "You have nothing to be sorry about. Another article, a good one, came out shortly after, so in a way they kind of cancel each other out, I guess."

"I'm glad," I say, staring straight ahead at the stream of glowing red taillights.

We've passed three different exits when I start shouting out clues on traffic signs for where we might be going, but Bennett refuses to answer my guesses. Maybe he figures out what ideas to steal at a dumpling restaurant in the San Gabriel Valley or at an art museum. At this hour, though, museums are closing. I lean back against the car seat and search for stars against the October night sky. I only find the quiet appearance of the moon with a glowing half halo, its illumination gaining strength as the minutes pass.

Bennett taps his hand against his leg to an imaginary song, keeping his eyes safely on the road. When he slows the car and pulls into an outdoor drive-in movie theater, I'm slightly confused. Bennett pays for our tickets and is instructed by a man in a neon orange vest where to park.

"The drive-in? This is where you get your best ideas?" I ask disbelievingly as I watch cars line up in front of a massive screen. I've been tricked!

"I wasn't kidding!" Bennett turns the wheel into our spot. "Movies help me get out of my own head. My thoughts are clearest here."

"Clearest when you're watching..." I look over at the poster of tonight's screening. "...*Practical Magic*?"

"A good movie transports," Bennett says, undoing his seat belt. "This one's witchy, and it's what happens to be showing tonight. Have you seen it?"

"I have. It's good," I say nonchalantly. I watch it every single year in the lead-up to Halloween, but he doesn't need more data points on me.

Bennett reaches behind his seat to grab something. "Dinner," he says, holding up a brown paper bag with plastic containers piled to the top.

"Don't they sell food here?" I ask.

"I wanted to prepare something special for you." Bennett sets the containers on top of the dashboard. He passes me a paper plate and wooden chopsticks. "And this way we know what the food we're eating is actually made of."

Through the plastic, I spot rolled rice and seaweed, but it can't be what it looks like. "Is that," I say, leaning closer to the containers, "sushi?"

"Handmade. I also brought popcorn, Peanut M&Ms, Twix, and Red Vines for dessert. The candy here is way overpriced."

"Right. So this is where you came up with your idea for ZodiaCupid?" I ask as Bennett removes the lids off the containers.

"No, that was somewhere different."

"I see. Then what kind of ideas do you get here for your business?" I probe. Tonight cannot be a waste. "Is this where you thought up the idea for this mysterious product launch happening?"

"All my best ones, and actually, yes. But you still have to wait to find out what that one is." He ignores my groan of protest and reaches for the bag of candy, setting it between us.

I look toward the backseat. "Any chance you've got a slushie machine back there?"

"You sure do ask a lot of questions, don't you?" he says with a laugh. "I like that about you. One second." He jumps out of the car. I watch him run to the concession stand and return with large blue raspberry slushies in each hand. "I'll splurge for slushies."

I poke the straw into the blue icy slush. "Any chance you've got a money machine back there, too?" I ask.

"If only," Bennett says, resettling into the driver's seat. He twists a button on the radio to find the right station for the movie.

"Does this radio even work?" I ask in a teasing tone.

"It's the first thing I fixed," he says.

The screen in front of us lights up, shining light onto the hoods of everyone's cars. "You didn't have to handmake sushi! This must have taken you so long," I say, picking up a piece of sushi with my chopsticks and biting into it. "Whoa. What's that flavor?"

Bennett rolls up the sleeves of his slate-gray sweater and watches as I try to figure out the flavor pairing. "It's pumpkin, sage, and brown butter," he finally says.

"Sage! Yes, that's it. Unexpected. I don't stray too far from my usual sushi suspects. This is different." I take another look at the center of the sushi. Soft grains of rice wrap around cooked pumpkin with minced fresh sage and brown butter, the crispy dark seaweed exterior adding a salty finish.

"I know it's unconventional, but I think the flavors really work well together." Bennett pops the entire piece of sushi into his mouth.

"They surprisingly do. It's nice, actually," I acknowledge.

Bennett smiles. "I'm happy you like it."

We watch the opening scene of the movie as we alternate between bites of sushi and sips of slushie. There's a comfortable silence between us as we eat.

"Can I tell you something?" I whisper to Bennett.

"Okay," he whispers back.

"I've always wanted to experience a drive-in movie."

"I hope it's to your satisfaction."

"Four and a half stars," I say.

"That's my highest review yet," he says gratefully.

I try to stifle a laugh. "Why are we whispering? We're not in a theater," I continue speaking quietly.

"Then I can do this?" Bennett rips open the bag of Peanut M&Ms and crunches a handful of candy between his teeth.

"And this." I chomp down on the Twix bar but there's hardly a sound.

"Shhh!" he says playfully.

Amusement bubbles up inside of me. I hug my arms around my body, my sweater the only barrier against the cool evening air. Bennett pulls two blankets from the backseat and offers me one.

"Thanks. You're like a magician," I say, accepting the blanket.

"I come prepared." Bennett holds his blanket in front of him, shielding his face before dropping it and ducking as though he's disappeared.

"Impressive," I tease, fluffing the blanket over my lap. The glow from the screen illuminates his face.

"What's your favorite movie?" Bennett asks.

"I can't pick just *one* movie as a favorite," I say. *"Love Story* for a good cry, *To Catch a Thief* for love in a stunning setting, *10 Things I Hate about You* for the dialogue, anything and everything by Nora Ephron. It depends on my mood."

"Great choices. You could be in the love business." Bennett grabs a handful of popcorn. "So you prefer the rom-com classics?" he asks before I have to respond.

I run my hand along the edge of the striped blanket and nod. "I do. The humor was wittier, less vulgar."

"I couldn't agree more. Movies now have to involve capes and powers or over-the-top visuals to be a hit. Is it too much to ask to watch regular people trying to figure out life?"

"Movies now are a literal escape from reality. But to me, love stories are the best escape. What's *your* favorite movie?" I ask, taking a sip of slushie.

"Don't laugh, but it's *Big*," Bennett reveals.

"Why *Big*?" I ask, assuming it's because he's in such a hurry to get to the end destination.

Bennett sits back against the driver's seat, placing his arm up on the window. "I watched that movie so many times, thinking about how cool it would be to turn into an adult overnight. All I wanted to do was grow up."

"Were you trying to grow up to impress a girl and ride on the adult roller coasters like Tom Hanks did in the movie?" I prod. "Or were you trying to rush to the finish line? It would be very Rat-like of you."

Bennett rests his free hand on the steering wheel. "Yes, it's true, the Rat won the Great Race."

"The Rat played tricks on the other animals to secure his first-place spot. He got his free ride on the backs of others—"

"Like the Ox who helped him cross the river," Bennett interjects.

"Um, yes, that's right," I say, surprised by how much he actually does know. "Then he jumped onto land before the Ox could move fast enough to get to the finish line. I googled this out of curiosity."

"Uh-huh. Well, sounds like a smart animal to me," Bennett says, smiling. "You don't think that's all a myth?"

"I like to believe there's a tiny bit of truth to it," I say. "Whether it's legend or the zodiac itself, these are bigger concepts for people to believe in. To find comfort and reasons for why things are the way they are. A way to make sense of the world."

He quickly blinks a few times. "And you think *Big* being my favorite movie has something to do with ... the Great Race somehow?"

I shrug. "You tell me."

Bennett raises his left eyebrow. "I wanted to be bigger because I had a pretty tough childhood. I became obsessed with anything that promised an escape," he explains, a wave of sadness seemingly washing over him. He clears his throat. "My mom died when I was six."

"Oh," I whisper, my pulse quickening. I redden with shame for all the assumptions I carelessly made. For the conclusions I jumped to in my article. So much for Vent Drafting. "I'm so sorry, Bennett. I can't imagine how hard that must've been."

Bennett speaks toward the screen, the creases between his eyebrows deepening. With his profile facing me, I can look at him for as long as I want. "When I'd ask my dad about her, he'd just get sad and change the subject. He couldn't feel his way through the pain to teach me. I grew up wanting to know who she was, what her favorite flower was, what kind of music she listened to when she did the laundry ... would she be proud of the man I've become?" He grunts softly.

"I'm sure she'd be proud of you," I say. Even with the slushie, my throat feels dry when I swallow. My heart pounds so hard

I wouldn't be surprised if it burst its way through my chest and flung itself over the convertible's windshield. His honesty only reminds me of my own lies. The weight of my secret is like a rolling snowball gathering more and more snow. I can't keep pushing off telling him who I am. He needs to know the truth.

Bennett glances over at me with sad eyes. "Everyone handles their grief differently. That was his way," he says, justifying his father's actions.

I stay quiet, listening to him open up.

"I was so mad that she was taken away from us," he continues. "Taken away from me and that I knew nothing about her. I felt like I lost control." Bennett keeps his tone steady. "I spent weekends at the library learning everything I could about my culture so I could feel like she was a little more familiar. A little less gone. I took back control."

"Which is how you know so much about the zodiac," I say, more to myself than to him.

"I only experienced it through Lunar New Year parties and children's books up until I was six, but that was so long ago I hardly remember. I taught myself the rest. I'm still learning." Bennett's expression is unreadable. "I became obsessed with things that were tangible, in my hands or in my mind."

"Like data," I say.

Bennett dips his head. "Numbers don't lie to you; they don't make fun of you. They're reliable." He laughs somberly. "A few years ago, I found my mom's diaries."

"And you read them?" I ask.

"I did," he says, a flicker of guilt flashing across his face.

"I'd do the same," I confess. "I have a theory that people write diaries so that their children discover and read them. It's a way of documenting history and to be seen when time has wiped the memories of us away."

Bennett relaxes. "I hope so. She wrote a lot about how important the Chinese zodiac was to her and how it helped her understand herself as a woman, as a wife, as a mother."

"Well, I think that's poetic. You learned about your mom through her own words. In the way that she would've wanted you to know her."

Bennett nods. "What surprised me most was that she used the zodiac to learn more about herself. History informing the present. She wasn't so strict about compatibility and who belongs with who." He flashes me his crooked smile, and under the navy sky, it looks more pronounced. It nearly melts my heart. "Honestly, she and my dad were incompatible, but they had the happiest marriage. I always found it fascinating that they were incompatible on paper but still had the best relationship."

"I see," I say, looking down at my blanketed lap.

"It's not like now I know everything," he says. "But it was a starting point to learning more about who she was. And in a way, who I was. That's why the article was so upsetting earlier. I've felt like a walking identity crisis for most of my life, and it was called out."

The best I can do is muster up the courage to nod. It's a weak attempt, but it's better than nothing.

Bennett looks up at the moon. "You wanted to know where the idea for ZodiaCupid came from. My mother."

My stomach twists into knots. Now is not the right time to tell him the truth. Exposing myself will have to wait.

"Sorry, I'm being a big bummer right now," Bennett adds. "I

don't usually share this with people. Kind of a habit I picked up from my dad."

"No, I'm glad you told me," I say. All I want to do is make him feel better. What's happening to me? Instead, I just grip my slushie tighter. "Thank you for sharing such an important part of your life with me. An important part of you."

Bennett nods and looks down at his hands. "I watched *Big* shortly after, and well, from then on, I begged my dad to take me to the amusement park every weekend so I could find that fortune-teller machine in real life."

"Also, Tom Hanks." I nudge him gently. "You can't go wrong with any movie that has Tom Hanks in it."

"He's the, what is the term people use? G.O.A.T.?" he says with a hint of sarcasm.

"He's a Goat?" I ask, trying to make him laugh. "When's his birthday?"

"No, the Greatest of All Time," he says, grinning.

"Oh, right, of course," I agree. "He's such a goat."

I can sense Bennett watching me intently. Emotions stir inside me that I haven't felt in a long time. I almost don't recognize myself. Why do I want to hug him and not strangle him right now?

Ahead of us on the screen, Sandra Bullock runs into town to kiss the man she loves. A chill runs through me at the awareness of my proximity to Bennett.

Bennett adjusts in his seat and says, "Did you know that Thomas Edison was responsible for the first on-screen kiss in a movie?"

His fun fact comes out of nowhere, and I dissolve into laughter. His mood seems to lift.

"It was 1896," he continues, "during a time when kissing publicly was scandalous. People went wild for it. It's hard to calculate the percentages of how many chemicals are released when two people kiss, like oxytocin, serotonin, and dopamine, but—"

"Hey, Bennett," I say, still smiling.

"Sorry, you're trying to watch the movie," he says, shifting his position.

"No, it's not that. I know there's a lot happening with chemicals in the brain when people kiss, but what they're trying to portray up there is a relationship. Here, give me your hand," I say.

Bennett skeptically reaches his hand toward me.

At first, I hesitate but then grab his hand in the name of proving a point. "Do you feel that?"

"Do I feel what?" he asks, looking at my hand on top of his. The tips of my fingers graze against his knuckles.

"A sensation running through your body?" *Or is it just me?* "That's not numbers and data. It's a connection between humans. That's what matters."

Bennett dips his head. "Right. Connection." He flips his palm up, and our fingers lock into place.

"When two people find each other and connect...it's an inexplicable kind of magic," I say.

It isn't until Bennett gives my hand a light squeeze that I realize our hands are still touching. I quickly pull my hand away and tuck both between my legs. Bennett draws his hand back and rests it on his knee.

"The only magic I'm used to is the one that happens when numbers properly add up or how data can give you greater insight into making better decisions and products. Through data, we can better understand people," Bennett explains.

I shake my head. It takes time to really know someone. Compatibility doesn't just magically happen through computer code. "Not completely."

I look toward the movie screen, pretending to be particularly interested in the scene. We cast side glances at each other every few seconds.

Bennett grabs the Peanut M&Ms and tilts it toward me in an offering. "Here, you can have the rest," he says, giving the bag of candy a little shake.

"Are you sure? I don't have anything to exchange for it," I joke, "unless you like melted slushie."

There's a glimmer of amusement in Bennett's eyes as he places the candy into the palm of my hand. "Being here with you is all I need."

CHAPTER 9

There's been a slight change of plans. No big deal. Apparently one of the panelists dropped out, and she's being replaced. I know you did your research on everyone to ask them specific questions, but you may need to improvise a little," Alisha says reassuringly. We stand together backstage at The Theatre at Ace Hotel, waiting for the live podcast to start.

"Do you know who it is?" I ask suspiciously. *Please don't let it be Bennett.*

"They didn't say. It's supposed to be an all-women panel, though," she says, as though reading my mind. "There will be four of you up there."

I push down the growing stress about my article that was sent out yesterday. Since it went live, it's been shared around on social media...a lot. The only reason I know is because Lunar Love has never been tagged so many times before. Good for Lunar Love. Bad for Bennett.

Still dialed in to the same wavelength, Alisha adds, "It's a good thing you made that article anonymous with CakeGirl. I thought it read a little harsh, but it's not like ZodiaCupid is playing fair. When I searched through the folders, that's the only one I found. I should've checked with you before I sent it out. I'm so sorry."

I wince. "You have nothing to be sorry about. It was completely my fault. I should never have put my emotions on paper like that. It was...awful."

"Hopefully it'll just disappear in a few days," Alisha says. "Maybe Bennett won't even see it. He's busy, right?"

Not quite. I know he's already seen it. I had to watch it live in real time as he took in the words. Words that *I* wrote. Even if they weren't meant to be put out into the universe, they were. And that's on me.

I acknowledge her optimism and attempt to refocus on being excited for the afternoon. Today, I get to focus on promoting Lunar Love and all the work we're doing to help people find love.

"I need to compartmentalize. Right now, all I care about are my talking points." I sneak a look out into the gilded theater and gawk at its carved columns and intricate plasterwork. Excitement slowly overtakes my anxiety. "I can't believe we're here, in this venue. I feel like a rockstar. How did this event attract so many people?"

"It's about love and dating in Los Angeles," Alisha says, "and people need guidance."

"True. How's my hair?" I ask, running my hand through the strands to fluff my loose waves.

"Waves still intact," Alisha says. "Close your eyes. Okay, all set, no eyeliner or mascara smudges. I have blotting paper in my purse if you need any."

I peek out from behind the curtain at the growing crowd.

"I keep getting bombarded with ZodiaCupid sponsored ads," Alisha says with a sigh directed toward her phone. "That's what you get for looking at something once. How do I report them?"

"Your expertise is going to be useful when Lunar Love finally goes social," I say. "Social media is the biggest, most immediate move we can make right now. I'm glad I secured the social media handles for Lunar Love months ago." Without Auntie knowing, of course, since she dismissed the idea of social media as vain and self-serving.

While I share Pó Po's and Auntie's sentiments about online dating, I am pro–social media. Lunar Love may have thrived on word of mouth in Auntie and Pó Po's time, but now people are moving online. No. They've *been* online. And we need to meet them where they are. I want to lean into the traditional elements of our business, but it's time people know we exist. We can use digital marketing to bring people back to in-person connections. That's the goal anyway.

"For sure! It looks like ZodiaCupid is really playing up the animal angle and providing trait fun facts," Alisha analyzes.

"We need to be different."

"We can share our favorite quotes about love!" Alisha says.

"And the moon! I can share songs and lyrics from my moon playlist," I offer.

Alisha side-eyes me. "Wait, do you really have a moon-themed playlist?"

"Of course! Lots of Billie Holiday, Stevie Nicks, and Ella Fitzgerald. It's the soundtrack to my matchmaking. It also doubles as the perfect background music for baking," I explain. "What do you think about pushing the hashtag #LoveInTheMoonlight? Our clients can tag us on dates they go on, and we can respond with a first-date moon-themed song or something. I haven't worked out the exact details."

"Ooh, love that. Interactive. Doing a hashtag campaign can be a great way for people to learn about us and build community," she confirms. "Look at us being more modern." We snicker to each other.

A producer calls out something, and Alisha squeals. "I'll leave you be. Enjoy the view from the stage. Good luck!" she says.

"Thanks! See you after," I say, taking a deep inhale to calm my nerves. Alisha winds her way through the growing crowd to Randall, who has secured front-row seats in a show of support. I cross my arms over my stomach to self-soothe. I close my eyes and try to think of something calming when a memory of being curled up next to Bennett at the drive-in interrupts my meditation. A sense of calm washes over me. Guilt shortly follows.

When this podcast episode airs today, Bennett will know who I am. So much for only caring about my talking points. I need to speak to him first. I reach for my phone and craft a short text message: Hi! Do you have a second? Have something to talk to you about.

The timing isn't ideal, but I have to tell Bennett who I really am for real this time. I can deal with his reaction later. No big deal. I'm sure he'll understand, being a fellow small business owner. I hope. Then I can concentrate on doing this podcast. This is my first bit of press for Lunar Love, and I can't let distractions derail my focus.

I turn to find Marcus, the *Dating in La La Land* host and

moderator, approaching. He's dressed in a sharp navy suit and smells strongly of cologne.

"Olivia! Are you ready? I never get to dress up like this. Usually we're in sweats behind a microphone," Marcus says in a peppy tone.

"Oh, true!" I laugh nervously, sneaking a look at my phone for a response from Bennett.

"Thanks, by the way, for your flexibility with the slight change," he says. "The producers thought it might be fun to get a dialogue going about love and matchmaking."

"Of course! I'm excited to meet everyone." I stand up straighter, pulling at the sleeve of my plaid blazer.

"Absolutely. So how this will work is, I'll introduce everyone when I'm on stage, and then you come out when your name is called. Simple enough, right?" Marcus says as he cracks his knuckles.

"Can you repeat that? I don't think I followed," I joke. "Kidding, just kidding." I gulp my nerves down. Nothing yet from Bennett.

"Actually, would you mind repeating that? I was told we'd get our own song to walk out to," a deep voice behind me says.

My eyes widen at the sound of the person's voice.

Marcus grins. "Ah! Here's the last-minute fill-in now. Allow me to introduce you two. Olivia, Bennett just started ZodiaCupid."

No, no, no.

"And Bennett, meet Olivia. She's the new owner of Lunar Love," Marcus says, articulating every word. Before I can stop him, he's exposed me. There it is. The truth's out.

"I thought this was supposed to be an all-women panel," I whisper to Marcus between gritted teeth.

"The ladies we reached out to were unavailable. Bennett generously canceled his afternoon to join us. We'll have to find another angle to market this episode," Marcus explains casually, like he hasn't just blown my cover and set fire to my plans. "I'll allow you two to get acquainted, but keep your ears out for your name. The audience may get testy if they have to wait too long." He takes off before either of us say anything.

I slowly spin to see Bennett looking at me with an unreadable look in his eyes. For seconds that feel like hours, we stare at each other, speechless.

"We have to stop meeting like this," Bennett finally says. "I assume that's what your cryptic text message was about?"

"I—" I start. "I was going to tell you. I'm now in charge of Lunar Love."

A deep blush spreads across Bennett's cheeks. Oh no, he's mad.

My stomach flips. I should've told him last night, especially after how honest he was with me. If he never wanted to see me again, I'd understand. Please say something, Bennett. I'll take any vowel, verb, or expletive you want to throw my way. I'm ready.

My apology is on the tip of my tongue when Bennett meekly says, "I know."

"You know..." I trail off confused, waiting for him to finish my sentence. "What do you know?"

Bennett looks at me with careful eyes. "I know who you are."

I choke down my "sorrys" and "I meant to tell yous." I was not ready for that. They're just five simple words, but they hit me like a meteor.

"Wait. What?" I finally say. I feel the blood drain from my face. Someone from behind the curtain shouts, "Places everyone!"

On stage, Marcus gives an opening speech but I can't process full words in this moment.

"I don't understand," I say, my mind running through all the different scenarios. At what point did he find out? Or did he know this entire time? Why wouldn't he have told me? "Did you know who I was when we met at Lucky Monkey? I knew you were spying on me!"

"What? No! I didn't know who you were until the end of the baking class," he calmly explains.

"You knew who I was almost every time we saw each other, and you didn't tell me? Why? Why did you ask me out last night?" I ask, processing it all. Was he trying to finish off Lunar Love? Is he trying to steal more of our ideas? I let my guard down for one night so this Rat could manipulate me. I know better.

Bennett looks down at the floor. "I was thrown off. I really was testing out the app on our first date. After having just seen you at Lucky Monkey, I don't know, it was weird. When you started bombarding me with questions, it clicked. I brought up Lunar Love to see if you'd bite, but you didn't. I caught on to what you were up to when you pretended to want to see my office, and I decided to join in. Knowing who you were made it easier to take a risk and ask you out. I had all the facts. It made me more comfortable."

I lift my eyebrows in surprise. "You had all the facts on me so you felt in control? That's why you asked me out?"

"No, that didn't come out right. I—"

"And what do you mean it clicked? How do you even know who I am?" I ask, my tone edgier.

"Hey, remember that you lied to me, too," Bennett says. "You're also complicit in whatever this is. For all I know, you could've known who I was before our first date." He scrunches his forehead in thought. "Wait. Did you?"

"Did I what?" I say obliviously.

"Did you know who I was before our first date?"

Caught again. I bite my lip. "I knew who you were since the Matched with Love conference, okay?" I say, finally conceding. "You were there yammering on about how opposites can attract and handing out beta codes and surprisingly soft eco-fleece like candy."

Bennett studies my face. "That was *you* I was debating with?"

I look past his shoulder to avoid making eye contact with him.

"Good for you. You had me fooled. So you, what, saw me at the conference and then purposely used my app to match with me?" he says in a slightly joking tone.

I don't answer.

His mouth drops open. "No...way. And here I am thinking fate played a role."

A small snicker tumbles out. We may have coincidentally run into each other at the bakery, but we were brought together because of *my* matching abilities. Sure, they may have been on *his* app, but that's beside the point.

"Fate? Please. I *am* fate," I mumble. I regret ever wanting to tell him the truth.

Out of nowhere, Bennett breaks into laughter, his entire body shuddering in amusement.

"You think this is funny?" I ask, looking around at the stares we're attracting.

"I laugh so I'm not completely freaked out. We both lied so we could see more of each other," Bennett says.

"I don't know if *that's* true," I say, though this isn't entirely accurate. Part of me did want to see him again, and now after this, we'll probably never see each other again. That's a discomforting thought.

Bennett presses a hand against his chest. "You're acting like *I'm* the bad guy here. You do realize how manipulative what you did was, right?"

I cross my arms, probably looking pouty and petty, but I don't care. "You're right. I never should've tried to match with you," I say, exasperated. "Now you know how I know who you are. How do you know who I am?"

"We should talk about this after," Bennett says, remaining calm. "I'll explain everything."

"No. We're going to talk about this right now. My taking over Lunar Love hasn't been announced yet publicly. In fact, today is the announcement. You would've found out once you heard the podcast. Did Marcus give you a list of panelists with our titles?"

"He didn't," Bennett says matter-of-factly.

"Then tell me how you know who I am," I command, growing in confidence.

Bennett pushes his hands into his dark jean pockets and looks over at the crimson velvet curtain. "I can't really say," he mumbles.

I close the distance between us. His musky scent sweeps over me and chips away at my assurance. How dare he unnerve me like that!

"What, did you take a blood oath? Bennett," I say sternly, "tell me."

His eyes scrunch as he processes something. "I know about you," he starts slowly, "because of your Pó Po."

"Pó Po as in...June Huang?" I ask with a laugh. "No, seriously. That's not funny."

Bennett nods. "Seriously."

I stumble back. "What the—"

"Olivia Huang Christenson, everybody!" Marcus announces from the stage.

Bennett gently grabs my shoulders and turns me around. I somehow manage to put one foot in front of the other and walk across the stage. I even get a wave in. Randall points to his cheeks and mouths the word "smile!" I force one across my face and then see him shaking his head and mouthing "too much!"

Under an ornate arch spanning the width of the stage, five armchairs are arranged in a half-moon formation like we're about to be in conversation with Oprah. Even she wouldn't be able to soothe me right now. Small tables with microphones are placed artfully in front of each seat. The third panelist, a woman who I recognize as the relationships editor from *El Lay Daily*, is already settled into the farthest chair to the left of Marcus. The fourth panelist, the consumer market research person, is seated directly next to him. She looks up at me and gives me a polite smile. I sit in the chair opposite her, meaning Bennett will be between me and Marcus. Just the two of us sitting stage right pretending to act like everything's normal. How hard can that be?

"You look like a celebrity caught in paparazzi headlights! Relax. This won't be too painful!" Marcus whispers to me with a chuckle before announcing Bennett.

I watch Alisha's and Randall's jaws drop as Bennett crosses the stage and sits down next to me. He gives the crowd a small wave before his eyes flit over to mine. I want to glare at him, but if I look at him for too long, I fear I'll forgive him before he's even had a chance to say sorry.

We spend the next ten minutes giving brief introductions, explaining the work we do, and fielding easy questions. I try to remember my talking points, but my thoughts feel like mush as I try to overanalyze every interaction I've had with Bennett. It isn't until Marcus directs a question to both me and Bennett that my brain perks up.

"Olivia, Bennett, both of your companies match people using the Chinese zodiac, but from what you've both said, it sounds like one focuses on compatibility, and the other, not so much."

I speak before Bennett has a chance to. "That's right, Marcus. One of us—Lunar Love—actually matchmakes based on complementary traits of the Chinese zodiac. Which is the way it's supposed to work. My grandmother started Lunar Love over fifty years ago. We're the original here in LA," I explain proudly.

Marcus leans forward into the microphone. "Bennett, did you know Lunar Love existed before you started ZodiaCupid?"

I turn my body to face Bennett. "Great question, Marcus," I say.

Bennett coolly smiles. "I always do my due diligence. But I actually knew about Lunar Love in a more personal way," he says. "June Huang, the founder, your grandmother," Bennett continues, looking me in the eyes, "matched my parents."

My smirk drops from my face. "That can't be right," I say. He told me his parents were incompatible. This guy can't even keep his story straight.

"It's true. I followed the path of my parents' history, and it led me to you. To June," he quickly corrects.

"I think you're getting your paths mixed up," I mutter. But even as I say those words, I falter in my conviction. Pó Po couldn't have done that. She's careful and meticulous. Mistakes like that are only made by me. I shift my attention back to Bennett.

He nods. "June was an excellent matchmaker, and she built an incredible business. You're very lucky, Olivia. I'm sure you're just as good as she is."

Jerk! What's this guy's deal?

"Well, if that's not adorable!" Marcus says. The audience claps along with him.

"It's something, Marcus, it's something," I say. "But Bennett, just because Pó Po, I mean June, *allegedly* matched your parents, it doesn't mean you *know* her. Or me."

Marcus and the other panelists look confused as I pick up my conversation with Bennett where we left off backstage. Bennett realizes right away. He gives me a look. *The* look. The let's-not-do-this-here look.

Addressing Marcus, the panelists, and the audience, Bennett says, "I see our businesses as complementary to one another. The Chinese zodiac can't be monopolized. We offer a similar service but in different ways." He looks smug with his political correctness.

"Our business isn't a digital identity crisis. That's the only difference," I reveal in the heat of the moment.

Bennett's smile melts off his face. His eyes turn so cold that they extinguish the fire behind mine. "That's not—" Bennett says before stopping abruptly. He thinks for a moment, his eyebrows lifting. Under his breath he asks, "Were you the one who wrote that WhizDash article?"

Oops.

"You're CakeGirl, aren't you?" Bennett asks, the hurt on his face cutting deep into me.

"No sidebar conversations!" Marcus says with a nervous laugh. "Speak up so we can all hear. This is a live recording, all made possible by our generous sponsors."

Bennett leans onto one of the armrests. "You know, it can be really hard for people to let go of the past, Marcus. Change isn't easy for everyone. But we're living in modern times so it's time to stop getting stuck in our old ways. Digital is the future. What do you all think?" he asks the audience.

The audience claps and cheers to answer his question, their excitement bouncing off the walls of the theater. Everyone except Alisha and Randall, of course. They sit with their arms crossed, looking appalled and shouting boos as shields against the crowd's enthusiasm.

I try to think of a witty comeback, but instead I become defensive. "Why do people feel the need to get rid of traditions? They're an important part of history that will be forgotten if we," I say, motioning my arms around the stage and out toward the audience, "don't keep them alive. Why are you so against tradition, Bennett?"

Bennett adjusts the collar of his amber cashmere zip-up. "I'm only against tradition when it distracts you from the truth of what's good. When you operate in a state of denial because you're stuck in the mud of the past," he says, his tone icy.

"Poetic! For our listeners at home, the tension in here is palpable," Marcus says, crossing his hands over his lap. "And remember, panelists, we're live. We can't edit anything you say afterwards."

I look out into the crowd and up at the faded murals above the balcony. The vaulted ceiling glimmers from the thousands of tiny mirrors sprinkled across it. It's as though we're in our own

Spanish Gothic–style world, the indoor mirror-stars a glimpse of the past. Except instead of the sensation of feeling unconfined by the vastness of the universe, I feel trapped. All eyes are on us—on me—as I form my response.

"Tradition is steady. Reliable. Lunar Love has lasted this long for a reason," I explain, twisting one of my rose-gold rings around my pointer finger. "We're not some flash-in-the-pan start-up that's only around until people move on to the next shiny thing."

Bennett scoffs. "Sounds like someone's worried that technology will obliterate what's old and outdated."

The fire behind my eyes is back and burning brighter than ever. I feel the heat radiate through my body so rapidly that I'm not fully aware when I stand up and announce, "We're not outdated. Our methods may be rooted in history, but we make real love happen. I'll prove to you that we're better. I bet I can match you up with someone so compatible that you'll be in love by the end of the year."

The room goes quiet. Marcus, pro that he is, speaks first. "I'm not a betting man, but that sounded to me like a wager."

Bennett sits up straighter in his chair, looking pensive. "That's—I don't know about this," he says. "You don't want to do this."

"I don't want to do this, or *you* don't want to do this?" I take my seat confidently. "Scared your scam will be outed?" I say quietly, offering Bennett a smug smile. "I've been in business long enough to know what it takes to make a successful match. Your business hasn't even launched yet. Who's better? Well, it's as clear as the sun and the moon."

Instead of scaring Bennett off, I've only intrigued him. He

settles into a more comfortable position. "More like, I can't be held responsible when ZodiaCupid's results are better than you think. Better than Lunar Love's outcomes."

I bite my lip. "Impossible," I say, growing panicky. I keep a neutral and unwavering look on my face. "Like I said, I'll prove it to you."

"Based on traits?"

"Precisely."

"And you think you know me?"

I half smile. "Oh, I have a decent idea about who you are."

"Fine. You've got yourself a deal," Bennett agrees. Warmth has returned to his eyes, but I can still see the hurt behind them. Hurt *I* put in them.

"Wait, so I'll take the time to handpick you a custom match, and you'll let your algorithm do the work?" I ask.

"That's how our businesses work, isn't it?" Bennett says. "You pick a match for me, and I'll let my algorithm pick one for you, and we'll see who finds love."

I narrow my eyes at him. Little does he know, I'm never again letting myself fall for someone incompatible. This wager's already been won. "Absolutely."

"And I don't need until the end of the year. In my world, two and a half months is too long. I bet I can match you using ZodiaCupid with someone you'll be in love with by the end of the month," Bennett counters.

"You're kidding," I say, letting out an unamused laugh.

Bennett shakes his head. He crosses his arms and leans back casually against the seat. The other two panelists look slightly stunned, but amused.

I blink furiously. "See? This is my point exactly! That isn't about how fast it happens. Love isn't some careless word you throw around!"

"That's right!" Alisha shouts from the audience. I'm relieved when a couple others in the crowd agree with her.

"Well, folks, this just got very interesting," Marcus says excitedly, as though he can already envision the ratings his show's going to get. "Even the audience is getting into it. Olivia, you think Lunar Love and compatibility is better. Bennett, you don't. How about this? Whoever can match the other with someone they fall in love with first gets an exclusive one-on-one podcast episode, a shout-out on our social media channels where we have over one million followers, and a feature on our website. Heck, we'll even throw in a dating package for ten giveaway winners, paid for by us."

"And a feature in our dating column," the relationship editor chimes in. She sits cross-legged in her chair looking way too entertained.

I'm stunned by how quickly this all escalated. That's huge exposure. And ten new immediate clients? That may be nothing to ZodiaCupid, but it's a lot to us. That would reduce our need to find people right away, and we could focus on what we do best. I can physically feel the seconds passing as I process the situation.

"Well?" Marcus asks me before turning back to his microphone and adding, "Listeners at home, we can practically hear Olivia thinking. What will her decision be?"

I've always admired how Marcus builds anticipation in his shows, but now that his tactics for keeping listeners tuned in is directed at me, I'm not such a fan.

I extend my hand out to Bennett. "I'm in."

"Excellent," Bennett says, wrapping his fingers around mine. The contact sparks memories of last night: touching hands, homemade sushi, stolen glances under the stars, the rare feeling of unbearable lightness. It was like being with a completely different person. I shake off the drive-in version of Bennett. He's long gone.

"Folks, it looks like we have ourselves a Match-Off!" Marcus announces.

Pulled back into the moment of being watched by thousands of eyes, I lock my own two with Bennett's. He gives me a private, small, crooked smile. The breath in my chest catches. I hate what that does to me.

This is going to be fine. I know for a fact his app doesn't work and that my matching record is way higher than his. I'll get lots of press for Lunar Love, ZodiaCupid will be exposed for the sham that it is, and Bennett will find love. It's a win-win for everyone.

I grip his hand tighter and pull him closer. Our cheeks graze as I bring my lips up against his ear. "I hope you're ready to fall in love."

CHAPTER 10

Six days and one very important match later, I claim an empty seat under a palm tree wrapped in twinkle lights and set my tray of dumplings and cup of boba beer onto the sticky table. I drag the metal chair a foot to the left along the concrete ground until I have a clear view of one table in particular across the courtyard. I keep my sunglasses on, even though the sun has already started to set.

"Do you have eyes on the targets?" Alisha asks, her voice booming through my earbuds.

"Rat and Dragon are now seated. I repeat, they just sat down," I say quietly, feeling like an undercover agent in a spy movie. Why haven't I been doing this for all of my clients' dates?

Lines of people form in front of food trucks, dessert booths, and the beer garden outside of the San Gabriel Mission Playhouse, the backdrop to this year's Dumpling and Beer Festival. Laughter fills the air as families, couples, and fellow singles hunt down dinner and taste test delicious beer flavors like matcha and mango.

I bite into my mac and cheese dumpling and prepare to witness sparks flying. Across the courtyard, Bennett and Harper toast their beers and dig into their dumpling assortment and pile of mochi waffles.

"I hope they like each other," I say into the headphone microphone. "He *needs* to fall in love."

"You combed through the entire database and thought through each of their traits. I think they're going to like each other," Alisha says reassuringly.

"They're both entrepreneurs and share a similar work ethic. She has big ideas for the future, and he's resourceful enough to support them. She's interested in food, he's creative with his food pairings and is actually a decent cook—"

"This is according to the sushi he made you on your *date*, right?" she asks dramatically.

I draw hearts into the condensation on my beer glass. "It wasn't a date, Alisha. It was research."

Alisha snickers. "Uh-huh. Whatever you say. Speaking of research, Harper doesn't know you're there, right?"

"No! Neither of them do. I just want to make sure everything goes smoothly for them. I can't wait to see the look on his face when he realizes how wonderful she is."

I watch as Bennett and Harper smile politely at each other. Harper laughs at something he says, and I become acutely aware of how she's angled her body toward him.

"They're sitting awfully close for a first date," I mumble.

"That's a good thing, remember?" Alisha says.

"Yeah. Yes, definitely. Of course," I repeat like I'm trying to convince myself. "There's usually some warm-up time involved, that's all."

"You're good at what you do. You've already warmed them up. Now it's game time," Alisha says, slightly distracted. On the other end, I hear the opening song of *My Best Friend's Wedding* in the background.

I nod to myself. "Right. We've got this in the bag. By the end of the night, he'll be swooning."

Harper drops her fork, and Bennett reacts before she has a chance to, picking up the utensil and standing to grab her another one. "I wonder if he'll throw himself on the ground for her, too," I mumble. At the thought of him doing that for Harper, my breathing becomes shallower.

"He did what?" Alisha asks, humming along to the movie's song.

My heart thumps hollowly. "He was a gentleman, that's all," I say, not wanting to give more life to a kind gesture that probably meant nothing.

The crinkle of a plastic bag cuts the first part of Alisha's sentence off. "—hope she's into him. From the way you described him, he sounds intense. Now that I think about it, though, he could've reacted to the article a lot worse, so maybe he's not so bad."

I take a sip of beer through the wide straw, a mouthful of tapioca coming up with it. "He's not a bad guy. Besides, he's *our* enemy. Not hers."

"By the way, have you talked to your Pó Po yet?" Alisha asks.

A group forms around a table to cheer on a dumpling-eating competition. "Not yet. I need more details first. He could be messing with me. Trying to get into my head."

"That'd be a bizarre way to do it, don't you think?" she says.

I narrow my eyes in Bennett's direction. "This guy's capable of anything."

I lean onto my elbow to see around a family who has stopped

to huddle in my line of sight. When they finally move, Harper's alone at the table. I scan the crowd and find Bennett paying for more dessert at a booth.

"I wonder if he'll scrape the frosting off that cake, too," I say. Instead of going back to the table, he turns in my direction. "Uh, let me call you back."

"I'm a big boy. I don't need a babysitter, you know," Bennett calls out to me as he approaches. He slides a plate of matcha cake across the table. "I brought you this. Thought all your sleuthing might make you hungry."

"That was unnecessary," I say, my mouth watering. "How did you know I was here?"

"I sensed a disturbance in the Force," he jokes. "You only sat next to one of the few decorative palm trees and are wearing sunglasses at night. You might as well have strapped a neon light to your chest that blinks, 'I'm discreet!'"

I lean my forehead into my palm. "Does Harper know?"

"Oh. Yeah. She thinks you're really committed."

I push my sunglasses over my head. "Because that's what in-person matchmaking allows me to be. Committed. You're not left to your own devices like all the poor souls in Digital Purgatory."

"In what?" Bennett asks.

"Nothing. You wouldn't understand. You didn't tamper with this, did you?" I ask suspiciously, hovering my chopsticks over the icing.

Bennett shakes his head. "Too many witnesses."

The corner of my mouth lifts into an almost-smile before I remember why I'm here and my mission of taking down Bennett—I mean, finding Bennett love.

"Are you sure you want to go through with this? We can call it off right now, no hard feelings."

"Your date's going *that* well already, huh?" I ask, crossing my arms over the section of table in front of me. "We can call it off if we both agree that I win."

"No one has won yet. But you know what happens if one of us does, right?" he adds with a peculiar shyness.

I drop my hands into my lap. "The details of the competition were pretty clear," I state. But deep down, I know what he means. If I win, I lose Bennett. But he's not mine. Never has been. Any chance of there being an *us* is over before it can even begin. What am I saying? There is no *us*. There could never be an *us*.

Bennett lingers in the drawn-out silence. "Okay. As long as we're clear."

"Perfectly," I say hesitantly, my voice shaky. I clear my throat. "Harper's great, isn't she?"

Bennett looks caught off guard by my quick transition. "She really is," he says. "I have to thank you for not sending us to salsa dancing or anything. The night would've ended before it started."

"Very interesting," I say. "How do you know there's not going to be dancing here?"

"Here in public? Where? On the tables?"

I motion toward the tables. "This date could be one giant flash mob. You don't know."

"If that happens, I'm gone." Dread ripples across Bennett's face. "I had an embarrassing junior prom moment that put me off dancing forever," he explains.

I'm immediately intrigued, but he's already been over here

long enough. "Hates dancing. I'll make a mental note," I say, "for the next time that there won't be because, I mean, come on!" I motion toward Harper across the square, who's watching the live band that's just started playing.

"She's open to trying all the different food, she does interesting work, and she's very pretty," Bennett says. A pang shoots through me. "I admit you're good. Though that was never in question."

"Exactly. So how about we just call it for what it is? I win, you lose, we both move on."

Bennett braces his hands against the back of a chair and leans forward. The veins in his forearms swell, shadows pooling in the grooves of his defined muscles. I pull my attention from them, remembering that they belong to the competition in front of me.

"The bet was on who would fall in love first. Last I checked, I'm not in love with Harper," he says.

"Yet," I say, not meaning to sound so hesitant about it.

"You're not getting out of your date," Bennett says, the corner of his mouth sloping upward.

I catch myself staring at him and look away before he notices me. "Speaking of date, I see what you're trying to do here. The only rule was that you have to give it a fair shot. Don't you dare sabotage this," I say quickly. "Just ignore me. Pretend I'm not here."

"That's hard to do, but I'll try," Bennett says, his eyes sparkling in the palm tree's lights. A flicker of electricity shoots through me. We linger in the moment for longer than I expect. Suddenly, he adds, "Hey, did you know Oktoberfest started in 1810, and every year, over two million gallons of beer are consumed?"

I lean forward in my chair. "Keep those fun facts between us,"

I instruct. "I don't know yet how Harper feels about trivia or you being a piñata filled with useless, but interesting, fun facts."

"There's only one way to find out," Bennett says, walking backward away from me slowly. He pauses briefly and then turns and heads back to Harper.

When he's gone, I become highly aware of his absence. He doesn't look over in my direction for the next thirty or so minutes, as though there's an unspoken agreement between us. He does something animated with his hands and makes Harper laugh more. I so badly want to know what he's saying.

Twenty minutes later, I abandon my prime viewing position at the table and find cover in a shadowed arched doorway closer to Bennett and Harper. I check my phone for new emails and confirm the balloon delivery details for tomorrow's Cookie Day.

"Would you like to join us at the table?" Bennett asks, appearing beside me in the doorway.

My hand flies up over my heart. "You scared me! Don't do that!"

"You're lurking creepily in the shadows." Bennett positions himself next to me, resting his shoulder against the wall. "Do you do this for all your matches?"

"Remember what I said about pretending I'm not here?"

"Harper found a few of her chef friends. I think she's bored with me," Bennett says.

"What? No! She's just being friendly," I say, standing on my toes to look over the crowd. She's surrounded by a small group of people in chef jackets. "Go back over there and charm her. Meet her friends."

"Before I do that, I wanted to clear up something between us. What I said at the panel, about your Pó Po," Bennett starts.

"You were just trying to rile me up. You were mad about the article," I say, glancing up at him to gauge his reaction. It doesn't matter whether I meant to send the article or not. The fact is, it's out there. And for that, I do owe him an apology. "I'm sorry about that. And for using the *digital identity crisis* line. And then throwing it back in your face at the panel. And for sneakily matching with you and lying about who I am."

Bennett smirks. "Is that all?"

"Yes. That's all I'm sorry for. Nothing else," I say, watching him carefully.

Bennett reacts to my expression with one that looks like surprise. "I appreciate that. Though the word *mad* sounds extreme. Hurt, yes. But I can handle a little bad press. I wish it didn't come from you, is all. The manipulating-a-match thing I honestly can't be mad about. You beat the algorithm. That's impressive."

I lift my chin up. "That's right. Remember that's who you're dealing with. Someone who beats algorithms."

Bennett inhales sharply before finally saying, "I'm sorry, too, for not telling you I knew who you were."

My shoulders relax in relief. It feels good to come to some kind of understanding. "Now I guess we're back to being even."

"How about we make a pact not to lie to each other anymore?" Bennett says.

I tilt my head forward. "Why?"

"We've lied to each other enough, don't you think?"

"You're probably right. I guess I can agree to that," I say. "So you'll tell me what the product launch is then?"

Bennett's face glimmers with amusement. "That's a surprise, not a lie."

"Fine, then be honest with me about Pó Po."

Bennett takes a step closer, and I can feel the heat of his body take the chilly edge off. "That would be a weird and specific thing to lie about. She really did match my parents."

I think for a few seconds. "I'll have to ask her to confirm."

"Want to stroll?" Bennett asks, glancing over my head at Harper.

I look over in the same direction. She's engrossed in conversation with her group of friends. "Quickly. Tell me more about Pó Po. Then get back there and be social."

We weave around families and children munching on dumplings, making our way to nowhere in particular. I unzip my jacket to release some of the heat forming in my chest. Too much boba beer probably.

"You didn't expose Pó Po on stage. Why?" I ask as we walk side by side under colorful archways.

Bennett lifts an eyebrow in surprise. "What was there to out?"

"That she made an incompatible match," I say grimly.

He tucks his hands into the back pockets of his jeans. The curves of his upper arm muscles are accentuated as the fabric of his sweater pulls tighter against his body. My heart rate quickens when I notice the way he's looking over at me. "Your Pó Po made a successful match."

"Not technically. You could've delegitimized our entire business in ten seconds."

"The legacy and credibility of Lunar Love isn't hanging by the thread of one incompatible match," he says. "You're known for your quality matches, period. I think it's you getting hung up on needing every match to be perfectly compatible."

"It's how relationships should be," I say firmly.

"Olivia, you'll miss out on good people if you believe

compatibility is the one and only way to love," Bennett says. "Trust me on this."

"No, I'll only avoid the wrong people if I do," I retort. "Pairing incompatible animal signs together only leads to trouble."

In the courtyard, the live band finishes their set and switches out with a guitarist who starts playing an acoustic version of "What a Wonderful World." A few of the older couples slow dance in the courtyard, their heads resting against one another. Unexpected longing for something indescribable strikes me suddenly. I swat the emotions away.

"Look, it's your nightmare," I joke, swaying to the music.

Bennett ignores the dancers. He doesn't even tap his foot to the beat. Instead, he just examines my face. "Life is restrictive as it is. Why set more boundaries for yourself?"

"You never answered my original question backstage about how you know me through Pó Po," I push back, changing topics.

"She talked about you," he says casually.

"What, did you meet every week for brunch or something?" I ask sarcastically, lifting and dropping my shoulders to imitate his nonchalance. "Elaborate. I need more details. Where and when did you meet? What did she say exactly? You have to tell me. We just made a pact!"

"She told me that you would be taking over Lunar Love soon. She showed me photographs. You were a pretty cute kid." Bennett grins, the beauty mark on his cheek lifting with the corner of his eyes.

I bury my face in my hands. "Oh, god."

"What's so bad about childhood photos?" he says with a laugh.

I spread my fingers over my eyes and peek at Bennett through them. "It's not that. You were both conspiring!"

Bennett turns to walk sideways, bending closer to look at me through my window-fingers. "You make it sound a lot shadier than it was. She didn't mention me to you at all?"

"Definitely not," I say on an irritated exhalation.

Bennett sighs. "Your turn. What really happened at the baking class?"

We find an empty spot to sit at the Mission Playhouse's curved fountain, the sculpture in the center spilling over with water from top to middle to bottom. From here, I can see Harper, who's laughing and chatting with her friends, not looking like she's missing Bennett at all. That's not a great sign.

I refocus on Bennett. "I told you, it was a friend from a past life. That's all there is to know."

"Pact," Bennett says, holding his hand over his chest.

"Was that a trick? Just so I'd tell you?" I ask defensively.

Bennett crosses his ankle over his knee and rests his elbow on his thigh. "You promised."

I sigh. "She really was an old, close friend. Colette." Saying her name brings her ghost to life. Water splashes into the center of the fountain, sending ripples outward toward us. I bite my lip, trying to find the words. "I destroyed her life."

Bennett doesn't laugh or scoff. He sits and waits patiently for me to continue, his calmness encouraging me.

"I didn't know she was back in town," I add. "Seeing her was surreal."

"How did you destroy her life?" Bennett asks without a trace of judgment in his voice. He's in the middle of a date but is acting like he has all the time in the world for me.

"By matching her with someone incompatible." I stare at the mossy floor of the fountain to avoid eye contact with him. The lights around the circumference of the fountain wall power on, making the water glitter in the lavender dusk. "I convinced her to let me match her. When she finally agreed, I was in a place in my life where I thought incompatible matches were harmless. I learned my lesson. I'll never let that happen again."

"That's tough," Bennett says.

I spiral deeper into my memories, reflecting on what happened. It wouldn't be the first time these thoughts have taken over.

"I must've missed something in the background check," I try to reason. "The guy convinced Colette to make a sketchy investment, took her money, and then vanished. That happened because of me. He tricked us both."

"That's awful," Bennett sympathizes.

"As her matchmaker and friend, I should've known something wasn't right. I was too distracted with my own life," I admit. "I let what I was going through influence me. I refused to listen to Pó Po, to my gut, or to anyone who knew better."

The noise of the crowd around us fades away. I confide in Bennett like it's the easiest thing in the world. Like I've done it before a thousand times. He listens carefully, focusing on my face. Feeling him watching me is unnerving and wholly satisfying at once.

"I haven't talked to Colette in years, and it's all my fault," I continue. "Our friendship ended overnight."

"Have you tried reaching out?" Bennett asks.

I turn my head side to side slowly. "It was pretty clear she wanted nothing to do with me. The blowup was intense. It was a rough time." I move my ring up and down my finger, twisting it around and around.

"I'm sorry to hear that," Bennett says softly. "That's hard to lose someone like that."

I wave my hand through the air. "I was reckless. I had—have—a responsibility. What I do, what we do, affects actual human lives. It isn't a game. The consequences are very real," I say breathlessly. It's been years since I've talked about this. For a moment, it's as though the weight of the world isn't my burden to carry.

"Hence what you said about incompatibility only leading to trouble." Bennett angles his body toward me, the expression on his face compassionate. "Thank you for telling me."

"Is that a good enough reason for you throwing yourself on the ground?" I joke, trying to lighten the mood.

"I would've done it for less," Bennett says earnestly, a small grin playing across his lips.

His smile is contagious, and I can't resist mirroring it. I bite down, blushing.

I look over the crowd to check on my client, who's no longer with her group of friends. Bennett stands to greet an enthusiastic Harper, who's spotted us. She waves excitedly and jogs the rest of the way to us.

"Hi, Olivia!" Harper says with a big smile, her lips painted blush pink.

"Harper, hi," I say in my most professional tone. The optics of this must look bad. I form excuses in my head to say to her. But really, there's no excuse for taking her date away. None that I could tell her anyway.

"I just needed some coaching," Bennett says, covering for me. "She came by to make sure we were doing all right."

"That's so nice of you! Sorry, Bennett, I got caught up with some people I know from work," she says, gesturing toward the food trucks. "One chef was having a bit of drama, and I had to report for friend duty. The food world is small."

"Pea-sized," Bennett says with emphasis.

I let out a laugh. Betrayed by my own heart.

"I thought you two were talking shop over here," Harper asks conspiratorially.

"What? No, definitely not," I say.

Harper rests her hand casually on her hip. "I thought you were kidding at first when you told me that this date was with the founder of ZodiaCupid. Who knew he was using Lunar Love! But he uses both like me. I guess why limit yourself?" she says. "How nice that the two of you get along so well."

Bennett lifts up his eyebrows in agreement with her. "We're all just trying to bring more love into the world. Isn't that right, Olivia?"

"One compatible match at a time," I say sweetly. "Don't let me hold you up. Enjoy the dumplings and the unlimited beer, on Lunar Love."

"In that case, round two in the beer garden?" Bennett asks, offering his arm to Harper. She links her arm in his and smiles. I gulp down my envy as their bodies move together as one.

"Bye, Olivia!" Harper says giddily.

"Enjoy your date! Love is in the air!" I shout awkwardly, attracting stares from children challenging each other to stuff entire dumplings into their mouths.

Bennett glances over his shoulder, making eye contact with me one last time before entering the beer garden. Rat and Dragon are on the move.

CHAPTER 11

My sister, Nina, was right when she predicted my future. I balance stacked dishes in my arms and distractedly set plates around the outdoor dining table. Against the olive tree in my parents' yard, teal balloons are tied together to create the shape of a crescent blue moon. Opaque white and silver glass candle votives are scattered on the tables and deck railings. Mom wrangles with the streamers while Nina finishes lighting the candles.

"What's with Dad's apron?" Nina asks. We all turn our heads toward Dad, who's rocking a *Scottish and Proud* tartan apron at the grill.

"Don't get me started," Mom says with a laugh. "He's been going down the rabbit hole of his ancestry."

Pó Po brings over a box of silver mesh bags. "This is looking lovely," she says, looking around the backyard. "Olivia, will you please help me bag up some cookies?"

I haven't been alone with Pó Po in over a week. This will be my opportunity to talk to her about Bennett. And her alleged incompatible match. I pull out a chair for Pó Po to sit in at the table, and she shows me how she wants the cookies packaged.

"So this is basically the wedding shower, right?" I ask, dodging what I really need to say.

Pó Po looks up from the stack of cookies and smiles. "It's kind of like that. The tradition is that the groom's family sends pastries and cookies to the bride's family. Marriage is about the bonding of the couple, but also of our families and ancestors."

"I like that," I say. "I had never heard of it before."

Pó Po takes a moment to restack some of the misplaced pastries. "It's not easy to keep traditions alive when you're far from family. But over time, traditions, and the way they're celebrated, are adapted. Isn't it great knowing about it and enjoying it in our own way?" she asks.

"I don't know," I say. "Aren't traditions traditions because they stay the same?"

"Liv, life is not all or nothing, and traditions are better alive in one form or another than nonexistent."

I place two cookies into a bag and pull the strings tight. "Like Lunar Love," I say.

"No one would hire me when I moved here," she continues. "I barely spoke any English and had three kids. I could've kept Lunar Love the way it was, but it wouldn't have worked. I had to adapt."

"How'd you keep it all together?" I ask.

"You just keep going. Make the best decisions that you can at the time," Pó Po shares. "It was quite the culture shock. Even with the kids wanting to live a more traditional American life."

"Yet you still got Auntie hooked on the zodiac," I say.

Pó Po laughs. "I did, but your mother was surprisingly stubborn for a Dog. And your Uncle Rupert was too absorbed with his dinosaurs to care about any other animal. It's no wonder he chose paleontology over matchmaking." She shrugs. "Lunar Love was my life. This never came up when you were transitioning to take the lead, but I hope you know this legacy doesn't have to be yours."

I stop mid-tie to look up at Pó Po. "I—I love Lunar Love and matchmaking. Why would you think that I don't?"

"I just want you to know that you're never stuck. You're independent, and working in the family business might sometimes feel counterintuitive. Lydia felt that way at times. There was a point she almost walked away."

"I didn't know that," I say, searching my memory for conversations Auntie and I may have had about her wanting to leave Lunar Love behind.

"Oh, well, that's a story for a different day." She pulls a bag's strings as tight as she can.

"I'm not giving up on Lunar Love," I say. If Pó Po was able to create a successful business out of nothing, surely I can build off the solid foundation she constructed.

"I'm happy to hear that. You were presented with a challenge to overcome. Is everything going okay? I may have some savings that I can put toward whatever you need at Lunar Love."

"No, no! Don't eat into your retirement fund. I'm handling it," I reassure her.

Pó Po reaches over to tap my hand. "Remember, where there's a negative, there's always a positive. Now, tell me. Have you given any more thought to the gentleman Auntie introduced you to over email?"

"The one with a ten-year strategy? I appreciate a well-thought plan but that's a bit much." This man, like all the others Auntie tries to pair me with, is compatible to my Horse sign. I also know from her email that he's a doctor and an off-hours tennis buff.

"She vetted him herself. Maybe he can be your plus one to Nina's wedding. His Tiger is a match to your Horse. A Fire Tiger, too. His optimism might rub off on you. And he plans on being a heart doctor. You'd both have something in common," Pó Po offers.

"How can I say no to Dr. Love-Fifteen? Pretty easily, actually. I can see it now. All those long hours he's away will give us distance that will make us appreciate each other, but when he's back, he'll drag me to the courts to be his doubles partner so he can exhaust his nervous energy."

"This man is compatible to you, and you're *still* not interested." Pó Po sighs. "Careful, Liv. Your heart's been broken, but it's stronger than you think. Isn't it time you make room for someone new?"

"You know my resistance isn't because I don't believe in love. I'd rather focus on finding love for others, not myself, that's all," I tell her.

When Pó Po lost Gōng Gong, she never remarried, and Auntie's still single. They poured themselves into matchmaking and leaned into their independence. Maybe that's the fate of those who lead Lunar Love. I had my great love. Or at least what I thought was love. Maybe that was it for me, and now, like the women before me, it's time to focus on work.

"Lunar Love comes first," I add. I decide to finally say what I need to get off my chest. "Speaking of Lunar Love, I heard something interesting the other day."

"Hmm?" Pó Po hums as she diligently packs, ties, packs, ties.

"I met someone who had already somehow known who I was. Because of you. And it turns out you had matched his parents."

Pó Po's small hands come to an abrupt stop.

"But he says that his parents were incompatible. Which I told him couldn't be true," I continue. "But is it true?"

"The O'Briens," Pó Po finally says softly. "You were out on a Singles Scouting when Bennett came to find me about a year ago."

"A year ago?" I interrupt. "You've been hiding what could potentially destroy Lunar Love from me for a year?"

Pó Po's thin, lined eyebrows furrow. "Destroy Lunar Love? With his little app?" She scoffs. "Matchmaking is more than just swiping. There are so many people using these apps, how do you sort through everyone? You can't trust what or who people claim to be online. Hands-on matchmaking services are dependable. Safe."

"*I* know this," I say, "but that didn't stop the guy you shared confidential information with."

Pó Po smiles. "Lunar Love has been through it all. Don't worry."

The advice is vague at best. "Please, continue," I say, choosing not to fight it. Her calmness about this is mystifying.

Pó Po fidgets with a loose string. "Bennett learned through his mother's journals that later, after she was married, her birth year wasn't what she had believed all along. Her birthday and year on the birth certificate had been recorded incorrectly, since she had been born just one day after the Lunar New Year."

"So she was a Borderliner," I say, referring to a term we use to call people whose birthdays fall so close to the days of a different animal sign that some of the traits blend.

Pó Po nods. "The years had been mixed up. His mother spent her entire life believing she was born in the year of an animal she actually wasn't. This affected the matching."

So she did make an incompatible match. Like I did. But the reasoning behind hers is understandable. Borderliners can be very tricky.

"He said his parents were happy," I say, reassuring her.

"It was a sloppy mistake," she says as though she's scolding herself.

"It was an accident. It's not like you purposely made an incompatible match. That'd be a different story," I justify.

"What you did was an accident, too, Liv," Pó Po says in a soothing tone. "You did what you thought was best for your friend at the time. We can't always make perfect, blissful matches."

I wrinkle my eyebrows. "You warned me but I didn't listen. At least yours resulted in a successful marriage."

Brightness returns to her face. "Bennett's parents were good together, incompatible or otherwise."

"Why didn't you tell me about him? He knew about me," I ask. "You never hide things from me."

"I was ashamed about his parents' match," she says. "And you never cared much about the men I bring up to you. How is Bennett different than Mr. Love-Fifteen?"

"He just is," I say after a moment.

"He knows about you because I talked about you. How could I not?" Pó Po says. "I'm sorry that you were caught by surprise, but everyone's entitled to their own secrets every now and then."

I have a million more questions but I sense she wants to drop it. I've already questioned her enough. Pó Po goes to her room to rest before the festivities pick up while I bundle the bagged cookies together and bring them to the front entrance for guests to grab on their way out. More friends and family have started to arrive, evidenced by the growing stack of shoes in the entryway. A knot in my stomach forms at the anticipation of having to field questions about Lunar Love and if I've managed to save it yet.

"Olivia! Can you grab this?" Dad asks as I pass by the kitchen. With a plate of raw meat balanced in one hand, he hands me a plate of cheddar cheese slices that have been individually shaped with a cookie cutter to be perfectly round. "Moon cheese. I paid extra for expedited shipping. The fee was astronomical!" He laughs at his own joke.

"Looks good," I say to Dad, following him back out to the grill.

"Everything all right?" Dad asks when I don't even pity laugh.

"Oh, yeah. I just have a lot on my mind. Nice apron, by the way."

"You like it? It's the exact tartan pattern of our family clan from Scotland," he explains. "I had it custom-made. Let me know if you want one." He nudges a burger patty so it lines up evenly with the others.

Dad places the plate of rounded burger meat onto the grill's side table. "You want a Full Moon Burger Special?" he asks, flipping his metal spatula into the air, barely catching it. I narrowly dodge the spinning utensil.

"Definitely. Medium rare, please. I'll be back for it." I pat Dad on the shoulder and make my way over to the dessert table where I see Nina and Asher, Nina's fiancé, lingering.

"Do we have enough food?" Nina asks us, fidgeting with her sapphire engagement ring.

"There's four platters of wife cake, walnut cookies, sponge cake, Chinese shortbread, two trays of chocolate cake, a plate of macarons, two bowls of fruit, a box of doughnuts, burgers, chips, drinks...I think there's plenty," I say.

"If we run out, I'll go whip up a fresh batch of cookies myself," Asher says reassuringly. He rubs Nina's shoulders.

"Okay," she says, exhaling a relaxed sigh. She adjusts one of the plates so that it's angled closer to the tray. "Thanks, Ash."

Mom joins us with two cookie cakes. "Grandma and Grandpa sent these for you. They told me to tell you that they're sorry they can't make it, but they're looking forward to seeing you at the wedding."

"Well, there we go! More food. Problem solved," Asher says with a smile. "Let's get this party started. Drinks, ladies?"

"Just a little bit of wine, please," Nina says. "Don't go wild with it."

Asher, a Universal Studios tour guide, raises his eyebrows. "Speaking of wild, did you know that *Psycho* was the first American film to show a toilet flushing on screen?"

"A real toilet?" I ask, pretending that this is the first time he's told me this fun fact. He must be working overtime on his comedic timing.

"Just go," Nina says, gently pushing Asher toward the beverages.

We look around the backyard, which looks like a galaxy of blue and white decorations.

"You really went all out with the Over the Moon theme," she observes. "I didn't know there were pumpkins on the moon."

I nod. "Only when it's feeling festive. Everyone agreed that we should go big since you're planning a courthouse wedding."

"Whoa. I'll officially be married in two weeks!" Nina says dreamily.

"Asher's a lucky guy. I'm glad his family was able to join us today."

"Can you believe Pó Po allowed it? You know how selective she is about traditions. She's not ready to let me go, I guess."

"It's not like you're going off to live with his family, never to return," I say. "Unless you are, then..." I move my hands up and down as though I'm weighing the options.

Nina grabs me by the arm. "Hey, let's go to The Spaceship."

"Right now? Don't you have to mingle?" I ask.

"I just need a minute." Nina leads the way to the front yard and climbs up the ladder of our treehouse. Dad built it for us when we were young enough to believe that the structure had magical powers. Now we just like to pretend that it does. We named it The Spaceship because it took us on journeys beyond our wildest imaginations.

"Can this thing still support both of us?" I call up to her.

"If not, we go down together!" she yells back.

I grip each bar tightly and slowly climb the ladder, pressing my body against the metal rungs. "Remember when we used to play up here and pretend we were flying to the moon?" I ask, finally making it up the ladder. The treehouse floor is patterned by the shadows of the tree branches, creating a thousand different ever-changing shapes.

"It was just us and the stars and that parrot that would never stop squawking," Nina says. She leans back against one of the treehouse's walls. I join her on the floor.

Nina pulls out a little red box from the pocket of her dress. "I got you something. Just a little maid of honor gift, even though there's technically not going to be bridesmaids."

"No! Today's supposed to be about you!" I pop open the lid, revealing a little gold horse charm. "Thank you! It's so pretty!" I string it onto my necklace so it dangles next to the moon pendant.

"I know you don't agree with compatibility, but Asher's the one for me. It's like you with baking." When she says the word *baking*, I think she's about to say Bennett and my entire body breaks out in a light sweat. "When all the ingredients are mixed together, it tastes as it should."

I look into Nina's round eyes, her short dark lashes curled. "You don't have to convince me," I say. "I think you two are great together. Why are you even mentioning it? I thought you don't believe in compatibility or the Chinese zodiac."

Like Mom, Nina wanted to do something completely different than the family business. Her interest in the zodiac didn't stick like it did for me. The irony with Mom is that she married someone compatible to her Dog sign.

"But you do. And Pó Po and Auntie do. I know you all worry that I'm going to end up with someone who I compete with all the time because we care too much about our own opinions." Nina tucks a light brown strand of hair behind her ears.

"Sounds like someone's been doing research," I say.

"I may have flipped through one of Pó Po's zodiac books," she admits. "It was a little nerve-wracking seeing all those traits laid out like that."

"And you worry we'll think that you'll have to compromise too much and that you'll be too critical of each other because you're both Roosters?" I ask.

She angles her head. "Something like that. I don't want to disappoint anyone, but I also believe that Asher and I, while yes, we have our differences, are supposed to be together."

"You only disappoint me when you're late for our brunch dates," I joke.

She laughs. "But you have to admit that you didn't agree with our relationship at first," she says. "I don't want to feel like I'm betraying my family by not marrying someone who isn't a match in the way you all believe."

"*Betraying* is a strong word. The family just wants you to be happy. That's what matters."

"I hope so," she says.

"The zodiac helps us understand ourselves and our partners. It's like Pó Po said, life is not all or nothing." I lift a fallen, waxy leaf and turn it between my fingers. "At first, yes," I continue, "I was hesitant about the incompatibility. My life's purpose is to help people find their compatible partners. And I know first-hand how incompatible boyfriends can turn out. But now that I've gotten to know Asher and have seen you two together over the years, there's no question in my mind that you were meant to be."

"You promise?" Nina asks.

I nod. "Asher's confident and fights for what he wants. You're considerate and take the time to make sure things are done the right way. Sure, you might butt heads every now and then, but I see two people who are strong individuals who are even stronger together. If there were blockers that you both felt you couldn't get past, that would be a different story."

"Mmm," Nina groans and leans her head up to face the sky. "You don't sound like you. You can't really believe all that."

"I believe in compatibility, *and* I want you to be happy. You're my sister and my best friend. You're the exception." I give Nina a light nudge on her knee.

She gives me a small smile. "It must be nice to have guidelines for yourself. Love is so messy."

I laugh humorlessly. "Want to know a secret?" I draw in a quick breath. "Sometimes I envy your freedom of not being tethered to the confines of the zodiac."

Nina reaches out to hold my forearm. "Olivia, neither are you."

I make a disbelieving face.

"You've always been determined," she continues. "You act tough, but you're a romantic. Love is your oxygen. Maybe you need to put your mask on first before helping others."

My phone lights up with a text message, and I quickly pick it up. I tap into a text from *Asshole*, a code name I assigned to Bennett in case anyone looks at my phone when a message comes through. An uncontrollable smile spreads across my face.

We moved up the product launch just so I could use it to find you the best match possible. Get ready for a good time.

"What's that smirk for? Was it something Asshole said?" Nina asks, her voice thick with curiosity.

"It's just spam," I say offhandedly.

"Yeah, right. And don't tell me it's a client. You are way too professional to name a client Asshole in your phone."

"Fine. His name is Bennett," I answer after a long pause. "He's the founder of ZodiaCupid, Lunar Love's new competitor. I tried to gain intel from him at a baking class. It's a long story that I don't want to get into now, but trust me when I say it's nothing."

Nina stares at me with a look of surprise and amusement. "It's nothing, but he's texting you? Bennett," Nina says, trying out how the name sounds. "What are you, dating or something? The irony."

"Please. When's the last time I went on a date?"

"Uh, sounds like when you went to this baking class," Nina says, like it's the most obvious fact in the world.

I balk. "That wasn't a *real* date. I don't have time to spend on anyone with all the work I have. The to-do list never ends."

She rolls her eyes. "Don't let your need to get ahead stand in the way of love."

"Isn't success ultimately more satisfying?" I ask, half joking.

"How very American of you. You know the two aren't mutually exclusive, right?" Nina asks. "If you want, you can totally bring him to the wedding!"

"Not you, too!"

Nina laughs. "Sorry! Maybe Pó Po's matchmaking is rubbing off on me. Is she still trying to find you a plus one? Either way, the invite stands for you to bring him."

I cough out a laugh. "God, no! He's not...anything. We're not dating, and I definitely can't bring him to your wedding," I say. Because he's my archenemy who I'm in the middle of taking down. There's absolutely no future for us as prospective partners, and mixing business with my family would be disastrous.

"Why not?" Nina asks, humored. "Are you going to get in trouble if you do?"

"Well, he is a Rat," I say.

"And that makes you, what, opposites or something?" Nina

asks, looking way too entertained. Her eyes widen as though she's figured something out. "Wait. This is why you're being so positive about me and Asher."

"I'm always positive about love, Nina. It's my job!"

Nina smirks. "Not like this."

"This guy...he's my complete opposite," I articulate, thinking out loud. "I can see it now. His hunger for money and obsession with data will be too overwhelming for me and how I make decisions, which some might call too emotional. He's secretive and doesn't show his cards right away, whereas I like to know things immediately. I wouldn't be able to tell what his true motives are, and that would annoy me. He'll want feedback on every little thing, and I'll be turned off by someone who isn't self-assured. You see? It's useless to even pretend there could ever be something between us."

Nina leans over, her elbows digging into the side of her knees. "I haven't decided yet if it's charming or exhausting when you do that 'I can see it now' thing. You know, just because you and your ex weren't compatible doesn't mean you can't ever be with someone incompatible again, right?"

"He has nothing to do with this," I say, putting my hands up in defense. "I'm providing context based on what I've learned about Bennett so far."

"You really learned a lot about this guy at one baking class," Nina says skeptically.

"I get paid to analyze people quickly," I rationalize.

"I think it's a matter of perspective. His data is numbers. Your data is traits," Nina says.

"My data? That's not how I view love. Based on traits and elements, I help create a—"

"Spark, right?" Nina asks.

I hold my hands out toward her. "Exactly."

"Just like an algorithm, you're trying to make sense of love. You bring order to it for others."

"I'm not trying to have a debate about this."

Still, her words linger.

She sticks out her lip to pout. Nina lives for a good debate. It's what makes her a respectable, albeit exasperating, comic book editor. If authors can reasonably explain their points, Nina's willing to go along with them.

"I just want you to be as happy as I am," Nina says. "You used to love being in love."

I stretch my legs out in front of me. "I am in love. With my work."

Nina leans her head back against the treehouse wall and laughs.

"And I am happy," I continue. I reach for the moon and horse pendants around my neck. "I have Lunar Love and my clients and my family and my health and Pinot and *you*. And cake. There's never a shortage of cake. Honestly, what more do I need?"

CHAPTER 12

I wake to the sound of buzzing against my wooden nightstand. Sensing movement, Pinot climbs over my body to meow in my face for attention. Half-awake, I feel around for my phone.

A cryptic text from Bennett appears on my screen. Date details coming later today, just need you to make sure your profile is up-to-date.

I flop back against the pillow, checking the time on my alarm clock. 6:15 a.m. I hold my phone up in the air with extended arms, my eyes adjusting to the bright glow of my screen in the dark.

I check ZodiaCupid, remembering Bennett's text on Saturday about the product launch. Where's this app update you keep alluding to? I respond.

Bennett messages back immediately. Happy Monday to you, too! It's launching this afternoon.

Before I can respond, another message appears.

Breakfast on me? I can give you a sneak preview.

Obviously, I need this sneak preview. I check my phone calendar for any client sessions—nonexistent—and meetings before agreeing to his offer. Except for a few check-ins with Alisha, my schedule is worryingly open.

After a couple hours of anticipation, I meet Bennett outside of Urth Caffé in downtown LA. I almost don't recognize him in his white T-shirt, workout shorts, and running shoes. We take our place in line, which luckily isn't as long today as it is most days.

"Looks great," Bennett says, looking around at the quiet morning crowd. "I looked up this place on a buddy of mine's newly launched dish-rating app and found a few items with four stars that we could try."

I make a face. "It's Urth. Most everything is good."

"Two hundred and eighty-nine people rated the egg sandwich four point three stars. Let's make sure we get it."

"Two hundred and eighty-nine people? Wow. Well, it must be good then," I tease. "You order what you want. I already know what I'm getting." I look him up and down. "Important meetings after this?"

"I just came from a hike, actually. I texted you on the way up and didn't have time to go home and shower." Bennett tugs at his neckline a few times to air his shirt out. It's still slightly damp from his workout, the fabric clinging to the curves of his chest.

I imagine he would be firm to the touch. Like he works out and takes care of himself, but not obsessively. The tips of my fingers pulse with the desire to reach out, just to see if I'm right.

"Mmhmm," I mumble absentmindedly.

"I run to Griffith Observatory three times a week, then meet my Shoot for the Stars group up there every Monday. Why? Does this outfit bother you?" he asks, his questioning eyes sliding down my face. I flush, becoming hyperaware of what expression I'm making.

"It's fine. Don't feel like you have to get dressed up for me,"

I say, watching him fan himself. Despite having just run up a mountain, he looks surprisingly great. His skin glows, and his musky smell is earthier than usual. In a good way. Is it possible he looks even more handsome?

"Noted. You, on the other hand, didn't need to dress up so much," Bennett says in a joking tone.

I glance down at my black jeans, front-tucked pink sweater, and plaid blazer. "I may not be seeing any clients today, but I'm a professional," I say. I immediately wish I could take back the tidbit about the lack of client meetings.

"I'm only teasing. You look great," he says. His gaze lingers on me and heat blossoms from my toes up to my chest.

"What's Shoot for the Stars?" I ask, changing the subject.

"It's a program to try to get young kids interested in STEM. What better place than the Griffith Observatory to do it?"

"It's perfect," I agree. "Griffith's actually my favorite place to hike in LA."

We shuffle forward in the line.

Bennett nods. "It's incredible being able to escape into nature in the middle of a city. I'll never take it for granted."

"Exactly!" I say excitedly. I catch myself and tone down the energy. "And you bring the T in STEM, I assume?"

Bennett smiles. "I do. I try to make data analytics, computer programming, and machine learning sound fun. Which, it is, but some kids don't always see the appeal at first."

"I'm sure you leave quite the impression," I say with slight sarcasm in my voice. "Do you make the kids run up the mountain, too?"

"It's the first thing they do. I like to make them earn their knowledge," Bennett says with a laugh.

He sets his menu down on the register counter as we approach. We place our orders, and he pays, as promised. We take our number to a metal table outside, settling into a spot next to the building's painted brick wall.

"Let's see this new feature," I say, refocusing on the purpose for being here.

Bennett taps his screen a few times. "Here," he says, placing his phone on the table between us. He moves his chair to the other side so he's sitting next to me. His knee bumps into mine under the table but I don't move my seat back. "I'll walk you through how this feature works."

I notice that the updated dashboard emphasizes the designed animal icons. A light pink swipe-through instruction panel pops up with illustrated peonies in the background, introducing me to the latest additions. I'm caught off guard by the use of peonies. Did Bennett think I'd like this feature because it uses my favorite flower?

I swipe through the mini-tutorial and learn that people receive a peony flower petal when they message with all twelve animal signs.

"When users message other users or go on dates, they earn more petals," he explains. "When they fill out feedback about the date to help the algorithm improve, a petal is added. Ultimately, the petals add up and form a blossomed flower."

"What do you get when you have a blossomed flower?" I ask, still focused on the screen.

"They all get added up into a bouquet. Besides the public acknowledgment of being active on the app, we're playing around with the idea of sending users actual deliveries of flowers when they reach a certain number of bouquets."

A waiter brings our food to the table. Bennett, surprise

surprise, ordered the tried-and-true egg sandwich and green juice. I pour maple syrup over the top of my Belgian buttermilk waffles after taking a sip of my Earl Grey iced tea.

"The number next to the peony shows how active the users are on the app, so you know if someone's serious about being on it. Basically, the higher the number, the more people they're probably talking to," Bennett elaborates, moving his egg sandwich around spiritedly. He bites into it, consuming the sandwich slowly and methodically.

Somehow, he looks cute chewing. No one looks cute chewing.

"Does it live up to the hype?" I ask as I cut my waffle into smaller pieces.

"Four point three stars did not do this sandwich justice!" he says excitedly. "This is definitely four point five stars." He swallows and covers his mouth with his napkin as he laughs. It's so endearing and innocent that my heart could burst. "Here, try some."

Bennett twists the egg sandwich around so I'm eating from the side he hasn't put his mouth on. I hesitate, but he looks excited for me to share his enjoyment. He holds the sandwich closer to me. We make awkward eye contact as I bite down, and my body shakes with nervous laughter at how intimate this is.

"That makes two hundred and ninety-one satisfied customers," I say teasingly, my face flushed.

I scroll past Bennett's peony petal count on his profile. It's much higher than I expected. I would only have one petal.

I can feel Bennett watching me, waiting impatiently for my reaction.

"You gamified the app," I say slowly, processing what I'm seeing. It's a tacky addition, ultimately making the zodiac look like a game. People are now players in a different sense of the word.

"I was inspired by your favorite flower," he says. "I thought it was beautiful and kind of perfect that they symbolize prosperity, good luck, and best of all, love and the rebirth of relationships. So much meaning!" Bennett wipes crumbs from his mouth.

I want him to know how insensitive his gamification move feels, but he's clearly proud of this. I choose my words carefully. "Wow" is all that comes out. I can do better than that.

"I see what you were trying to do. What if you, I don't know, focused on deepening the elements of the zodiac itself instead?" I propose.

Bennett's smile falls. "Oh, do you not like it?"

I pause midbite, a piece of waffle hovering awkwardly between my plate and mouth. "How honest do you want me to be?" I ask.

Bennett shifts in his seat. "Well, I wanted your opinion, so . . . I guess tell me what you really think."

This is where I can edge ZodiaCupid out and encourage him to continue down the path of something that would be bad for his company. I can see it now. Beta testers feel played and leave his app for us because we actually value love and match people based on compatibility. To us, love isn't a competition.

I watch Bennett carefully. I could lie and say this is a good move, that people will love it. But when I look into his eyes, I can only tell the truth.

"I'm generally not a fan of adding gaming elements into nongaming spaces, especially when it comes to love," I admit. "I think it has the potential to make people feel bad if they don't have a high peony count. Or they might feel pressure to reach out to people just to look popular or desired, as though it's better to have a higher score so the peony fully blossoms."

Bennett listens carefully to my words.

"Does success look like high petal counts or quality matches that can't be assigned numbers?" I continue. "Gaming elements can also be really addicting, which, I get it, you want to encourage people to be on the app, but it feels a bit forced."

Bennett drops his head in disappointment. Maybe I've said too much.

"I'm sorry," I continue. "I didn't mean to upset you."

"That's tough to hear," he says, rubbing his hand over his face. "But maybe you should try it before you fully judge it. This feature will help me find the love of your life, after all."

My entire body shudders at the thought. "How exactly?" I ask, unconvinced.

Bennett leans forward, and I feel his arm heat against my own. "From what I know about you so far, I suspect you'd want to be with someone who doesn't have a lot of peony petals. This feature lets me know who's active but not too active. I can see which animals you interact with most and the reviews from the dates. Because I won't have access to your profile from your phone, I'll have to look on the back end who you match with. I'll have to coordinate your date details with whoever I choose for you while pretending to be you."

"Is this your ploy to mess with the algorithm? You can only match me with someone I actually matched with."

Bennett bends closer. "I want you to fall in love. Someone matching on your profile is the best way for me to find love for you. Which reminds me. Can you update your profile as though you were using the app for real?"

"This is ridiculous," I say, launching ZodiaCupid on my phone and reviewing my profile. More fun facts pop up on the screen. "Did you know Rembrandt was a Horse?"

"He was," Bennett says. I can't tell if that sounded more like a confirmation or a question.

"When I learned that little detail—from your fun facts, thank you very much—I wondered what traits he embodied. Who was the man behind some of history's most iconic paintings?" I muse. I fill out the prompts on my profile with more detailed information about myself.

"I wrote those fun facts, thank you very much. And it was passion. The man had passion. He wouldn't stop until he reached greatness," Bennett clarifies. "He achieved great wealth in his life...until he lost it all by not getting enough commissioned portrait work and making some bad invest-ments." He lifts his green juice glass in a toast. "But hey, to passion!"

I fight back the impulse to laugh but Bennett's flirty smile has rendered me defenseless. I lift my iced tea in a mock toast.

"There. Updated," I say, setting my phone next to my plate. "So, about the whole love thing. When are you going to finally tell me about your feelings for Harper? I haven't had a chance to catch up with her yet."

Bennett shifts his footing and leans back against this chair. "She's impressive, outgoing, accomplished, and has a contagious love of food," he starts. "But—"

"But? No buts," I say.

"But I don't think she's the girl I can see myself loving. Like, falling *in love* with."

"You've only been on one date! Don't tell me you also believe in love at first sight?" I sigh in exasperation.

Bennett laughs. "I'm sorry," he says, sounding like he means it.

I shake my head from side to side. "I don't accept that. If

Harper wants to see you again, you need to go on a second date. Give her a chance. You both seemed to hit it off."

Bennett fiddles with the straw in his now-empty juice glass. "She was interesting to talk to," he says as though he's actually considering it. "If she wants a second date, I'm open to it."

I breathe out in relief, though a sliver of anxiety creeps in. "Great. I'll keep you posted."

"Don't forget, your date is next." Bennett's lips firm into a straight line, his gaze quickly wandering over my face.

"The thought keeps me up at night," I say melodramatically. "There's no way I'm forgetting about it."

Bennett knocks his knee into mine, and I can't tell if it's on purpose or not. The contact makes the hair on my arms spring to life.

"I do appreciate your honesty, no matter how brutal," Bennett says. "Everyone on my team acted like they loved the idea. Maybe a couple of them were holding back their real thoughts. Thank you for not lying to me."

My heart flips. No grudges here.

"Thanks for the waffles." I shrug. "And it's your business so you should do what you think is best."

"In surveys that we sent out to users, fifty-eight percent said they'd like this," Bennett says. "I thought this could increase user engagement."

I shrug my shoulders. "People using your app are looking for human connection and love. Gamification plays up data too much for my taste. You've essentially made their dating lives a game. Love isn't a game to everyone."

"I'm trying to make it fun," Bennett explains. "Especially for those who are already on the edge about the zodiac. This might keep them interested."

"Maybe. But is that really why you want people using your app to begin with?" I push a strawberry into my mouth as I think. "Remember the scene in *Big* when Tom Hanks is sitting in a marketing meeting playing with a building that turns into a robot?"

Bennett's eyes light up. "Yes. He breaks one of the arms off."

"Right!" I say. "The guy running the meeting is shooting off all these data points and numbers about what kinds of toys kids are playing with. But it's not what kids really want. Tom Hanks knows this because he *is* still a kid. He ignores what the numbers indicate and thinks up a different great idea based on gut instinct and emotion. He becomes a successful toy designer because of his *feelings* about toys, not because of data."

Bennett furrows his brows and holds his hand over his mouth and nose. "You're right. I can't believe I've never thought about it like that before. I've always found comfort in numbers. They're consistent, reliable."

"Until you're driven purely by numbers and all you make are purely financially motivated decisions," I say in a gentle tone. My entire body aches at the recollection of his mother and why he does that. I have to actively resist the urge to hold him, hug him, and rub his back in support.

"Money keeps the lights on." Bennett scoots back in his chair half a foot and leans his elbow up against the back of the chair. "In defense of numbers, they're not always such a bad thing. Numbers give you feedback and a direction to move toward."

"Maybe," I say, unconvinced.

"Here's an example. We found that eighty-eight percent of the users we surfaced the zodiac sign fun facts to enjoyed the app experience more than those who didn't see them. They referred us to their friends and gave us high scores in our surveys."

"Really?" I ask with a hint of skepticism. Bennett runs his hands down his thighs, the fabric of his shorts pulling tighter against his skin. I look away before he catches me staring.

Bennett lets out a short laugh and smiles. He caught me staring.

"In fact, they even requested more information about the Chinese zodiac," he says.

"Well, that's good," I say, biting my lip. I mean it, even though I don't want to in this moment. Anything that gets people excited about the zodiac is a positive in my eyes.

"Anyway, I'm glad I ran this by you before launching. I have a lot to think about and discuss with the team."

"Anytime," I say as a comfortable silence falls between us. "Well, I should get going. Some of us have real work to do."

We stand to head our separate ways. "I'll be in touch with your date details," Bennett says, pushing his chair into its original spot.

"Can't wait," I mumble. If Bennett asked me when the last time I went on a date was, I wouldn't be able to tell him because I can't even remember when that was. I coach people all the time about how to date and remain calm about it, yet my own advice doesn't bring me solace.

"Hey, I went into your date with an open mind and a good attitude," Bennett says, snapping me free from my negative thought spiral. "You owe me that."

"I owe you nothing," I say, "but I'll be on my best behavior."

Bennett looms over me, studying my unamused expression. "I think watching you fall in love is going to be the highlight of my career."

CHAPTER 13

H is name is Owen Rossi, and he's Year of the Tiger," Bennett explains, listing off the key points from my date's profile. I try on a blue hat in the souvenir shop at Dodger Stadium, where I'll apparently be meeting my perfect match named Owen. The store is filled with zealous fans eager to spend hard-earned money on overpriced tees and hats to prove their loyalty to their favorite team and players.

I give Bennett an impressed look. "A compatible sign," I say. "Interesting. Worried that your incompatible theory wasn't going to pan out?"

Bennett lifts the hat off my head and drops a pink one in its place. He looks at my reflection in the mirror and shakes his head, pulling the pink cap off.

"We do both," he says.

"Did you really need to buy a ticket to be here? I can handle this on my own."

"Mine's a nosebleed seat. I need to make sure you do this the honest way. At least I'm candid about being here," Bennett says. "You're meeting Owen at the seats. You'll be behind home plate."

I whistle in a low tune. "These tickets must have cost a fortune. I thought you haven't raised money yet?"

Bennett flips through the replica player jerseys on hangers looking for a specific size and turns his head toward me. "Normally, users pay for dates, but because of our arrangement, ZodiaCupid treated you two to this. Our hope is that users aren't going on a lot of dates, and that the ones they do go on are enjoyable."

I rummage through key chains in a basket. "I'm not complaining. I haven't been to a game in years. I used to come here with my dad all the time. He loves baseball."

Bennett holds a jersey out in front of him and then drapes it against himself, looking down at it and then back up at me. "How does this look?"

It's a simple, casual question that forces me to look at him. No. Not *look*. Observe. To evaluate how the width of the shirt aligns with his shoulders. Perfectly. To follow the buttons down his torso to ensure the length works for him. It does. The polyester top falls against his chest flatteringly, the shallow V-neck drawing my attention to places that are wildly inappropriate given the circumstances.

Suddenly my neck is warm, and my entire body tightens in response. I grip one of the key chains tighter between my fists. It feels too intimate viewing Bennett in this way and helping him decide what to wear.

I tilt my head, not committing to a decision either way. "It's sporty," I say vaguely. Now, if Owen wants an opinion on how to clothe himself, I might be willing to give it. Because Owen is my date. Bennett is not.

"So your dad loves baseball?" Bennett asks, following up from before.

I avert my eyes from the top that's still pressed against his body. "What? Oh. Yeah. He writes low-budget horror flicks. Some of his past films are *The Green Monster* and *Field of Nightmares*. Have you heard of those? He's still trying to write a movie that will earn a cult following."

Bennett looks amused. "I sadly haven't, but they're now on my list."

One of the sleeves has fallen across his chest, and in this brief moment of not being put together, he looks so boyishly handsome that I almost can't handle how adorable it is. "You going to buy that or something?" I ask, probably coming off more flustered than I intend to.

Bennett slings the jersey over his arm. "I think so. I don't know who this player is, but it feels right to blend in."

I feel the corners of my mouth turn upward. "That's the team spirit," I say playfully.

"You want one, too? We can match."

I hold up a hand. "I'm good. Baseball was an astute choice," I say, considering its environment for first dates. "It's a fairly quiet game that allows for small talk, it has the best stadium food, and there's a good view from most seats. I'll admit I'm impressed." I look up at Bennett with an approving smile.

Bennett's lips form a straight line. "Actually, Owen chose this."

"Well done, Owen." I push down on the head of a bobblehead and nod along with it. "Or was it because of the profile matching? At least he read what I wrote. Let's hope that's a good sign."

Bennett plucks the bobblehead out of my hands and replaces

it with my ticket. "It's time for you to get to your seat. And remember, keep an open mind."

I march down the steps toward my seat and find a man already seated. My heart pounds nervously when I see him. The idea of meeting him was easier as a concept, but a real person in front of me makes this uncomfortably real. I make eye contact with who I think is Owen and say his name in a question form. He nods and stands. He's maybe four or five inches taller than me. We're luckily on the outside of the row so I can make a quick escape if need be. I extend my hand for a shake, and he mimics my movement.

"Is that seat good for you? I'm happy to switch," Owen says as I secure my spot on the aisle. I tilt my head to get a better look at him. He has bright blue eyes, sandy blond hair, and fair skin covered in pale freckles.

"I'm fine here, thanks," I say, noting his manners. I enjoy the expansive view from the seats. Two scoreboards stand tall across the field with the crisp mountains illuminated by the lowering sun behind them. Fans carrying food and drinks slowly occupy the multicolored pastel seats while music blasts around us.

I tap my knee self-consciously. Talking to strangers isn't usually such a challenge for me. I could pretend I'm on a Singles Scouting. Nope. No. I'm here to give this an honest shot. Don't think about business right now.

"So, what number date am I?" I finally ask, not being able to help myself.

Owen looks over, appearing confused. "Excuse me?"

"On ZodiaCupid. How many dates have you been on?"

"Oh! I've only been on a few. Everyone I've met through the app has actually been lovely. I just haven't hit it off with anyone in the way that I'm looking for," Owen says in a way that sounds rehearsed. He must be nervous.

"Sure, sure," I say, dipping my head. "And you like the app?"

Owen narrows his baby blues at me. "You don't work for ZodiaCupid, do you?" he asks suspiciously.

I successfully avoid letting out a laugh. "Definitely not!"

"What do you do then?"

"Right, you only know what's on my profile," I say. I consider lying again but instead try the truth. What have I got to lose? "I work in my family's business. I'm actually the new owner of our matchmaking company that matches people based on their Chinese zodiac animal signs, too."

Owen gestures in understanding. "Sleeping with the enemy. Nice."

"What? No!" I recoil back into my seat. "I'm just testing out what's available now. Why limit yourself, right?"

"That's what they say," Owen agrees.

I shake my head. "That's what who says exactly?" I tease.

"Just people," he answers frankly.

"Oh. Okay." I scan over the crowd, looking for good people-watching opportunities. "Did you want anything to eat or drink?" I ask after a particularly long stretch of silence.

"I can get it," Owen says, starting to stand.

"No! I'll do it. One of my favorite things to do as a kid was contemplate my food options. Who am I kidding? That's my favorite thing to do now," I say with a tongue-tied laugh.

"Okay, then, I'd love a beer, please," Owen says. "It was a long Wednesday. And I had a big lunch so I'll skip the food."

"You sure?" I ask. "They have Dodger Dogs here! Where else can you get that?"

"That's basically just a branded hot dog," he says, clearly not sharing the same enthusiasm over baseball food.

I sigh. "You're probably right."

"Please, let me treat." He pulls a twenty-dollar bill out of his wallet, reconsiders, and then adds two more twenties to the pile. "I remember stadium food being expensive."

"It's one of the tastiest scams," I say. We share our first laugh, and suddenly I'm caught off guard. ZodiaCupid matched me not only with someone compatible, but with someone I'm not completely miserable being around. Awkward, but not miserable. It's still early.

With a stack of money in hand, I scurry up the stairs and find Bennett in his new jersey waiting at the top.

I clutch the sixty dollars to my chest in surprise. "Can you stop doing that? It scares me every time."

Bennett leans against a pole with his arms crossed. "I'm just standing here."

I jerk my thumb toward the field. "Shouldn't you be out there? Your teammates are depending on you."

He smooths out his jersey. "I'm doing my daily autograph round," Bennett says with a smile.

"You're making me nervous! Do you need to be creepily watching from the top of our row?"

"Just making sure you're okay," he says.

"From the guy . . . you matched me with?" I ask. "Oh, right, you don't do background checks on your users, so for all we know, I could be rubbing shoulders with someone who burgles or texts while driving!"

Bennett's shoulders shake when he laughs. "That's the worst you can think of?"

"I'm the one who has to mingle with the shoplifter for the next nine innings," I say. "I'm not letting my mind go to darker places."

"What's he like?" Bennett asks.

"What's he *like*?" I repeat. "You don't know anything about who I'm on a date with right now, do you?"

Bennett makes a face. "Our app is the matchmaker, not us."

Chanting starts below us as music plays, stops, plays, stops. The food level is packed with eager fans elbowing each other out of the way, rushing to stand in line for greasy, starchy concessions. Children sprint around with packs of candy and trays of fries in hand. I step to the side to dodge a man balancing three cups of beers when a little girl with strawberry ice cream crashes into me cone first. I feel Bennett steadying me with both hands, his firm grip around my shoulders sending shivers down my arms.

"Are you okay?" I ask the girl, who stands looking stunned, her scoop of ice cream now decorating the front of my white tee. With wide eyes brimming with tears, she nods slowly.

Bennett pulls his wallet from his jeans and takes out a five-dollar bill. He kneels down and uses his thigh as a flat surface to quickly fold the bill into the shape of an ice cream cone. The little girl watches on, amazed. When he holds the ice cream bill up in front of her, she breaks into a wide toothless smile, no tears in sight.

"It looks like you gave her a giant pink belly button," Bennett says to the girl, holding back a laugh. "Looks kinda cool, huh? Go get yourself another ice cream. And stay close to your parents." The little girl takes the ice cream bill and runs back to a little boy at the ice cream kiosk.

"That was sweet of you," I say quietly.

"That's literally the only thing I know how to make with money," Bennett says, "so it's a good thing she didn't run into you with a soft pretzel. Are you okay?"

"Oh, yeah. Pink is all the rage nowadays, didn't you know? I actually told her to do that," I say with a smile. Bennett laughs before running over to the nearest food stand to grab a wad of napkins as I wipe chunks of strawberry off my jeans with my hands. Bennett returns and hands me a small cup of water. He steps closer, lifting my right arm and gently wiping the cold pink ice cream off with the rough napkins.

"I can do that," I start.

"I got you," Bennett says in a low voice. Being this close to him requires tilting my head back further. He dips the napkin into the water and cleans off the stickiness that the melted ice cream left behind.

Bennett releases his grip, sliding his hand down my arms. His touch is disorienting. Then he unbuttons the jersey and takes it off, looking like his usual self again in a simple navy tee. He wraps the jersey around my shoulders, and I lift my arms to tuck them into the short sleeves. I look like I've been swallowed whole by a white Dodgers jersey.

"Thanks," I say distractedly, elongating my neck to see what his hazel eyes look like from this distance. Still soulful.

Bennett brings the collar together at the base of my neck and fiddles with the top button. I can sense the presence of his hands, every nerve in my body tingling. It drives me absolutely wild. He pulls his hands back for me to finish the buttoning.

"You smell like a hot dog," I say, regaining my awareness.

My fingers fumble around the buttons, a new nervousness over-taking my motor skills.

"Is that a good thing?" he asks. "I ate a Dodger Dog earlier. You can only get them here."

"Right!" I nod. "You get it!" I take the remaining napkins and wipe up the now-absorbed dessert from my jeans.

"You should be talking with Owen, not up here waiting in lines," he says somewhat begrudgingly.

"The food's up here, and the game's down there. Unless you have suggestions?" I say, holding out the money toward him.

Bennett takes the money. "Fine. What do you want?"

"Ooh," I say, tucking a hand under my chin while I think. "What sounds good? Let's start with a soft pretzel with extra salt, a chili dog with extra cheese, curly fries, and one of those long red licorice things. And a beer for Owen. Thanks!" I turn back toward my seat.

"Be back here in ten minutes!" he shouts behind me.

There's a wave moving around the packed stadium that reaches us just as I make it back to my seat.

"Nice jersey!" Owen says as he flings his arms up. "Where's the food?"

"It's being prepared," I say, raising my arms in response to the crowd. "I'll grab it in a few. What'd I miss?"

"Honestly, I couldn't tell you," he says. "I don't know any of the players' names or anything that they're doing. Baseball's fun to watch, but I just can't get into it the way others can."

"Baseball shows us who we are, whether we know the plays or not," I say dramatically, rattling off a line from one of my dad's most popular movies.

"Isn't that from *Homer, Run*?" Owen asks. "I love that movie."

I eagerly turn toward him in my seat. "You know that one?"

"It's a classic. I'm a bit of a horror film buff."

"Cool," I say, realizing I haven't actually had a chance to look at his profile myself. "What is it you do, Owen?"

"I work in my family's business, too," he says. "We run a winery in Malibu."

My ears perk up at this information. "Tell me more!"

"I'm the fourth generation of California farmers," Owen explains. "I manage the operations of the vineyard, and my sister runs the tasting room. There's a lot more people involved, but we're starting to take over more of the responsibility."

Owen shares more about his family's winery and his desire to execute new ideas while maintaining the history and reasons why customers have remained loyal. It's nice to be able to chat about similar business struggles and hear about someone else's worries for a change.

"Think that food is ready?" Owen says after describing how the wine-bottling process works.

"Oops! Let me go find out," I say. I check the time on my phone and see a few texts from Bennett. It's been thirty minutes.

I climb the stairs two at a time and find Bennett waiting at the top.

"Food's cold, beer's warm. Here's a foam finger," Bennett says. I hold my arm out, and he slides the foam finger over my hand, balancing the tray of food on top. "Did you get lost or something?"

"Owen and I were talking," I say. "I can see why you picked him."

Bennett's posture stiffens. "Oh, great. So it's going well?"

"Surprisingly," I say, tossing a curly fry into my mouth.

"You think you'll see him again?" Bennett asks, his eyebrows furrowed.

"We're only in the"—I say, looking back toward the field—"third inning. We're just talking. If we take off to elope, I'll send you a courtesy text."

Bennett scrunches his mouth into a smile. "Well, uh, good. I'm glad it's going well."

"Okay. Good. So then why do you look concerned?"

Bennett puts his hands up on his hips. "Who, me? This is what I look like when I'm right. Because of ZodiaCupid. You're hitting it off with someone you met on *my* app. Maybe we know what we're doing after all, huh?"

I rip off a piece of cold soft pretzel and dip it in the cup of mustard. "I see why you picked him. He's cute, though you couldn't have known that, so you got lucky on that one. He's also excited by the challenge of running his family's business. I can respect a legacy. From what he shared with me, it sounds like he makes good instinctive decisions. It's clear he cares about both his work and family." I pop the mustardy pretzel into my mouth.

"You were easier to crack than I thought." Bennett looks perplexed as he shifts his footing.

"Don't get too excited." I wrinkle my nose. "This is me having an open mind. This is good! You want some?"

"Did you know that, in the seventeenth century, soft pretzels were incorporated into weddings? The bride and groom would make a wish, break the pretzel, then eat it. Kind of like a big, soft, loopy wishbone." Bennett yanks a chunk of pretzel off, dips it in mustard, and then crams it into his mouth. "Good," he says between a full bite.

I laugh out loud at his goofiness. "You have mustard on your lip," I say, tentatively reaching forward. "May I?"

"Oh, this? I want that there," he says, angling his head back.

With my foam finger–free hand, I tuck my thumb into a napkin and delicately wipe the yellow smudge off his face. The backs of my fingers rest against his cheek as I press against the edge of his lips.

"There," I say, my fingers grazing his jawline. Heat shoots through the center of my body, and I quickly inhale a breath of air.

"Thanks," he says quietly. A smile disrupts Bennett's serious face.

I follow his laugh lines over to his gold-flecked eyes and down to his rosy lips. They're slightly parted, as though something important to say is on the tip of his tongue. The shouting of "Sweet Caroline" in the stadium grows louder, pulling me out of my daze.

"I know our animal sign traits match well together, but compatibility is, well, it's complex," I say, picking up where I think we left off. I crumple the mustard-stained napkin in my hand. "Like I said, we're only in the third inning. Don't start thinking of podcast talking points yet."

Bennett eyes me up. "It's complex, or you make it complex?"

I look down at the tray of cold food. "Hey, next time I come back here, think you can bring one of those small plastic Dodgers caps with nachos in it?" I ask, ignoring his question completely.

"What? Oh, yeah, sure," Bennett says, looking distracted. He leans over the railing in the direction of where Owen and I are sitting.

"Also, good news. Harper said she's open to another date," I add. "This Friday work for you?"

Bennett refocuses on me. "I promised you I'd be open to it, so I'll be there."

"Fantastic. I knew you two would hit it off," I say. "Okay, I should probably go down to my seat. Don't forget the nachos hat."

"Do you want dessert? I can buy you dessert after you eat your nachos," he asks.

"I don't think it's a good idea to mix nachos and ice cream."

"What about a churro?" he offers.

I shake my head. "That might be too much greasy food for one game."

"That could be true," he says, seemingly disappointed.

I carry the food down to Owen, who's in the middle of a phone call talking about grapes and corks.

"Take these," I whisper. "I'll be right back. I forgot something."

I race up the stairs, foam finger slicing through the air as I run.

"Bennett! Bennett!" I yell.

He turns around, looking surprised.

"I almost forgot to tell you," I pant. "It's very important."

"What is it?" he asks.

"Don't forget the jalapenos!" I say.

A look of amusement flashes across his face.

"Got it. Jalapenos," he says. "Anything else, my Queen?"

I tap the foam finger against my chin as I think. "Cheese. Don't forget the cheese."

"I get it. You want nachos. They're pretty straightforward. Cheese, tomatoes, beans, some kind of meat. Preferably a pickled jalapeno or a red pepper. Maybe even some sour cream. Understood."

I wiggle my giant blue finger in front of his face. "No sour cream." I boop the tip of his nose. "I want ice cream, too."

Bennett shrugs. "I can make this faster and mix it all together."

"No, go to the nacho stand first, then have the ice cream guy top it all off."

Bennett chuckles at this, and I join him. The laughter is contagious, our shoulders rippling in sync.

"Okay. Get going. I don't want to keep you from your date," Bennett finally says, his eyes still watery from laughter.

"Don't worry about him. He's down there fermenting." I burst out in another fit of laughter.

Bennett smiles but doesn't seem to understand the reference. "He's what?"

I side-eye him. "You don't get it because you don't know anything about him! He's in the wine business," I explain.

"Ah, so he only gets better with age," he says with a smirk.

Once again, I'm giddy with laughter. I head back to my seat with a stupid grin on my face.

By the top of the fourth inning, Owen and I have exhausted our small talk and have formed an understanding. We'll leave at the top of the eighth so we can get out of the parking lot before everyone else. I say I'll visit his winery's tasting room, and he vows to look up Lunar Love if ZodiaCupid doesn't work out.

A text from Alisha buzzes in my lap. Have you seen the social media numbers lately?

I pull up the Twitter app on my phone and tap the notifications bubble. 80 retweets? 200 likes? I respond.

Your moon song pairings with zodiac signs is by far the most popular strategy so far. A few people have reached out to learn about what we do, she messages.

Feeling rude, I glance up at Owen, who's luckily busy managing his own messages. I can at least appreciate the man's work ethic.

That's amazing. Let's keep going with that. See if we can double that number. If we're attracting potential clients, it's worth pursuing. These numbers give us a direction to move toward, I write.

Oh no. I'm starting to sound like Bennett.

I stare out over the field, mindlessly eating my licorice rope and watching the sun disappear behind the stadium lights. The fact that my first date through ZodiaCupid was not a total nightmare is slightly worrying.

But the biggest curveball of today—and perhaps the most distressing realization—is that for the rest of the inning, all I can think about is Bennett O'Brien and when I'll get to see him next.

CHAPTER 14

I wait at the handoff point near the bottom of the Getty Center Tram for Bennett and Harper to arrive. The Drinking with the Stars event at the Getty Center was so perfect that I full-on squealed when I discovered it was happening. An hour of learning about the history of the Getty's most famous paintings followed by a wine pairing under the "stars" of Los Angeles. And with the view from the top, they won't be able to resist each other.

While I wait, I check for any new emails. The name Carol Rogers sits at the top of my inbox.

Hello Olivia,

Lovely meeting you last week! Let me know when you're available for a coffee chat and we can nail down a time. I'll be bringing by interested clients next week, if that's okay? We'll be quick and quiet. Talk soon!

Stay silver, Carol and Poppy

I sigh and close out of Carol's email. I'll respond later.

Bennett arrives early, looking dashing in an olive cashmere sweater and dark jeans. He smells like pine trees and shampoo, as though he just stepped out of an outdoor shower in the forest.

His face lights up as soon as he sees me. I return his smile and reach forward with the tickets.

"You look very nice. Will you be lingering again tonight?" he asks.

"Not this time. I want you two to have a real chance," I say. "That's probably hard with me being distracting."

Bennett exhales a disappointed-sounding *oh*. "Too bad. I was hoping for a food runner," he jokes, his mouth turned downward.

"You're on your own tonight," I say with a laugh. "We still need to debrief about Owen."

"So formal. Normally, users figure it out among themselves, but you're right, this is a different situation. Let's debrief," Bennett says. "What's your verdict?"

I reflect for a minute. "He was nice, but I can see it now. The required hours of working in our family businesses might take time away from each other because we'd both be so committed. We'd enjoy each other's company, but how long can that really last? As a Tiger, he's adventurous enough to do what he wants while giving me my freedom, but he mentioned something about expanding into different vineyards in various regions around the world, and while that sounds cool, it might be a little too much unpredictability for me." I cross my right foot over my left. "I think that's most of it."

Bennett stares at me, his eyes widened. "What happened to all the good things you said a couple of days ago?"

I watch a cloud float by overhead. "I didn't despise his company. And he did laugh at my jokes—"

"Did he make *you* laugh?" Bennett asks. His question is oddly specific.

"Uh, I can't recall specific examples," I say.

"So then, it wasn't love?"

I laugh. Definitely not. "Maybe," I say, stringing him along. "Isn't that what you want?"

Bennett's jaw flexes. His tenseness makes me want to keep talking about Owen, purely to see what he'll do. "I just didn't think it would be that easy," he mutters.

"Wait, you believe me?" I say, playfully thwacking his arm with my hand. "Of course it wasn't love! First dates are for sparks, like with you and Harper. And date two, well, date two can lay the groundwork for L-O-V-E. You'll see tonight."

"Were there sparks? With you and Owen?"

I let the silence drag on to make him squirm. "No," I finally admit. "Owen and I didn't have the initial fireworks that I like to see in long-lasting couples."

"We'll have to try again on date number two," he says. "Unless we decide right now to call the whole thing off?"

I fold my arms. "And why would we do that?"

"I think we've established by now that while you see the zodiac one way, I see it in a slightly different way. But we're essentially talking about the same thing."

"You really also think the Chinese zodiac is a language for love and guide to better understanding ourselves and relationships?" I ask.

Bennett is quiet for a moment. "It's a tool in the toolbox.

There are more variables at play when it comes to love, but I don't disagree with your version."

"Of course there are other variables, but no. No one's calling anything off," I say. I will prove that my way is the best way. That Lunar Love is right.

Bennett drops his shoulders forward in an exhale. "Okay then. But since I'm having a second date, you need to have a second date."

I consider this. Can ZodiaCupid strike twice with a decent match? Highly doubtful. "Fine. One more date. But that's it. I'm a busy woman with podcasts to record and features to be interviewed for," I say with a winner's confidence. "I'm having dinner with Pó Po tomorrow but I can do it on Sunday."

Bennett smiles, looking relieved. "Sunday it is. I was between a few choices for the first date so I already have someone in mind. I'll see if he's available on short notice."

My phone buzzes with a call. "One second, it's Harper," I say, wiggling my eyebrows at him. "She must be running late."

I step aside to answer the call as Bennett looks on curiously.

"Harper? Hey! Are you on your way?" I ask.

"Olivia! I'm caught up at a restaurant launch that I completely forgot about. I won't be able to make it. I'm so sorry. Is Bennett there?"

"Oh no! He is. Do you want to talk to him?" I ask.

"Can you just tell him I feel awful? I look like such a flake. Between you and me, though, I don't know if he's quite what I'm looking for. He's a great guy, but we didn't really hit it off. Sorry! Do you have any other matches lined up?"

I deflate with disappointment. Tonight's event was so perfect for Bennett and Harper! "Don't think another second about it,"

I say in a strained upbeat tone. "I'll get started on your next match. Good luck with your event."

"She's not coming, is she?" Bennett asks when I return.

I shake my head. "How many fun facts did you tell her?"

"Actually none!" he says with genuine surprise.

"I'm sorry for the trouble, Bennett."

"Was this your plan all along?" he asks, reading my face.

"My plan was for you to have a second shot with Harper, but she's caught up at work," I say, maintaining my professional tone.

Bennett nods in understanding. "I get it. No problem." He holds up the two tickets and extends his elbow in my direction. "Shall we?"

"Shall we...what?" I ask, looking at his arm.

"Attend the event," Bennett clarifies.

I narrow my eyes at him. "Together?"

I imagine slipping my arm around his and being interlocked with Bennett as we peruse beautiful art and drink probably not inexpensive wine. Even that simple gesture would allow me to confirm all the thoughts I shouldn't be having about his arms. Get it out of the way so I don't have to ever think about them again. An evening drinking under the stars. With Bennett. It shouldn't be a thrilling thought, but it is.

Bennett gives the tickets a little wave, shaking off my thoughts with the movement. "It would be a shame to let this night go to waste. I don't know what drinking with the stars is like, but I want to find out," he says.

I try to stifle the zing of excitement that zips through me. "This date was supposed to be for you and Harper. I can't—"

"How about we don't call it a date then?" he says. "It can be a meeting. We're two dating service professionals. We can even talk about work all night long."

"You running out of ideas and need some of mine?" I retort.

Bennett slips the tickets into his back pocket. "If you don't want to, I'm not going to push you," he says. "Have a good night."

"Wait," I blurt out. "It's been a while since I've been up there. They have one of my favorite paintings. It wouldn't be right to let those tickets go to waste. They cost real money."

Real money that Lunar Love doesn't have a whole lot of. This can be research.

Bennett's crooked smile spreads across his face. Once again, he holds out his arm to walk me to the tram. The zing morphs into more of a zap, all the initial enthusiasm draining from my body. What am I doing? This is not a good idea. Bennett is my competition. A pseudo-client.

But it's just one night. And as we've established, this is not a date. Rats and Horses do not date. We're two professionals having a professional meeting. Maybe I could even turn this into a Singles Scouting. I let out a long breath to still my hammering heart, and before I can make up an excuse to leave, I tuck my arm up into his.

At the top of the mountain, the sky looks like a series of pale orange and lavender brushstrokes straight out of a Monet painting. The moon is in its first quarter phase, half of its glowing surface beaming down on us.

"Look at the legs on this one," Bennett says. He tilts his wineglass and watches as maroon droplets slide down the inside of the stemware. He inhales just above the glass, as instructed by the sommelier. "I'm getting hints of old saddle leather and crushed rocks."

"Very nice!" I say, mirroring him. "To me, it smells more like freshly printed paper and that feeling when you're sitting under the moonlight looking up at the stars thinking about how small you are in the world."

Bennett smirks before sniffing his wine again. "I'm not getting that. Wait. There it is. Ah, nothing like the smell of insignificance and toner."

We both quietly laugh together, trying not to draw attention to ourselves.

"You really knocked this date out of the museum," Bennett says, looking pleased. "I learned so much in that class. If date planning was a competition, you'd win. You're good."

I *knew* Bennett the Historical Buff would love what I planned for him. And Harper. Him and Harper.

I lean back against the railing and admire the museum's imposing architecture, the warmth and permanence of the stone marking its long-lasting presence. Situated at the top of a hill in the Santa Monica Mountains, the Getty is an escape from the city, an isolated retreat from a city of millions. The buildings are so grand and stunning that it's easy to forget there's art inside. The various buildings, fountains, and gardens create more of a campus feel than that of a typical museum.

"Where *does* your interest in history come from?" I ask.

"Well," he says slowly, "I've always been fascinated with the past. It's oddly comforting to know that there are different interpretations and perspectives of events that took place in time."

I spin and face the mountains alongside Bennett. "If things

can be interpreted so many different ways, how do you know what to believe?"

"That's the point. All we can do is act on what we know in this moment in time."

"That makes me anxious to know that anything can be re-invented at any point." I tilt my glass and stare into the inky wine.

"Nothing's permanent or guaranteed," Bennett says softly.

"So you like history because there's room for interpretation?" I clarify.

His eyes search mine. "Some of the best creations in history were because people were willing to look at the same thing differently. So yes. Though going against what others think often feels like trying to turn a cruise ship in a puddle."

"You've got a point," I say, "but that sounds a little bleak."

"Sometimes being bleak is easier." Bennett pushes his hair back and rests his hand over his mouth. When he looks back at me, his face looks more serious than usual. "Like this pitch, for instance. I'm going to be trying to convince people about my interpreta-tion of the Chinese zodiac. It's not for another two weeks, but I've been preparing every day. I need my delivery to be spot-on."

"What, are you nervous?" I ask, intrigued by this information.

Bennett hesitates for a moment. "Honestly? Yes. There's a lot riding on this. It's not like I've never pitched for funding before, but this business is more personal to me. I don't want to look like an imposter."

This takes me by surprise. "You don't come off as worried to me," I admit.

Bennett goes quiet for a moment. "I'm decent at compart-mentalizing. I want to enjoy this time with you."

He tugs gently at his sweater neckline, drawing attention to the base of his neck. My breathing quickens watching him.

As much as I don't want him to raise money, I also hate seeing him stressed. "I've never pitched to investors before, but I have a thought, if you'd like to hear it?"

Bennett turns to face me with eager eyes. "I'd love to hear what you think."

I tentatively place a hand on his shoulder as I consider my words carefully. He looks at my hand and smiles. "Focus on the human element, not just the numbers. Really sell them on why you started this business," I say.

His lips narrow into a thin line. He nods, looking as though he's trying to make sense of his thoughts. "Thank you. You're probably right, as hard as that sounds to not focus on the data. I'm just not great at expressing emotion outwardly. I learned to shut it off a long time ago. I find comfort in numbers. They're concrete. You can manipulate them to make them work for you. Emotion, love, those are completely uncontrollable."

"But they have the highest payoff," I say, removing my hand quickly.

Bennett rolls the sleeves of his sweater up to his elbows, settling into our conversation. I feel myself start to relax in a way I haven't in a long time.

Bennett motions toward the view of the ocean. "Isn't fall in Los Angeles charming?"

"Crisp mornings and sunshine all day? Sunsets like these? Absolutely," I say. Absentmindedly, I reach up to twist the moon on my necklace.

"That's beautiful," he says, noticing the necklace.

"Thanks. It was passed down to me for taking over the family business," I say. "And the horse is from my sister."

"Is she into the zodiac, too?"

"Actually no."

"Darn. I would've given her beta access. Oh wait! She's getting married, so never mind."

"Yeah, she's off-limits as a client. For the both of us," I add, smirking.

"How's it been taking over the family business?" he asks cautiously. "Is it okay if I ask you that?"

I think through all the various politically correct statements I could answer with. *I'm excited for the opportunity. Lots of challenges ahead, but nothing I can't handle.*

Maybe it's the wine or the fact that Bennett's so easy to talk to, or maybe it's the magic of the moon hanging in the distance, but instead of saying something, anything, that makes Lunar Love look like it's doing well, I just croak, "It's been kind of rough."

Hearing those words escape from my mouth feels wildly revealing. I look down at the ground beneath me. It's still intact. The world didn't end. Bennett doesn't even look smug or happy to hear this. Instead, he looks surprised.

"Really? How so?" he asks, taking a step closer.

"There's a lot of pressure from my family to turn the business around," I say, continuing to divulge more than I probably should. "I took it over during a challenging time. Sometimes it feels like the business is too set in its ways to ever change. Or maybe people are just too focused on the new."

"To turn the business around?" Bennett asks with an empathetic tone.

"We're going through growing pains," I say, using Pó Po's choice of words. "I'm sure Pó Po told you everything there is to know, even though she's in denial about it."

"She didn't say anything about needing to save Lunar Love," he says. "I'm sorry that you have to deal with that."

"There have been challenges for a while," I confess, maybe more to myself than to him. There were challenges long before Bennett was in the picture.

Bennett takes a sip of wine. "How'd you even get involved in your family's business? Was it something that always interested you?"

"I haven't known anything else, really. I love what I do. I basically grew up in the business, yet I still don't fully feel like I fit into the culture of what it represents."

"Lunar Love is more traditional," Bennett says. "Are you considering making it more modern?"

"Even if I were, you think I'd tell you?" I say suspiciously. "You're still my competition, right?"

Bennett swirls the base of his wineglass in the center of his palm. "You know I don't see it like that. I wish you wouldn't, either."

I sigh. "I love how traditional the business is and what it represents. Tradition tends to become diluted and reinterpreted over time, which is important so it doesn't completely disappear, but I don't want the business to lose its original charm. I know that's a different way of thinking than the tech world you're used to."

"I think of it as iterating upon what's already been done," Bennett says.

"Right, traditions were meant to be broken," I say flatly.

Bennett holds his free hand up in defense. "I said that in *one* interview, and you're taking it out of context. I think traditions *are* meant to be broken when they're rigid like rules and run the risk of being lost to history. My way of going about it is probably bolder than you're used to."

I tap my finger against the stem of my glass. "Maybe."

"I do think it's incredible you're trying to preserve what your Pó Po started. In this day and age, that's rare." His eyes dart down at me before he refocuses them on the city view ahead of us. "Who in your family is involved?" he asks.

"My pó po and auntie were involved, as you know," I say, emphasizing my last words. "My mom followed a different path. So did my sister. But I was hooked from the start. I purposely went to college in Los Angeles so I could keep working in the business part-time. I even tailored my major so I could be better at my job."

"Business degree? Communications?" Bennett asks.

"Psychology. I wanted to better understand how people act and think and how they fall in love," I explain. "I care about the work I do but I might've lost sight of who I am in order to keep the family legacy alive. And if I don't succeed, I think I'll be proving something that, deep down, I feel about myself."

Just as quickly as the words float out of me, they're carried away on a breeze across the hillside. How long have I felt this? I've been so in the thick of everything that I haven't had time to fully process my emotions. Sometimes it's easier to stuff down uncomfortable feelings than to deal with them head-on.

Bennett nods thoughtfully. "You feel like you're overcompensating so you don't fail and feel less of . . . something . . . than you already do."

"Maybe? Probably."

His face relaxes into a soft smile. "Vague, but I can relate."

I look over at him. "You can?"

"If ZodiaCupid fails, or doesn't live up to its potential, it'll be a huge blow. More than any other business I've started before. This one's too personal to me."

I tilt my head in understanding, remembering what he told me about his mother.

"With this app, I learn something new every day about the Chinese zodiac," he continues. "About people. About myself. And I love that. Even to this day, though, I feel like that little kid learning about himself at the library. I've never had to explain to people that I'm Chinese more than I do now. I love being mixed and celebrating all of my cultures, though, even if I often feel like I don't fit into any of the communities."

"I know the feeling," I say, crossing my arms over my chest. Realization dawns that maybe how I feel is that if Lunar Love fails, my insecurities about not being Asian enough to run this business are true. Most of the Chinese zodiac resource books at Lunar Love are in Mandarin, a language I can hardly hold a conversation in. In the early days of the business, client sessions used to take place exclusively in Chinese until Pó Po's English improved. But what's Asian enough?

"If I fail, it'll confirm things I think about myself, as you said," Bennett divulges. "Like an imposter."

"The syndrome is real," I say.

"Sorry, I made this about me," Bennett says. "Please, continue."

I bite my lip. "No, go on."

Bennett scrunches his face. "It'll be as though I'm not Chinese enough or I don't belong doing this because I didn't grow up one hundred percent immersed in the Chinese culture. As though the bits and pieces of the culture that my mom did choose to celebrate and teach me won't be sufficient. It's silly."

The emotion hits differently when it's said out loud. "I don't think it's silly. If it's something that you experience, that makes it real," I say with more confidence than I feel.

The sun lowers in the sky, the temperature dropping with it. I readjust my grip on the wineglass and hug my arms against my chest, pulling my oversized, colorful, geometric sweater tighter around my body. Bennett notices and moves even closer.

He smiles, and for a moment it's just us under the pink and purple clouds. From this vantage point, we can see the rhythm strip of the downtown skyline—the heartbeat of Los Angeles— the San Gabriel Mountains, and the Pacific Ocean floating in the distance.

We fall silent, our eyes locked on one another's. Feeling his eyes on me makes me nervous in an excited sort of way.

"Let's go see the *Irises*," I say abruptly.

I set my wine down on a table and cross the patio to a building across the way as Bennett follows closely behind. Inside is quieter at this hour as museumgoers flock to the patio to catch the sunset. We wander through the halls until we find Vincent van Gogh's *Irises*.

The iconic painting hangs in front of me, and I'm swept up in the swirling movement of the leaves, the violet petals twisted together, their figures carefully captured in vivid hues.

Bennett sidles up so close next to me that our arms touch. I tilt my head toward him without removing my eyes from the painting.

"You can almost feel the flowers moving," I say, dreamily.

"He painted this in, what..." Bennett takes a closer look at the museum label next to the painting. "1889. So this was after he had been hospitalized. If memory serves me right, these flowers are based on the ones that were in the mental institution's garden. He painted nearly one hundred and thirty pieces during his stay there." He looks over at me and quickly adds, "It's also nice to think about how seeing these flowers in the garden must've helped him through a tough time."

"Nice save. That's the emotion I'm looking for," I say. "What *don't* you know random facts about?" I look from the flowers to his face. They're both quite the sight.

His voice is soft as he says, "You."

I feel my face become hot. "You know some things," I say shyly.

"I know that you enjoy art and wine. I know that you care about your family and their legacy. I also know that when you're nervous, you twist your necklace, like you're doing right now."

I drop my hand from my neck.

Bennett's voice softens even more. "I know that you're curious and smart as hell, that your eyes look like milk chocolate in the sunshine, that when you're not sure what to say, you bite your bottom lip." He hesitates at first before grabbing my hand. I don't pull it away. "I also know that my worries don't feel so heavy when I'm with you, and that your laugh is my new favorite sound." He looks down at the ground and then back up into my eyes. "I also know that I'd like to kiss you. If that's all right?"

Thoughts of us being incompatible compete with emotions I haven't felt in a long time. My head and heart battle one another, elbowing their way to the front of my mind. The room spins around me, becoming a blur of paint. Then I look into Bennett's eyes, and I feel steady. Stable. And all at once, despite everything I believe in, this is what I know for certain: I want to kiss this man.

"Yes," I whisper.

I wrap my arms around his shoulders as his arms find their way around my waist. I stand up on my toes to close the distance between us.

Our faces inch closer, mouths parted. I stare at the gold fleck in his eyes until our lips connect and my eyes flutter shut. When our lips are pressed together, I feel as breezy as irises swirling in a Van Gogh masterpiece. I grab a fistful of his sweater and hold him tight. His lips are soft, just like I imagined. We quickly move into a steady rhythm, our kiss deepening.

It's as though Bennett's the painter and I'm the canvas; every kiss a stroke of the brush, revealing, little by little, the unexpected masterpiece that is our embrace.

CHAPTER 15

"Are you sure you don't want any?" Pó Po says as she wrestles the cork out of a wine bottle.

"I'm all wined out from last night. Here, let me help you," I say, reaching for the Pinot Noir she's chosen. I pull the cork out and pour the bottle's contents into a stemless glass, the ruby liquid splashing up against the sides.

"What happened last night?" Pó Po asks.

I give Pó Po a sheepish smile. "I was out...at a Singles Scouting," I lie.

"You expect me to believe that half-assed lie?" she says skeptically.

I cough out a laugh at her word choice. "No, I don't," I admit.

My phone vibrates with a text from Nina. "Nina's not coming!" I inform Pó Po. "She has to do something with her dress and menu planning for the wedding."

"Too bad. Is she still wearing white?" Pó Po asks.

"Yes, her jumpsuit is still ivory, Pó Po," I say. "It's off-white."

"Aiyah! You know that color is what people wear to funerals. And it's not even a dress!"

"But in Western culture, it symbolizes purity. It's traditional for brides to wear white on their wedding day."

Pó Po shakes her head to the side. "I don't like it."

"She'll be wearing red for the wedding dinner. She's also making sure to incorporate traditional elements. You may not like it now, but I think you will!" I exclaim, giving Pó Po a stern but loving look.

"Fine," she says, giving me a face right back.

"Let's enjoy ourselves. You know I live for these dinners." I start pulling dumpling ingredients from my parents' kitchen, relying on muscle memory to guide my movements.

"I'm glad you were still able to make it," Pó Po says.

"I wouldn't miss it," I say. And I haven't. Not one. Our Dumplings and Rom-Dram Dates are the highlight of my month.

Pó Po folds up the sleeves on her lavender linen lounge set. "Have you—"

"—given any thought to Auntie's latest match? No," I blurt out.

"I was going to ask if you've figured out what you're wearing to the wedding," she says patiently. She pours soy sauce over ground pork meat.

"Oh, sorry," I say as I slice scallions and mince garlic.

She shrugs, moving onto a new topic. "I think you'll enjoy what I've picked for today. *In the Mood for Love*, directed by Wong Kar Wai. It's a masterpiece. Very moody. A slow burn."

"Ooh, moody. That's exactly what I'm craving," I say, scooping salt out of a ramekin with a spoon. After last night's kiss with Bennett, I haven't been able to think about anything else. "LA is charming in the fall, don't you think?"

"Aiyah! Stop! That's sugar, not salt!" Pó Po manages to catch some of the sugar as I pour it over the pork mixture.

"Oops."

"It's bright, like every other time of year here, but sure, I guess you could call it charming," Pó Po says, giving me a weird look.

"Apple and pumpkin picking in sunshine, vibrant sunsets, cooler evenings, sweaters!" I rattle off.

She watches me closely. "What were you saying about last night?"

"Did I say something? I don't think I said anything," I tell her.

"You're red! Are you blushing, or lying, or both? You're face turns red when you lie."

I fan myself with my hand. "This kitchen is hot!"

"Let me ask you a serious question, Olivia. Do you take me for a fool?"

I laugh. "You? A fool? That's the last thing you are."

"Good. And accurate. So tell me what it is," she presses. Pó Po stops mixing the dumpling filling and leans against the counter.

"Are you feeling okay, Pó Po?" I ask. "Do you need to take a seat? I can take over."

"Don't fuss! I just need a quick break. When you get to be as old as I am, you're always tired. Enjoy your body while you're young and healthy," she says, waving me off. "Besides, you still haven't perfected the dumpling fold. Pay close attention."

I watch as she pleats the dough swiftly. Following her lead, I spoon filling into the center of the wrapper and mimic her movements, folding the dough into a half-moon shape. "Whoops, too much filling," I say, glancing up at Pó Po watching from the stool.

"That one's yours," she says, placing a plump dumpling on the plate in front of her. "Let's not play this game. Tell me. Are you in love?"

"Love?" I laugh. "Come on, Pó Po. You can't be throwing the L-word around like that. I can't be happy? My marketing ideas for Lunar Love are starting to show traction. That makes me...joyful."

Pó Po laughs and wipes flour off her hands with a dish towel. "Very good, but that's not it. Liv, I've spent my life around those in love. I know it like astronomers know the craters of the moon."

I half smile. "My mind's just a little...preoccupied."

"Go on." Pó Po looks over at me with an upturned eyebrow. She reaches for an apple pear in the fruit bowl and a paring knife from the knife block. "Could you please get me two bowls?"

"I think I'm just a little in over my head," I say, my walls slowly coming down. I grab two bowls from the cabinet and slide them toward her. One month in and I've done the opposite of proving myself worthy of taking over Pó Po's business.

She frowns. "How so?" With a few swift turns of her wrist, the skin of the apple pear curls off against the knife's blade into spiral shavings.

"It's nothing I can't handle," I say. She can probably sense how hard I'm trying.

"You know you can tell me. You're letting the business get between us. I know how you want to be perceived, especially by me, but I don't care about business owner Olivia. Right now I care about my granddaughter Olivia."

Pó Po cuts the skinned apple pear into smaller slices, arranging them into a bowl. She pushes it toward me. Pó Po's cut fruit is always a treat, calming me in stressful times. I love watching her efficiently and swiftly skin apples and pears, score and cube juicy mangoes, and cut through melons with ease. Fruits always taste sweeter when they come from her.

Frozen in place, I stare at the shiny fruit. Once Pó Po knows the truth, I fear that she'll regret ever having made me owner. That she'll be so frustrated that she'll revoke my status and send me on my way. I'll have humiliated myself and, worst of all, be a disappointment and bring shame upon the family name. I bite into a slice, crunching the fruit between my teeth slowly. "Thank you," I say, trailing off.

Pó Po must sense my hesitation because she holds her pinky out toward me. Slowly, I bring my pinky up to hers, and we press our thumbs together.

"I . . . made a bet," I say, staring down at the plate of dumplings. "I bet that I could make Bennett, you know the one, fall in love. If I can, which I will, I'll get great press for Lunar Love. And ten new clients paid in full, which would be huge for us."

Pó Po slowly sips her wine. "You think you can make Bennett fall in love?" she says, amused.

"I know I can," I say. We resume our dumpling pleating. "Do you not think I can?"

"He's a very determined man. And he's focused on his business," she says.

My hands stop. "Pó Po, what do you know?"

Pó Po only moves faster, her fingers filling, folding, filling, folding. "I know nothing."

I give her a look.

She sighs. "During the times I met with him, I noticed he doesn't like to get too attached. He can be pretty unemotional."

"Well, yeah, this I know," I say, conflicted. That kiss last night wasn't unemotional.

"From everything he's told me about his mother," Pó Po says, "well, I suspect he doesn't want to fall in love with someone only to lose her. I don't think he can bear to lose someone else important to him. I could be wrong. This is just one old, wise woman's take on it."

"You're probably right then," I say, distracted. Her words add weight to our wager. I think through Bennett and Harper's compatible traits. They were a good match, but I guess it didn't click for either of them. And the last thing I want is for him to be heartbroken again, *especially* because of the Head Matchmaker at Lunar Love. Heartbreak is the worst-case scenario for any of my matches. "I matched him with someone who was great. I'm sure I can find someone else."

The thought of another person being with Bennett is discomforting. But kiss or no kiss, and despite blurred lines, the bet is still technically on, and I have to see that through. For Lunar Love's sake.

I can feel Pó Po analyzing my expression. "I see," she finally says.

I pour oil into a pan and turn the heat on the stove on high. "What do you see?"

"You like him."

"Who? Bennett?" I laugh awkwardly.

"No, the mailman," she deadpans. "Yes, Bennett."

"No. I can't like him. He's maybe not as horrible as I made

him out to be when I first learned about him, but he's still my rival."

Now Pó Po laughs. "Rival? What is this, high school football?"

"It's not funny! His app launches in less than four months. You won't be laughing when Lunar Love's boarding up its doors."

Pó Po laughs harder as she rises from her stool. "Lunar Love has been in business for over half a century," she says, waving her hands in the air. "You don't think we faced any competition in our days? Our roots are strong. We've survived many competitors. You'll do the same. I know you can handle the pressure." She takes the plate of dumplings and arranges a handful of them onto the hot oiled pan.

"Exactly. This is me handling it."

"After Bennett came to me to learn about his parents, he wanted to pair up and work together," Pó Po says casually.

I smush hardened dough between my fingers. "No..."

"You know my stance on trends and technology. Auntie and I turned him down, so he branched out on his own."

"You knew ahead of time that he was going to steal your business concept?"

"I didn't invent Chinese zodiac matchmaking, Liv," Pó Po says.

"I know, but still," I say.

Pó Po neatly folds a kitchen towel and places it next to the stove. "I may have told him about you, but he was the one who said no to my idea to matchmake you two."

"You tried to matchmake him? With me?" I bury my face in my hands.

"As I said, he told me no."

"Even better," I groan. "He was repulsed by me."

"Quite the opposite," she states. "He didn't want to lead you on, is what I think he said. He was preoccupied with his business and didn't want to get in the way of yours. He's a good guy. In fact, you told me no, too."

"When? He must've gotten lost among all the men you try to match me with," I say.

Pó Po lifts her eyebrows. "You never listen."

I dust flour off my hands, the white powder floating down onto the counter. "That's for the best. We're both professionals," I say. As professional as making out in a museum gets. My heart pitter-patters at the thought of potentially seeing Bennett again tomorrow for my second date. I hope he'll be there.

"As I said before, it's okay if you like him," Pó Po says, not dropping her previous statement. Her eyes make the slightest of movements as she looks into mine. I can't tell if she's happy or if this is the tip of a soul-crushing iceberg of disappointment. "So do you?"

"It's not like it matters. We're incompatible."

Pó Po narrows her eyes at me. "You didn't answer my question. When you think about this man, how do you feel?"

"At first, I wanted to hate him. For obvious reasons. But . . . he's actually pretty great."

Pó Po adds water to the pan and covers it, the steam billowing and enveloping the dumplings in the heat. "But how do you feel?" she repeats.

I watch water droplets collect under the glass lid and drop back into the pan. "Like I don't want him to fall in love with anyone else." The realization is like a punch to my stomach.

"Okay," Pó Po says. "You're incompatible, yet you've gotten this far."

I laugh humorlessly. "Hardly. I can see it now—"

"—Why do you do that?" she asks.

I look at her, my mouth hanging open. "Do what?"

"That 'I can see it now' nonsense. Ever since you and that incompatible ex-boyfriend of yours broke up, you've used that line followed by a bunch of negatives to get out of ever having to date anyone. I know it's your coping mechanism, especially after that incompatible match with your friend. You do it all the time with Auntie and her matches. You did it with mine every time."

"I don't do that," I say defensively over the sizzling dumplings.

"You might lie to this man about how you feel, and you might lie to me, but don't lie to yourself." She narrows her eyes at me. "You're a matchmaker, not a psychic. Where's the fun in everything and everyone being predictable? Where's the magic in that? You have no clue what's going to happen with the couples you match. You're not responsible for every element of their relationships," she says with vigor.

"I can't all of a sudden change the way I think," I explain.

"But you can try. And if that doesn't work, then just try *feeling*."

Pó Po's words linger in the air.

"I can't remember the last time I let *myself* do that," I concede, remembering what I told Bennett at the drive-in.

Pó Po grabs for my hand and gives it a squeeze. "Then maybe now is a good time to start."

"Bennett said something to me about how I'll miss out on good people if I believe compatibility is the one and only way to love," I recall.

"The man has a point," she says resolutely.

"Why do you sound like you're trying to convince me of

something?" I ask. "Are you telling me that *you* are not only supporting an incompatible relationship, but are actively encouraging it? There's no way."

Pó Po taps my hand and then lets it go.

Not finished with my thought, I grasp for examples. "What about with Uncle Rupert? When he married Aunt Vivienne, weren't you mad?"

"At the time, it was a surprise," she explains. "It was always in one ear, out the other with that boy. But he loves her. What could I do?"

I stare at Pó Po in disbelief. "What could you do? What you've done to every other client who came in wanting to test out incompatibility. Tell them no and find them someone compatible."

Her face remains neutral. It's as though the roles are reversed.

"I don't understand," I add. "You and Gōng Gong were compatible, you started a business around compatibility, Mom and Dad are compatible, all your matches have been compatible. Well, mostly. Your entire life and career are built on compatibility." I grab two plates from the cupboard.

"You don't have to be compatible with someone in order to love them, Olivia. There is such a thing as attraction that not even a chart or algorithm can explain. It's an indescribable science." Pó Po gives me a small smile. "I'll say this. Everyone is different and may have varying viewpoints of the Chinese zodiac, whether they use it as something bigger to believe in, a guide for compatible partnership, or to better understand themselves. Take the moon, for instance. Farmers rely on the moon in times of harvest, sea creatures synchronize their biological clocks with the moon's light and phases, and sometimes the moon is used as a mystical backdrop for spooky nighttime campfire stories."

"The moon represents something different for everyone," I agree. "It has more of an impact than we give it credit for."

"True. When's the last time you heard someone ask, 'Wow! Did you see the sun today?' It's always 'Wow! Did you see the moon last night?' For good reason, too," Pó Po says. She peeks through the pot lid to check on our dinner. "Speaking of, keep an eye out for the moon next weekend. It's a rare blue moon. Two full moons in one month!"

"The sun is only pretty when it's rising or setting, but the moon is always beautiful. It's bold, bright, mysterious, elusive. We only see it in glimpses, catching it here and there from lucky angles."

"Ah, you are my granddaughter," Pó Po says, nodding. "Remember, Liv, our greatest qualities can also be our most inhibiting. You are similar to me in that way. Our stubbornness prevails."

"Being persistent is one of the traits I'm most proud of," I declare.

Pó Po uses chopsticks to move the cooked dumplings from the pan to our plates. "My stubbornness has served me well over the years. When I was buying the building Lunar Love is in now, the previous owner wanted to sell it to me for double what it was worth. He thought I didn't know better. I made him my offer, then in my broken English I told him to take it or leave it. Two days later, he called and accepted."

"You knew your worth," I say, scooping mounds of rice next to the dumplings.

Pó Po sighs. "I knew how to bluff. I had a week to get the money together. I had lied and told the owner I had the money ready to go, but that money was beyond my wildest dreams. Luckily, I made some kind friends like Mae and Dale who helped keep my head above water. Anything and everything helped. Don't misunderstand, being stubborn has helped get me where I am. I was determined to improve my English, put my children through college, and make a new life after Gōng Gong passed." Pó Po quickly inhales. "But perhaps I've been *too* stubborn in some cases."

"You didn't want Lunar Love to fail," I say.

"And neither do you." Pó Po rests her hand on my forearm. "But don't let your stubbornness get in your own way."

It takes a few seconds to process what I'm hearing.

"The last thing I want to do is disappoint you," I say.

"What would be disappointing is if you don't take a chance to try to make Lunar Love your own. If you don't put yourself out there, even when it means humiliating yourself. Don't get in the way of your own future," Pó Po instructs. "Now let's eat! Our food is getting cold."

We settle onto the couch in the living room and hit Play on the movie. In a toast, we tap our dumplings together with our chopsticks.

I'm finishing up my third dumpling when a message from Bennett lights up my phone screen. Pó Po is enthralled with the movie, hardly noticing that I'm using technology in the Movie-Screen-Only Zone.

I had a great time with you yesterday, he writes.

I balance my plate on my lap. Me too, I respond. What else do I say? Do I mention our kiss? Do I ask about the date? There are no manuals for what to do when your business competitor turns into your pseudo-client and then turns into someone you kiss.

Another text from him comes through. So your date to-morrow...

I craft my response: What about it...

It's tomorrow... he replies.

Right...I text.

What feels like an unbearable stretch of time passes before Bennett responds again.

He seems like a great guy and everything is paid for...Bennett writes.

Are we... I start to write at the same time his message comes through. I want to know everything he's thinking about what happened between us last night. After a few seconds, I delete the message. I guess I do owe you a second and final date. Are you going to be there?

Bennett responds faster this time. Do you want me to be there?

I don't want you to not be there, I reply.

I watch three dots bounce on my screen as Bennett types. I hold my breath.

Then I'll be there, he messages.

I grin when I read his response.

"Are you in the mood for love, Pó Po?" I ask, giving her a light nudge with my shoulder.

As the movie plays on the screen, Pó Po pats my hand and smiles. "Always," she whispers. "I hope you are, too. It's about time."

CHAPTER 16

I smell the ocean before I see it. The cloudless sky is a stunning cerulean blue, but the gorgeous day doesn't quell my nerves about how close I am to the water.

I miraculously manage to find parking and walk the rest of the way to the address Bennett provided in his vague text message. His instructions were to bring a sweater and sunglasses and to meet him in Fisherman's Village in Marina del Rey.

I look up from the directions on my phone to gauge my surroundings. Dozens of gleaming white sailboats and power-boats of all sizes are docked, bobbing up and down in the teal water.

You're still on land, Olivia. Breathe.

My heart pounds faster in anticipation of seeing Bennett again, a welcome distraction from my wobbly knees. With my cream-colored sweater slung over my arm, I find Bennett standing next to a kiosk holding a bag. Today he's wearing a cornflower blue tee that looks soft from years of wear and khaki shorts. He adjusts his light blue baseball cap a few times in a way that almost looks like he's fighting off nerves. Is he doubting his ZodiaCupid match for me?

"Hi," I call out, adding a small wave.

Bennett smiles deeply when he sees me. "Hey!"

As soon as our eyes meet, I feel instantly at ease. I force myself to avoid looking at the area of his face beneath his nose. If he so much as licks his lips, I'm a goner. After Friday night, my unsteady knees wouldn't be able to handle it. It's just my luck when Bennett crosses into my space to give me a kiss on the cheek. He lingers, the sides of our faces pressed together. When I blink, my eyelashes graze his upper cheek, sending a jolt of heat through me.

"So, who am I meeting today?" I ask dizzily, looking around for someone who looks like they might be going on a first date. "And shouldn't you be hiding behind a buoy or something? Is this weird?" An awkward stream of laughter comes out.

Bennett laughs. "Probably. But we're here, so I'll go get him. Are you good? I think you're really going to like him."

"Yeah. Let's see who you found this time," I mumble.

Bennett rounds the corner of the pay station. A few seconds later, he jumps out from behind it.

"Ta-da!" he shouts.

I snap my head back toward him. "Ta-da what?"

"Your date's with me! I matched you with someone compatible last time, yet that wasn't good enough. Now it's time to try it my way," Bennett says confidently.

"This is a total violation of the rules," I say, holding back a grin.

"We agreed to go on dates with people we match with, and we both found each other compatible people. We *did* match on ZodiaCupid, after all, did we not?"

"That was a different profile!" I protest playfully. "And that was with someone named B.O.B.! You and I have been on a date, Mr. Mooncake-Filling-On-Your-T-Shirt. We both know how that turned out."

"Because you were grilling me the entire time." Bennett smiles. "We still matched. I'm your date. No more stalling." He lifts a bag of unbleached flour from his bag. "This is for you. I couldn't find peonies and figured this was the next best thing."

I'm amused by his sweet gesture. "Fine. You're my date." My heart swells traitorously.

Before I can grab his offering, he pulls the bag back. "Actually, no. I'll hang onto this for now so you don't have to lug it around. Follow me." He leads me around the kiosk and down a dock.

"Should we be over here?" I ask, looking at the signs condemning trespassing.

Bennett slows his steps and gestures toward a small power-boat rocking back and forth in the waves. "I know Horses are adventurous so I wanted to plan something fun for you," he says, beaming. "We're having a picnic on the boat! Oh, good, you brought a sweater. I may have underestimated the temperature today, but it should be cooler on the water."

I grip my sweater tighter. "We're eating on a boat. Like, docked, right?"

Bennett jumps into the boat first, placing the flour on the seat. "More like on the water. I opted for the seventeen-footer so that we'll be more comfortable for our lunch. The water shouldn't be too choppy right now."

I feel the blood rush out of my face. I place my hand in his, grasping it a little too tightly as I step one foot onto what's pretty much just a floating tub. When our fingers touch, the same thrill runs through me that I felt at the Getty. The boat wobbles, and I let out a loud shriek.

"Are you okay?" Bennett asks, alarmed. I back up from the boat, keeping my feet firmly planted on the dock. His smile drops. "Did I mess up?"

I straighten my shoulders. "I'm . . . fine."

"I don't want to be presumptuous, but . . . are you scared of the ocean?" Bennett looks nervous that I actually might be.

"Were those the actions of a scared person?" I ask over-confidently. "Okay, I might be a little bit scared of it."

I see Bennett's eyes pop behind his sunglasses. "Say no more, we'll do something else," he says, starting to climb out of the boat.

"No, no! I'll be okay. You planned a picnic and rented a boat. I'll feel bad if I ruin your plans," I say, holding my hands up to stop him. "Honestly."

Bennett looks unsure. "Okay. You'll let me know if you feel like it's too much? Say the word and I'll turn this ship right back around."

I laugh. "Sure."

Bennett whips out his phone and starts tapping on the screen. "Horses tend to be adventurous, but I may have interpreted the term *adventurous* too loosely. Let me see here," he says, staring at his device.

"What are you doing?" I ask, looking around at the other tourists on the dock. "Are you reading an article right now?"

"I'm trying to see what other traits I may have missed," he says, moving his finger up the screen. "I totally missed the mark."

"What? No," I say, somewhat pleased to be continuously proved right. "Not every animal sign embodies every single one of their traits. Or if they do identify with a trait, it takes getting to know someone to truly understand what that means to each specific person. Sorry to say, but you're going to have to get to know me."

"I would love that," he says before scrunching his forehead. "I'll need to think through how to handle that on the app better. See? I'm learning every day."

"Don't worry about it. But if I don't walk onto solid ground or get in the boat, my legs won't be able to support me for much longer."

Bennett springs into action. "Right. Sorry. Let's try this again."

He steadies himself in the boat and holds both arms out toward me. I place my hands on his shoulders, stepping slowly into the boat. Our bodies are as close as they were at the Getty, sending my mind down a dangerous path.

"There we go," he says, watching me closely.

Bennett pulls out what looks like a life vest for a baby out from under one of the seats.

"Thanks," I mumble, distractedly reaching for the vest.

"This isn't for you," he says. He straps the baby life vest around the sack of flour.

I laugh out loud at the absurdity and feel slightly more relaxed.

"*This* one's for you," Bennett says, handing me a neon yellow life vest.

I speedily tighten the life vest around my body and carefully wobble over to the seats. I plant myself onto the bench in the front of the boat so I have clear visibility.

"Ready?" he asks. Bennett starts up the boat, the engine roaring to life and settling into a rumbling purr. "Let me know at any point if you want to turn back."

"So far so good," I say, focusing my eyes on the waves in front of us. I look to see how far I'd have to jump from the boat to the dock. In my dreams, I could probably successfully stick a five-foot landing, but before I can make this a reality, we're ten feet away from the dock.

I don't say anything while Bennett navigates us out of the marina for fear of him losing focus and the boat capsizing.

My body remains tight and curled as I focus on my breathing. Once there's enough fresh air in my lungs, I attempt to make small talk.

"Why didn't you start ZodiaCupid over here?" I ask, gesturing toward the beach. "I'd have pegged you as a Silicon Beach guy."

"Way too expensive," he says, casually holding the steering wheel in one hand. "I won't deny that being able to walk to the beach for lunch breaks would be a huge perk, but then I never would have met you."

I smile to myself. "Are you a big boater?"

"Not as much as I'd like. My dad loves fishing, so I spent a lot of time on the water with him as a kid."

A wave rolls toward us, rocking the boat from side to side. I quickly grab for the railing. The flour baby bounces in the seat and then goes overboard. We watch as it bobs up and down in the choppy waves. Bennett looks over the side of the boat and laughs.

"Don't look at me! I'm not going in there," I say.

Bennett maneuvers the boat closer to the flour. He reaches out for it, lifting the bag out of the ocean by the life vest straps.

"Last I checked, fish don't eat paper or flour," he says. "You want to steer? It's like driving a car, but instead of asphalt the roads are made of water."

"You can't drown in the roads," I murmur. I shakily waddle

over to the middle of the boat and position myself between him and the helm. I tightly grip the sun-warmed silver wheel. "Look, I'm steering!"

Bennett shifts behind me. "You're doing great!"

Ahead of us, a large boat angles in our direction.

"What do I do?" I scream, rotating the wheel frantically.

"Just stay the course, captain," he says, wrapping his hands over mine on the wheel. "They'll move."

The other boat navigates away from us.

"See? Trust me," he whispers into my ear. I shiver when his breath meets the side of my neck.

A long, deep breath helps calm me after my slight over-reaction. His hands are still covering mine as we steer the boat to our own patch of open sea to free float. When Bennett removes his hands from mine, my fingers immediately feel cold.

"Hungry?" Bennett reaches into the tote bag.

"Very," I admit, slowly walking to the front of the boat.

Bennett follows closely behind, keeping one hand under my arm to help stabilize me. "I wanted to make you my famous cacio e pepe but thought Italian sub sandwiches were a more practical choice."

"I love cacio e pepe. Few but quality ingredients. Creamy, spicy, cheesy. It's—"

"—true love, I remember," Bennett says.

Bennett reveals a container with two large sandwiches. He holds it out to let me choose from the two options.

"Oh, right. Of course. My original profile." I pick up one of the sandwiches and study its contents. Between the vinegar-and-oil-drizzled sliced loaves are tomatoes, lettuce, thinly sliced onions, herbs, salami, ham, and a variety of cheeses. My mouth begins to salivate at how fresh the ingredients smell. "These look promising. Should I expect any odd flavor pairings in here?"

Bennett laughs and hands me a plaid paper napkin. "Not this time. I went more traditional for this lunch."

"Interesting," I say, curious what his version of traditional tastes like. I sink my teeth into the sandwich. "Yum. My compliments to the chef."

Bennett lifts his sandwich in the air. "Great, I'll let Elvis know!" His laugh is lost in the waves, but seeing his lit-up face is all it takes to make my heart flutter. He prepares the rest of our meal of chips, precut watermelon slices, and bubbly water.

A gust of wind sends my hair flying into my face. Bennett lifts his hand up next to my cheek and pauses. "Do you mind?"

I shake my head. He gently pushes a strand of hair back behind my ear before pulling off his baseball cap and offering it to me.

I reluctantly accept, wiggling his hat over my head, the inside of the cap still warm. "Thanks," I say softly.

Bennett takes a sip of bubbly water, smiling at me with his eyes. "What is it about the ocean that scares you?"

I pop a chip into my mouth and adjust my grip on the railing. "When you're in the ocean, you have no idea what's swimming beneath you." *A certain parasite comes to mind.* "Right now there could be a twelve-foot eel beneath us, and we would never know. And I used to think sharks somehow had access to pools—you know, through the drains—so you can imagine how wild my imagination goes when it comes to the ocean. Also, drowning and riptides."

"All completely valid reasons." Bennett's face remains unchanged, unjudgmental. "I used to be scared of the water, too," he continues when I don't respond. "I was at a birthday pool party where we had to take a swim test to participate. Guess who didn't pass?" He points a finger at himself. "I was terrified of not being able to breathe underwater, so I had a tough time learning how to swim. I pretty much flailed around for five minutes in front of all my friends. It was so embarrassing that it took a couple of years before my mom could persuade me to swim again."

"How did she convince you?" I ask.

"She surprised me with water wing arm floaties that had shark fins attached to the sides," he says, motioning toward his arms. "She said that when I wore them, it meant she'd be right there beside me. And that when I did the breaststroke, it would look like I was swimming with sharks. She made it sound really badass. Mind you, I was five. It took some time but I eventually learned how to swim on my own."

"Your mom sounded like a smart woman."

Bennett's smile vanishes as he looks out at the ocean. "The smartest," he says quietly.

I reach for his hand and give it a light squeeze. "Maybe we overcome our fear of our businesses failing by learning how to swim. Metaphorically, of course."

His smile reappears, dimples and all. "We'll just have to find adult-sized shark fin floaties. You know, swimming with the sharks isn't terribly far off from how it feels to run a business. Because of their olfactory organs, sharks have acute senses of smell and can detect low concentrations of odors that help them identify prey or potential mates. They're incredibly aware of their environment and are impressively in tune with what's around them and what they need to do to survive."

"Sharks could also be below us right now. Trust nothing," I say jokingly. The rush of an old memory swells in me. "I was also broken up with on a dock once."

"The thought that anyone could leave you blows my mind," he says quietly. "Was he someone you were serious about?"

I play with a thread on the sleeve of my sweater. "I thought I was. He was actually incompatible with me."

"Really?" Bennett asks slowly and in a surprised tone.

"He was a Snake."

Bennett exhales and leans back against the railing. His eyes flicker out toward the horizon and then back to me. "What happened?"

"He was jealous and possessive, never trusting me when I had male clients to match. He belittled my work and always said how he never understood why I do what I do," I say, trying to piece together fragmented memories. "He'd always remind me that we were incompatible and questioned why I was obsessed with matching compatible people. Of course at the time, I thought I loved him and our relationship. So enamored, in fact, that I dragged my friend into an incompatible relationship, too."

"Dragged doesn't seem like the right word," Bennett says, lightly squeezing the aluminum can of bubbly water.

"No," I admit, "we were both excited about the match at first. I really thought I was happy, and that she would be, too. I never wanted to hurt her."

"Of course not," Bennett says, bending his knee and draping his forearm over it, leaning in closer as though he doesn't want to miss a single word I say.

"I'm the one who taught my ex about the different traits, which of course he laughed about at first," I continue. "Then he got a big job opportunity in New York and expected me to go with him. But I stayed here. We tried long distance because he didn't want to give us up. He said he'd be back."

"Did he come back?" Bennett asks.

I shake my head. "Turns out his ex from college was living in New York, too."

"So he broke up with you to be with his ex-girlfriend?"

"Well, not exactly," I say, trailing off. "Apparently he was dating her long distance while he was living here in California. He moved to New York to be with her, turning me into the long-distance girl. When I found out and we broke up, he had the nerve to say that it was because they were more compatible." That was the last time I'll ever be a pawn in someone's game.

"That's shitty," Bennett says. "He sounds like a piece of work who didn't realize he had something great right in front of him."

"I knew better." I adjust the baseball cap. "I've worked with a lot of people who have been scorned by love. And it's not like I've never been through a breakup before. But I let him manipulate me. The signs were there. His traits were obvious the entire time. I let myself get so swept away that I only saw his positive traits."

"And now you only see the incompatible traits in people," he says, pausing a moment before adding, "Not everyone is him. Have you ever considered that maybe your ex wasn't possessive because he's a Snake but because he was just an asshole?"

A laugh sails out of me. "Probably. Definitely." I think for a moment on this, soaking in the silence. "Losing my friend was worse than losing my ex," I say. "After all of that happened, I actually took six months off from matchmaking. I questioned everything about myself, the Chinese zodiac, and the concept of relationships. I took some me-time, and when I came back to LA, my friend was gone. Nowhere to be found."

"She left without saying anything?" he asks.

"Yeah. She never wanted to talk to me again."

"Oh, so she told you that."

"Well, no. But her actions told me everything I needed to know."

"I see," Bennett says, looking like he's gathering his thoughts. "When my mother died, I thought my father hated her because he never wanted to talk about her." He bends the silver tab back and forth on the can until it comes loose. "What I realized is that he never wanted to talk about her because he loved her so much it hurt to bring her up. Our actions don't always reveal our true intentions."

"You're probably right." I fiddle with the buckle on my life vest.

"You know it's never too late," he says kindly.

"We'll see," I say with a shrug.

He reaches for his bag and pulls out a plastic container of cut strawberries. "What brought you back to Lunar Love?" he asks, offering me the tub of fruit and a fork.

I pierce my fork into a sliced-up strawberry. "I missed it too much. The zodiac is in my veins. But I vowed to never let something like that happen again. For myself or my clients." Even as I say the words, I feel my resolve slipping.

With his free hand, Bennett grabs mine and lets our intertwined fingers rest on his thigh. "You think you'll know exactly how things will turn out because of people's personalities?" he asks.

"No?" I answer in the form of a question. "But I try."

"That sounds...exhausting," he says.

My eyes widen at his bluntness. "I love what I do, but

yes, it's pretty damn exhausting," I say before cracking up into laughter.

"Thank you for sharing all that with me," he says. "I like knowing more about you."

"Those are the only insights into my soul that you're getting," I inform him.

"I'll take it," Bennett says. There is a hint of a smile at the corners of his lips.

I run my thumb along the back of his hand. "Hey. My sister's wedding is happening in a couple of days. Would you...do you..." I start. "Do you want to come with me?"

I didn't intend to say it, but there it was. Out in the open sea. Maybe there really is something to the smell of saltwater, the sound of the waves splashing against the boat, and looking out into the endless distance.

Or maybe it's because I'm out of my comfort zone that I suddenly feel a sense of calm. But I've been out of my comfort zone for weeks now. Because of this man in front of me.

Bennett squeezes my hand as he gives thought to my question. I lose my train of thought, hyperaware of our skin-on-skin contact. "As your plus one?" he asks.

"You could also come as my bodyguard. It'll make me look important."

"Bodyguard it is," Bennett says with a laugh. "I would love to. Thank you." He removes his sunglasses and looks out over his shoulder at the ocean. With the glittering blue water reflecting in his eyes, the hazel looks jade green. He looks at my face with his mossy eyes, my skin burning beneath the life vest.

No more words come. Instead we just smile at each other and continue to hold hands, our knees gently knocking back and forth with the rhythm of the waves. His gaze sends shivers down my spine, and I forget that we're miles from shore, miles from where I ever thought we would be.

Admittedly, being on this boat with this man who's still largely unknown to me also feels oddly exhilarating. For a second, I think I might actually be enjoying myself. Maybe this whole water thing isn't so bad.

Suddenly, out of nowhere, a speedboat roars by, breaking our gaze and sending a series of huge rolling waves in our direction. The way the boat rocks feels like riding a roller coaster, and all the cozy feelings I had about the water evaporate.

I grab the nearest solid thing next to me for stability, which happens to be Bennett. I loop my arms around his neck while Bennett wraps his arms around my waist to help steady me. In a matter of seconds, the distance between us has vanished. My stomach does a flip, but I don't think it's because of the rocking. I send down thanks to Poseidon for helping us close the distance.

The boat steadies, but we stay where we are. I run my hand along the back of Bennett's neck, gripping it tighter. He pulls me closer by the straps of my life vest.

"About that bet..." Bennett whispers.

"Should we just..." I whisper back.

"Call it off?" he asks with pleading eyes.

I thought I could tread water and stay afloat, but it turns out I'm not such a strong swimmer after all. I'm swept up, swept away. Too far gone.

"Deal," I say.

We linger for just a moment, our faces inches apart. Then, like the water crashing on rocks, an explosion of tension is released as we bring our lips together. I gently bite his bottom lip, craving his taste again.

He reaches under my life vest and runs his hand along my lower back. I hang onto his biceps, a wave of want washing over me. Bennett's breath on my neck creates a cooling sensation, the condensation evaporating as quickly as it was formed. I run my fingers along the spots where his dimples indent and brush my thumb along his lips.

"Just tell me if it's enough," he breathes, cupping his hand under my chin, "or not enough."

At that, he kisses me deeply, tenderly. A tide of emotion rises in me. In the pressure of his mouth, I feel his want, too.

I push him back against the salt-sprayed vinyl seats, leaning down onto him. We angle our heads to find a way to reach each other under the rim of the baseball hat until he finally lifts it off my head and throws it onto a nearby seat. He softly pushes my dark brown hair behind my shoulders, letting his fingers drag down through the loose strands. We press our foreheads together, the tips of our noses touching. Electricity crackles through me like a bolt of lightning.

His fingers wrap around my thighs, silencing any thoughts of *I can see it now*. The glimmer in his eyes makes me forget everything I know about incompatibility.

He pulls back to look at me, his eyes a shade darker. I memorize the lines and curves of his face. If Bennett's the ocean, I'm already in too deep. No life raft can save me now. This riptide pulls me farther and farther out to sea until I can hardly see the shore.

CHAPTER 17

I carefully lean over Nina to work on her eyes, adding an extra layer of mascara to her short lashes. Pó Po looks through her jewelry case for Nina's "something borrowed" while Grandma, who's in town for the big day, takes photos of Nina getting ready. Mom finishes combing Nina's hair and pulls it into a low bun.

"I can't believe you brought Asshole as a plus one," Nina says. "I'm so glad."

"He seems like a nice young man," Pó Po says, winking at me when we make eye contact in the mirror.

"Let's just see how today goes," I say, keeping my face neutral. "He's meeting us at the courthouse."

I fluff a section of white feathers around Nina's strapless bodice. With her long brown hair swept up and pearl earrings glowing on her ears, she looks, in a word, breathtaking. I finish buckling the ankle strap on her baby blue, open-toed heels.

Nina steps back, adjusts a curled wisp of hair, and smiles. "Great job, ladies! I think this'll do."

Pó Po slips one of her rings onto Nina's finger and then looks her up and down, nodding with approval.

Grandma snaps another photo with her film camera. "You remind me of myself on my wedding day," she says to Nina in admiration. "Except I had a dress that resembled a tiered cake."

"It's been so long since we've seen those photos," Nina says, snickering with Grandma.

"Your father must have them in an album somewhere around here," Grandma says, looking around the bathroom as though they'd be in here. "I'll ask him."

I grab the emergency makeup kit and Nina's change of clothes, double-checking that everything's there before heading out to the courthouse.

Everyone piles into my parents' and Auntie Lydia's cars. As she climbs in, Pó Po reaches for the grab handle but misses and stumbles into the backseat. Mom and I sprint to her from across the front yard, our heels digging into the grass.

"Mom! Are you okay?" my mother asks Pó Po.

"Aiyah! I'm fine! I'm fine!" Pó Po says, waving her off.

"What are you doing trying to get in the car by yourself? We'll help you," Mom says with a low level of irritation.

"I birthed three children. I can get in a car." Pó Po buckles her seat belt and faces forward.

Mom shuts the door and shoots me an apprehensive look.

With a free second to myself in the car, I check to see if any messages have come through. There's one from Alisha.

Exciting news! One of your tweets has gone low-key viral. Looks like the hashtag is working. Yayyyy!! Have fun at the wedding! Congrats to Nina!

Our social media campaign has sparked new interest like I'd had a suspicion it would. This week alone, there have been more #LoveInTheMoonlight tags, and ever since we increased how many moon songs we pair with animal signs, I've answered over thirty direct messages about our services. It feels good to have an idea turn into reality. Maybe things will actually start turning around for real.

When we arrive, I find Bennett lingering in the lobby of the courthouse, looking sharp in a navy blue suit with a crisp white button-down. There's a sweeping rush of emotions inside me seeing him here, dressed like this, looking at me like that.

"Hey, you. You look beautiful," Bennett says. He twirls me around as he admires my robin's-egg blue silk dress before pulling me in for a hug. I bury my face in his neck, wrapping my arms around his waist.

I steal another look at him. "You're looking very handsome."

"June, it's lovely to see you again," he says, looking excited. He opens his arms for a hug, and Pó Po seems thrilled to accept it by the way she pats him repeatedly on the shoulder as they embrace.

Bennett gently places his hand on the small of my back as we follow my family into the courthouse room at our designated ceremony time.

Inside, I pull Asher to the side before the ceremony begins. "Asher," I say in my most serious tone.

"Olivia," Asher says back with a hint of nervousness. We've never spoken directly about his animal sign incompatibility with Nina, but she must've told him about our conversations.

"You're a lucky man, Asher. Treat my sister right. Don't ever lie to her. If you do, well . . ." I drag my pointer finger across my throat. I adjust his tie and spin him around by the shoulders. "Don't disappoint me."

His eyes are wide as he nods speechlessly before hurrying back to Nina.

Both sides of family and friends gather around the bride and groom. Everyone falls silent as Nina and Asher take their places in front of the judge.

I watch behind glassy eyes as Nina and Asher read their vows aloud and exchange rings. I'm hyperaware of Bennett standing next to me, his presence overwhelming and extremely distracting. Every so often, our eyes catch, and we quietly laugh to ourselves. He reaches for my hand, our pinkies linking in private.

Near the end of the ceremony, Asher's mother comes up to the front and gives a blessing. Both sets of parents carry sticks with a linen blanket attached by the corners and hold it over Nina and Asher. Together, Nina and Asher smash their heels against a bag, breaking the glass inside. The glass sounds like it shatters into a million pieces.

"Mazel tov!" the group cheers and claps.

Nina and Asher seal their love and promises with a kiss. Asher spins Nina into a dip, and she dramatically kicks her leg up. My little sister found her match. Another incompatible couple finding real love.

I ride with Bennett to Ming's Garden in the San Gabriel Valley, where the family gathers for the wedding feast. This spot is Nina and Asher's favorite weekend dim sum spot and the location of their first date. Where better to celebrate their love than the place it all started?

A waiter leads us to the private room in the back where several large round tables are set up. Seeing Bennett in an important family setting stirs in me a whole new level of nervousness.

Votives and flowers decorate the tabletops, the light from the candles emanating a warm glow throughout the room. A portable dance floor is set up in front of a microphone stand, drum set, flute, saxophone, and piano keyboard.

Pó Po grips my arm as I lead her to her seat. Walking with us is Dad along with Grandma and Grandpa, who hold hands as they shuffle toward the tables.

"What do you think all this is about?" Dad asks us. "I don't remember paying for a band."

Pó Po gives us a mischievous smile. "It's my surprise for Nina and Asher," she says.

"Has Nina seen this yet?" I gesture toward the dance floor and look around for her, but she must not be here yet. "Didn't she specifically not want dancing?"

"A wedding isn't a wedding without dancing!" Pó Po says in an all-knowing tone. "She'll like it."

Asher's family and ours split up so the families are intermingled at the tables. Bennett offers his arm as Pó Po lowers into her seat. We take our places next to her.

I thank the waiter and ask for a couple of glasses of water in Mandarin.

"I didn't know you spoke Chinese," Bennett says, looking impressed.

"Not fluently. A lifetime of Chinese classes and I can order water and ask what time it is," I say with a sigh.

Bennett nods in understanding. "I'm not fluent, either, but I've tried to learn. It's not easy to pick up or practice when everyone around you speaks English."

"Yeah. We never spoke it at home growing up. My mom can speak Mandarin, but my dad doesn't, so..." I trail off, reflecting on this particular shortcoming. "All the Chinese I heard at Lunar Love didn't even soak in like I hoped it would. Sometimes I have the cruel realization that I'll never know the language my own mother grew up speaking."

Uncle Rupert and Aunt Vivienne claim spots between Bennett and Asher's godparents at our table.

"Olivia! How are things at Lunar Love?" Aunt Vivienne asks. "I should introduce you to my sister's husband's cousin's son. If anyone can work wonders, it's you! Things are improving, I hope?"

I shift uncomfortably in my seat, knowing Bennett's listening.

"Stop with all that! You're going to make her a nervous rex before her speech!" Uncle Rupert, a paleontologist with a penchant for dinosaur puns, interjects with a sly grin.

Pó Po, who by now has heard every one of Uncle Rupert's puns, looks genuinely charmed by his humor. He looks pleased as he arranges his chopsticks across the top of his plate.

Soft music plays overhead while we wait for the bride and groom to enter.

Pó Po must sense the way I clammed up. "I'm glad you're both able to set aside your differences to be here," she says bluntly.

I'm startled by the callout, and we both laugh nervously.

"Me too," Bennett says agreeably, though I remain quiet. "How did Nina and Asher meet? Did you matchmake her?"

Pó Po waves her hand. "Goodness, no! Can you imagine?" she says, elbowing me gently in my side. "Three matchmakers in the family, and you'd think there'd be more *compatible* couples." She makes air quotes around the word compatible. I'm distracted by where she learned to do that, and by her unexpected dismissal of compatibility that she's been hinting at for weeks now.

"You know, in my matchmaking days in Taiwan," she continues, "I paired people based on their zodiac animal sign, education, and family background. My focus was matching clients from families of equal social status. In the old days, matchmakers used to be a lot more esteemed. But now we have a different relationship with clients."

Pó Po suddenly sounds like she's feeling reminiscent, and while I normally love it, I don't know how much of it Bennett would want to—or should—hear.

"Starting Lunar Love here, I dropped all the other details of matchmaking and focused on the zodiac. That was my interpretation of it. My way of modernizing it, I guess you could say. To keep it simple," Pó Po explains. "Now matchmaking can include looking at assets, salary, profession, and even blood type."

"Modernizing. *Very* interesting," Bennett says, raising his eyebrows theatrically at me.

"In China, matchmakers can charge tens, even hundreds of thousands of dollars," Pó Po says. "Lunar Love's practically giving away our services! Maybe I should've stayed in Asia. I read that a man paid one and a half million dollars for a match. I'm sure it took a lot of time and effort for the matchmaker to sort through thousands of women, but with that price tag attached, I'd welcome the challenge."

Bennett listens intently, focused on Pó Po and her stories.

"Is that even real?" I ask, suspiciously.

Pó Po clucks her tongue. "We could be making bonuses upwards of thirty thousand dollars."

"Can you imagine?" Bennett asks, leaning forward.

"Maybe we should be charging even more than we do," I say, even though I don't feel this way. I've already considered restructuring the fees. Less exclusive, more inclusive. After all, if we want to attract a younger clientele, our prices can't be as high as they are. When ZodiaCupid launches and offers free profiles with paid upgrades, how can we compete with their $9.99 per month? I tuck my hands under my thighs and focus on the candle's flickering flame.

"But now people want everything immediately, and love no longer has to be considered a big investment when there are free options available," Pó Po adds, giving Bennett a dramatic side-eye. To my surprise, he laughs.

All this talk about Lunar Love only reminds me how much work there is to do, especially if we want Lunar Love to be around for much longer. A pang of guilt forms when I think about how much time I've spent allowing myself to be distracted by my competition. I try to shrug off the stress and enjoy the wedding.

Without warning, we hear the door kicked open and see Asher walk in carrying Nina in his arms. Nina has changed into a long, ruby-red silk dress. I glance over at Pó Po to gauge her reaction and watch as her tight-lipped smile relaxes.

My focus turns back to Nina as her eyes flit from the group to the dance floor. She breaks into a giggle reserved only for those hopelessly in love.

"Looks like we're dancing after dinner!" Nina announces. "Thanks, Pó Po! We love it."

Pó Po slaps my thigh with the back of her hand. "I told you!" she says, pleased. There's no one else who could go against Nina's wishes and get away with it.

The newlyweds position themselves in front of the dance floor. "Before we eat dinner," Nina starts, "Asher and I would like to take a moment to have a toast and incorporate a Chinese tradition that I recently learned about and love." She looks over at me and smiles. "It's our interpretation of a tea ceremony. I chose my favorite green tea, and Asher chose chamomile."

At that, a few waiters glide over to our tables with platters of white teapots. They start pouring hot tea into the teacups next to each guest's dinner plate.

Asher continues where Nina left off. "The two teas have been blended together, representing our union and families coming together as one. To those who were able to be here, to those who aren't here with us today, and to love."

"And health!" Pó Po shouts out, holding up her teacup.

"And happiness!" Asher's grandmother chimes in.

We all hold up our teacups to toast and then sip the green-chamomile concoction.

Nina and Asher take their seats and more waiters come out with platters and bamboo steamers filled with food. A whole steamed fish is placed in the center of each table, the silvery gray of the fish's scales and sliced green scallions vibrant against the bleached white tablecloth. Around the fish are bowls of steamed rice, stir-fried vegetables, hot and sour soup, long-life noodles, and platters of Peking duck with steamed buns and hoisin sauce. Plates of garlic-and-ginger shrimp are squeezed in wherever there's room to fit them. Baskets of dim sum are piled on top of one another, welcoming interaction between guests at the table.

I fill my plate with a mound of steamed rice. Before I can add more, Pó Po takes over.

"No, no! Not enough food for you," she says. Pó Po grabs my plate and piles more food onto it. "You need to eat so you have energy to keep up with me on the dance floor."

Bennett follows suit, filling his plate with enough food to make Pó Po proud. Within minutes, he and Uncle Rupert are engaged in deep conversation about when dinosaurs last roamed the earth.

Pó Po watches me over the course of the meal. At the very least, I finish off the rice so that she doesn't have to remind me of the importance of eating every last grain.

"Bennett reminds me so much of Gōng Gong. Strong-willed, earnest, patient, and handsome," Pó Po leans over and whispers. "Things seem to be going well."

"I don't know. Maybe?" I mumble. Since my last talk with Pó Po, more has happened between me and Bennett. "It's been nice, but we've been together because of work. Who knows what will happen once we sort out this podcast situation. That bet I made, well, we called it off. I'm not sure what will happen now, but with Bennett being a Rat—"

Pó Po shakes her head. "Incompatibility. Compatibility. If you let it, they'll all rule your life."

My mouth goes slack. "Uh, isn't that the point?"

Pó Po tucks a curl behind her ear. "Sometimes in life, there isn't a point. Sometimes we demand that there is. We pray that there is. And sometimes, we make a point when one isn't needed. When things are actually quite simple."

"I don't understand," I say. "One day you're pro compatibility, the next you're not."

Pó Po's dark brown eyes glimmer as she grabs for my hand. "Liv, can I tell you something that you promise to keep secret?"

I look back to make sure Bennett's still talking to Uncle Rupert. "Of course, Pó Po. You can tell me anything. What is it?"

Pó Po folds the cloth napkin across her lap and then looks up at me like she's only going to say what she's about to say once. "Gōng Gong and I weren't technically compatible," she finally tells me in a hushed tone. She looks around to make sure no one else heard.

My hand loosens its grip, my chopsticks dropping into my lap. "What's that now?"

"I rejected my parents' arranged marriage for me and married Gōng Gong instead." She continues when I don't say anything. "They matchmade me too late. He was my first and only love, and he happened to be incompatible. I wish you could have known him. When I say his death quite literally tore my world apart, I mean it. My children were the only ones who got me through that dark time. Which leads me to why I started Lunar Love."

"I had no idea," I whisper. "How could you never have told me this? This is huge."

"No one knows," she says. "How would it look if the founder of Lunar Love was promoting compatible love when she herself never had a compatible marriage?"

All my thoughts rush to me at once. I sit frozen in place, my hands gripping the sides of my chair. "I don't understand. Did you both agree to lie about his birthday?"

A small smile lifts Pó Po's cheeks. "Something like that. For so long, I believed that my husband died because I rejected my parents' safe, compatible arranged marriage. Lunar Love was my repentance, what I promised myself I'd do. I committed to a life of compatibility and would make it work no matter what."

"You stubborn woman," I say with an amazed laugh, my shock slowly wearing off.

"You see why my stubbornness was inhibiting," she says. "The thing with spending more than fifty years of your life doing something is that you gain a good sense of what's important, compatible or not."

"Compatible or *not?*" I whisper.

Pó Po reaches for my hand and pulls it into her lap. "Don't get me wrong. Compatibility is the bread and butter of Lunar Love, and there's truth in the system. But here's something else I've learned in my lifetime: you should be with someone who not only makes you happy, but who challenges you."

"Who *challenges* me?" I repeat. What is happening right now? "I can't believe this."

"If you really boil it down, Lunar Love provides people with the knowledge and tools for making relationships work." Pó Po gives my hand a light squeeze. "I didn't want you to be disappointed in me, so I didn't tell you sooner," she says.

"Disappointed in *you?* You could never disappoint me. Thank you for telling me," I say, squeezing her hand gently. "Your secret is safe with me." Pó Po leans in for a hug, and I hold her tight.

I'm still processing this information when the room quiets for my toast as maid of honor. I grab my glass of champagne and overcompensate with a forced smile that makes my cheeks burn. My already shallow breathing quickens until I feel like I'm going to burst. Bennett turns from his conversation and picks up the napkin that slides off my lap, placing it on the table.

"I consider myself lucky that love is my life," I start, my voice shaky. "I am literally around love every day. In the thick of it. Helping create it. Which means, when I say I've never seen a love quite like Nina and Asher's, you should believe me. It's an honor to witness a partnership filled with respect, laughter, intense debates, a flair for the theatrical—as evidenced by Nina and Asher's entrance—lots of love, and honesty."

Light laughter fills the room. "I know a perfect match when I see one," I continue. "Nina and Asher, I love you both. Congratulations, and may your best days be ahead of you." I hold up my glass and a chorus of clinks rings out in the room.

Once the carrot wedding cake—in the shape of a Rooster for Nina and Asher's signs, made by yours truly—is cut, the band members trickle in. Dressed in all-white tuxedos and sequin bow ties, five older Chinese women take their places at their instruments. No one knows what to anticipate. The woman with the flute begins to play familiar, high-pitched opening notes.

"It's time for their first dance!" Pó Po squeals, having already moved on to the next event of the evening.

The singer opens her mouth to sing and out comes a Mandarin version of "My Heart Will Go On" by Celine Dion. Bennett and I glance at each other and burst into laughter at how unexpected it is. Nina and Asher look confused but dance anyway to the romantic crooning. They hold each other close, their feet moving in sync on the temporary dance floor, and laugh together. Pó Po closes her eyes and sings along, swaying back and forth in her seat.

The last note of the song ends, and I'm excited to hear what they play next. It's anybody's guess. The saxophonist leans forward with her instrument, the smooth notes of "Crazy Little

Thing Called Love" filling the room. Pó Po drags me with all the strength she can muster to join her, while I try to pull Bennett up to join us.

"You can't not dance!" I shout to him over the music.

"I don't dance in public!" he says. "Remember? Junior prom."

"What could've been so bad? You were what, seventeen? We all look ridiculous at seventeen."

He shakes his head. "It involved a pulled hamstring, sweaty bangs, split boxers, and my entire grade laughing at me."

"I promise I won't laugh when you pull your quad this time," I say very seriously.

Bennett stays put in his seat.

My shoulders drop. "You're really going to make me dance alone?"

Bennett visibly tenses. "Sorry," he says, "but honestly? You don't want me dancing with you. It'll just be humiliating."

"Okay, if that's what you want," I say, disheartened.

"Love is crazy, and that's the thing!" Pó Po sings, reinterpreting the lyrics. The song is performed in English this time so even I can sing along if I want to. She dances her heart out and tugs at my arm. I follow her, abandoning Bennett at the table. I recall what Pó Po said about him not wanting to get too attached. A cloud of uneasiness looms over me, but Pó Po's excitement pushes it away.

Pó Po doesn't move fast, but she wiggles with passion. She throws her head back in delight, her happiness contagious. Auntie, Mom, and Dad join in, each of them taking turns to show off their dance moves. A few minutes later, Nina and Asher bop their way over to us.

"This was a great idea, Pó Po!" Nina shouts over the music.

"You're right. I would've regretted not having this. Maybe you really do know best!"

"Don't ever forget that!" she shouts back.

When the slow Mandarin version of "Can't Help Falling in Love" booms over the speakers, I go back to the table to sit with Bennett.

I lean in closer to his ear. "You okay?" I ask.

Bennett drapes his arm around me, and I rest my head on his shoulder. "I'm great. Thanks for inviting me. This means a lot."

"Thanks for coming," I say, angling my face up toward his. "You're sitting this next song out, too?"

He nods.

For the next slow song, I find my way back to Pó Po. She wraps her arms around my waist, and we rock back and forth.

Pó Po leans back to look me in the eye. She holds her pinky up. I link mine with hers, and we press our thumbs together.

"Liv," Pó Po says, "you are worthy of love. Let people in. Your heart is stronger than you think. And always remember that I am so proud of you." She cradles my face in her hand and looks intensely into my eyes. In this simple act, it's as though she can sense all my worries and fears and wants and desires that are deeply embedded in me. "You were never, and will never be, a disappointment."

CHAPTER 18

It's ten minutes past 11:00 a.m., and Harper still hasn't arrived for her session. Is it possible I scared her off for good with Bennett or she already found someone using ZodiaCupid? Did I miss an email about her canceling? In a panic, I google *small business loans.* Dozens of links populate the page, and I scan over topics like fixed assets and working capital.

I log in to the online banking dashboard to check on Lunar Love's financial health. The numbers have dropped, even with the addition of Harper and a few others. Social media and the live podcast episode have drawn some attention, but they're still not converting enough clients.

I lower my head into my arms, racking my brain for ideas. I remember Pó Po's offer to loan Lunar Love part of her savings, but I can't accept that. There's something there, though. I log in to my own bank account and do some budgeting and calculations. If I significantly cut back on going out to eat, don't buy new clothes, and limit travel for the next few years, I could invest my own savings into the business and still be able to make rent on my apartment. Barely, but it's doable. It would be owner's equity. Not a *lot* of owner's equity, but enough to cover the past-due bills and the ones for next month.

I initiate a transfer and watch my personal savings drop down to a terrifying new low. I'm betting big on Lunar Love. I *should* put my money where my mouth is.

As I'm on the verge of having a full-blown panic attack, the front door swings open. Harper!

"I'm sorry I'm so late. My previous meeting ran long, but the good news is we locked in that client I was telling you about." Harper exhales a happy sigh as she settles into the chair in the session room.

After a flood of cancellations, I'm just thrilled she showed up at all. "Congrats! That's exciting."

"Their social media presence is not great right now, but we're going to turn it around. Speaking of, I noticed you joined the world of social media. Welcome! Your last tweet was great. I like that you're keeping the messages true to who you are as a business. Don't lose that."

"Thanks. Coming from you, that means a lot," I say, relieved on many different levels. We just need that content to result in sign-ups. "Let's start by talking about Bennett. I know you said on the phone that he's not what you're looking for. Can you elaborate on that? For my learning purposes." Saying his name out loud feels revealing, as though I may have said it too affectionately.

Harper adjusts the waistline of her jeans and props her left calf under her right thigh, getting comfortable before divulging her emotions.

"I understand why you paired me with him. He's confident,

opinionated, enjoys good food, and is easy to talk to," she reports.

I maintain a neutral expression. I've made out with one of my clients' matches. One of my clients' dates! The word *professional* doesn't exist in my vocabulary. I'm a complete fraud.

"But..." She trails off.

"But what?" I grip my pen tighter.

"He wouldn't stop talking about you!" Harper says with one raised eyebrow.

I wrinkle my nose. "I hope my being there didn't dominate the conversation. I shouldn't have shown up like that."

"No, I didn't mind that. I mean, he kept bringing you up in conversation. Whether he was aware of it, who knows, but he did."

"I'll have to discuss first-date etiquette with him," I mumble, scribbling into my notepad. "So just to confirm, you *don't* want another date with him?" I hold my breath in anticipation.

Harper grins. "You think I missed that last date on accident?"

I eye her doubtfully. "Did you not?"

"It's like I said last time, the matchmaker needs, well, a matchmaker," she says with a wink.

"I see." *I'm* the matchmaker here, but I can't be upset at a paying client.

"We grabbed lunch last week to work out some details. He had a whole plan. It was so sweet. I could tell there was something between you two at the dumpling festival," Harper says matter-of-factly.

"Oh, no," I say, shaking my head. My jaw clenches as I process what she's told me. Bennett maneuvered me to get what he wanted: a date. How else has he manipulated me?

"And here I was thinking you only did strictly compatible matches. Aren't you a Horse?"

I sit upright in my chair. "We do. Conflicting traits can pose real problems sometimes. A lot of misunderstandings, opposing opinions and values, qualities that might be endearing at first but end up being dealbreakers. Compatibility is tried and true. That doesn't mean perfect, because nothing is, but it's like mixing butter and sugar together for a cake. Incompatibility is like mixing butter and salt. Sure, someone might like that flavor combination, but when you eat enough of it, that cake's going to make you feel not so good," I say, starting to ramble. It's starting to get exhausting defending the core of our business that no one but me seems to care about anymore.

"Got it. At the end of the day, I want someone nice who I can go to Italy with and gorge on endless pounds of pasta together. Is that so much to ask?" Harper asks with a laugh.

I guess for her that nice, pasta-loving person won't be Bennett. A surge of relief runs through me.

"You and me both," I tell her. At the thought of pasta, my mental rolodex flips to Parker T., the Rooster I matched with on ZodiaCupid. He loves Italian food, and if he likes historical landmarks, then he probably enjoys traveling. The hours aren't great as a restaurant owner, though they're typically better than a chef's hours, so I won't rule him out. If Harper doesn't want Bennett, it's on to the next.

But Parker's a Rooster. If I can find out his birth hour, there might be a chance his ascendant aligns with Harper's Dragon sign. I'll message him on the app and find out, reveling in the irony of Lunar Love poaching ZodiaCupid's clients. That's what they get for invading our territory.

As soon as Harper leaves, I open ZodiaCupid and scroll through my matches until I find Parker's name. I start typing and hit Send on the message before overthinking it.

A light pink swipe-through instruction panel pops up with illustrated peonies in the background, catching me off guard. Bennett went through with gamifying the app. Despite our conversation at breakfast and his saying he wanted to rethink things, I guess I didn't make a convincing enough case to scrap the feature.

I hover over Bennett's profile, recollecting his peony count. How much higher is it now? I press my thumb to the screen and soak up the information that appears. Apparently much higher. My stomach tumbles over itself. Who else has he been seeing and talking to besides me? In this moment, the past becomes my present. I can't be hurt again. Not like this. Not by him. I'm nobody's pawn.

To take my mind off Bennett, I click into one of our most recent tweets to respond to a comment. One person tweets asking if he can change his sign to a Dragon because it sounds cooler. I type up a friendly response informing him that all clients must be their real sign in order to find true compatibility. We're not in the position to be turning paying clients away, but that's just ridiculous. I check the numbers and see that the latest moon song pairing has over three hundred retweets. As much as I try to push Bennett out, in the back of my head I can practically hear him gloating about how useful data is. In a message, someone asks what our process and rates are. It's small, but it's something.

I lean back in my chair, close my eyes, and listen to the sounds of Lunar Love. There's a low murmur outside from the afternoon crowds, sporadic creaks from the building, and the sound of my own heartbeat, which feels like it hasn't stopped racing since I took over the business.

The locals and tourists passing by in front of our window catch my eye, and I notice a woman's pastel lilac suit. Carol? Not today. Not now. But she's not alone. She comes bearing clients. Probably developers. I completely forgot to respond to her email. What else am I forgetting?

Carol strides down the path to Lunar Love. Her two clients catch up to her, the three of them walking side by side as Carol gestures excitedly at the building. I first notice red plastic glasses. Elmer? Is that Bennett next to him?

I jump up from my seat. Bennett's here. *Here.* At Lunar Love. The nerve of that man.

I open the door and stand with my hands on my hips, blocking the entryway. "Can I help you?" I direct my question to Bennett.

Bennett offers a firm smile. "Hey, sorry! Ignore us. We're leaving." He calls out to Carol and Elmer, "Hey! We're not going in there."

Carol waves her hand toward the building. "I emailed you last week that I was bringing clients by," she says to me, lugging the same bag, different color, up her arm. Poppy pops up from the depth of the purse and yips. "I never heard back from you but assumed it was okay. We won't be long."

To Bennett's credit, he actually looks annoyed. He could win an Academy Award for that level of commitment. "I didn't know this was the building she was talking about. We're on our way to the next one," he says to me. He's wearing a button-down with the sleeves rolled up, a business casual type of handsome.

As he leans in for a hug, I swing my arm around for a side pat, my brain fortunately taking over before my body has a chance to. By the way Bennett angles his body, I can tell it's awkward for both of us.

"Right," I say disbelievingly. "You just follow her around without asking any questions?"

"This was a last-minute addition," he says.

I don't know what to believe anymore. "A week is last-minute?"

"Elmer's in charge of coordinating the new office tours," he explains. "We have five that we're looking at, and this was on the way. I didn't know it was Lunar Love, I swear."

Carol taps her foot. "Well, fine, okay. Let's go to the next one, if you're sure. But this place is really special," she says, walking down the path away from our building. "We'll let you know if we change our mind."

Elmer pushes past Bennett. "I'd like to take a look," he says, his red glasses framing his smug eyes. "You came to our office to snoop around. Now it's our turn."

I wait for an explanation from Bennett.

"He wasn't too thrilled about learning who you really are," Bennett reveals in a low tone. "I honestly didn't know she was bringing us here."

I remind myself of the information I just learned. We're on my turf. I extend my arms out under Lunar Love's pink door-frame. No one's getting past me.

Elmer peeks around my head to see inside. "Those walls could be knocked down. There's so much potential!" he says like he's trying to be provocative.

Alisha pokes her head out of the back office. "We have

company, I see!" she says, strolling over to us. I drop one of my arms to let her pass. "Bennett up close in the flesh. Man, I wish Randall wasn't on lunch break so he could witness this."

Bennett extends a hand. "And you must be?"

Alisha purses her lips. "Olivia, glad you're speaking so highly of me," she says with mock annoyance. "I'm Alisha, Olivia's matchmaker-in-crime."

"Great to meet you," he says with a smile.

I shouldn't have filled Alisha in on everything because the look she gives me in front of Bennett is a clear giveaway. He notices, and a small laugh through his nose comes out.

"When was the last time that carpet was replaced?" Elmer asks, peeking through one of the windows.

"Oh, let's see," I say, pretending to take his question seriously, "sometime between the first moon landing and when the Spice Girls broke up."

Alisha grabs my arm. "Now that was a sad year."

Elmer rolls his eyes and continues to critique the space. "First thing I'd do is get rid of all the pink and red."

My jaw drops at his audacity. "Don't get too comfortable," I call out to Elmer with an edge in my voice. "We're not for sale." I look up at Bennett. "You know we're not for sale, right? Because we're definitely not for sale." My chest feels heavy with the pressure of feeling like Lunar Love is being kicked out both physically and digitally.

Bennett nods quickly. "I know that. Elmer, let's go. I'm sorry about all this."

"Since when did he become your business partner anyway?" I nod toward Elmer, who won't let up.

"He's not my business partner, but he does like to involve himself," Bennett says, shrugging. He leans over to whisper to me, "He's surprisingly ill-mannered for a Rabbit."

I resist laughing at his joke, forcing the corner of my lips down and out of a smile. I resume a stoic expression and assertive posture.

Alisha watches Elmer carefully. "You know, I may have a great match for him."

"Keep our clients away from him," I say sternly. "We have a reputation to maintain."

"I heard that!" Elmer says, finally breaking his gaze through the window.

"Okay, I'm in the middle of date planning. Fantastic meeting you, Bennett, or should I say B.O.B.?" Alisha says, winking at me before heading back to the office.

Bennett laughs as heat rises in my cheeks. "So you're telling people about me?" He takes a step closer.

I avoid making eye contact with him. It never ends well. "She helped me solidify the details of your date with Harper. She deserved context," I explain in a professional tone.

"I'll accept that," Bennett says.

"Clearly you're talking about me, too, but not in a good way," I say, nodding toward Elmer.

Bennett smiles, one corner of his mouth pulled higher. It's infuriating. "I save my best words for talking about you."

Internally, I roll my eyes and smile unconvincingly. After everything I learned today, he almost feels like a stranger. But then I think about the past few weeks and I've never felt closer to anyone.

"Hey, I don't know if you got the email about the Halloween

party ZodiaCupid is hosting on Saturday for all beta testers, but I'd love for you to be there," Bennett says. "Would that be weird?"

"I'll have to look at my calendar," I say coldly. I'm not in the mood to run into other women he might be going out on dates with. Somewhere along the way, we became too friendly. Lunar Love and ZodiaCupid are not friends. An alarm of panic rings through me when I remember that I agreed to call off our bet in a moment of passion. From now on, I need to only make important deals on solid ground.

"I really hope you'll be there. It's come-as-your-animal-sign."

"Cute," I say, unsmiling.

He leans over. "Is everything okay?"

I put on a happy face. "Fine. Everything's fine."

I gave up press, potential clients, and proving Lunar Love's efficacy for what? So that I could freely kiss my competitor? Was everything just an elaborate ruse? Worse, did I fall for it? He did work with Harper to manipulate the situation. To date me. So that he could prove me wrong? I don't know what to think or believe anymore. Especially now that Bennett is here in front of me, shopping for buildings— including ours—for his copycat business. But hey, *I'm totally fine.*

"Alrighty!" Carol sings from the end of the pathway. "Thanks a billion, Olivia. We'll be in touch."

"Nope," I call out after her.

"This is a fine place you got here," Elmer says. "Maybe I saw some documents through the window, maybe I didn't."

"Sorry again," Bennett mouths. "I hope I see you soon."

I walk him to the edge of the welcome mat. "We'll see. And

do me a favor and remind Carol that we are *not* for sale," I say, accentuating every last word.

I unconsciously slam the door shut, rattling a framed photo on the wall of me, Pó Po, and Auntie outside of Lucky Monkey Bakery. Our arms are wrapped around each other, and we're laughing. We all look so young, so happy, so innocent.

CHAPTER 19

I'm greeted on Saturday afternoon with a delivery to my apartment. I open the box to reveal a spooky chocolate cake for Halloween and a card with the words "No tricks here, just treats. Sorry for showing up on your pink doorstep like that. Hope to see you tonight. —Bennett."

I break off one of the chocolate gravestones and let it melt in my mouth. It's possible I'm being irrational about him influencing me, but I can't risk being hurt again. It's like Mom says, "Evidence is what matters, not speculation." As much as I don't want to go to the party, I need to know the truth.

Several hours later, I follow signs for ZodiaCupid's Halloween party and take the elevator up to the rooftop. With sweeping views of downtown LA and a glowing blue moon as the backdrop, the hunched plastic skeletons and spider-filled cobwebs strung throughout the space look spooky in a fun way.

Dressed as Rembrandt, I wear a vintage black cloak and beret that Pó Po was able to find in her boxes of old clothing, and I'm armed with a plastic painter's palette. The outfit wouldn't be complete without a stick-on mustache and mouche.

Around me, people dressed in skintight tiger costumes, snake-print jumpsuits, and Cupid outfits carry drinks and mingle. Michael Jackson's song "Thriller" blasts from a speaker near the bar. I scan the crowd for Bennett so I know the general vicinity to hang around.

I wind through people in animal costumes and walk toward a woman with long, wavy platinum-blond hair cascading down her back. The guy next to her in a chef's outfit lifts his toque and immediately I know it's Bennett from the way his hair falls. My palms break out in a light sweat at the sight of him.

My steps slow as I observe the situation. I take cover behind a witch's cauldron of punch bubbling over with dry ice fog. The woman with platinum hair smiles at something Bennett says and rests her hand on his shoulder. In my mind, I see his peony count number increasing. He's the start-up world's most eligible bachelor, after all. Why wouldn't he be dating other people? Other people clearly want to date him.

I crouch lower to get a better angle of him and the woman who's giving a solid A-effort to imitate Daenerys Targaryen, Mother of Dragons. She leans forward to better hear him and then laughs vivaciously at whatever it is he said that probably wasn't even funny.

I'm bumped from behind by a man circling the cauldron, and he almost knocks me off balance.

"Olivia?" a voice says.

I hold my beret to my head and angle my face up toward the stars. Standing over me is the host from our live panel interview.

"Marcus?"

Marcus waves from above. What was a stylish suit at the live podcast interview is replaced by a bright red bacon strip costume. His face appears through a cutout hole in one of the pink layers.

"Well, well, I didn't expect to see *you* here tonight," Marcus says. "Especially after everything with the wager. That's very big of you."

"It was a last-minute decision to come. Don't tell anyone you saw me," I instruct as I stand to face him.

"Are you meeting your date here?" he asks excitedly. "Or rather, your *love*." He squeals. "I can't believe ZodiaCupid actually worked. Secretly, I had my money on Lunar Love."

"Hold on." I smile to be polite but am downright confused. "What do you mean, ZodiaCupid worked? And did you say love?"

"We were notified yesterday that a winner had been established. You both went on dates, and apparently, *you* fell in love. Congrats!" Marcus says with a laugh.

The pieces fall into place. Finally, I have clarity. I've been played.

"I'm not . . . I can't be in love," I stammer.

Marcus grins. "You've got the glow of a woman in love."

Never in my life have I hated a piece of bacon more. My thoughts race in every direction as Stevie Wonder's "Superstition" flows from the speakers. I abandon Marcus mid-sentence and make a beeline for Bennett.

"Who do you think you are?" I blurt out, interrupting his conversation with one of his probably many women.

The Mother of Dragons awkwardly backs away.

Bennett's caught off guard when he sees me, his eyes widening. "Olivia!"

I should've trusted myself. Of course he's exactly who I thought he would be.

"I'm leaving," I say, gathering the fabric of my cloak and turning to go. I push through a group of partygoers in uninspired dog ear headbands.

"Wait," Bennett calls out. He catches up to me faster than I expected. "Slow down. I'm so glad you made it." He bends down to hug me, and my cheek smushes into the shoulder of his chef jacket. Sweat forms on my lower back, and I'm thankful my perspiration won't be visible through the cloak.

"I'm sure you are," I say. "I'm going now, so you and your dragon lady can get back to your date, or whatever this is."

"Our what?" he asks, his eyebrows scrunched. "We're not on a date. I don't even know who that was."

"Says the man with the high peony count. Looks like you gamified, after all."

"Uh, what? You know my peony count is high because my profile is how we test features. You're the only peony for me." His look of excitement to see me turns to confusion.

I scoff. "How can I believe that?"

He frowns. "We spent a lot of time and money building the gamification feature. We at the very least had to try it. I owe that to my team."

"I had a long talk with Harper and heard about your plan to manipulate me," I say. My heart thumps wildly inside my chest. How could I have let this happen? I can't fall for a Rat. It won't end well, it never does.

Bennett thinks for a moment. "Manipulate you? I wanted to spend more time with you. That's the only reason why I worked with her. I thought we had a good time."

I laugh bitterly. "You can manipulate numbers all you want, but you shouldn't manipulate people."

Bennett gently guides me to the side and out of earshot from an eavesdropping Easter Bunny. We tuck under an arch of plastic skulls while a group of Monkeys watches us from the dessert table.

"I have explanations for everything but you're not listening," Bennett says, getting visibly frustrated. "You did some things for us to meet. I did some things for us to keep seeing each other. Our efforts brought and kept us together. I wasn't trying to work you over or sabotage you. Never have, never will. And there's definitely no one else."

I hear him, but his words aren't convincing me otherwise. "This isn't a situation that you can handle or control," I inform him.

"I'm not trying to control you," he says. "Though that's perfect for you of all people to say that. You think you can control who loves who and the outcome."

"I just want people to be happy. Oh, and you haven't heard the best part yet. Yesterday, you go and tell Marcus that *I'm* the one who fell in love and that Lunar Love lost." I clap a hand against my palette. "Power play. Very nice. Kick the small, old, traditional, boring matchmaking business while it's already down and going under."

Bennett holds his toque against his chest. "I did no such thing. I haven't talked to Marcus since our panel."

I cough out a laugh at his denial. "Bullshit. I just saw him, and he told me everything." I'm such a fool! On what planet did I think being with Bennett and running Lunar Love could work?

Bennett thinks for a moment and looks like he has a realization. "Elmer," he mumbles. "Elmer must've told him. He's probably still feeling resentful for being tricked."

I shake my head. "Everything's Elmer's fault, isn't it? Even though it's your business. We had a pact. And we called the bet off! There wasn't supposed to be a winner."

"And I honored that. I don't care about the wager," he says, his voice rough. "I care about you. I want to be with you. If I haven't made that obvious enough, I'm sorry."

"Of course you don't care about the wager. You don't need it! Your business is going to be fine. I, on the other hand, needed those clients. I gave up those clients for you. Well, congratulations," I say sadly. "We're at the end of the month, so I guess you also win the article and the podcast episode. Marcus is probably already making plans for it."

We step closer to let someone dressed as a parrot pass by. "Parrots aren't in the zodiac, you know!" I call out after her. I survey the scene around us, shaking my head.

Bennett steps sideways to block my view of the rainbow-colored bird-person. "I thought agreeing to the wager would show you that we can both coexist as businesses; that our companies offer different things for different people," he says.

"Coexisting is out of the question. You were the one who turned down my pó po's matchmaking efforts. Yet now you want to be together? Please."

A strand of loose hair falls across his forehead. "I was focused on building ZodiaCupid. Can you blame me?"

"And you did. You built ZodiaCupid. Once we're officially

out of business, you'll be able to proudly say that you destroyed Lunar Love."

"I don't want Lunar Love to go out of business," Bennett says defensively. He shifts his footing, and a clip-on rat tail swings around his leg. "You know that's not why I started ZodiaCupid." His eyes plead with me, and my heart flip-flops back and forth disloyally. This is what happens when I become too attached, too emotional.

I straighten my shoulders and steady my voice. "You're my rival, nemesis, competitor...take your pick. I can't believe I ever trusted you and...your stupid little Rat chef outfit."

"Hey! Don't disrespect Ratatouille like that," Bennett says, tucking his tail back behind him. "He may have been a rodent, but he had big dreams. In fact, he—never mind," he says when he sees my serious face.

Bennett's head is tilted to the side, his jaw clenched. He's uncomfortable.

"Seeing me was probably just some way of collecting data points on how long it would take for me to fall for you," I say, adjusting the stick-on mustache that has slipped down over my lip.

"All of that is not true. Please, Olivia. Let's just forget about this stupid wager. I want to be with you. Let's not fight."

When Bennett's this close, I can't stop myself from thinking about the way he smells. His smile. His lips. I can still feel his arms wrapped around my waist pulling me into him. My heart aches at the memory. But there's no use. It's too late.

I look at the ground. "It's pointless," I say, my sadness crystallizing into something firmer. How could I have let my guard down? "Honestly, what's the use? All roads lead to moments like this. I don't make the rules."

"Yet you're so good at enforcing them," Bennett says.

"We believe in different things," I say.

"You have this idea in your head that we're incompatible, but I disagree," Bennett urges in a low voice. "I think that people can surprise you. That's what love is about. That's what the zodiac you've worked to promote your entire life is about."

"You don't get to tell me what the zodiac, love, or my life is about."

Bennett rubs his hand against his forehead. "Do you really think I started ZodiaCupid to put Lunar Love out of business? Do I come off as that terrible of a person to you? That I'm single-handedly trying to destroy the zodiac itself?"

"I don't know what your scheme is!" I shout-whisper defensively. "You're such a Rat! I figured you out early on, and I should've known I'd be right. You take other people's ideas to get a free ride, you try to please everyone so you're not rejected by anyone, you're dishonest and secretive, and you mislead for your own advantage."

As soon as the words come out, I regret them.

Bennett looks at me stunned and quiet, any trace of a smile wiped clean from his face. "Maybe you're right," he says dejectedly. "I've been trying to figure out who I am for a long time, and you figured it out after knowing me for what, a month? You're never going to trust me, are you?"

Trusting is a dangerous game, especially when it comes to the rules of compatibility. I've already bent those rules too much. We're incompatible, and I should never have let myself get this far with him. I bite my lip.

Bennett gives a small, humorless laugh, the upturned crease next to his typically happy hazel eyes nonexistent. "I'm not your ex-boyfriend, Olivia. I'm not going to leave you or hurt you. I may not be a compatible animal sign, but I'm definitely not him," he says, looking pained.

"Neither of us should have to change who we are to be together," I say, trying to swallow the aching. "And I don't think either of us can stand another heartbreak."

Bennett's face clouds over with hurt. "No one's asking you to change. You speak so highly of emotion and human connection, yet here I am trying, and you're not willing to see it from another perspective. You're being so damn stubborn. We've been getting along, despite our so-called incompatibility, despite our jobs."

"Lunar Love isn't a job. It's my life."

"Isn't what we feel real? Because it's real for me." He takes a step closer and reaches for my hand. "Can't you give us a chance? I don't want to lose you."

"This way you won't," I tell him.

I stare at Bennett as all my conflicting emotions wear me down. For a fleeting moment when our hands touch, a life together feels possible. But it's an illusion. We were born when we were born. We are what we are.

"I'm sorry. I just...can't." I extract my hand from his and turn to leave, disappearing into the herd of animals.

A throbbing sting crawls its way up the back of my throat, working its way to my eyes. Tears stream down my cheeks and onto the sticky ground, carrying my mustache with it.

CHAPTER 20

The sun slowly appears over the horizon, its rays poking up from behind the jagged hills. I push my sunglasses up the bridge of my nose to cover my puffy eyes from a week of on-and-off crying. Bennett and I are better off without each other. Our traits won't clash to the point of destruction, and he won't have to lose someone again. Neither will I.

I find Alisha, who's graciously agreed to join me this morning, at the bottom of the trail stretching out her quad muscles. Even at 6:00 a.m., she looks stylish in her leopard high-waisted leggings and crop top.

"Ready?" I ask.

Alisha stands with her hands placed firmly on her hips and nods begrudgingly.

We begin our journey up the path toward the Griffith Observatory, home to space and science exhibits and telescopes that transport visitors to the cosmos. Used as the backdrop for many Hollywood movies, Griffith Observatory is a white concrete structure topped with penny-colored domes resting on the slope of Mount Hollywood in Griffith Park. In the morning light, the cobalt blues and dusty purples of the park glow.

"I don't know how you got me to do this. Thank god for gel undereye patches. You've got to try this new brand I found. My eyebags look nonexistent, right?" she says.

All week, she's tried to distract me from thinking about Bennett. Her energy is usually contagious, but as of late, it hasn't quite caught on.

"Like it was fifty percent off at Chanel. Not a bag in sight," I deadpan.

Alisha laughs. "Oh, sweetie. As if Chanel would ever have a sale." She stares up at the mountain with a look of dread. "You promise the view at the top will be Instagram-worthy?"

"It's worth the burn," I assure her.

We follow the zigzags of the well-worn path, nodding to fellow early birds getting their heart rates up. Alisha breathes heavily and stays a few steps behind me. We take a few breaks around every other bend so her heart doesn't "pop."

I'm quiet for the first half up the mountain, trying to sweat out any remaining tears still inside of me. It's for the best, I repeat to myself. There's a Bennett-sized hole that can't be patched up. I'm walking at a snail's pace, trying to work through my thoughts while stepping one foot in front of the other.

"Liv," Alisha starts, "we can head back down if you're not up to this."

"I can do this," I say, pushing through the hurt. "I know I'm no fun to be around right now."

We pass a girl using her phone. On her screen is a monkey icon. "Give me a break!" I shout. "We're on a mountain. This is a ZodiaCupid-free zone."

The girl glances up and shoots me a dirty look.

I stand on my toes to get a better look at her screen. "You're a beta tester, though? On a scale of Strongly Dislike to Absolutely Despise, how much do you hate the app so far?"

Alisha grabs my arm and pulls me away from the hiker. "Sorry! Have a lovely day!" she calls out to the girl, who's already started jogging away from us.

"You're scaring innocent hikers," Alisha says, tugging me along.

"If they're using ZodiaCupid, they're not so innocent," I mumble.

We find a spot on a bench just below the Observatory, overlooking the city, and sit for a water break. I stretch my legs out in front of me, recalling out of nowhere that this is where Bennett has his Shoot for the Stars volunteering every week.

A more serious look settles on Alisha's face. "You know I love you. And I love Lunar Love," she says. Then in a more playful tone, she adds, "But damn, you are stubborn."

A laugh escapes me.

"Joining your family's business was the best thing I've ever done. Helping people find love is truly a dream job," she adds.

I nod. "You've made Lunar Love better."

"Thank you. We always talk about how people are complex and that their signs aren't the only thing that makes them who they are," she says. "Right?"

"It's true," I agree. "Humans are more complicated."

"I've never seen you be so die-hard about compatibility until your last breakup. And I don't only mean the one with your ex-boyfriend."

"And the one time I dated someone incompatible, well, we

know what happened," I say defensively. "Since I was a kid, I've been learning about and promoting compatibility."

"But not like this." Alisha tugs at her leggings. "I know you're the matchmaker who can't be matched, but what if you're the only one who believes that?"

I draw circles in the dirt with the tip of my shoe and stay quiet.

"What happened is in the past, but it's very much affecting your present and future," Alisha says. "It seems to me you're clinging to the idea of compatibility because you're scared. You're scared that you'll lose someone you love again, and that by not honoring the traditional way of matchmaking, you'll also lose Lunar Love."

"I've lost love before," I say, "but I don't think I could bear losing Lunar Love."

"No one doubted your ability to matchmake after what happened with your ex and friend. So what if you dated an animal sign that didn't pair well with yours? You could've had the same result even if he were compatible."

"But when I doubted my beliefs, that happened. It's better to not question them anymore," I say. I distanced myself to avoid feeling the way I feel right now. So if I still feel like this, what was it all for?

"So you want to stay on the safe path," Alisha says, air quoting *safe*. "You're not someone who sits back idly while others take risks. You go after what you want. You always have. Just as you'd do everything you could to save Lunar Love, why wouldn't you do everything you could to be happy?"

Her words cut to the core. I'll risk everything I have for Lunar Love, for clients, for family, but not for myself.

Alisha smiles. "Remember the woman who came in because

her parents sent her to us when they discovered that the guy on her screensaver was Henry Golding, and her engagement ring was actually costume jewelry? You worked day and night, went around town on Singles Scoutings, and thought through different trait matchups to find her someone to bring home for Lunar New Year. You wanted their relationship to be more than that, though."

For the first time all week, I feel my cheeks widen in a smile. "She had to want to find love for the right reasons. I still remember her face when I told her we weren't a rent-a-boyfriend agency."

"Exactly." Alisha nods, her high ponytail swinging from side to side. "You worked with her, coached her, taught her. And she eventually came around to wanting love for herself, not for her family's sake."

I nod. "You're right."

"You work hard to put love out into the world. And your method works." She pulls her phone from her waist pack and taps into Twitter. "Look, two of your clients posted using the #LoveInTheMoonlight hashtag."

Two smiling faces shine back at me, along with a few nice words about us. A surge of promise jolts through my veins. What was once an idea is now a living concept out in the world. Two strangers were brought together because of Lunar Love.

"But your method is also not the law," she continues. "I can't tell you what to do. No one can. Maybe think of yourself as your own client. Maybe you'd be telling her something different than what you're telling yourself."

I consider her words. "Thank you," I say, leaning over for a hug. "I may have been slightly irrational."

We sit quietly for a few minutes. "You know, Hugh Grant and Colin Firth are both Year of the Rat," Alisha offers, breaking the silence.

"That changes everything," I joke.

"There's also something else I wanted to show you," Alisha says, scrolling through her emails.

"We're supposed to be disconnected right now. Immersed in nature," I say.

"The word *disconnected* is not in my vocabulary. This morning, my friend sent me a link to the latest *Dating in La La Land* episode. Lunar Love gets a shout-out at eight minutes and twenty seconds." Alisha looks nervous when she shows me her screen. "It's the podcast episode with Bennett," she says. "Do you want to listen?"

My heart starts pounding in my ears. It's *the* podcast episode. The one we wagered on. The one that I lost.

Alisha already has the podcast launched on her phone. She slides to the specific time in the episode and hovers her finger over the Play button.

"Play it," I say, bracing myself. If he has something to say about Lunar Love, I need to know what it is.

My throat tightens when the sound of Bennett's voice fills the air.

"The only reason I'm on this podcast is because of a silly wager," Bennett says. "But—"

Marcus's voice interjects. "That's episode thirteen, for those who want more context. I'll link to it in the program notes. Please, continue."

By the way Bennett clears his throat, I can tell he's annoyed. "As I was saying, I'm here because of three very important women who paved the way for a business like mine to even exist. And I'm not talking about apps. I mean Chinese zodiac matchmaking. In 1970, a woman named June Huang started Lunar Love, a matchmaking company here in Los Angeles, and she built it up to be one of the most special matchmaking businesses that exists today."

My nose and eyes sting as I hold back tears.

"Lunar Love is truly one-of-a-kind," Bennett continues. "I honestly don't consider ZodiaCupid to be their competition. They're in a league of their own. June was my inspiration, and I'm lucky to have learned a lot from her. Over the years, one of June's daughters took over, and now, one of June's grand-daughters, Olivia, is in charge. I consider myself lucky to have also learned a lot from Olivia, too. She was actually supposed to be on this podcast today instead of me. In no way did I win this wager. In fact, I lost pretty badly."

"How so?" Marcus asks.

There's a long pause. "I fell in love," Bennett finally says.

I gasp, my breathing becoming faster. I bite my lip and lean closer to listen.

"So, per the terms of the agreement," he adds, "Lunar Love should get the social media placement and new clients. They deserve it. I met an amazing woman because of them. I may not be what she's looking for, but if I'm lucky enough to have a second chance, I won't mess it up. Someone much smarter than me once told me, if it's something that you feel and experience, that makes it real. What I feel, it's real."

Tears prick my eyes. "You didn't think you should lead with this?" I ask Alisha.

"I had to let you get there on your own first," she says. Alisha hits Pause and grabs for my hand. "He really sounds like he misses you. What do you feel?"

"That it's real," I say softly.

My phone buzzes with a ZodiaCupid notification with a message from Parker. He's open to talking, even though he chose to use ZodiaCupid for whatever reason in the first place. He didn't flat out reject Lunar Love. Maybe he's even into the zodiac, and at the end of the day, isn't that the type of excitement we're trying to instill in our clients?

I look out over Los Angeles as the city starts to wake up for the day. It's the city where people come to make their dreams come true. Where anything feels possible. The place where anyone can freely reinvent themselves over and over again. The town where competition is fierce, but ambition is fiercer. Competition doesn't stop people from chasing after what they want. It's not going to stop me, either.

Even Lunar Love is in its own process of reinvention. Maybe it's not completely unreasonable to think that the merging of traditional and modern can actually do some good in the world.

"I have to go," I say, checking the time on my phone. I take off running down the mountain. I have a pitch to get to.

CHAPTER 21

I arrive at the Pitch IRL venue in downtown LA to find Bennett. The venue is small enough where every angle is considered a good seat. On the large screen behind the stage, I see the ZodiaCupid logo displayed. Perfect. I made it just in time to catch Bennett in the middle of his pitch.

Up on stage, Bennett paces back and forth. He looks nervous. This isn't what I expected when I envisioned him pitching all his past businesses. As he starts to describe ZodiaCupid, he fumbles over data and statistics. He takes a second to drink water.

I approach the stage looking sweaty and disheveled in my leggings and oversized T-shirt. When Bennett places the cup down and looks up, I'm able to catch his eye. I give him a small wave and mouth the words "From the heart," pointing to the left side of my chest. He returns the smile and quickly inhales before letting out a long breath.

"People are more than just line items in an Excel spreadsheet," Bennett says. He stands up straighter, his grip on his notecards relaxing. The confidence that was lacking in his voice before is now present and commanding.

"There's no algorithm in the world that can capture what it's like to laugh uncontrollably with the person you love or that feeling when you're sitting next to someone for the first time at a movie and wondering if they want to hold your hand just like you do," he says, taking deliberate pauses and steps across the stage. "Or when you bomb so badly on a date but don't care because every second you spend with them is more important than any second you had without them."

Just when I think he's finished, he looks up at me and dives into why he started ZodiaCupid. He shares a condensed version of the story he told me about finding his mother's journals, and how his parents were mismatched yet perfectly matched, and the importance of discovering your culture no matter what age you are. It's when he speaks from the heart that I notice the young audience shifting in their seats and focusing on him instead of on their phones.

He hits his stride and returns to the data and statistics. He discusses the beta version of the app, who they've been able to hire with savings, their marketing plan and how the strategy has been working, estimated expenses and anticipated revenue, and potential user numbers post-beta. At first, he captured their hearts— a feeling I know well—and then he captured their wallets.

As I watch him in his element, I think about all the ways that online dating has benefited me. While Lunar Love lost clients, it made me figure out how to be smarter about the business and our offerings. Without the app, I may never have found Parker to match with Harper. Without ZodiaCupid, I may never have found Bennett.

On my phone, I see my dad's name light up the screen. I decide to call him back after the pitch, letting his call go to voicemail. When he calls a second time in a row, I can't ignore it.

"Hello?" I whisper, ducking out of the audience and into the lobby.

"Hey sweetie," Dad says quietly. "Where are you? Can you talk?"

Through the windows, I watch as Bennett speaks animatedly. The crowd loves him.

"I'm actually in the middle of something."

"Would you be able to get out of it and come home?" he asks.

"Why? What happened?" I ask, my tone more urgent. "Can you tell me now?"

Dad clears his throat. "I hate to tell you over the phone..." I sense a shift in his voice. I press the phone harder against my ear and search for a private corner.

"Dad, what is it?"

"Pó Po passed away in her sleep last night," he says sadly.

Everything goes quiet. People in my line of sight blur. I freeze in place but the room feels like it's spinning around me. A hollow silence hangs between us as I process what I've just heard.

"It was very unexpected," Dad continues. "I'm afraid I don't have good news to follow this up with. Are you there?"

"Nn-hnn," I mumble, half listening. My dry throat and eyes burn. "She seemed fine." My mind jumps to when she fell into the car, triggering a reminder of her feeling tired when we made dumplings. My pulse races. How could I not have seen that she wasn't well? "Wasn't she?"

"Honestly, we don't know. The Huang women have always

put on a strong face. If she was sick, she never let on how bad it was," he says.

I lean back against the poster-covered wall and curl forward, tears streaming down my cheeks onto my leggings. Everything in my body stings. "How are Mom and Auntie? Does Nina know?" I manage to ask. My heart feels like it's going to climb its way up my throat and out of my body.

"They're being practical about it all. I've been delegated to making calls. The paramedics came this morning. We don't know what happened yet."

I nod, even though he can't see me. Remaining calm is Mom's specialty. My theory is that it comes from her years of lawyering—*If I let myself feel all the emotions I want to feel working in this legal system, I'd never make it through the day*—and being raised by Pó Po, the most practical of them all—*Everything comes to an end. That's life!*

"I'll come over in a bit," I say, dazed.

When Dad and I hang up, I bury my face in my hands and sob, not caring who's watching. Pó Po can't be gone.

After one last look at Bennett on stage, I head to the only place that can provide real comfort right now.

I push forward on the door of Lucky Monkey as I've done day after day after day, only to remember I have to pull. The door feels heavier. While normally butter and sugar welcome me in, today I don't smell anything. I wind my way past browsing customers to the back counter and find Mae Yí-Pó shuffling back and forth. I can tell by the look on her face that she already knows.

"Olivia," Mae Yí-Pó says. She extends her arms, and I bend down, letting myself be cocooned in her embrace. I squeeze my eyes shut to prevent tears from leaking out onto her shoulder, but no luck.

"I can't believe it," I say, sniffling.

Mae Yí-Pó holds me as my tears cascade down my cheeks. She gently pushes me back, holding me by the shoulders. "Come with me," she says.

I follow her to the back office of the bakery where there's another person sitting in a chair. My steps slow as I process who's in front of me. She must've heard about Pó Po from her mom, who's close friends with Auntie.

"Colette?" I whisper. "What are you doing here?"

Colette jumps up from her seat and takes a step toward me before stopping herself. She looks exactly the same as she did three years ago but has longer hair. People confused her, Nina, and me for triplets. We all may be mixed-race Chinese American, but we don't look the same.

"Hi, Olivia. I heard about Pó Po. I'm so sorry," Colette says sadly.

Mae Yí-Pó clears another chair covered in aprons and papers. "Please, both of you sit," she directs to us both. "I'll be back in a second."

I walk past Colette and take a seat on the edge of the chair next to hers as Mae Yí-Pó leaves the room and quietly closes the door behind her.

"When did you get back in town?" I finally ask.

"Five months ago. I was in New York City for the past few years after..." She trails off.

I twist my ring. "How'd you find me?"

"When my mom told me the news, I had a sneaky suspicion you'd come here. It has always been our safe place," she says. "I meant to get in touch earlier, but I wasn't sure how. Then I saw you at that baking class, and you totally ditched."

An unexpected laugh slips out at the thought. "I didn't. My date slipped," I respond, surprising myself by how natural our interaction feels. It's as though no time had passed since we last saw each other.

Colette's eyes widen, her mascaraed eyelashes framing her light brown eyes. "You have a new boyfriend? I...that makes me so happy to hear, knowing that you didn't let your ex ruin love for you."

Before I can correct her, she adds, "I saw the recent press on Lunar Love. You're in charge now. That's amazing. It's what you always wanted."

"It is. I am. I learned a lot ever since..." I start.

"About that," she says, adjusting her position toward me. She crosses one leg over the other, her bare knees peeking through the rips in her baggy Levi's. "I owe you an apology."

"You—wait, what?" I say, stunned. "It's me who owes you an apology. I hurt you with that incompatible match. I made you leave LA. I'm so sorry I messed up. I will always regret my mistake."

Colette sweeps her long bangs to the side and shakes her head. "Mistake? Are you kidding? You were just doing what you thought was right. If there's anyone to blame, it's the men who we thought we could trust. It wasn't your fault. But I'm sorry I cut off communication. I thought you were mad at me for the match not working out and for disgracing Lunar Love and you and Pó Po. I couldn't face you. I couldn't handle the embarrassment."

I huff out in disbelief. "Never once was I upset with you for either of those things."

Colette laughs humorlessly. "You were going through your own stuff, and I should've been there for you instead of running away. But I'm here now. And I'm not going anywhere."

"I'm not going anywhere, either," I say. Colette pulls me in for a hug, and I soak her oversized sweater with new tears.

There's a light knock on the door, and Mae Yí-Pó pokes her head in. Seeing her sends me into another sob.

"What am I going to do without Pó Po?" I ask, hunching forward on my knees. The pit in my stomach grows. "What will happen to Lunar Love? I don't know how to do this without her."

"Too many questions." Mae Yí-Pó sits across from us in her own chair. "You're going to keep doing what you're doing. She prepared you for this moment. You already have everything you need. I know your pain right now feels unbearable, but the last thing Pó Po would've wanted was for you to be sad."

"How can I not be?" I weep. Colette hands me a tissue from Mae Yí-Pó's desk.

"She lived to be ninety years old! That's worth celebrating!" Mae Yí-Pó says in a more optimistic tone.

"That sounds so . . . cheery," I say between sniffles.

"She hit a longevity milestone most of us could only hope for. The long, full life she lived is worth being happy about. I know that's how she felt about it." A small smile spreads across Mae Yí-Pó's face. "By no means was she perfect, but she was as close as one could come. Her life is worth celebrating."

"I never thought about it like that," I say, more tears pricking the back of my eyes. "I can't stand the thought of her suffering alone."

"Oh, honey." Mae Yí-Pó reaches over and grabs my hand. "She

never felt like she was doing anything alone. She loved many and was loved by many. Your Pó Po was never one to make things about herself. She knew that if you were too busy worrying about her, you wouldn't have been able to worry about yourself. And she cared for her family more than anything else in this world. It would've destroyed her more to see you all fuss over her."

"I just..." I trail off. "I didn't get to say goodbye."

"Because it's not goodbye," Mae Yí-Pó says. "This feels like an impossible loss. It will for a while. But you'll soon learn that this isn't the end. We take care of our ancestors when they're gone, and while that doesn't bring them back here to us, we become connected to them in a different way."

I look over at Colette, who nods along with me, even though we seem to have no clue what she means. At this point, I'll believe anything if it means I can be close to Pó Po.

"I have an idea." Mae Yí-Pó stands and reaches for three aprons, handing us each one. "Let's bake," she says reassuringly.

"Now?" I ask.

Mae Yí-Pó sharply nods. "Right now. Like we used to."

I feel the tension melting out of my shoulders. "Okay."

"Let's do it," Colette says as she sweeps her dark brown hair into a low ponytail.

Mae Yí-Pó, Colette, and I sift flour, whisk sugar into yolks, and whip egg whites into stiff peaks. It's a dreamlike feeling that brings me back to when we were kids.

"The secret to the Swiss roll's fluffy sponge cake is how gentle you are with adding the egg whites into the mixture," she says, delicately using her spatula to scrape the sides of the bowl and fold the airy peaks over themselves. "Don't overdo it."

I watch her skilled movements, allowing myself to get lost in the soft folds of batter. She pours the mixture into a parchment-lined baking pan and slides the tray into the oven. While the cake bakes, we make the filling.

"Do you remember the first time I taught you how to bake?" Mae Yí-Pó shouts out to me as she pulls heavy whipping cream from the walk-in fridge.

"Barely. That was so long ago," I say. "Do you?"

Mae Yí-Pó nods as she mixes cream and sugar together. "You were so bored waiting around at Lunar Love for your Pó Po and Auntie. You told me that they allowed you to come here, when instead you had actually just left to do your own thing." She laughs.

I smile. "Sounds about right."

"Your Pó Po called to make sure you got here safely."

"How'd she know I'd come here?"

"Because she knew you," Mae Yí-Pó says kindly.

"I guess some things never change," I say, shaking my head with a laugh.

Colette laughs along with me as she opens the oven door. "This is ready," she says, removing a clean toothpick from the center of the cake.

"She waited all afternoon until you came back on your own time," Mae Yí-Pó explains, lifting the sheet tray out of the oven with mitts.

"Was she mad that I had just disappeared?" I ask, the smell of vanilla permeating the air.

Mae Yí-Pó waves her hands. "She could never stay mad at you for long. You'd come sometimes, too, Colette."

"What did we love making most?" Colette asks.

"Swiss rolls," Mae Yí-Pó says with a wink. "You always

wanted to make an entire roll to bring back to your family. Your Pó Po said it was the best cake she had ever eaten."

After letting the cake cool slightly, Mae Yí-Pó delicately pushes the warm cake into a parchment-covered log. "It's all about the pre-roll," she says, tiptoeing her fingers skillfully along the edges. "This gives the cake its shape so that when it cools, it's still flexible."

"So that's the secret," I mumble. "I could never get that right."

"It just requires a little guidance, patience, and a light touch," Mae Yí-Pó replies.

While we wait for the cake to drop in temperature, we fall into silence, moving around one another as we wash the workspace clean with damp rags. Once the drips of batter have been wiped from the counters and the mixing bowls and testing spoons are loaded into the dishwasher, we're ready to fill and reroll.

I smile to myself about the resurfaced memories as I spread lightly sweet filling over the golden center. The edges of the cake slightly curl, the parchment paper crinkled beneath it.

"All yours," Mae Yí-Pó says, gesturing for me to do the final roll.

I slowly turn the cake onto itself as filling spills out over the spiraled edges. Colette sprinkles our creation with powdered sugar, and Mae Yí-Pó cuts the treat into slices.

"To June Huang," Mae Yí-Pó says. We take bites of the Swiss roll. "Mmm."

"These are always so much better right out of the oven," Colette says between mouthfuls.

The airy cake comforts me. "It's the best one yet. Do you think Pó Po would like it?" I ask.

Mae Yí-Pó takes a second bite. "She'd absolutely love it,"

she says, wrapping her arm around me. "Never forget that, no matter what happens, your Pó Po is watching over you, just like she always has, and she's very proud of you, just as she always has been."

I slowly nod to acknowledge Mae Yí-Pó and what she's saying. The creamy Swiss roll filling coats my tongue as I swallow down a fresh batch of tears.

CHAPTER 22

"She wants it to be what?" Nina asks, sounding as shocked, sad, and defeated as everyone else. She and Asher have joined us at Mom and Dad's house, having been able to cancel their honeymoon with a partial refund.

We're in the thick of coordinating Pó Po's funeral with Uncle Rupert on speakerphone contributing his thoughts. It's been a few days since Pó Po passed but there's a lot of planning to do.

"Fun," Mom says. "Her words."

In the kitchen, I skin an apple pear and slice it, dividing the halves into quarters, the quarters into smaller pieces. I set the bowl of fruit and a handful of forks on the table when Auntie joins us bearing two bouquets and a pastry box.

"Mae Yí-Pó dropped by. This one's for the family," Auntie says, placing one flower-filled vase on the kitchen counter. "And these are for you. Apparently someone came by the bakery to see if Mae Yí-Pó could get these to you."

Auntie gives me a wink as she hands me a vase stuffed with pink peonies and the box.

I tentatively accept them.

"It's from Asshole, isn't it?" Nina murmurs, wiggling her eyebrows.

"It's probably from Alisha and Randall or something," I murmur, even when I know it isn't. Alisha and Randall brought flowers over yesterday.

I carry the flowers and box to the counter and pluck out the tucked-in card.

Olivia—I'm very sorry to hear about your Pó Po. I know they can't do much, but I hope these flowers and Swiss rolls (vanilla only, of course) will help provide the slightest bit of comfort. —Bennett

I dig my fingernails into my palm. After pushing him away, Bennett still has the heart to do this. A twinge of regret and guilt forms inside of me. We didn't get to talk at the pitch, but he saw that I was there. I trace my thumb over his name and then tuck the note into my pocket and return to the table with the rolls.

My mom lifts a piece of paper filled with instructions from Pó Po on how she wanted her funeral to happen. In addition to sketching out a loose timeline, she had three requirements: the funeral needs to be on an auspicious day, she gets to choose most of her paper funeral offerings, and it should be a celebration of her life, which in Pó Po speak means "fun and magical."

"Mom made it clear in her letter that she didn't want everyone to be so sad, Rupert. I think we should honor it," my mother says into the phone set in the center of the table. "She's had her share of hardship during her life. There will still be traditional elements. This is Mom we're talking about."

"Okay, okay. Let's do it her way," Uncle Rupert agrees.

"Olivia, you're in charge of figuring out the music," Mom tells me.

"The noise signifies the end of the ceremony and the moment for lowering the casket," Auntie clarifies. "The music has to be loud enough to frighten away spirits and ghosts."

"I saw in a movie once that out-of-work actors are paid to cry loudly at funerals?" Asher asks. "Is that true?"

"Having someone else loudly crying encourages others to shed more tears, since by that point, they've already grieved so much. Traditionally, a lack of tears at funerals makes it look like the deceased wasn't loved, and this disgraces the family," Auntie answers. "But funerals are starting to become simpler and more modern."

I only need to think for a moment before I know. "A saxophone. She always loved the sound because it reminded her of Paris."

Auntie and Mom nod in approval.

"How appropriate!" Uncle Rupert says over the speaker. "Here's a bone to chew on: Should we hire a magician?"

We look around at one another.

"She wants it to be magical, doesn't she?" he adds.

"I think that's exactly what she would've wanted," I say, breaking the silence.

On the auspicious evening of the funeral, family and friends gather to wish Pó Po a safe journey into the afterlife. There are more than one hundred guests in attendance, everyone wearing various shades of white and cream. In what seems like minutes, the one hundred guests grow to what looks like a thousand, with a line of people forming outside waiting to come in and find their seats.

The magician Pó Po matchmade years ago jumped at the opportunity to take part. He quietly performs a dialed-down act in the corner of the chapel next to the casket. He reaches into the arm of his jacket and reveals a single white chrysanthemum. He does this one by one, handing everyone in the room a flower.

"Pó Po really would have loved this," Mom whispers next to me.

"I wish she could've been here to see it," I whisper back.

I take in the white streamers and silver balloons filling up the space. The room looks more like her ninetieth-birthday party, just as she wanted it to. I turn a hard candy with my tongue, the sugar dissolving slowly.

"The bitterness of the day is counteracted with the sweetness of the candy," Auntie explained to me at some point in the past week.

I sneak a few more pieces of candy to try to offset the bitterness of life in general. It's a tasty gesture, but it doesn't work.

Hundreds of white, yellow, and pink lily and chrysanthemum flower arrangements are lined up in layers surrounding Pó Po. To the side of the flowers are baskets for food offerings. In them, I spot containers of rice, fruit, plastic-wrapped chicken, and pastries, gifts from the guests who offer these edible goods for Pó Po to take with her on her journey into the afterlife.

I've spent the past week learning about and executing traditions that I had never heard of before. While Nina stuffed small red envelopes with paper money and a quarter, which we'll give to guests to ensure they get home safely and to spend and pass on the good luck and fortune, I put together white envelopes filled with candy that guests could consume once the funeral is over.

I look around at the crowd and spot Alisha and Randall. My heart bursts at the sight of them. Randall spots me first and nudges Alisha. Randall gives me a small wave while Alisha mimes a hug.

The funeral director clears his throat to command attention and breaks our gazes. He welcomes everyone and reads a brief biography of Pó Po, known to everyone else as June.

He doesn't mention her contagious laugh, her sharp wit, her even sharper memory, or the look she gives after hearing about a successful match or tasting a spicy Pinot Noir but instead captures a loose essence of who she was generally, a kindhearted woman who spent her life in the service of others. To everyone, she meant something different.

The funeral director moves on to read selected poems and words about moving into the afterworld, the spirit life that sounds so far away, so unattainable, and so imaginary. I hear guests blowing their noses and wiping away their tears and watch others stare blankly ahead of them. Most, though, subtly glance lovingly over at Pó Po in the open casket, dressed in her favorite outfit, her cornflower blue vest and white polo, to look good in the afterlife.

Beneath Pó Po are two extra sets of clothing for her to use in the next life. These clothes, along with the blankets that Mom, Auntie, Uncle Rupert, Nina, and I will drape over Pó Po, will keep her warm and protected on her journey into the spirit world. We approach the casket one by one with blanket in hand, slowly covering Pó Po.

After Mom, Uncle, and Nina have their moments, my time comes. I approach the casket slowly, fearfully almost, even though earlier I mentally prepared myself for what to expect. Pó Po's hair has been restyled in her usual permed curls, and at once I relax at the familiar sight of her. With her makeup and personal clothing, she looks like the Pó Po I've always known. I lift my blanket, being mindful to remember this moment, and gently layer it on top of Nina's blanket.

"If you want to say something, now's the time," Mom says. "Auntie and I will say something at the end."

I look out toward a mix of familiar and strange faces, finding comfort knowing that we're all here for one purpose: to honor Pó Po's memory and the life she led. I twist the dangling crescent moon around my neck.

Standing where the magician was just minutes ago, I address the group.

"June Huang was an extraordinary woman," I start, my voice shaky. "Her legacy proves it. In all her stubbornness, for better or worse, she owned who she was. Her life wasn't perfect or easy. She never expected it to be. But even in hard times, she kept going. She persevered. Life won't ever be the same here on earth without her, but it brings me some comfort knowing that she'll be working her magic in the afterlife and continuing to make others happy. Pó Po, we love you, and we miss you. It goes without saying that you've made this world a better place just by being in it.

"My love for you is fuller than the fullest moon," I whisper to Pó Po, stealing one last look at her. Tears fall from my eyes onto the blanket. They absorb into the cloth, little pieces of me to accompany Pó Po on her journey.

I lift my pinky to her and imagine her linking hers with mine, our thumbs pressing together in unison. I want it so badly that I can feel the pressure against my thumb.

I make eye contact with Mae Yí-Pó in the group and say out loud, "Someone wise taught me that long lives are worth celebrating. So that's what we're going to do."

I pull out my phone and tap Play on the first song on my moon playlist. The high opening jingle of King Harvest's "Dancing in the Moonlight" floats out of the speaker.

Slowly shimmying my shoulders to the beat, I hold two sideways peace signs in front of my tear-filled eyes and pull them apart. I tap my foot and move my body to the rhythm.

As the beat picks up, I extend my arm diagonally up to the ceiling with a disco finger and then bring it down across my body. I twirl a couple of times over to Pó Po, extending my hand out to her and pretending to spin her around. My family watches on, momentarily stunned.

I sidestep across the room before salsa stepping back to the other side. Uncle Rupert starts snapping but doesn't fully commit to the cause. Even Colette, who loves to dance, stays seated. Having used up all the dance moves I know, I move my body to the beat, making it up as I go.

I'm dancing alone until someone sitting in the back stands up and starts swaying his arms side to side, snapping to the beat. The man does the Twist around amused family members, making his way to the center of the room. All eyes are now on him as he does the Electric Slide between dangling streamers.

As he gets closer, I see that the man doing the moonwalk

down the aisle is Bennett. My breath catches in my chest. Even after everything, seeing him here is more than I could've hoped for. Bennett and I don't exchange words. We just keep dancing to the music, our eyes locked on one another.

Following our leads, Nina and Asher finally jump up and join us, holding their hands up in the air. Auntie shyly stands and wiggles her hips. Dad holds his hand out for Mom and twirls her in place. Mae Yí-Pó and Dale Yí-Gong pump their arms up and down enthusiastically, encouraging others to celebrate with us.

Before I know it, the entire room is up and dancing. Smiles form on everyone's faces. Some people even sing along.

Wherever she is, I know Pó Po is smiling and dancing right along with us.

CHAPTER 23

When the service concludes, I search for Bennett among faces I both recognize and don't. I wind through the crowd, hoping to find a towering man in a white cashmere sweater.

An older woman in a vanilla-colored velvet shawl gently places her hand on my arm. "I wanted to say how very sorry I am about your grandmother. I was one of June's clients back in the day," the stranger says.

"Thank you for being here," I reply, distracted.

"My granddaughter's here with me. Tiff!" the woman calls out, slowly lifting her arm to wave a younger woman over to us. I look past the woman's shoulder to see if Bennett's behind her.

"Hi, I'm Tiff. You're Olivia, right?" Tiff asks in an excited tone.

I'm too determined to find Bennett to pay much attention to the women in front of me. "I am, yes."

"Your grandmother was a legend. I'm sorry for your loss," Tiff says.

"I appreciate that," I say, growing antsy. "It was nice to meet you both."

"Olivia! Before you go," Tiff says. "Could I give you my card? I write for the *LA Times*, and I'd love to do a profile of you and your grandmother, and I believe your aunt? Lunar Love is a gem in LA. I haven't found any in-depth pieces about your business. Sorry to bring up work right now, but I think Lunar Love's story deserves to be told."

I refocus on the woman in front of me. "Wow, yes. Of course. Thank you," I say, caught off guard by the offer. I tuck her card into my tote. "Sorry for being so out of it right now, but I'd love to share Pó Po's story."

I say goodbye and continue my search. With no luck inside, I walk outside into the chilly evening air. Under lit pathways, guests gather and reunite. They discuss what a shame it is to have fallen out of touch with one another and how wonderful it is to see one another again after all these years. Pó Po always loved bringing people together, no matter the occasion.

For a few minutes, I stand silently looking out over the dark, sprawling, green-sloped lawn in the cemetery. Rows of neat round hedges line the man-made paths. Mountains surround the land, serving as a peaceful backdrop in this final resting place.

I miss Pó Po so much that my entire body feels numb. I remind myself what Mae Yí-Pó said about being connected to family in a different way when they pass. I'd do anything to stay linked with Pó Po.

When I have no luck finding Bennett, I follow the path around the building to a grassy patch for the next part of the ceremony. The containers of food offerings have been brought outside, along with dozens of finely crafted paper objects.

I spot Auntie hovering on the side of the group and settle in next to her. Moments later, someone else walks up and finds his place next to me.

"Hey," Bennett whispers.

I turn and gasp, surprised to see him standing in front of me. "Hi," I whisper back.

Mom moves to the front to face the group, positioning herself next to a large red enamel burn bucket. "Thank you for joining us as we send goods to Pó Po in the afterlife," Mom starts. "She left us with a list of very specific items she wanted."

There are many knowing chuckles from the crowd.

"Classic June!" someone in the crowd yells, drawing more laughs from the group.

"In Chinese culture, it's unlucky to arrive empty-handed in the afterlife," Auntie explains, elaborating on her trainings from the past week. She nods hello to Bennett.

"Unlucky?" Bennett repeats.

"Families burn joss paper and paper funeral offerings crafted to look like and represent items that their loved ones might need in the spirit world: a house, car, money, clothes, a Mahjong kit, a television, and a chest to hold their money and belongings."

"So, things you had on earth," I say in understanding.

"Some people even throw in a jet plane for their ancestors. The sky's the limit, depending on what you can afford to buy or have made."

"Those paper offerings look so real," Bennett observes.

"It's how we take care of our ancestors. The items must be burned so they can make it to their final destination in the other world and be used by the recipient," Auntie says.

Bennett and I listen closely, soaking in the tradition we're about to witness. I'm surprised that he didn't know about this custom, either. This bit of knowledge about him is oddly reassuring. We're learning together.

"In the afterlife, you can give the deceased a life they never got to live," Auntie adds. "It's a way of providing comfort."

"I'm relieved knowing that Pó Po's next chapter is only just beginning, and that it'll be a comfortable one," I say. Part of me wonders if she'll be reunited with Gōng Gong in the afterlife.

Auntie nods. "And then some. You want Gucci shoes but never had the ability to afford them here on earth? We can offer up a pair during the ceremony. Of course that's an extreme example. First things first, we need to make sure Pó Po has the necessities."

"That's wild, but I also kind of love it," I say, looking up at Bennett. I never thought there would be a nice way to move forward into death. When there are designer loafers involved, maybe the afterlife isn't so bad.

"The point is to keep our family happy," Auntie explains.

"Does this only happen at funerals?" I ask.

"This tradition is integrated into different holidays through-out the year, but also on birthdays and special occasions. It's up to you," she says, giving me a small smile before joining Mom and Uncle Rupert at the front. Together they move the various paper objects into the bucket. Somewhere among the pile of goods is my contribution of handwritten notes so that Pó Po would have my words to keep her company. I also decided to sneak in some copies of client profiles so she could do what she does best: matchmake.

I'm entranced by how intricate each item is, their bright colors and careful construction on the verge of being . . . set on fire.

"This is how we stay connected," I say out loud to myself. Realization dawns that this is my way back to Pó Po. She's only a fire away.

Up front, Nina points out various objects. "A yacht?" she asks. "Does Pó Po even know how to operate a boat?"

"That's what the ship captain is for," Auntie clarifies. "We can't forget to add a wine cellar and a sommelier. She may not have had those luxuries in this life, but in the next one, she can." Auntie and Mom share a small laugh.

"There's a disco ball in there," I inform Bennett, nodding toward the bucket up front. "I wonder what dancing in the afterlife feels like."

"Less joint pain probably," Bennett says, his crooked smile appearing. How I've missed that smile.

Our faces glow as the objects go up in flames, the yellow and orange flickers dancing against the ink-black night sky. We watch in silence as the paper funeral offerings are transformed into smoke, a form that escapes the natural world.

Around me, people softly say prayers while the items burn. Smoky strands of Pó Po's new paper house, bottles of wine, money, food, and clothing float up into the air, swirling and spinning above our heads. I'm overcome with emotion, but this time, it's with hope. This tradition, the act of honoring ancestors and spirits, is a foreign concept to me, but I find more comfort in it than I would've thought possible.

My eyes fill with tears, this time happy ones. The last time I felt this moved was with Bennett at the Getty. I peek over at him, and he looks just as enthralled. He must sense me watching him because his eyes dart over to me.

"I've never seen anything like this," he says quietly. "So the paper is burned...but then where exactly does it go?" He glances toward the paper goods, his eyebrows bent in interest and determination to figure it out.

"To our ancestors in the afterlife," I say, repeating what I've learned from Auntie. I can see how hard Bennett is trying to visualize this concept.

"How do you know if they have everything they need? How do they receive the actual goods?" he asks. "Where is the afterlife, even?"

I give him a small smile. "It's about believing. I don't think there are clear-cut answers. It's kind of like a leap of faith."

After a moment, Bennett nods and then reaches for his wallet. From behind a few dollar bills, he reveals a small receipt. On it are the words *Lead with your heart* written in Pó Po's handwriting.

"What's that?" I whisper.

"It's from my first lunch meeting with your Pó Po. After I paid, she wrote this down. I've kept it with me ever since, but her words didn't fully sink in until you taught them to me," he says. Bennett smiles and looks at the receipt thoughtfully before folding the rectangular slip of paper into a mini ice cream cone. He walks up to the front and drops the paper ice cream into the flames.

I blink my tears away when he returns to me.

"I hope her house comes with a freezer," he says, nudging me with his shoulder. I soak up his presence, observing his expression as he watches the fire work its magic.

"Hey. Tonight my family and I are making dinner together in honor of Pó Po. I'd like for you to be there, and I think Pó Po would've, too. Of course, only if you want to."

Bennett doesn't even try to fight the smile that immediately forms on his face. "There's nowhere else I'd rather be," he says.

There's so much I want to say to Bennett, but for now, our quiet understanding is enough.

CHAPTER 24

I'm wrist-deep in flour when Bennett arrives at my parents' house.

"Bennett, it's nice to see you again," Mom says in the entryway before leading him into the kitchen. When our eyes meet, his tense shoulders drop three inches.

"You can help Olivia with the dough," Mom instructs. "Have you ever made dumplings before?"

Bennett drops his bag on a chair and rolls up his sleeves. "Only once, but that was a long time ago," he says.

"I'll show you how to do it, per Pó Po's instructions," I offer, using my palm to roll a small piece of dough against the floured table. I flatten the dough with a rolling pin, turning it until the wrapper is round and thin.

"I'll follow your lead," he says without any resistance. Bennett watches me intently, mimicking my movements with invisible dough.

"No highly rated recipe up your sleeve?" I ask good-naturedly.

He smiles. "I wouldn't stand a chance against your Pó Po."

I cut the dough in half and hand him his piece to divide and roll into wrappers. We work diligently as Mom cuts scallions, Nina minces garlic, Asher measures sauces, Dad chops ginger, and Auntie preps ingredients for the side dishes. Dad throws Bennett softball questions as I focus on my rolling and breathing to steady my hands and hammering heart. Bennett moves surprisingly fast, looking as though he's loving every minute.

Over one hundred rolled wrappers later, Bennett covers our hard work with a damp towel. He beams at what we've created together.

"We'll take it from here," Mom says. "We'll eat in an hour. Nice work, both of you. Olivia, you're getting as fast as Pó Po." I bask in her words. Bennett does, too.

"You can come with me," I say to Bennett after we wash flour off our hands. He follows me up to the second floor, out the deck, and up to the roof.

"Should we be up here?" he asks, crouching low as he mimics my movements until we reach a flat section where I've set up a blanket for us to sit.

I pat the ground next to me, and Bennett doesn't object.

"Hi," I say in an exhale.

"Hi," he says.

"Thank you for coming to the funeral. And for the comfort food." I think for a moment. "You danced. In public."

"It was my honor," he says. "Thanks for coming to the pitch."

"I wish I could've stayed longer."

"When you saw me on stage stumbling over my words, all I could think about was you and if you would ever forgive me. You saved me from making a fool of myself. My words only came out clearly because I imagined that I was only talking to you."

"You spoke from the heart," I say.

"I'm not so good at that," he says, gently nudging me with his elbow.

"It's a start." I bite my lip. "It sounded like you spoke from the heart on the podcast, too."

Bennett lifts his shoulders up in a half shrug. "I told them I didn't want to do it anymore and to replace me with you, but they said that if I wasn't going to do it, neither of us would. So I figured I'd use the platform to talk about Lunar Love. I hope that was okay." He sighs. "And for the record, I meant what I said."

"You *were* the winner, so it was right for you to be on it," I say.

"I was the winner?" Bennett asks curiously. "That can't be easy for you to say."

I dip my head. "You were a formidable opponent, I'll admit."

He holds up his phone. "So this was true then?"

On his phone is my second WhizDash article. When I sent it to Alisha's friend last week, I promised her three months of free matchmaking services if she could expedite posting it. Luckily for me, she's still Team Lunar Love and was open to trying something new.

In my last list, I wrote about all the things that ZodiaCupid wasn't. Turns out, the only one with an identity crisis here . . . is me. Instead of figuring out who I am or what I want to be, I projected my insecurities onto a digital app. Truth is, through the app I bashed, I met someone great.

He reads a line from it out loud. "This Horse fell in love with an incompatible match by accident, but it turned out to be the best thing for her." His eyes flash up at me. "Do you mean it?"

My eyes flick from his phone to his eyes. "Every word."

His face lights up. "Well, this Rat fell in love with a Horse, but I don't think we're mismatched."

Heat rises in my chest. "As much as it shocks me to say, we did match on the app so I guess you really technically did win."

"That's *technically* true," Bennett says happily.

"Even though we're the signs that we are," I say.

Bennett laughs. "Right! So, if I recall correctly, your evaluation of me being a Rat is that I'm a freeloader, afraid of rejection, dishonest, and misleading?" he says, throwing the words I directed at him at the Halloween party back at me.

I cringe hearing those words again. "No. Because you're resourceful, ambitious, easy to get along with, and caring. You're a good listener, have a great sense of humor, and have a kind heart. And I...I'm sorry," I say, stretching out the words.

"We may have different approaches to life, but I think that can be a good thing," Bennett says.

I reach out to grab Bennett's hand. "Even though we're incompatible according to the Chinese zodiac, I've never felt more myself than when I'm with you. And life's too short not to be with someone you feel most yourself with."

Bennett clasps my hand in return and scoots closer to me on the blanket. "You're not the only one who feels that way. You've made me a better version of myself."

"It's safe to say that you've been slightly influential on me, too," I admit.

Bennett pulls me closer. "I hope you believe that I never tried to put Lunar Love out of business. I may not completely change your mind about compatibility, but I hope I can at the very least change your mind about me."

I take a deep breath. "I can see it now. My need for adventure will balance nicely with your intellectual pursuits. Your flexibility and forthrightness will help counteract my stubbornness, which, let's be honest, I need. You'll respect that I crave my independence while I'll appreciate, after learning over time, that being together can be just as fulfilling."

"I'll do my best, but I like how independent you are," Bennett whispers, leaning his forehead against mine.

The nearness of his face to mine almost derails my train of thought, but I push on, considering the other ways Bennett might help balance me. "Sometimes I'll want control, sometimes you will, but the natural leaders in us will value that we're in an equal partnership where one of us isn't just following the other. And since we both, for the most part, know each other's traits, we can work on compromise and come together from a place of understanding."

Bennett looks impressed. "You forgot one thing."

I look at him with skeptical eyes. "What?"

He holds my hand against his chest. "My data-driven mindset will always be balanced by your heart."

I shake my head. "You have more heart than you think. There's no doubt we both need control. For me, it's who gets to be matched together. For you, it was in your approach to how those matches happened. I so closely follow predetermined rules for myself and others."

"Maybe love isn't something that can be controlled to the level we were trying to manage it," Bennett says. "It's not something where either of us can guarantee an outcome. For most of my life, I needed to be able to take charge. But, Olivia, you make me want to lose control, go with my gut, delete the spreadsheet, and take the risk."

I smile, my heart overflowing with emotion. "I have something for you," I say, reaching for a metal bucket I covered in a towel earlier today.

Bennett peeks over my legs. "What is it?"

"I thought it could be nice to do our own joss paper burning," I say, bringing out an envelope from under my side of the blanket.

His eyebrows knit together in confusion. "Do you have more items to send to your Pó Po?" he asks.

"For your mom," I say, handing Bennett the envelope.

He delicately holds the envelope between his hands and pulls out a stack of papers.

"What are these?" he says, reading the writing on the paper. After a few seconds, understanding settles on his face.

"They're your parents' Lunar Love files," I explain. "They include the notes Pó Po took when she matched your mom and dad."

Bennett's eyes glisten. "I don't know what to say," he says, falling quiet. "I thought about my mom a lot today. In my mind, she's forever this brilliant person who never missed a bedtime reading, always ate the frosting first, and taught me how to dance. These details make her feel real again."

"It's the best match Lunar Love ever made," I admit.

Bennett flips through the pages, absorbing every last detail.

I lift the towel from the bucket and reveal an assortment of small paper goods. "I was able to track down a paper shop today. I found a guy who makes the most beautiful paper items I've ever seen. I took the liberty of picking up some necessities for your mom."

Bennett gently lifts out a paper house, clothing, money, shoes, and food. "You even included little paper journals and pens," he says, surprised.

"For her to write about her experiences," I say. "I'm sure she has more great stories to tell." I hand him a folded piece of paper. "I'd also like to add this, if that's okay with you."

He takes the paper from me cautiously. "What's this?"

"It's a letter to her, from me. I'd love for her to know how incredible her son is, and how proud she'd be of who you are."

A tear trails down Bennett's cheek. "This is . . . thank you," he says, wrapping his arms around me and pulling me closer.

I hug him back, breathing him in.

"This means everything," he adds, placing the items back in the bucket and sliding my letter in with it. "These files. I can burn them, too?"

I nod. "I still have the originals for you. When your mom receives these, maybe she'll think to find Pó Po. Then they'll have each other in the afterlife."

Bennett places the files in the bucket and grabs the match-box from me. With just one strike, the match crackles into a small flame. He drops it into the bucket and watches as the paper goods fuel the flames, the blaze growing in height and heat.

Shadows on Bennett's face dance to the flicker of the golden sparks. I nestle into him while the smoke rises up, disappearing into the night. When he turns to face me, his hazel eyes have intensified. All sense of time disappears as we look at each other. It's as though we're really seeing each other, not for our jobs or for our signs, but for who we are without all that. It feels like I'm seeing him, seeing myself, for the very first time.

His face relaxes into a dimpled smile. "If I didn't make it clear enough before, I love you."

A wide smile spreads across my face. "I love you, too."

We slowly lean closer into each other until there's no space left between us. I pull his arm around me tighter as I wrap my arm around his shoulders. I tilt my head back, waiting for his lips to reach mine. Under the waning crescent sliver of the moon and the navy sky sparingly dotted with stars, we abandon our fears and insecurities, hold each other tightly, and embrace being compatibly incompatible.

CHAPTER 25

Three months later

Easy on the flour, doughboy," I say playfully as Bennett rolls rice flour dough into little balls on a wooden cutting board.

"Hey! I have feelings," he says with a mock-serious tone. "I want these rice dumplings to be perfect. Auntie Lydia will never approve of me if I can't get tāngyuán right."

I nod in agreement. "They are her specialty. Better to be safe than sorry." I scoop another spoonful of flour onto the board.

"Okay, you go get the other desserts ready," Bennett instructs, gently nudging me out of the kitchen with his elbows. "Clearly, I'm the expert here."

"You don't need my help? I know you like following the steps together."

"I'm cool with doing these on my own. I got this."

"Okay," I say uncertainly. "If you're sure?"

Bennett flashes me a crooked smile meant only for me to see. "I'll meet up with you outside once I'm done filling these."

I smile back, a feeling of freedom and deep connection swelling into me at once. I hold my floured hands up in surrender. "Fine! You're on your own!"

Mom walks into the kitchen with a tablecloth. "Olivia! Take these out, will you?" she says. "For the dessert table."

Dad lugs in a box filled with *Extra Serving Plates* written on the side. "I don't know what we have up in that attic, but this is the last time I'll ever go up there. I swear I heard the pitter-patter of tiny feet."

"Damn Rats," Bennett says with dramatic mock irritation, his eyes sparkling at the irony.

Mom lifts the lid open and takes a peek in. "At least they're not broken."

Dad sighs. "Guess I'll have the honor of cleaning these later," he says.

Mom slaps a pair of purple rubber gloves against his chest. "You'll need these."

"Bennett, those are looking lovely!" Auntie says as she breezes through the kitchen. She gives the dough a soft squeeze. "Very nice."

Bennett stands up straighter with pride as he folds the dough around black sesame seed filling.

"Lydia, are you wearing perfume?" Mom asks teasingly.

Auntie blots her matte red lips with a tissue. "Walt will be here soon. How do I look? Oh, never mind. I know I look fabulous," she says, sauntering out of the room.

Once Auntie didn't have my match to worry about, she quickly resumed her own search for a man worthy of her love. Alisha found Walt in the Lunar Love database. Turns out, he had been there all along, too.

The doorbell rings, and Mom slips off her apron to answer the door.

"Xīnnián kuàilè!" two voices boom from the front entryway. Randall and his husband, Jonathan, pass through the living room carrying trays of sweets and Randall's special peanut snack.

"Happy Lunar New Year!" I repeat back to them.

"Olivia! It's been forever," Jonathan calls out. He sets his tray down and greets me with a big hug.

Seconds later, I spot Mae Yí-Pó and Dale Yí-Gong slipping their shoes off at the front door.

I grab the tablecloth, Randall's bowls of peanuts, and my latest baking creation, a Year of the Ox–shaped Incompatibility Cake, and head outside to the backyard.

Paper lanterns in the shapes of accordions, horses, and fish dangle between the trees. The moon balloons from Nina's Cookie Day are surprisingly still floating, so we placed them by the back door to give them a second life.

I fling the tablecloth over the dessert table and arrange the bowls of melons and pears, plates of sweets, and pots of tea so everything looks presentable.

"I just had a little chat with Bennett," Nina says, sidling up beside me. She places a tray of two chicken dishes, hot and sour soup, and homemade dumplings onto the table.

"And?"

"He's great. Listening to me paid off, huh?" she says with an all-knowing look on her face. She lays out the spoons and forks and examines my food arrangement. She pushes a teapot one inch back and looks satisfied.

"Don't get used to it," I say playfully.

Asher calls out, and we see him struggling to start a fire in the fire pit.

"Not again," Nina says, running over to help.

"Let me know if you need help finding the spark!" I call out after her. "It's how I make the big bucks!"

Through the glass windows, I see Bennett and Dad laughing about something. I spot ZodiaCupid team members chatting with the Lunar Love team on the back patio.

Auntie makes her way over to me with a bowl of green beans. "Are you ready?" she asks.

"More than ready," I say, taking the dish from her and placing it next to the rest of the food.

"I'm proud of you, Liv. I'm still trying to wrap my mind around the changes. And learning how to let go. Whatever you choose to do long-term, you will always have my full support," Auntie says emotionally.

"Thank you."

She picks up a tangerine from a pyramid of fruit, tosses it back and forth between her hands, and looks around at the guests. "It was a good idea only limiting this year's festivities to close family and friends. We've had enough big events for the year."

"It's been nonstop, hasn't it?" I reflect. "The *LA Times* and *El Lay Daily* articles were the cherries on top."

"The *LA Times* profile was beautiful. Pó Po would've been shocked by how much attention it received," Auntie reflects.

"It meant Lunar Love and her legacy will live on."

Auntie places the tangerine back on top of the pile and winks. "Would you have thought four months ago we'd both have boyfriends?" she asks.

"Never in my wildest dreams," I say with a laugh.

"One way or another, we had to get you matched!" Auntie says mischievously.

"And you, apparently!" I say.

Auntie throws her head back in laughter before heading back to the house to greet Walt. She waves to Colette, who has arrived bearing a box of what must be more baked goods. Over the last few months, we reconnected, catching up on the past three years. I didn't fully realize how much I missed her until she was back in my life.

"I've missed your family's Lunar New Year parties," she says. "My mom can't be bothered to throw one together."

I take the pastry box from her and slide it between two other plates of food. "Where is she now?"

"Who knows? Probably off on a yacht somewhere in the French Riviera," she sighs. "Bennett said he'll be out soon. I'm glad you found a good one. He's nothing like the last ones we dated." Colette nudges me, and we laugh.

"No. Definitely not," I agree with a shake of my head.

Once the food and decorations are set up and all the guests have arrived, I tap my teacup to get everyone's attention. I stand to the side of the fire pit and feel the warmth from the flames. Bennett joins me as we face our group of friends and family.

"Thank you, everyone, for joining us tonight. It means a lot that we can celebrate together. It's fitting, considering this holiday celebrates new beginnings and intentions, both of which we have a lot of." A few people in the group chuckle. "This year's Lunar New Year looks a bit...smaller...than other years, but even after everything, we wanted to make sure we celebrated. Many of you didn't have the chance to meet Pó Po, but I know she would've loved all of you." I look up at the night sky and raise my teacup. "Tonight, we celebrate her and the start of new traditions."

Everyone lifts their teacup in unison, and we all take sips of our tea.

"There's also something we wanted to share with you first, though most of you already know. It's not public yet so don't tweet about it or anything," Bennett jokes. "We were ecstatic to receive funding from a couple of investors, but we were even more floored when they got on board with our second pitch for a Lunar Love and ZodiaCupid merger."

I look into the group to find Alisha and Randall's faces. They give me thumbs-up signs. Bennett's team cheers and whoops. Even Elmer, who actually is a nice guy once I got to know him, looks excited.

"We're over the moon that, starting Monday, Lunar Love and ZodiaCupid will be sharing the same orbit," I announce.

"Hopefully, together we can see a boost across both platforms," Bennett adds. "Especially since Valentine's Day is right around the corner."

"It's a merging of tradition and modernity. It's not all or nothing," I say, thinking of Pó Po. "There's room for both of us. And there's room for adapting."

In the group, I locate Harper and Parker, the original Lunar Love and ZodiaCupid collaboration before it was official. Their signs and ascendants weren't compatible according to the Chinese zodiac, but based on my evaluation of their traits, we paired them up to see what would happen. Three months later and they're still going strong.

"Sometimes traditions can be reinterpreted, but that doesn't mean they go away completely," I say. "We think this route could help us bring something we're passionate about into the modern day. Lunar Love will have a more updated database, in a sense, while being able to use data to assist with our in-person matchmaking."

Our friends and family excitedly clap and raise their drinks.

I hold my teacup up. "Thanks for coming along with us on this journey. It's been a wild ride so far."

After our announcement, Bennett finds me standing alone by the dessert table. He comes bearing a bowl of rice dumplings in warm water.

"I made these especially for you," he says, handing me the bowl.

"What'd you put in it?" I ask suspiciously. I lift a rice ball to my nose with the spoon and sniff it.

He laughs. "Just my love."

I take a bite, the warm black sesame seed filling running into my mouth. "This *is* good."

"Excellent. I have a one hundred percent success rate so far then," he gloats, kissing the top of my head as I lean into him. "What's that supposed to be?" He nods toward the cake on the table.

"It's an Incompatibility Cake. The Ox's horns got a bit tricky," I explain.

"I hope it's not red velvet," he jokes.

"It's made with Earl Grey and beet. Flavors you wouldn't typically expect to work well together but actually do." I use a knife to cut into the middle of the cake and add slices to our plates. "I made it for you."

At the same time, we dig into the cake. I scrape the frosting off, careful not to disrupt the cake beneath it. Meanwhile,

Bennett cuts in vertically, scooping up an even ratio of the cake and frosting.

Bennett gives me an odd look. "Frosting first?" he asks.

"This is me trying to see things from your perspective," I say.

"Likewise," he says.

We take our bites. Bennett shakes his head. "This is strangely delicious. These flavors..."

"They're a perfect match," I say, finishing his sentence.

Bennett smiles, and my heart tumbles and turns, even after all these months.

"I think that went well?" I ask.

"Very. This'll be fun."

"Or a complete disaster."

"Maybe this is my way of infiltrating your business now," Bennett says with a conspiratorial tone. "Or at least to stop you from poaching people off my platform."

"We may be partnering, but the magic of Lunar Love can't be replicated," I inform him.

Bennett squeezes me tighter. "I think we have what it takes to make this work."

"Just keep your hands off my buns, and we won't have a problem." I eat another spoonful of frosting. "So, do you happen to know what time you were born?" I ask casually.

"I was wondering how long it would take you to ask me that. Do you even know yours?" Bennett asks, polishing off the last of his cake slice.

"Of course I do. Year of the Horse, birth hour of the Horse."

Bennett laughs. "I should've known. You're a Horse through and through."

I look up at him and wait. "So? What about you?"

"You want the truth? I don't know what time I was born."

"Can't you find your birth record or something? There are ways to find out," I say.

"Isn't it kind of romantic not knowing?" Bennett asks, wrapping his arms around me.

I lean my head into his shoulder. "That's one word for it."

Bennett wiggles his fingers playfully. "Secretive. Mysterious. Ooh."

"You joke, but this is our livelihood *and* culture *and* relationship," I say teasingly, turning to face him.

Bennett shakes his head. "I'm just leaving room for magic!" he says playfully.

"Okay, okay!" I laugh. "Just kiss me." I tug Bennett's hair tenderly to bring him closer to me and give him a deep, hard kiss.

Maybe there is beauty in opening yourself up to the love you don't expect and the traits that will keep you guessing. Because compatible or incompatible, we're all just trying to love and be loved, however that might look.

We look up into the dark February sky, our attentions pulled toward the glow of the jade-white moon. The moon is practically invisible in its waxing crescent phase, its outer edge a thin pearly glimmer shining against the stars. New love a barely there whisper in the night sky.

As a matchmaker, I'm constantly learning. My most recent lesson: love is *mostly* like the moon. Whereas the moon and all its phases are predictable, love is not. Where I once thought I could predict how my relationships would turn out, I now realize that was as foolish as trying to keep the tides from rising and falling.

In the end, gravity always finds us, bringing us right back where we belong.

ACKNOWLEDGMENTS

If you've skipped ahead to read the acknowledgments first, I'm right there with you, and I hope you enjoy the book. If you've already read this book, thanks for reading and for sticking around until the very end.

The very fact that these words exist in book form is incredibly meaningful. I grew up reading, watching, and loving romantic comedies, even when the heroines and leading ladies looked nothing like me. Being mixed-race Chinese American, I rarely read about or saw characters who I could relate to. Putting mixed characters into the forefront has always been, and will always be, important to me.

Thank you to my agent, Ann Leslie Tuttle, for seeing the promise and potential of this story and for helping me take it to new heights. Thank you to my editor, Alex Logan, for championing this story's heart and purpose and for supporting Olivia and Bennett and the book's underlying themes. Thank you to my film agent, Mary Pender, for being an early believer and supporter of this story even before edits came back. I am endlessly grateful to you all.

Thank you to Estelle Hallick, Daniela Medina, Abby Reilly, Dana Cuadrado, Sabrina Flemming, Ambriah Underwood, Grace Fischetti, the production team, the sales reps, and everyone on Team Forever. It's a thrill to join the Forever family.

It's emotional for me to see a mixed-race illustrated character on the *cover* of a book. Thank you, Sandra Chiu, for capturing Olivia's spirit and making this cover look like a piece of art. Thank you also to Rosemary Gong and Eugene Moy for your encouragement in this journey.

To the authors who replied to my cold emails, met for coffee, picked up my calls, and responded to my direct messages, I think about your kindness often and am so glad to know you. Thank you for helping a new author through the daunting yet exciting publishing process.

To my parents, for a childhood filled with good books and good food. Thank you for supporting my journey full of twists and turns every step of the way. To my mèi mei, I am grateful for your unwavering support and encouragement. To Auntie Rae, thank you for your cultural and Mandarin language insights.

To the booksellers, librarians, bookstagrammers, book bloggers, book clubs, and podcasters, your vast knowledge of books never fails to impress me. Thanks for all that you do in spreading the love of books to others and for always knowing just the right story to recommend.

Thanks to you, reader. I know that there are thousands of books out there for you to choose from, so from the deepest depths of my heart, thank you for choosing to spend time with mine.

And finally, to my best friend and husband, Patrick, the Snake to my Horse. Thank you for reading literally every single version of this book and for caring just as deeply as I do about these characters. You are my living proof that happy ever afters can be found through online dating. I am the luckiest that the algorithms brought us together.

ABOUT THE AUTHOR

Lauren Kung Jessen is a mixed-race Chinese American writer with a fondness for witty, flirtatious dialogue and making meals with too many steps but lots of flavor. She is fascinated by myths and superstitions and how ideas, beliefs, traditions, and stories evolve over time. From attending culinary school to working in the world of Big Tech to writing love stories, Lauren cares about creating experiences that make people feel something. When she's not writing novels, she works as a content strategist and user experience writer. She also has a food and film blog, *A Dash of Cinema*, where she makes food inspired by movies and TV shows. She lives in Nashville with her husband, who she met thanks to fate (read: the algorithms of online dating), two cats, and dog.

Reading Group Guide

Dear Reader,

Thank you so much for choosing to spend time reading Lunar Love. *This book is my love letter to Chinese traditions and the ways we make customs our own. I am proud to be mixed-race Chinese American. My Chinese, Scottish, Welsh, and Danish ancestries inspire my writing, but they also inspire me to learn more about the family who came before me and their traditions, culture, language, and food. Through stories and photographs and by asking a lot of questions, I'm constantly uncovering new tidbits of information about my family. All of these nuggets of knowledge build a bigger picture about where I come from and who I am.*

When my mom moved to the United States from Taiwan in the 1970s as a young girl, her family celebrations and traditions always incorporated specific types of food, such as long-life noodles for birthdays, mooncakes for the Mid-Autumn Festival, and zongzi (sticky rice dumplings) for Qingming. Beyond food, my mom passed down other Chinese traditions and superstitions to my sister and me: No shoes on in the house! Don't wear white in your hair! Eat every grain of rice or your husband will have pockmarks!

But there are also traditions that I have both discovered and made my own later in life in my personal attempt to learn more about my heritage. As a few examples, I wore both white and red at my wedding. My husband and I had a tea ceremony before our wedding dinner in which we blended our favorite teas together to create one that guests could enjoy. I now not only happily accept hóngbāo, but I also give red envelopes to my nieces as a proud auntie.

Learning more about one's background seems to be a desire shared by people of all ages. My dad had clothing made after discovering our Scottish clan tartan a couple of years ago.

I'll forever be on a journey to understand where I come from while fully understanding that things change over time. I am fascinated by how myths and superstitions, ideas, beliefs, traditions, and stories evolve. What advances? What comes back around? Who has the responsibility and/or pleasure of keeping customs alive? Maybe we all do, for whatever we value in our lives, carrying these things of importance from the past, making them relevant in the present, and pushing them forward into the future.

With Lunar Love, I hope to show that there can be joy and fulfillment in bringing traditions into the present day, and that there's nuance and complexity in being mixed. Ultimately, my greatest desire is that you see a part of yourself in these pages, however that might look.

With love,

Lauren

Discussion Questions

1. A lively debate takes place at the Matched with Love Summit about whether or not opposites attract. Do you think opposites attract? Why or why not? Do you think that being opposites is a good basis for a relationship?

2. Olivia thinks compatibility in partners is important. Does compatibility matter in relationships? If so, how? If not, why not?

3. Learning about new traditions and keeping them alive is important to Olivia. What family traditions do you keep alive? How have they changed over time?

4. One of Olivia's challenges is to bring a traditional business into the present, while thinking about its future. How do businesses need to change with the times? Over time, how has Lunar Love changed and adapted?

5. Olivia and Bennett make a bet to prove to each other that their version of Chinese zodiac matchmaking is best. Whose method—Olivia's in-person matchmaking or Bennett's dating app—do you think is better? Have you met someone through online dating? Was that experience positive?

6. Olivia and Bennett sometimes felt like outsiders because they don't see themselves as fully fitting into their Chinese

heritage. When have you ever felt split between two parts of yourself or as though you weren't "enough"?

7. Olivia puts a lot of pressure on herself to make Lunar Love successful. Why do you think this legacy is so important to her?

8. Olivia's grandmother is the revered and beloved matriarch of her family. Did you feel the family's grief when Pó Po died? Who is the senior member that leads your family? What are the reasons that you respect and value them?

9. What role do you think food (Swiss rolls, dumplings, mooncakes, animal-shaped cakes, cookies, etc.) plays throughout the book? Are there any special recipes or foods that have been passed down in your family?

10. Olivia and Nina have a heart-to-heart in their treehouse named The Spaceship. Where do you go when you want to escape or think or have a private moment with someone?

11. The various flowers throughout *Lunar Love* have significant meaning to Olivia (Bennett gives Olivia white chrysanthemums, Olivia's favorite flower is the peony, ZodiaCupid is gamified with peonies, and they view Van Gogh's *Irises*). What types of flowers have significant meaning to you and why?

12. Now that Olivia and Bennett have merged businesses, what do you think the future holds for their relationship?

Q&A with the Author

Have you always wanted to be a writer?

I always wrote, but I didn't approach writing in a formal way. I spent a good amount of my childhood at my parents' office writing stories in empty conference rooms on my gifted, beloved typewriter (likely provided to me so I would stay out of my parents' way during meetings). When I wasn't making up stories for my family to read, I was reading. I consumed book series like Sweet Valley High and Nancy Drew, loving getting lost in worlds other than my own. Because that's what stories do for us. They give us peeks into worlds and lives that are different than our own. But something else that stories should do is show us ourselves. I didn't have books or movies that featured characters who looked like me or my family. After years of writing non-fiction, I missed creating my own worlds and characters. When I started writing fiction again, I knew I wanted to showcase people like me whose worlds aren't often shown in the media.

How do you celebrate Lunar New Year?

When I was growing up, my family would go to different aunties' houses for Lunar New Year, where there would be platters of dumplings, vegetables, fish, noodles, and desserts. It was always a very social event. The highlight for my sister and me was when the red envelopes were handed out. These days, I host Lunar

New Year for my family. We hang lanterns, put out decorations, and make an entire feast. My dad's responsible for cooking the whole fish, my mom makes her now-perfected recipe of bái táng gāo (white sugar sponge cake), my husband makes the side of vegetables, and I take the lead on the homemade dumplings. There's always freshly cut fruit and store-bought candies. We also celebrate New Year's, so Lunar New Year is a nice time to gather again to eat good food and spend more time with family.

Can you briefly explain the Chinese zodiac?

The Chinese zodiac, also known as Shengxiao ("born resembling"), is an important part of Chinese culture. The Chinese zodiac is a belief system based on the lunar calendar in which twelve animals represent a repeating twelve-year cycle. Each lunar year is represented by a different animal, in the order of Rat, Ox, Tiger, Rabbit, Dragon, Snake, Horse, Goat, Monkey, Rooster, Dog, and Pig. Each animal is associated with various personality traits, which is why people use the Chinese zodiac as a way to learn more about themselves and who they may be compatible with.

One common belief of how the animals got their order was that the Jade Emperor held a race in which all of the animals in the world were invited to compete for spots in the zodiac calendar. This competition has become known as the Great Race, and the top twelve animals who placed became the official animal signs. Because the Rat came ahead of all the other animals, it is the first animal in the cycle. The Chinese zodiac is complex and fascinating, and, similarly to Western astrology, is an interesting way to learn more about yourself, friends, family, and colleagues.

Which of your Chinese zodiac animal sign traits do you most relate to?

I'm the Year of the Horse, an animal sign I very much relate to. As a Horse, I'm very independent. I can definitely be stubborn and impatient. I prefer to keep busy so I balance a lot of spinning plates at once, which is exciting, challenging, and stimulating, but I do have a hard time relaxing. I'm also adventurous in that I will try most things once and I love having a variety of experiences that will take me to new places and keep my mind active. It is said that the Horse is unbridled in love and romance, which I think holds true.

Lunar Love shows both the pros and cons of dating apps. How do you feel about online dating?

I was always wary of online dating because there was a stigma around it. I'm a by-product of romantic comedies, so I thought my meet-cute would come in the form of some serendipitous, charming moment on the New York City streets like it did in books and movies. But after third-wheeling my sister and her now-husband one too many times, I created an online dating profile. I went into it the same way that I approach most things: with a strategy and a timeline. I signed up for a service that required that users pay, and I gave myself a six-month period to see if online dating was even a good fit for me.

Five days later, I met the man who is now my husband. Our first date was five hours long, and we moved in together after three months. On paper we are not "compatible," and we have both admitted that it wasn't love at first sight, but by Date Two we were in it for the long haul. When it comes to online dating, I really can't complain. It led me to the love of my life.

What inspired you to write about Chinese zodiac matchmaking and online dating?

I am inspired by how Chinese astrology can be used as a language for getting to know ourselves and others better. Your specific animal sign depends on the year in which you were born, but there are many factors beyond just the animal signs to consider, including the ascendant (determined by the time of day you were born) and five elements (water, wood, fire, earth, and metal) that align with the year you were born in. The nuances of Chinese astrology and all the elements that come into play with one another continue to fascinate me.

Matchmakers would pair people together based on the compatibility of their animal signs. Placing Chinese zodiac matchmaking in contrast with dating apps came together in my mind in an organic way having grown up learning about the Chinese zodiac, but also having met my husband through online dating. I found the concept of the highly personal compatibility matching within the Chinese zodiac interesting, especially when juxtaposed with Big Tech's algorithms and data that are also intended to find you compatible matches. I'm curious about how beliefs and traditions evolve over time, and matchmaking is certainly an area that has progressed in a variety of ways.

Your book features many iconic locations in Los Angeles. Have you lived there?

I have! I went to college just outside of Los Angeles and frequently drove into the city to explore and intern. After living in New York City and Seattle for a while, my husband and I moved to Los Angeles for a few years before moving to Nashville. The locations in the book are some of my very favorite LA spots, from Chinatown to the Getty to Griffith Park. Los Angeles is such a vibrant city with great food, cool bookstores, fun hiking spots, excellent museums, Hollywood, and beautiful weather. We also lived in Pasadena, which is such a gem with even more great food and things to do. It's also home to a few favorites of mine: Vroman's Bookstore; NASA's Jet Propulsion Laboratory; and The Huntington Library, Art Museum, and Botanical Gardens. Los Angeles will always hold a special place in my heart.

What is your next novel about? Does it also include a Chinese tradition?

My next novel is about an artist who deeply believes in the Red Thread of Fate: a Chinese legend in which Yuè Lǎo, the god of love and marriage, connects two people by the ankles with a red thread. One night, she meets a man from out of town and tours him around New York City. After a misunderstanding, the two aren't able to connect after their enchanted evening. But when an unexpected opportunity brings them back together, the woman can't help but wonder if this man is the one on the other end of her red string. This book is filled with more traditions, superstitions, and myths—I can't wait for you to read it in early 2024!

Chinese Zodiac Character Chart

Zodiac Animal	Birth Years	Character	Personality Traits
Rat	1984	Bennett O'Brien	Resourceful, entrepreneurial, intelligent, opinionated
Ox	1937 1961	Harold Christenson (Grandpa) Rupert Huang	Down-to-earth, reliable, follows head over heart
Tiger	1938 1962 1986	Etta Christenson (Grandma) Martin Christenson Alisha Lin Owen Rossi	Generous, romantic, optimistic, quick-tempered
Rabbit	1987	Elmer Han	Thorough, ruthless, self-indulgent, moody
Dragon	1976 1988	Carol Rogers Harper Chen	Confident, takes initiative, decisive, driven
Snake	1989	The Ex	Elusive, possessive, private, demanding

Zodiac Animal	Birth Years	Character	Personality Traits
Horse	1930 1966 1990	June Huang (Pó Po) Lydia Huang Olivia Huang Christenson	Quick-witted, impulsive, multitasker, stubborn, high-spirited
Goat	1955 1979 1991	Mae Zhang (Mae Yí-Pó) Jonathan Chastain Colette Curtis	Gentle, compassionate, kindhearted, determined
Monkey	1956 1968	Dale Zhang (Dale Yí-Gong) Aunt Vivienne Huang	Innovative, intellectual, clever, competitive
Rooster	1981 1993	Parker T. Nina Huang Christenson Asher Green	Meticulous, opinionated, organized, responsible
Dog	1958 2018	Lisa Christenson Pinot	Honest, loyal, straightfor-ward, capable
Pig	1971	Randall Zhu	Patient, courageous, trustworthy, overoptimistic

Mae Yí-Pó's Swiss Rolls with Vanilla Cream Filling

Chinese Swiss rolls are light and delicious without being overly sweet. You can find them in most Chinese bakeries as slices or entire rolls. The filling can be whatever your heart desires: vanilla cream, matcha, jam, chocolate cream, you name it. The result is a fluffy cake living its full spiral potential.

Makes 6–8 slices

INGREDIENTS

Cake:

- ½ cup cake flour
- ½ teaspoon baking powder
- ⅛ teaspoon salt
- 3 eggs at room temperature, separated into egg yolks and egg whites
- 4 tablespoons light brown sugar
- 3 tablespoons vegetable oil
- 1 teaspoon vanilla extract
- 2 tablespoons whole milk
- 3 tablespoons white sugar
- ¼ teaspoon cream of tartar

Filling:

- ⅔ cup cold heavy whipping cream
- 3 teaspoons white sugar
- 1 teaspoon vanilla extract
- 1 teaspoon powdered sugar (to sprinkle on top)

METHOD

Preheat the oven to 350°F and line a 9" × 13" baking pan with parchment paper. Make sure the parchment paper is large enough to neatly fit the pan but also has edges that you can use to lift the baked cake out of the baking pan.

Into a bowl, sift the cake flour, baking powder, and salt.

In a separate bowl, whisk the 3 egg yolks and light brown sugar together. Add the vegetable oil, vanilla extract, and whole milk and then whisk until completely smooth and free of any lumps.

Add the flour mixture into the egg yolk mixture, and mix until the batter is well blended and lump-free. Set the batter aside.

In the bowl of an electric mixer with the whisk attachment, add the remaining egg whites and the 3 tablespoons of white sugar and whip until you get stiff peaks. You can also mix these ingredients by hand with a whisk. Once you have stiff peaks, add the cream of tartar and mix again.

In batches, gently fold the egg white mixture into the flour-and-egg-yolk batter with a spatula. This will create an airy batter, but it is important to be delicate with this and not overmix or mix vigorously.

Pour this combined mixture into the parchment-lined baking pan and smooth the top so the batter is evenly distributed. Tap the pan against the counter to get rid of any air bubbles.

Bake for 15–18 minutes until a toothpick comes out clean. Be careful not to overbake the cake.

While the cake is baking, make the filling by mixing heavy whipping cream, sugar, and vanilla extract in the bowl of an electric mixer with the whisk attachment until you get stiff peaks. You can also mix these ingredients by hand with a whisk. Cover the filling and place it in the fridge until it's time to fill the roll.

Remove the baking pan from the oven, and let the cake cool on a cooling rack for 10-12 minutes. You don't want the cake to cool fully.

Carefully lift the parchment paper by its sides to remove the cake from the pan. Gently flip the cake upside down onto another large piece of parchment paper, and peel the original parchment paper off the cake.

Make 3 shallow cuts on one side of the width of the cake while it's still warm. Careful not to cut all the way through.

Starting on the side with the cuts, gently roll the cake, keeping the new parchment paper intact. Pre-rolling the cake while it's still warm should help make rolling the cake with filling easier. Keep the cake rolled up in parchment paper for 15–18 minutes.

Unroll the cake carefully. It doesn't need to be flat when you add the filling. Spread the filling onto the cake evenly with a spatula.

Gently roll the cake up again. This time, pull the parchment paper away from the cake as you roll.

Once the cake is rolled, slice the ends off for a clean edge. Sift powdered sugar on top, slice (cleaning the knife between each cut), and enjoy! To firm the cake up more, wrap the roll in parchment paper and refrigerate for 3–4 hours.

Pó Po's Pan-Fried Pork Dumplings

Dumplings (jiǎozi) are a traditional food for Lunar New Year. They are shaped to resemble an ingot, an early form of currency in China, because dumplings symbolize longevity and wealth. Dumplings can be stuffed with various fillings and can be pan-fried, boiled, or steamed. If you're looking for something quicker, opt out of making your own dough wrappers and buy pre-made dumpling wrappers instead.

Makes 60–70 dumplings

INGREDIENTS

Dough:
- 3 cups all-purpose flour, more for dusting
- 1 cup warm water (plus 3 tablespoons, if needed)

Pork Filling:
- 1 pound ground pork
- 2 ½ tablespoons soy sauce
- 1 tablespoon grated or finely minced fresh ginger
- 2 tablespoons minced garlic
- 3 scallions, thinly sliced
- 1 teaspoon Shaoxing rice wine
- 1 teaspoon sesame oil

Dipping Sauce:
- ¼ cup soy sauce
- 1 tablespoon Shaoxing rice wine
- 1 tablespoon chopped fresh ginger

METHOD

Dumpling Wrappers:

Add the flour to a large bowl.

Slowly pour the warm water into the flour and mix with chopsticks. The dough will look a bit lumpy, and that's okay. If the dough still feels too dry, add in the extra water.

On a floured surface, knead the dough until the water and flour are combined and smooth. Shape the dough into a ball and let it rest for 30–45 minutes covered in plastic wrap.

Dumpling Filling (make while the dough rests):

In a large bowl, mix the pork, soy sauce, ginger, garlic, scallions, Shaoxing rice wine, and sesame oil until combined.

Making the Dumplings:

After the dough has rested, remove the plastic wrap. Knead the dough once more on a floured surface.

Divide the dough into pieces weighing 11–13 grams.

Flatten each piece of dough with your palm and then use a rolling pin to roll them out into a circle about 3–3.5 inches in diameter. Keep a light touch here—you want the edges of the wrapper to be thinner than the middle. (This makes for easier pleating and a thicker middle to hold the filling.)

Place rolled-out wrappers on a plate covered with a damp towel to prevent the dough from drying out.

Using a spoon, scoop out no more than a tablespoon of pork filling for each wrapper. Add the scoop to the center of the wrapper.

Using your finger or a brush, add a little water along the edges of the wrapper to help the dough stick together better. Bring the edges of the wrapper together to create a half-moon shape around the filling. Pinch the edges to seal. From the center, make small folds with the dough down one side, pushing each new pleat against the previous one. Repeat this pleating on the other side.

Place the pleated dumplings on the plate or parchment-lined baking sheet with a damp towel over them so they don't dry out.

Pan Frying the Dumplings:

Add 1–2 tablespoons of vegetable oil to a nonstick pan and set over medium high heat.

Once the pan is hot and the oil is shimmery, place the dumplings in the pan (pleats facing up) without letting them touch each other. Cook for 1–2 minutes until the bottoms are golden.

Add 3–4 tablespoons of water and immediately cover the pan with a lid. Careful here: the oil sizzles and the steam rises quickly once you add water to the pan.

Steam the dumplings for another 3–5 minutes until the water has evaporated and the dumplings are fully cooked. The dough will appear softer and off-white. Cut open one of the dumplings to make sure it's cooked through all the way. This combination of pan frying and steaming adds a tasty crunch to the dumplings with a soft, chewy top.

Transfer the dumplings to a plate and serve with soy sauce or dipping sauce.

Make the Dipping Sauce:

In a small bowl, combine the soy sauce and Shaoxing rice wine.

Add the chopped ginger and mix it around the sauce to add flavor.